The Jihad's Messiah

Jihad Series BOOK I

NICK DANIELS

Risen Books
Portland, Oregon

For Jesus Christ, the true Messiah

What happened to America?

Marcus du Preez, PhD.
Professor of Political Science at UCT

The United States was once a powerful nation. In fact, as recently as five or six years ago, no one would have thought the U.S. could be so absent from the international political scene as it is now. My students still ask me to explain how this came about.

What swept America away from its position as a world superpower? It's hard to explain and I don't propose to have all the answers. What I can say is this: America entered into the current social and economic crisis due to supernatural as well as natural causes.

The recession that began in 2008 was one of the first signs. Everyone thought it was temporary, like any other recession—and it seemed so for a while. But the dollar kept plummeting, and the government couldn't halt the plunge.

Then came the earthquakes and tsunamis along the West Coast that leveled L.A. and San Francisco, the hurricanes along the East Coast one after the other, the terrorist attacks in Chicago and Houston, and the energy crisis. The Middle East, shaken by riots, pumped up oil prices and kept the oil flow going for a while, only to cut it completely when the Americans decided to pursue "clean energy"—alternatives to petroleum that never succeeded. Many despaired, many more just went to church.

But then something happened for which, surely, no natural cause existed. All of a sudden, millions of people around the world vanished. The mysterious disappearances affected every nation on the globe, but the already weakened Americans spiraled down into oblivion when all their essential institutions—from the police and the military to the health professionals and the senate—were decimated in an instant.

The scientists suggested complex and conflicting theories to explain the disappearances, none satisfactory. So people came up with their own ideas. Some blamed global warming (planetary revenge?), others swore they'd witnessed alien abductions. Conspiracy theorists blamed the government, and the religious called it the rapture.

Whatever the cause, with the vanishings all hell broke loose. Chaos reigned, and once the great wars of the Middle East were loosed upon the earth, the world forgot about the U.S.

Many share my belief that the transitional government in America at the time was too focused on internal affairs—and perhaps a bit too sympathetic toward Islam—to challenge the rising Arab nations. And so the Turks wielded their Islamist agenda unencumbered, only to be defeated later by the most radical Iraqi leader in history.

CONTINUES ON PAGE 9

Islamic Coalition 2015-2019

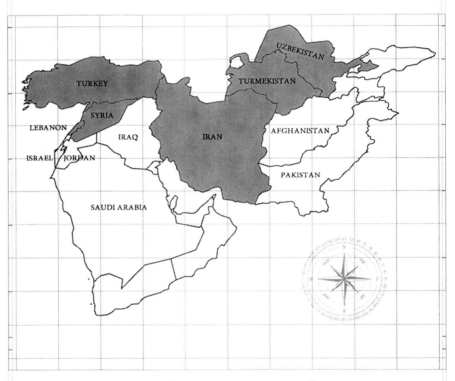

Great War of 2019

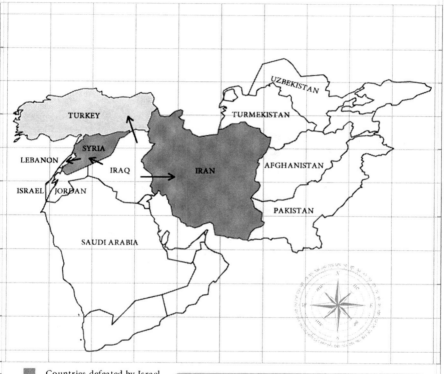

TURKEY

UZBEKISTAN

TURMEKISTAN

SYRIA

LEBANON

IRAQ

IRAN

AFGHANISTAN

ISRAEL JORDAN

PAKISTAN

SAUDI ARABIA

Countries defeated by Israel

→ Countries invaded by Iraq

After war, Iraq annexes Turkey, Syria, Lebanon, and Iran to form the Islamic Caliphate. Iraq signs peace treaty with Israel.

10 20 30 40 50 60 70 80 90 100 110 120 130 140 150 160 170 180 190 200 210 220 230 240 250 260 270 280 290 300 310 320 330 340 350 360 000

Islamic Caliphate
2019- Present

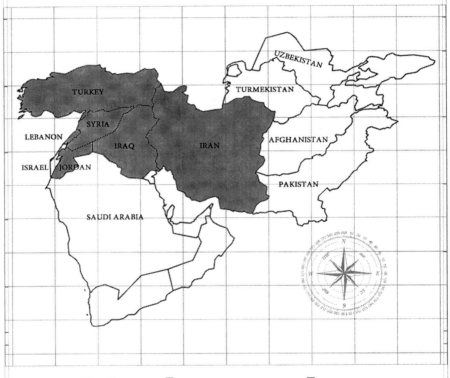

1

A rumor stampedes among the worshiping men. Armed soldiers have entered the mosque, seeking me.

I shoulder my way out to the purification area and see Hussai standing by the fountain with two soldiers. The calm of midday prayers leaves my soul as soon as I see the smirk he reserves for the torment of his enemies.

He nods at me to come closer, and in the warm light of the room I notice the blanket of dust on his zipped-up jacket. He's missed his prayers again, otherwise he'd be clean. His disdain for our faith makes me sick.

"*Aasalaamu Aleikum*, Farid."

I put on a smile. "*Wa-Aleikum Aassalaam*, Hussai. Are you coming to pray?"

"I must work, feed my family. But you wouldn't know anything about that."

The comment hits home, for today is Zainah's death anniversary.

"You'd do well to remember the words of Prophet Muhammad, peace be upon him: Prayer is the key to paradise. Not that I long to see you in paradise."

He hands me an envelope. "The army council summons you," he says, looking awfully pleased with himself.

"What does the council want?"

Hussai shrugs. "Only Allah knows."

Liar. Hussai is an *amid*, a brigadier general, not a messenger. I hold his stare until his eyelids flutter and his left cheek twitches—but he raises his hairy chin as if to look down on me, even though I outrank him. My stomach churns and I clench my fists, ready to teach him due respect for his superiors. But no. Not in this holy place, not in front of the imam.

Hussai nods to the envelope in my hand.

"You should open it. Perhaps they're expecting you soon."

I turn my back on him and face the high-ceilinged prayer hall, the hanging chandeliers, the columns with Qur'anic calligraphy. I won't give Hussai the pleasure of sneering at my expression as I read the letter, whatever it says.

I pull out a thick sepia sheet and unfold it. Water has soaked through the outer paper, wetting the letter and smudging the ink in one small section of the text. Signed by General Atartuk, the note summons me to the caliphate army council without delay. Two officers will escort me to the council's quarters in downtown Baghdad.

Why the urgency? And why do I need an escort?

Then I notice someone standing beside me—one of the soldiers. I spin and see the other one where Hussai stood before. There's no sign of Hussai. The soldier by my side is but a boy, some twenty years younger than I. The other soldier bears an old white scar on his right cheek.

"Please come with us, Major General." On his shoulder, he boasts two stars and the republican eagle. A colonel.

The boy pokes my side with the barrel of his M16 rifle and I give him a look of reproach. He draws the dusty rifle back, glances down at the carpeted floor, then at the colonel.

Bearded men wearing turbans gather in small groups around the room and overflow into the hall, staring and murmuring. Most of them are friends who welcome me every day, who have shared with me news of a successful business or a new wife over the tangy smells of the teahouse next to the mosque. These are men in whose eyes my honor and reputation are held high.

Why didn't they wait until I left the mosque? Until I returned to the base?

The colonel begins to say something, but I hold up one hand. "Let's not keep the council waiting." I stride toward the street. *"Bismillah-ir-Rahaman war-Raheem."* I begin in the name of Allah.

THE BLACK Mercedes Benz speeds along the new royal highway. I shift in the back seat, squeezed between the colonel and soldier boy. My shirt sticks to the white leather. I lean forward and reach with my hand to pull it away from my skin, hoping some air will make it down my back.

The sweaty skin tickles. Amazing–I've been in the desert for days, leading my troops against Sunnis and infidels alike, sweating like a donkey, and it never bothered me. Why should sweat make me uncomfortable now?

I know better than to ask the colonel the reason for my escort. He's just following orders. But what if I'm being framed? What if our enemies have come up with a ruse to have me killed? The Turks are still sour over their defeat—after all, we invaded their allies and decimated their army.

My palms tingle and I glance at the note again. It's clenched in my hand, wrinkled. The signature seems legitimate. The traces of the general's calligraphy are smooth and firm on the paper. It's a signature I've seen a thousand times and even forged once.

What if my worries are unfounded and this meeting will bring only good news—the awaited promotion to general, perhaps? No, it doesn't make sense to send an escort if this were a promotion.

I shove the note in my pants pocket and blow air as if whistling—a relaxation trick I learned from my imam in Palestine. I lower my chin and begin to mutter a passage from the Qur'an: "In the name of Allah, the Beneficent and Merciful…"

The Mercedes slows. The sandstorm's orange haze is not as thick in the Green Zone, and I can take in the city's skyline through the windshield above the traffic in front of us: glass and metal marvels that make Dubai look like a dumpster. The torn Baghdad the American troops left behind almost a decade ago has disappeared, and in its place the new capital of Babylon has arisen. *Allah-o Akbar.*

The vehicle plunges forward a little faster and I notice soldier boy staring at the gold and silver facades of shops lining the streets. His helmet bumps against the window as he turns to see the immense statue of Muhammad Al-Mahdi, the twelfth caliph of Islam, the sovereign ruler of our people, on his white horse. I stare too and pronounce a blessing for Al-Mahdi.

"Take the road toward the back of the building," the colonel tells the driver. "For discretion."

I nod, unsure whether to feel thankful or concerned. Why do they have to be discreet if this isn't a shameful matter? I mull over these questions but the image of Hussai's smirk at the mosque stings my mind, raising another one: What's his role in this charade?

The car halts at the Ministry of Defense building. They rush me through a dimly lit stairwell I've never seen before, though I've visited this building at least once a week for the past three years. The rusty handrail shakes under my hand. In fact, the whole structure vibrates with a low hum.

We're in the middle of April but it could as well be mid-August in here. I can feel sweat beneath my cargo pants.

My escorts have said nothing since we left the car. They move at a relentless pace, the colonel in front of me, the boy behind. We've climbed four floors already. Two more and we'll reach uncharted territory for me. Fear snakes into my gut, but I will it away. *I begin in the name of Allah,* I repeat a dozen times in my head.

The colonel stops and opens a narrow door to his left. "Please," he says, extending one arm.

I walk in and white light greets me on the public stairs of the building. We go through another door and into a hallway where I see familiar office modules and green walls.

"*Aasalaamu Aleikum*," a clerk in a red turban greets us, then scurries away with a stack of papers down a corridor like a rat.

It seems it's business as usual at the headquarters of the Islamic caliphate army, also known as the Mahdi's army.

"Wait here, Halid," the colonel tells the boy. "Major, this way."

Down the hall, he enters through the large ornate doors with Qur'anic inscriptions that lead to the general's office. As I follow, I catch a glimpse of a man chatting and chuckling with a group near the window. I turn to look at him—and Hussai averts his gaze. His graying hair and thick beard jiggle as he laughs, no doubt at me. I wish he'd look closer before I enter. Then he'd see that my face is stern and confident, that I have nothing to fear because Allah is my guide.

But he doesn't, and I move forward.

Across the reception area, General Atartuk's assistant is holding the door open. "They're expecting you."

The colonel moves to one side of the reception area and I nod at the assistant as I enter the room. Allah's will.

THE DOOR seals behind me and I'm left facing an empty desk.

"Farid," a voice calls to my right. General Atartuk stands at the far side of a ridiculously large conference table. Four men in black robes sit close to him, two on each side of the table. These are the permanent members of the council, the overseers of *Sharia* in the army, who punish those who fail to act according to the Islamic way.

"Please, take your place," the general says.

A sixth person I haven't seen before emerges from a dark corner and pulls one chair out. I sit across from the general and mutter a greeting, not sure my words come out right. It's as if my tongue is taped to the back of my teeth.

The four men scrutinize me, frowning, and only then, looking at their heads, do I realize I'm not wearing my black head wrap. They must think me a sinner for not covering my head, even though there's no set requirement to do so.

"Farid," the general says, in a paternal tone. "We've received some alarming information." The head-covered men nod and wring their hands. "There are accusations, Farid, grave accusations against you." The inflection of his voice is now harsh and tense.

"Accusations? Whatever they are, I'm sure they're false and easy to dismiss."

General Atartuk bends forward on the table.

"There appears to be evidence that you have ties with Zionists, that you're an infidel lover—a traitor, even."

A jarring sensation fills my head as I process the words, as if someone were shaking it violently.

"Who would dare call me a traitor? I'd give my life for jihad. I've pledged my allegiance to Al-Mahdi. I'm a servant of Allah. *Allah-o Ahkbar!*"

"*Allah-o Ahkbar,*" the council members respond like robots.

The general nods. "It's hard for me to accept these charges, Farid, because I know you and I knew your father. He wasn't the best Muslim, but he served his country and even gave one of his sons for the Palestinian cause."

My hands prickle at the mention of my brother, a suicide bomber now in Paradise enjoying the seventy-two virgins promised for the martyrs of Allah.

"In any case I refuse to believe this without hearing your defense."

I stand and breathe in some courage.

"You must never believe such nonsense, sir. I've faithfully served the Mahdi's army for the past three years since you brought me in from the Saudi air force. Have I not acquired all the weapons now held by the soldiers in the Islamic caliphate? Have I not proven my loyalty to Al-Mahdi, god give him peace? Where's the proof that I'm a traitor? What is the evidence?"

The general looks down to his hands.

"I have yet to see the evidence. But the source, an honorable Muslim, claims he has it."

"Is your source Brigadier General Hussai Siddiqui?"

"I should not reveal the identity of—"

"General, please." I realize my sharp tone can cost me my career, so I flatten my voice. "Is it Hussai?"

The general faces me for a few seconds, then nods. Too angry to trust myself to speak, I imagine Hussai's mocking laughter outside the office. Of course he's the source. No one else but Hussai wants the general's position as much as I do—and he wants it for power, not for Islam. Almost ready to retire, Atartuk will leave his job to the next in line: me. Hussai can only aspire to be in the pool of candidates if I'm out of the way. May he be deprived of Allah's blessings.

"Hussai has lied and defamed a Muslim brother," I say. "I demand an investigation for misconduct, General."

"He'll have his chance to show evidence for his accusations. If he doesn't, he'll be punished."

I'll punish him first. He'll regret the day he decided to lie to the council.

"Is there anything else, General?" He shakes his head. "Then if you'll excuse me, I must get back to the base." I start to leave, already tasting the satisfaction I'll feel when I break Hussai's nose.

"Wait."

One of the four men stands and points at me.

"You deny the charges of being a Zionist?"

"Of course."

"Do you affirm to hate every Jew and to be willing to slay them wherever you find them?"

My eyes narrow. Does he know I grew up in Israel? Surely not. Allah forgive me, but I have never been able to hate the Jews, as much as I've been taught to.

I try to wet my lips under the fixed stare of the councilmen. My former imam once told me that lying is allowed by the Qur'an if one's life is in danger. Muhammad lied and condoned lying many times. And if I don't lie about this, they'll behead me for sure.

"Yes, I hate those pigs. I hate the Jews. *Allah-o Ahkbar.*"

The men are shouting praises to Allah as I move out of the office. My heart is pounding and I hide my trembling hands in my pockets. Down the hallway, my eyes meet Hussai's. His mocking smile vanishes as I run toward him, fists clenched.

2

I want to shatter every bone in his body.

As I run toward Hussai he tries to block the punch, but I smack his cheekbone and knock him to the floor.

"Who's the traitor, you hypocrite?" I spit and grab his shirt below his neck. "You're the traitor, conspiring against your Muslim bro—"

Hussai slaps me and tries to pull away. I punch him in the belly, and as he writhes, the clerks of the Islamic caliphate army gather like spectators to a dogfight.

My mouth is dry again. I feel the crowd pressing in and glance at the wide-eyed clerks. Their returning stares nail me where I stand.

This was the wrong place to settle my score with Hussai. He's my subordinate. I'm the major general in the Mahdi's army, not a fresh soldier who quarrels with violence. Hussai is kneeling, scowling at me. Should I hit him again with everyone watching?

Fast steps approach behind me, and I hear the murmur of a clerk near me: "Time to leave." I start to turn—

Strong arms around my waist drive my feet into the air, and my back lands flat on the floor. Hussai's breath invades my nostrils and his weight threatens to crush my chest. His dark face rises above me against the backdrop of a white lamp on the ceiling. I hear his curses and expect the coming blow. Where's the anger that drove me here? I need it to get out of this asphyxiating chaos.

I close my eyes, then my lungs begin to move again, all the weight that pressed me now gone. My instincts, my training, or my common sense, something, kicks in and I spring up in an instant.

The scarred colonel holds Hussai back while soldier boy
points his rifle at me.

"Bring them to my office," the general says.

"YOU COULD go to trial for this. You have upset me, brothers."

The general's face reveals more shame than anger, which
makes me feel ashamed too. Of course, I would never let Hussai know that. He's sitting on a chair less than a meter from me.
Last time I glanced at him, his forehead glistened and his lips
quivered. He can't hide his emotions the way I do. I enjoy seeing
him defeated, but I've placed myself in a lethal mess. If we go to
trial we'll either spend many days and nights in Saddam Hussein's old dungeons or our heads will roll. Mercy is scarce under
the caliphate's law. And it must be so, because the world can't be
subdued under Islam with a lax regime.

"You disappoint me, Farid. And you, Hussai—well, I don't
know what to think about you. What has gotten into—"

"I was attacked."

I purse my lips and look away. What can I say in my defense?
This is not my usual self. My temper has betrayed me. My last
rage attack was years ago, I'm not sure how many.

"I'm partly responsible." The general turns to Hussai. "I
didn't hide from Farid the fact that you brought the accusations
against him."

"Without proof," I say.

Hussai looks straight ahead and cocks his head, acting as if
I'm not there.

"I won't back off from my claims against that infidel lover.
The truth will come out soon enough."

I stare at him. Is he planning to frame me? I imagine jump-
ing out of my chair and pounding him. By Allah, I must contain
myself. I close my eyes and grip the arms of the chair until I'm
sure my knuckles have turned white.

"You distort the truth, *Munafiq.*" Hypocrite.

His chair rattles and I pop my eyes open. The colonel has spared me from Hussai's jabs again, keeping him on his chair by pushing down on his shoulders.

"Enough! You two are suspended from service, effective immediately." The general stares at some point across the room, then shakes his head. "I want you to report back to your stations in five days. On Wednesday you'll receive orders. If I didn't need you for the imminent offensive Al-Mahdi is planning I'd put you both in confinement for a month before handing you to the radical overseers. Thank Allah I'm feeling merciful today."

Imminent offensive? We're in the middle of a peace treaty with our enemies.

"Are we going to war?" Hussai sounds as startled as I am.

The general nods.

THE COLONEL escorts me out of the building through the main exit. Soldier boy opens the door of the idling Mercedes, but I shake my head and walk away from the car.

"We can drive you back to your home if you want, sir," the colonel says.

I face him with a sly smile. "I'm not going home yet, colonel. I'll find my way later."

After the car melts into the traffic, I walk south until I'm surrounded by noise: gratuitous honks, indistinct shouts, all sorts of clattering. To my left, a young man sings out of tune, to my right an old merchant calls out to passersby, inviting them to browse the clothes hung on the rail in the center of the sidewalk.

What's worst—the suspension or the coming war? The peace of the last couple of years was beginning to feel comfortable, but Al-Mahdi knows better. Sometimes war is necessary for a lasting peace.

I need to clear my thoughts, grasp the meaning of this debacle, but the streets aren't helping. People have gathered at the plaza across the road, shouting an angry chant that piques my curiosity.

The crowd forms a human circle around three policemen beating a man. After a stint of brutal punches and rib-breaking kicks, the policemen let the thin victim take a respite. He doesn't plead for mercy, or cry, nor do his eyes show any resentment. Instead, a fragile smile and an impossible peace shine from his face.

"Who is that man?"

An onlooker by my side answers. "A Christian."

"I thought the council had eradicated non-Muslims from the country long ago."

"Nah. And I say they've shown enough mercy already." He raises a fist and shouts with the crowd. "Death to the enemies of god!"

As the policemen tie him and place his neck over the rock that will hold his head for the last time, the Christian's gaze turns to the eerie orange sky. His face is glowing, and it's as if he's seeing something no one else can see, something glorious.

I shake my head and step back, not wanting to see the execution of a happy man. He must be deluded or mentally ill to face death in such a manner.

A hand grabs my shoulder and I recoil, thinking it's a beggar, but the breath closing on my face belongs to a familiar man.

"*Afin, akhoya.*" Hello, brother.

"Ibrahim?" He's supposed to be dead. At least, that's what the intelligence reports said.

"Good to see you again." He shakes my hand with a strong grip, pulls his back and takes it to his heart. "Aren't you glad to see me?"

"Of course."

I last saw Ibrahim eighteen months ago, during a short trip to the West Bank to survey the remains of Ramallah. That time he didn't see me, but I spotted him among a group of protesters at the plaza. No, at the heaps of debris where the plaza once stood.

"What are you doing in Babylon?"

"Had to come and see for myself what your caliph has done with Baghdad."

Ibrahim opens his arms, palms facing up. "Maybe he should rebuild the Palestinian camps in the same way."

"Ibrahim, please." I glance back at the executioners. "Let's go to a quieter place."

I press him forward with my hand on his back for a few meters. "I know a nice teahouse not too far from here."

He tries to keep up with my quick pace. If he only knew. Any unfavorable comment against Al-Mahdi could cost him his head—especially around the crowd beheading the Christian. In a city where most sports and attractions are banned, executions provide the entertainment.

We walk a while in silence and I eye him every now and then. His dark boyish face is just as I remember it from our days in Israel, where our occupation was to pickpocket tourists—until the day we joined Fatah, the Palestine Liberation Organization. There's a wariness in the way he moves his eyes over the objects and people around him. He has the look of a man who does not trust. But then again, I know why. I too lived in Palestine for a time, where every child is taught to distrust and hate the outside world—especially the Jews, the root of every Arab disgrace. The answer then is jihad.

"Tell me Ibrahim, how's Ali Muhammad? Have you seen him lately?"

"I have. He's a proud *mujahideen*."

So my cousin is still fighting for the Palestinian cause. At least he's alive.

"Is he still talking about becoming a martyr?"

"Of course, it's an honor to die for jihad."

An honor to blow himself up? Better to keep my thoughts on this subject to myself or Ibrahim will be offended. I point with relief to the entrance of the teahouse.

"Over here."

Four men sit around a dominoes game near the door. I glance at the sixes and twos lying on the table. It's been a long time since I've played anything, but the Islamic council doesn't approve of army members participating in leisure activities. How I miss the weekend ATV rides at the Saudi desert with my Air Force brothers.

We pick an empty table in a corner. The edges of the flowered tablecloth are but loose threads waiting to be pulled and undone. It's a lot like the places of my childhood in Israel. I breathe the relaxing aromas of boiling herbs and feel at peace for a moment.

"Impressive," Ibrahim says as we sit.

"What's impressive?"

"The city. Baghdad. I'm sure there's nothing like it in the entire world."

"You should also see Mecca. Another city built to show the glory of Allah."

"Ah, yes, Mecca, but what about Jerusalem? Your caliph has let those pigs build their temple. It's so big and pompous the Dome of the Rock pales beside it."

"Don't talk like that. Al-Mahdi has brought peace between Sunnis and Shiites, has united four Islamic nations into one, and will soon rule the world. Don't you believe the prophecies?"

He laughs. "You really sound like one of those professors or an imam, Farid. What should I know about prophecies? You're the one who learned to read and all that. While you spent all those days at the mosque listening to sermons, I was throwing rocks and dodging Israeli rubber bullets."

"All right, listen," I say. "After the death of the Prophet Muhammad, peace be upon him, there were eleven caliphs. The twelfth caliph disappeared when he was a young boy, and the prophecies tell us that Allah was protecting him in the desert until the Last Days, when he would return to bring the world under Islamic law and justice. You've seen what Al-Mahdi has done in the past four to five years. It's just what the prophecies foretold. There's still much to be done, but look around you—he has created prosperity for each of his followers."

"Sure. And Palestine was supposed to benefit from the Islamic caliphate too. Or should I say Babylon? That's what you call it, no?" Ibrahim shakes his head. "Have you been to Gaza lately? To the West Bank? There's no prosperity, there's only bones, stones, and—"

"At least you have food in Israel. The rest of the world is starving."

"That food isn't for the Palestinians, Farid! Your caliph has forgotten his promise—"

I bang on the table. "Shut your mouth."

People stare our way and I lower my voice.

"You're talking like an infidel, Ibrahim. Every Muslim is obligated to support Al-Mahdi, including you. He's The Lord of the Age, the Awaited One. Soon he will restore justice to Palestine and the rest of the earth. Soon Islam will be victorious over all religions. Just wait and see."

Ibrahim leans back in his chair and cocks his head. "I'll believe that the day I see Jerusalem controlled by the believers and every Jew beheaded."

A waiter brings cups and tea and arranges them for us. I look away at the men playing dominoes. One of them, a bald guy with a graying mustache, glances just below the table with a frown. I see what he's frowning at: the player beside him is pulling a tile from his pocket.

"You cheated!" the bald man says. The cheater shrugs, then all of them burst out laughing.

Ibrahim says, "I want to believe you." He leans forward. "We can't wait any longer. Tell me something is going to happen, Farid. Tell me this peace covenant won't continue for another three and a half years. Tell me your powerful army isn't going to sit still while the Jews cavort in our land."

His stare makes me feel uneasy again and I look down at the

mantle. Imminent offensive, the general said. I'm supposed to go back to the base in five days and prepare an attack.

"I don't know."

THIS IS a dream. It must be, because I'm holding a bomb in my hands. It looks a lot like the bomb I held on my sole suicide attempt. But something is different this time because I'm not smuggling the explosives into the crowds at the Western Wall in Jerusalem, ready to blow myself up with hundreds of Jews for Allah's jihad. Instead I'm in the bedroom of my old house in Jeddah, my wife Zainah sleeping at my side.

Oh, Zainah. I want to touch her but my hands are glued to the explosives. Unlike the bomb of my youth, which I never saw detonate but threw in a trash can at the sight of Arab youngsters I dared not kill, this charge won't leave my hands. I know what I'll do next, even against my will. I will call on the name of god, click the detonator, and blow my marriage bed into a million fragments of death. Please forgive me, Zainah, please—

I awaken to the familiar hum of distant prayers. I run to the kitchen, glance out the window, and scan the color of the firmament. My heart skips a beat. The twilight must have disappeared from the sky no more than a few minutes ago. Did the *muezzin* recite the *Adhan*, the call to prayer? Is the loudspeaker at the mosque broken? No, I simply fell asleep.

I peer over the roofs of my neighbors at the dome of the Al Kadhimiya shrine in the distance. The prayers have started, and I can picture all the faithful men bowing in perfect rows, one behind the other, following the imam.

I hurry to the living room and stand upright. The solemn intention crosses my mind without effort: I offer this night prayer: four *ra'kah's*, seeking closeness to God.

I lift my hands to my ears. *"Allah-o Ahkbar."* The council members flash in my thoughts for a second. "In the name of

God, the Merciful, the Compassionate. Praise belongs to God, Lord of the World, the Merciful, the Compassionate, Master of the Day of Judgment."

Imminent offensive? Why didn't they tell us before? My parched lips cling to each other. I must pray.

"We worship only You, and from You alone do we seek help."

A secret attack. Against whom? A headache creeps in. I should have seen this coming. The war exercises, the intense training of the troops in the last few weeks.

"Lead us on the straight path, the path of those whom You have blessed, not on those on whom is Your wrath, nor of those who have gone astray."

The Americans are not a threat any more, nor the Turks nor the Russians. And there's the covenant with Israel. Who are we fighting, then?

"*Allah-o Ahkbar.*" I bow down and place my hands on my knees. "Glory be to my Lord, the Great, and praise belongs to Him."

I should be at the base, preparing for jihad, not sitting in my home, suspended. I promised Zainah to work for the peace of our people, but that will come when Al-Mahdi is victorious over all the nations. That's what I told her, that war is a means to peace, that jihad is our duty as Muslims. How I miss those arguments with her.

I stand and gasp as I realize I forgot to recite the second chapter of the Qur'an. I close my eyes and try to focus on my supplications. "God hears the one who praises Him. *Allah-o Ahkbar.*"

What now? Oh, yes. I kneel and rest my forehead against the carpet. What's wrong with me? Salah is my nature.

"Glory be to my exalted Lord, and praise be to Him."

Brrring, brrring. I jolt up and stare at the phone across the room, its small digital screen glowing green. Who would call during the time of prayers? Perhaps the congregational prayers have finished. *Brrring, brrring.* But I have a duty with God. I place my hands on my thighs.

"I ask forgiveness of God, my Lord, and turn towards him. *Allah-o Ahkbar.*"

A beep halts the ringing and I stare at the machine. I stand for the next unit in the prayer just as the phone emits a second, prolonged beep, indicating a voice message. Perhaps the general is lifting my suspension and they want me to go back right now. Not likely. What if Al-Mahdi asked for my presence at the base? The army needs me, my men need me. I'm their guide and inspiration. But I should finish my prayers. The phone's glowing screen fades into energy-saving mode.

"In the Name of God, the Merciful—"

God will forgive me since he's so merciful. I go to the phone, dial my voicemail—and a voice from the past upends my night.

3

So predictable. Hussai watches through his binoculars as Farid trots out of his building, four sharp in the morning. Hussai knows the routine by now: Farid will run five kilometers, hand-lift a dozen massive logs over his head near the gold market, and come back right on time to clean up before his prayers.

Hussai rubs the bruise on his left cheek and fills his chest with air. Patience. His payback will come soon. He leans back in the driver's seat of his Land Rover, eyelids heavy. A five-minute nap? He has more than two hours to find the evidence he needs to back his claims to the general. Maybe he won't find anything, but it's worth the try. He closes his eyes and lets lethargy pin him to the seat.

His eyes flutter open. Four fifty-three. He curses and his hands grapple with the door lock. When he stumbles out the street is deserted, but engines hum on contiguous streets. Four fifty-five, his Casio digital watch reads. Now he must hurry.

Although no one is watching him—as far as he can tell—Hussai tries to look inconspicuous. He's in Kadhimiya, the Shiite's holy neighborhood. Any interaction and his Sunni accent will give him away.

He scowls at the sand under his feet and keeps walking. His father called the long stretch of desert and palm trees that is Iraq a sandy beach with no ocean. The April winds blew two sandstorms over Baghdad in the past week, but he's accustomed to them. Only rain could halt the storms, but it hasn't rained for years. Some blame the two lunatics at the Temple Mount. The Two Witnesses, they call themselves, said to have supernatural powers, just like the Caliph. How can people believe such nonsense? Crazy or not, the Witnesses managed to rebuild the Jewish temple in Jerusalem. Almost finished, Hussai heard a few weeks ago—and covered in gold. People murmur their outrage at the erection of Solomon's old temple but soothe themselves with prophecies that one day everyone will serve Allah or meet the sword.

Hussai doesn't care much about the prophecies. History is enough for him to abhor the Jews. They have oppressed and slaughtered the Palestinians, attacked and conspired against Arabs, all from a land to which they lay false claim. What Hussai does care about is the gold lining the walls of the Jewish temple. If the Mahdi's army ever tramples that fancy synagogue—which is likely, as the caliph is a greedy military genius—he plans to be there to claim his reward. But Farid must go down first. Only as full general can Hussai dispose of the spoils as he wishes.

Two bright lights blind him. He lifts an arm to his face and looks below the silhouette of his hand. The lights approach fast. A horn blares and he jumps off to one side. A dark green Lada speeds by him. He whistles and puts a hand on his chest. A few seconds later, another car turns into his street. Hussai moves over to the sidewalk and strides towards Farid's building. He's wasted too much time already. His pace quickens. Is that a tremor in his hands?

He reaches the dark apartment building and looks up five levels to the top floor, where Farid lives. All seems dark but for a dim light that shines through a window on the third floor. He reaches for the door handle and pushes it down. Unlocked. He smiles and inches the door inward.

Thud, thud, thud, thud. Heavy steps rushing to the door. Hussai spins to his left and shoves his weight against the rail of a shop as the door of the building swings open. The cold rail clanks in the shadows. He cringes. A citric smell hits his nostrils, making

him want to sneeze. A fruit shop. He halts his breathing, waiting.
"Who's there?" The quivering voice of a woman.

Hussai exhales and glances at the black burka. She probably
can't see his face in the darkness.

"Mind your own business, woman." She hurries away.

How ridiculous he must have looked recoiling from a female.
He waits, fists clenched, until she vanishes at the street corner,
then jogs into the building.

THE COPY he made of Farid's key unlocks the bolt with a sharp
click. A dripping beep begins a countdown. Hussai storms in,
flashlight pointing forward, searching for the alarm. A lone
lamp in one corner of the living room spreads soft yellow light
across the clean carpet. Above the lamp, the alarm system emits
a stream of red blips like a detonator ready to go off. Less than
ten seconds to deactivate it.

Hussai pulls the Russian gadget Raskolnikov sent him from
his pocket. The infernal beeping aggravates his anxiety and his
hands fumble with the device. He hits the lamp with one elbow.
It topples to the floor. He curses. He presses the device against
the alarm and pushes a black button. There's a swirling sound,
like a tiny airplane engine coming to life. Swoosh. The beeping
stops. Green light.

Sweat covers his forehead. That was close. He picks up the
unbroken lamp from the floor, places it on the table, switches the
flashlight off and hangs it on his belt, then closes the front door.

Hussai scans the place. Clean and modern but too small for
his taste. It's one of those luxury apartments built by a foreign
developer right before the Americans left—when the city was still
divided and the so-called Messiah hadn't yet come.

As expected, Farid has a copy of the Qur'an at hand. It sits on
the coffee table beside the reclining leather chair by the window,
a stack of books on the carpet nearby. Any Zionist material? He

kneels by the pile and reads the spines, disgusted when he sees the book on top is a Shiite text. The Shiites put forty-three bullets in his father—the scars of hate are impossible to heal. He keeps skimming down the stack. A few poetry books by Hafiz Ibrahim and Mahmoud Darwish. Elias Kohury's *Gate of the Sun*. But no Zionist propaganda. On the contrary, some of these authors are Palestinian. Hussai doesn't read much himself but knows well the lists of approved and condemned books by the Islamic Council. He's been charged with finding rogue army members—and Farid has no idea. In almost six months he has yet to find a single traitor, but he plans to make one of Farid even if it means planting evidence. That would be a last resort—his head will roll if he's discovered framing the major general.

Hussai stands and walks toward the kitchen, where he picks up a cinnamon scent. Why Farid lives in this cramped one-bedroom suite, he can't understand. The army pays well enough. In fact, Farid must be earning twice Hussai's salary, and while Hussai has three wives and eight or nine children, Farid lives alone. He can afford a larger place. What a strange man.

Finding nothing out of the ordinary in the kitchen, Hussai moves to the bedroom and switches the light on.

"Ha!" So early and his bed is already made, though he has no woman to clean for him. What a pathetic life.

The matching set of bedside tables has no messiness or even dust, but an odd folder sits by itself at the base of a lamp. Hussai runs a finger over the cover, then flips it open. Newspaper clippings about the wars, some featuring Farid's heroic acts as a pilot during the war against Turkey. Hiding beneath the clippings is a book: *Peace in the Middle East*.

Hussai scratches the top of his head. He can't picture Farid, the ultimate warrior, reading about peace. On the first page of the book, two initials are written with blue ink—Z.Z.—and tucked into the middle pages, an article about the peace treaty with Israel.

Interesting but not particularly incriminating. Hussai pulls out his phone, takes a picture of the folder and its contents, then replaces the folder on the table. More, he needs more.

He shuffles carefully through the drawers of the large cabinet against the wall with their military-neat stacks of clothes. As he closes the bottom drawer with a thump he catches a gleam underneath the cabinet. He pulls out a picture framed in silver and turns so the light will fall on the dusty glass. A photo of a stunning woman with big rounded and a perfect smile. Beside her, a younger Farid. It's obvious the wedding took place before the Council's rule, or her face would be covered. When Farid came to Baghdad, he came alone, as far as Hussai can remember.

For a whole minute, he stares at the photograph. "Who are you? A bloodthirsty Jew, perhaps?"

The phone rings in the living room and Hussai jerks. The frame slips out of his hands, hits the border of the cabinet with a *crack* and falls to the carpet. He mutters under his breath. The phone rings a second time but is cut off. Hussai grunts and stares at the back of the picture frame. The tiny white label in the corner says: *Made in Saudi Arabia.* How peculiar. He picks up the frame but a piece of broken glass remains on the floor. He curses again and considers placing the whole thing back under the wardrobe, broken pieces and all. But perhaps he should take the picture and throw away the glass and the Saudi frame. Will Farid notice? Judging from the dust, probably not.

His Casio vibrates and he glances at it. Five-thirty. Time's running out. There has to be something. He walks out of the bedroom and paces around the living area, scratching his bushy beard, examining every corner. No safe, no mail, no paperwork. Farid's office at the base, maybe? That would be harder to break into.

A faint green glow catches the corner of his eye. The telephone. Who's calling Farid so early in the morning? Hussai grabs the phone from its base and reads the message on the screen: Call forwarded to cell. He presses the menu button, seeking incoming calls. The most recent is from a long string of digits in which

Hussai recognizes something familiar. He reads the number again: 7095613.

Raskolnikov's number also starts with the 7095 though the rest is different. A call from Moscow. Are the Russians working with Farid as well? Raskolnikov assured Hussai he was the only Russian spy in the caliphate. What's he supposed to make of this? And how long has Farid been talking to the Russians?

He scrolls down the list of recent calls, looking for the 7095. The second call seems also an international number, beginning with 9722. Nothing familiar about that one. The rest are local. He returns to the top, then types and saves the Russian number in his cellphone. If he can't find any Zionist connection, a Russian connection will have to do. He grins and pushes the menu button on Farid's phone, ready to place it back on its base. It is then that he notices the icon on the top right corner of the screen. The envelope icon.

He glances at the buttons below the screen—he loves this phone—and sees one with the envelope on it. The button glows when he presses it.

Hussai listens to the saved message of a man speaking strange words. What language is that? He presses the button to repeat the message. All he needs is one familiar word. The message lasts almost a minute. At the end of it, Hussai bites his bottom lip and scratches his beard. He closes his eyes and repeats the message a third time. He can almost make out the first two words. He replays the message again. Hussai laughs. The first two words are now clear in his ears: *Shalom*, Farid. Hebrew. A call from a dirty Jew.

"Just what I needed to hear." It's almost too good to be true.

4

I run, drenched in sweat, through the familiar streets of Kadhimiya, rushing past the old Camp Justice military base where Saddam was executed. This neighborhood is beginning to feel like a prison. Maybe I should try a new route, venture outside the Shia havens and into the open desert. Maybe I should fly somewhere until my suspension is over.

"*Shalom*, Farid." Last night's message is still replaying in my mind. "It's Jonathan ben David. I know it's been a long time and our lives have gone on different paths, but… I don't know who else to call. It's about Benjamin. He's… ah, hard to say. I mean, what I want to say is… well, it's too much to ask, but would you come to Israel? I'm sorry, I know you have your duties and all but I just thought … please call me. You know how to find me. *Lehitraot*." Goodbye.

What an odd message. And I remember the tension in his words, the long pauses, and how his voice broke toward the end. Whatever happened to his brother is tearing his soul. Why didn't he say it? Why can't I find the courage to call him and ask?

The cell phone strapped around my biceps vibrates. I slow to a trot and reach for it.

"This is Farid."

"Mr. Zadeh," a guttural male voice says. Slavic accent.

"Who is this?"

"A friend."

The way he says this prickles my skin. I move away from the open street and shelter under the umbrella of an outdoor cafe table.

"What do you want, friend?"

"Right to the point. Good." He sounds amused. There's no background noise, so I can't tell where he is. "I want to interest you in a profitable business."

"I'm not a businessman."

"Oh, you're wrong, Major General. You've done quite some business deals for your country."

I wait, not wanting to say anything compromising. I'm in enough trouble already.

"I would like to arrange a meeting," he says. "Would you—"

"What's your business?"

"I would rather have you discuss this in private with our contact there—"

"You're wasting my time."

He grumbles. A long pause. I try to sound resolute.

"Very well, then."

"All right, Mr. Zadeh. I won't discuss details on your private line, but be at the Lebanese restaurant in the Green Zone at nine p.m. and I will contact you again."

Click.

The cell phone's screen dims and fades to black. What just happened? How does he know about the armament deals I've done for Babylon with the Chinese and the Russians? And why would a Russian be interested in our weapons if I buy them from his own country? A stark thought sears my brain. They may be watching me, monitoring my every move, listening to my ins and outs in the apartment. Is it tapped? I must search for microphones. What if someone is there now?

I sprint to my place.

A LONE car drives in my direction as I turn onto my street. I hop onto the sidewalk and keep a steady pace. The car jerks to the left, picks up speed and rushes past me, lifting a thin cloud of dust.

I stop and glance back: an old Land Rover. I get a strange feeling—do I know the driver? I dart toward my apartment.

Once in the building, I climb the stairs two steps at a time. I pause on my floor and listen before moving forward. The door shows no sign of tampering. My muscles relax and I go in.

I walk to the table with the lamp and reach under the false drawer for my 38 special. As I stand, the green light of the alarm blinks at me. I stiffen. The alarm is disabled. But I activated it when I left this morning. Something else—the bedroom door is open.

I spin and hold the gun in front of me, pointing at every corner. I search the kitchen, push doors open, rip the shower's curtain aside, peek under my bed. Sweat covers my forehead. I sigh and put the gun down. My gaze catches the white line of a shirt through a crack in the wardrobe. The bottom drawer is ajar.

As I reach down to inspect it, a car screeches on the street outside. I run to the window just in time to see a green Lada veering off. Staring at the empty road, I wonder how hard would it be to find the owner of that Lada. It's a Russian car. Fortunately, I know a Russian man who owns a Lada and lives right here in Baghdad.

Hussai pushes the spinach omelet away and leans back in his chair. Aisha, his oldest wife, rushes to pick up the plate and pour fresh coffee.

"Was the food pleasing, sir?"

He shrugs and answers with a grunt. His eyes are fixed on the loaf of *samoon* still on the table. Aisha tiptoes out of the room.

He burps and shakes his head. Not even Aisha's fine *bigilla*, the bean dip, could wash away the bile that tints his mouth whenever he thinks of the Russian number on Farid's phone. When he dialed the number to find out who it was, a recording said it was out of service. And Raskolnikov, who might be able to shed some light on the issue, isn't answering his phone. That's unlike him. Hussai snatches the phone from his belt, snaps it open, and redials Raskolnikov.

"*Privyet*, Hussai."

Hussai recoils. "Why didn't you answer before?"

"I was unavailable."

"Doing what?"

"You sound impatient," Raskolnikov says. "I assume you have good information for me at last."

Hussai purses his lips. He hasn't had much to report in the past few months. Should he tell him about the imminent offensive?

"Anyway," Raskolnikov says, "it's good you called. We want to recruit another informant, someone closer to the top. I made contact this morning and want you to close the deal."

A lump forms in Hussai's throat. "Who is it?"

"Major General Farid Zadeh."

He knew it. "No!"

"What? Why not?"

"Not him, not Farid."

Aisha pokes her head out the kitchen door. Hussai realizes he's standing over the table and barking into his cell phone.

"I don't know who you think you are to make demands of me," Raskolnikov says. "We've paid you well for many years, and what have you provided?"

He scowls at Aisha, who disappears at once. Then says, "I told you in advance about the peace covenant."

"That was more than three years ago."

"It's hard, in my position—"

"That's why we need someone higher up. You don't seem to have access to the general any more."

Hussai's facial muscles tighten and he pushes the table away. Raskolnikov sighs.

"Look, Hussai. You are my friend. We know each other since, what? The 1990s?"

Hussai mumbles a yes. It was in the icy winter of 1997, the last one he spent training in Moscow, that he became a spy for the Russians.

"That's why I've put myself on the line for you. But without results, I can't justify your expenses to the Duma liaison. Iraq is getting too strong now. The former Soviet nations are all aligning with your country, making everyone here nervous."

"Give me some time, Raskolnikov. Farid isn't trustworthy. No matter what he may have said to you, he's loyal to the caliph. Don't believe him."

"Should I believe you instead?"

"Yes."

"Why, Hussai? Why should I believe you? You're just afraid another element would take your place, isn't that so?"

He grabs a chair, hurls it against the opposite wall. A framed photograph falls to the floor and the glass shatters.

"Don't threaten me, Raskolnikov. You still need me. I know your secrets and I can put you down."

A cackling laugh fills the receiver. Hussai grits his teeth, knowing he has no other option but to play his trump card.

"We're going to war."

The laughter stops.

"What?"

"The Mahdi's Army is preparing for an imminent offensive. Confirmed by General Atartuk."

Five seconds of speechless static.

"Are you sure?"

Hussai smiles. "Didn't Farid tell you?"

"No, he didn't. He was reluctant to meet at all."

"Of course."

"But tell me about the offensive. Are we the target?"

"I won't tell you anything yet. I think I'll give you some time to reconsider recruiting Farid."

"Are we the target? Are you attacking Russia?"

"Have you reconsidered?"

"Hussai, I warn—"

"Think about it, Raskolnikov."

"You're just buying time...." Raskonikov's voice trails off.

"I have time. Do you?"

"Come on, my friend, don't—"

"Think about it."

Hussai smashes the phone shut against his palm.

6

The massive research building housing the army's weapons labs is part of the Islamic Caliphate Army Base complex but can be accessed from outside the base as well as from within. Only civilian staff use the outside entrance, but that's the one I'll use today. Knowing General Atartuk, it's very likely he instructed the guards at the base not to let me in.

I lower my head as I pass the security cameras and push open the glass doors. Two soldiers stand near a metal detector and a conveyor belt scanner that's seen better days, probably at an airport.

"Good morning, soldiers."

They stand firm and salute. *"Aasalaamu Aleikum,* sir."

I address the one standing closer to me. "I have some business here but prefer not to take the long path around. Where's the reception, soldier?"

"Down the hallway to your left, sir." He looks apprehensive. "Shouldn't you reg—"

"Thank you. You're doing a fine job here."

The soldier smiles and I stride through the metal detector, ignore its beeps, and walk down the hallway without looking back.

The clerk at the reception desk seems as bored as the soldiers. "Yes?"

"I'm Major General Zadeh. I'm looking for Dr. Sergey Vasiliev."

The clerk dials a number. "Wait here, please."

"Thank you."

I scan the area. At least four high-tech cameras point to where I stand. The incongruity between them and the easily duped security personnel makes me smile.

"He's coming," the clerk says.

I nod and wait. If Sergey Vasiliev is connected to the break-in, he may be nervous to see me here. The truth is, I'm nervous myself.

All I know is that he has a green Lada, and he's not the man who called me—but he may be the contact the caller mentioned.

"I did expect a visit, Major General, but not from you."

Sergey's voice startles me and I spin around to see a pained glance at me over his gold-rimmed glasses, as if it hurts to lift his head and meet my eyes. He seems unchanged since the first time I met him, six or seven months ago at the Mahdi's palace.

My gaze is drawn to the white powder over his oily hair. "From who, then?"

His left cheek twitches. "What can I do for you?" He keeps both hands deep in the pockets of his lab coat.

"You didn't answer my question."

"If you don't know the answer, maybe you're not supposed to know."

"Know what?"

Sergey takes off his glasses, holds them up to the light, then rubs the lenses clean with the hem of his lab coat. His silence is annoying.

I look over his shoulder at the heavy doors with a bright yellow sign: CAUTION: Restricted Area, Radioactive Materials, Biohazard, Toxic Chemicals, No Food or Drink. My mouth twists and I wonder if the powder on Sergey's hair is more than dandruff.

"Major Zadeh, please," he says, replacing his glasses. "Just state your business directly."

He's working on something classified. As he's the chief nuclear scientist for the Mahdi Army, there are only a few things he could be working on—a few very dangerous things. Maybe this is a chance to discover more than I expected.

I fix my eyes on his. "I want to see it."

"You want to see *it*?" He frowns. "Don't you mean *them*? What's there to see but a bunch of missile heads?"

"Nuclear missile heads?"

"Shush, no!" He flaps his arms and looks around. "We shouldn't be talking here. Come with me."

Is he worried about spies?

He turns around and unlocks the lab doors with a numeric code. I see he presses the six and the two but then covers the rest with his body. Only one half of the double doors opens, and I wonder why they have two doors at all. Perhaps to move larger things in and out?

He enters. I hesitate at the sight of the skull and the crossed bones above the TOXIC CHEMICALS label.

"Hurry up, Major."

We walk through a wide corridor that extends at least a hundred meters in each direction. Sergey goes to the right and enters the third door.

"Didn't they tell you what you came to see?" He slumps on his chair. The desk is piled with thick books, most of them open and stacked atop each other. A computer monitor stands in one corner, an infinite pipe growing and twisting on itself over a black background.

I pull my eyes from the screensaver. "They only told me you have a new weapon for my troops."

He cocks his head and his expression softens. "It's Sarin and Tabun gases. The nuclear heads aren't loaded yet. General Atartuk said the chemical rockets were needed first."

Sarin and Tabun haven't been used since the Saddam era, as far as I know.

"What do they do?"

"They're nerve agents. You release the chemicals, people breathe them or absorb them through the skin, and in a matter of minutes their glands and muscles are overstimulated and eventually shut down. They'll stop breathing."

Fascinating. This imminent offensive is more serious than I imagined.

"Why are you smirking?"

Am I smirking? Perhaps I am. I shrug. If I excel in this battle, I ensure my promotion to general. Then I can start thinking about Zainah's dream of world peace.

"You guys love to fight, don't you?" He nods as if answering his own question. "But what do I care? I get paid enough."

I lean forward. "When will they be deli—" The phone chirps. Sergey picks it up before the first ring dies off.

"Vasiliev." His brows arch. "Good... He is? ....Oh, indeed. I'll be right out to receive them." He replaces the phone and stands. "The general is here with your president–I mean, your caliph."

I too jump out of my chair. "The caliph, here?"

"Do you want to come out and greet them with me?"

"It would be an honor to see Al-Mahdi," I say. Quite a surprise, too.

"Come, then." He walks around his desk toward the door.

I freeze where I stand. I'm not supposed to be here. If the general sees me—

"Wait!"

I realize I've grabbed his shoulder and release it at once.

"What?"

"I just remembered—I should be doing something for the general this very moment." I glance at my watch, then tap my forehead. "I'm terribly late, how could I have forgotten?"

He shrugs. "Well, that's not my problem."

"I'm sorry, but I must go."

He shrugs again and strides out.

"I'll be back," I say. "And please, don't mention my visit to the general."

I'm not sure if he heard me. I step out of the office and hear the heavy door to the reception closing. I have the hallway to myself.

7

The cigarette butt flies through the air, falls to the pavement, and rolls down the sewer drain. Above the sidewalk, past the security shack of what was once the entrance to the Baghdad University campus, a sign reads Islamic Caliphate Army Base.

"You shouldn't smoke, sir, much less in public," the checkpoint soldier mutters.

Hussai's youngest wife, Sura, got a black eye when she said something similar a few months ago. Too bad he can't do the same to the soldier. Hussai looks away and taps the steering wheel of his car. Another soldier approaches the first one and points toward the shack.

"Go clean your vomit. It stinks in there."

"Hey, it's not my fault I'm sick."

"I don't have to put up with your nastiness."

The sick soldier drags his feet all the way to the shack while the other stands by Hussai's window.

"I'm sorry, sir, but we have orders not to let you in until..." He flips through the pages on his clipboard. "The twenty-fourth."

Hussai reaches for his shirt pocket and extracts a pair of folded bills. He fans his face with them. The soldier's eyes follow the money like a hypnotized man staring at a pendulum.

"I'm sure those orders do not apply during the weekend," Hussai says, brushing the top of the clipboard with the bills. With a swift movement, the soldier takes the money and flips a page on the clipboard.

"I think you're right, sir." He steps back and lifts the barrier.

Hussai parks at the back of Building 6B, away from the other cars, between two garbage containers. He tugs his cap, exits the car, and enters through the back door of the old brick building.

The door closes behind him with a clang. Out of the corner of his eyes he sees two or three people glance his way, then continue down the hall. As soon as they're out of sight he heads for the second-floor stairs, toward Farid's office.

With luck, not too many people will have decided to work this Saturday. But as he approaches the end of the wide concrete stairs, he hears mixed steps, imposing voices, something like the buzz of a crowd. What in the world is happening here?

A man hurries down the stairs, another follows behind. Hussai frowns, then looks up. Dozens of people are pacing the hallway of the second floor. How will he break into Farid's office now? He hesitates on the second to last step, then grabs the wrist of a passing clerk.

"What's the reason for all this activity, brother?"

"Al-Mahdi is coming to the base, sir. We must prepare and gather at the auditorium."

Hussai nods and releases the clerk, who walks away. He hears marching footsteps, then stumbles forward. Who dares push him?

"Everybody out now to greet the prophet's heir, Allah's chosen, the Awaited One."

Hussai turns and sees two men in black: Al-Mahdi's personal guards.

8

There's no emergency exit, no windows. I try to open a metal door with a lethal label but it doesn't budge.

I retrace my steps and move right behind the exit to the corridor, placing my ear against the metal door. A deep clang resounds within. It moves, and I spin out of the way. Five feet off I see a wooden door with no knob, the only one like it in this place. I stumble inside. An acrid stench flows from a row of wet urinals and an old faucet under a stained mirror.

Voices and steps fill the corridor outside. How am I going to get out of here? I nudge the door and peer out to see the back of the general, entering Sergey's office. I wish I could be there and listen to his plans. Who is this enemy we must destroy with biological and nuclear weapons?

The general emerges from the office and speaks to someone I can't see. I push the door a bit further open and see a man dressed in black with a turban that extends down his face like a scarf, covering all but his eyes. One of Al-Mahdi's personal guards. He has about a dozen of them, dressed like ancient nomad Muslim warriors. They never show their faces in public but are said to have been the twelve leaders of his former jihadist militia—the infamous militia that drove the last remnant of the Allies out of Iraq and took over the government.

The general twists back toward the office every second, and after about half a dozen words goes back inside. Is there another guard? I hear approaching steps, fall back into the restroom. I hear the staccato thud of boots on tiles.

I stand in front of a urinal, my back to the entrance, my hands in front of me.

The door slams open and hits the wall. My muscles tense. Al-Mahdi's guards are known for spontaneous violence. But the guttural sound I hear next is anything but hostile.

I stop pretending I'm urinating and watch the rangy man vomiting over the sink. His eyes bulge from his pale face and his chest heaves with obvious pain. He looks young, and the fatigues are a little too short for his long limbs.

The stench of the vomit is so strong that even the originator steps back with a look of disgust.

"You don't look good, soldier. You should see the doctor at the base's clinic."

He wipes his mouth with his sleeve and turns to me with the sedate slowness of the sick.

"Can't do that…" He looks at the insignia on my shoulder. "Major General, sir. I can't leave my post."

"Where are you posted, soldier? You must have a comrade that can take your post for a while."

"I'm in charge of the surveillance room, sir, and today I'm by myself." He shrugs and rubs his abdomen. "There's a virus going around…."

The soldier rambles about his symptoms but I can only think of the high-tech cameras I saw in the reception area. This is the man behind the monitors. "So, the surveillance in this building is separate from the rest of the base?"

"Yes, sir, we have some new equipment and they wanted to test it here first—" He bends over the sink and retches violently. As his body shakes I notice a clanking set of keys attached to his belt.

My fingers tingle. Those keys can open the door to the information I need. With the power of those cameras, I might be able to see and hear everything the caliph and the general discuss with Sergey.

I place one hand on his back and with the other unclip the keychain from his belt.

"No reason a member of Al-Mahdi's army should serve in such condition. Go, present yourself to the clinic. That's an order."

He manages to mutter his thanks, then heads for the door. But what if he plans to stop by the surveillance room?

"Don't stop for anything, soldier. The sooner, the better."

He stares at the floor. "Sir, permission to spea—"

"Don't waste my time, now do as I said."

"Yes, sir."

He hurries out of the restroom and I breathe the stench with relief.

THE SURVEILLANCE room is the size of a large utility closet, with a chair in front of two big computer screens—one shows a mosaic of frames from each of the buildings' monitored areas, the other is open to an interface that lets you select one of the areas and watch it in full screen.

The hallway fills with people as Sergey comes out of his office, the caliph behind him. His personal guard walks two or three steps back, always observing, while the general walks by Al-Mahdi, bowing to answer each question.

At the end of the hallway, Sergey scans his thumb on a black wall pad and opens a door, holding it for the others. He says something. Can I hear them? On the top right corner of the full screen monitor, a headphone image floats. I click it and the speakers come to life. Still, no voices.

Of course, the hallway is empty now. I bring up the feed for the area they just entered and hear Sergey's voice.

"This is the storage area. The level three and four biosafety labs are located on the other side of that steel and concrete wall."

He points to the far north wall of the room. It must be the size of a soccer field. Hundreds of crates fill the south wall. To the west, a line of three forklifts drives through an open gate with more crates.

Al-Mahdi raises one hand and they stop. I zoom in on his face. His honey-brown eyes seem narrow under his bushy brows as he stares at the stacked crates.

"Those are the chemical rockets, sir," Sergey says. I zoom out to see the rest of them.

The caliph doesn't acknowledge Sergey, just stares.

Sergey clears his throat, then hurries to an open crate not far from them.

"Please. Come see."

I follow with the camera and the computer automatically switches to a closer camera. Impressive. I can even see the rockets inside the crate.

Al-Mahdi grins. "Enough to subdue Northern Africa, General?"

"Indeed. We could launch them from our borders or drop them with our planes. They would not stand a chance against you, Lord of the Age."

There's no way we could fire those rockets with the equipment we have. Why would the general say that?

"How fast can we deploy them?" Al-Mahdi says.

"Well, now...fairly fast, I'm sure. Our pilots could fire most of these rockets in no time."

I zoom in on the crates. There must be at least six rockets in each, and even if we only had to launch a few hundred, it would take several missions. I shake my head. Why is the general misleading the caliph?

Al-Mahdi walks forward and waves his hand back. The general nods and stays put as Al-Mahdi wanders further, examining other rockets. My eyes wander with him. His gait is elegant yet authoritative. Power emanates from him. I breathe in deep.

Sergey scoots close to the general and leans to his ear. "Are you sure of what you said? Those rockets can be a heavy load for a fighter jet. They should not carry too many—"

"I know that!" The general stiffens as if realizing he raised his voice. "I know that." This time he talks in an undertone. "But

THE JIHAD'S MESSIAH   49

don't you dare say anything that would upset the caliph. Never contradict him, nor talk against his desires, if you want to keep your head."

Sergey nods.

"Now, go and bring us a report or something."

Sergey looks up, startled, and walks away just as Al-Mahdi returns.

"How good is the Israeli defense now?" Al-Mahdi's eyes are shining.

The general shifts his weight from one foot to the other. "Well, now, not as good as it was three years ago. They have handed over their weapons to the U.N. as part of the peace covenant."

"That is not what I asked, General. Do they still have their high-tech radars, their anti-missile mechanisms, their nuclear weapons?"

"I don't think so, no."

"You *don't think so* is not enough for me. We don't want to repeat Syria's mistakes. Or have you forgotten?"

"No, Great One, of course not."

I have not forgotten either. That day at the base in Ridyah we were all glued to the television. It was like September 11, 2001, only this time the targets were Muslims. The Turkish-led Islamic Coalition was ready to launch nuclear missiles against Israel from Damascus and, some say, from Gaza as well. Somehow, Israel gained intelligence about the attack, and before the Syrians could hit, Damascus and Gaza vanished under a mushroom of fire. When Iran and Lebanon rose up in fury, Israel fired nukes at them, too.

That was the worst defeat in Islamic history—though also the turning point for the rise of Babylon. Turkey was the most powerful nation in the region then, heading the coalition with Syria, Iran, and the ex-Soviet nations. After Israel destroyed Damascus, Al-Mahdi invaded Syria and took it from Turkey. I was there, flying my F-16, furthering Al-Mahdi's power and eventual seizure of the Turkish and the Lebanese. Now Al-Mahdi wants the Israelis, too.

"I need facts, General," the caliph says. "What does our spy report?"

The general grimaces. "The spy was killed a month ago."

"And you keep that from me?" His face is relaxed, but his fists are clenched. "I care nothing for your other spies, but the one in Israel, that's another matter entirely."

"I'm sorry, your excellency, I did not want to bother you with details of—"

"Don't bother me with excuses, General. Send another spy—Major Zadeh, perhaps. He speaks Hebrew and he's an outstanding soldier."

My breathing accelerates and I feel a bolt of excitement. I can't believe Al-Mahdi thinks so highly of me.

"I'm afraid he's unavailable, excellent lord. Farid is on a very important mission in preparation for the war."

My jaw drops. A very important mission? I stare at the general. Is he protecting me or...? All he needs to do is call me back from suspension—the caliph would never know the difference.

"Send someone else, then. But I want reliable data about the Israeli defense. By Wednesday."

THE CALIPH orders Sergey to lead them out, and the entourage steps out of view onscreen. I search for the hallway feed, but my eyes won't focus. My head spins. Is General Atartuk confabulating with Hussai in all this? No, that's impossible. Perhaps he's having second thoughts about retiring and sees me as a threat? That has to be it, because I see no other explanation. Then Al-Mahdi wants me to lead his army? What a delightful thought.

The caliph enters reception. "They should be ready to move toward the Israeli border at any time," he says.

"Yes, my lord," the general says.

What if he sends Hussai? No, Hussai would not survive a day. The only person capable of fulfilling this mission—and Al-Mahdi's wishes—is me.

Al-Mahdi walks toward the exit and I try to find the exterior camera feeds. By the time I do, the caliph and his guard are already outside. General Atartuk comes out through the door, cell phone against his ear, and stands by his master's side. He shuts the phone and bows his head.

"The staff is in the auditorium and the troops have gathered in the south field."

Al-Mahdi smiles. "Where's my horse?"

"On its way, my lord."

"You still don't understand the power of a symbolic display to lift the morale of an army. I'm the incarnation of their deepest beliefs and dreams. This show will benefit us all."

"Yes, my lord."

An immense white horse walks briskly their way, the man with the reins trotting beside it. Al-Mahdi smiles and claps.

"This is my hour. Not since the time of the Prophet has the world contemplated the image of God."

He mounts with ease and pulls the reins like an expert rider. Most Arab leaders in recent history had white horses, hoping Allah would choose them to be the Mahdi, but this is the real one, the Chosen One.

He rides off and I can follow him no more.

What now? I can't stay still, I must do something. If I weren't suspended I'd be in my office. I reach for my cell phone and dial my office's number to check my voicemail. I should have at least a couple of messages—

The line is busy.

I hang up and dial again. Busy. And I know I didn't leave the phone off its cradle because I checked my messages last night.

Who's in my office? I'll catch them this time.

My steps echo in the empty stairwell. The hall is lifeless as well, and I walk with all the stealth I can manage. As I draw near I hear papers rustling. A shadow passes beneath the door. I reach for my weapon and push the door open, aiming forward.

A silhouette against the window is reading from a folder. My files and notebooks are spread all over the desk, the phone and its cradle on the floor. I narrow my eyes until the intruder steps away from the backlight that obscures his features.

"Hello, Farid." It's Hussai. He has no shame. "Just doing a little work."

I lower my gun and step forward. "In my office?"

His face twists into the smirk I hate. "Back from our suspension so soon? Me too."

"Are you a spy?"

"No. You are."

"What are you trying to prove, Hussai?"

"I'm the counterespionage agent of the army."

"Who's ever heard of that?"

"We know about your contacts with the Russians."

How does he—?

He points at me with the folder in his hand. "You're finished, Farid."

"I've done nothing wrong. Your lies are worthless."

Laughter ripples through the room and Hussai's belly shakes. Each cackle fans the fire of my hatred for him.

"You're not ruining me!"

Hussai's laughter dies as I pull out my gun. Through the window behind him the chanting of a crowd distracts me for a second. Hussai throws the folder in his hand and a flurry of papers flies between us.

He dives to his left and rolls on the floor with a cry.

The hot gun shakes in my hand. What have I done?

Hussai moves. He's not dead. Yet.

9

Hussai presses one hand against his bleeding shoulder. His heart knocks against his ribs and he gasps. This isn't what he expected. Farid is crazy after all.

He rolls once on the brick-color tiles, trying to hide behind the desk, but the pain in his shoulder is too strong. He stops, back against the floor, and waits for the second bullet. Farid is a killer.

But why should he give up so easily? Why not fight? His head feels light. The ceiling fades away, replaced by fog. His limbs stiffen and all sound is sucked out of his ears.

A few moments later his head is clearer and his body seems normal, except for the pain in his shoulder. In the distance he can hear a blaring noise, like a car alarm.

He sits, leaning on his good arm, and looks toward Farid. But Farid is not there, nor anywhere in the office.

The fool didn't dare to kill him. What a coward.

Hussai reaches for the desk to pull himself up, but the effort drains him and he slumps back onto the floor. He waits a couple of minutes, then manages to sit against one side of the desk. His arm is bloody and his body shivers with a deep coldness. Why is he losing so much blood? He has to stop it. Maybe he can tie a piece of cloth around his arm and stop the flow. Where—

He hears quick steps and noises in the corridor. A man bursts into the office. So Farid came back to finish him.

10

Thick drops of sweat cover my forehead and the skin behind my ears as I rush down the stairs, away from the man I shot. I go out through the back door, feeling conspicuous. How long until they discover Hussai in my office?

This is the center of the campus, with many buildings and fields between me and the outside. I must think clearly, but all I can hear is the sound of the shot that hit Hussai. The scene replays in my mind, frame by frame.

I hear the static sound of a radio. Someone is coming. I move behind a large garbage container and peer out.

"I heard something, sounded like a gun. On my way to investigate. Over."

"Clear. Over."

An Al-Mahdi guard passes close and enters the building. If Hussai is still alive, he will lie yet more. Perhaps I could go back, take both him and the guard down and—no, too late for that, too risky.

Behind me, a familiar Land Rover is parked between two trash containers. I try the doors but they're locked. I slap the car roof and the alarm goes off.

Just what I needed. I sprint south toward the base's back gate. There must not be much activity there on a Saturday.

I take cover in the shadow of a building and scan the walking trail leading to the next building. Clear. But as soon as I step out of the shadows I feel a presence.

"Hey!"

Another Al-Mahdi guard stands in the middle of the trail.

11

Hussai's heartbeat races like a horse. Fear is not what he wants to feel, but he can't feel anything else. What would happen after his death? Would the Prophet receive him in paradise? Would god let him in? Why hadn't he been a better Muslim, good enough to guarantee a comfortable afterlife at least?

The man walks in and squats beside him. He reaches for his belt—surely going for a gun. Hussai closes his eyes and searches his memory for a prayer. There's nothing but cold blind terror. He knows he's going into a thick darkness, forever. He—

"I have a wounded man in building 6B. Needs medical assistance."

Hussai opens his eyes and faces the man, who holds a radio. He sees only two eyes staring at him over a black scarf.

"Can you move? Keep pressure on the wound."

The radio beeps and static is followed by a voice.

"What's your location in the building?"

"Second floor. Last office on the south." The guard stares at Hussai's uniform and reaches for his insignia to read it better. "Brigadier General Sidiqqui. What happened?"

Hussai's lips quiver. "It was Major General Zadeh… he tried to kill me."

"Major Zadeh? Your major tried to kill you?"

Hussai nods. "I discovered he's a Russian spy."

"That's quite a story. Where is he now? Is Al-Mahdi in danger?"

Weakness drains Hussai and his chin drops to his chest.

The guard speaks into his radio. "What's the doctor's E.T.A? Over."

"Almost there. Over."

"Copy that. Inform the general there is a bullet-wounded brigadier at the base and we must move Al-Mahdi out for protection. And put out word about the suspected shooter, Major Zadeh. He must be held for questioning."

12

"Wait there, identify yourself."

I freeze.

The guard's radio comes on. "Code black. We're moving him out. Keep looking for Major General Farid Zadeh."

He walks toward me. "What's the matter? Did you hear me?"

I nod without looking him in the eyes.

"Wait, you are—"

I startle him with one quick punch to his left ear and send him down with a double kick on his chest. He tries to stand but I place my boot against his throat, my gun between his wide-open eyes.

"Not a sound from you, all right?" He nods, and I grab his weapon and radio before taking my foot off him. "Stand up and walk to the building."

He complies, but his black eyes pierce me with contempt. I shove him forward, showing him the barrel of my gun and my finger on the trigger.

"Open the door."

As he reaches for the handle, I hit his head with the butt of my gun and he collapses to the ground. I drag him inside and throw his heavy mass into an engine room. I take his coat, turban, and scarf as a disguise.

May god forgive me for hurting my Muslim brother.

WHATEVER "CODE black" means I'm sure it was issued because of me. Seconds after I snuck out the back gate, a truck screeched

to a stop and four soldiers jumped out to block the entrance.
Nobody will leave that way now.

I observe the commotion from behind the wall of a children's
park. A helicopter takes off from somewhere in the middle of the
base and hovers a moment before flying north. It must be taking
Al-Mahdi to his palace.

I feel eyes on me and turn to find a group of children staring at me. A few meters away, nervous women in burkas whisper
among themselves.

"Go to your mothers, go now."

Two girls do what I say but three boys remain, eyes fixed on
my head scarf. One of the boys is tall, probably about ten years
old, with big round eyes and abundant black hair. I start to choke.
My son would be around that age by now. I run from the park,
away from my memories, into the city.

I TOSS the turban, scarf, coat, and my own shirt in a store's garbage can. No one will give me a second look now, even in my
undershirt.

I signal a taxi to a stop and the driver peers out the window.
"Where to?"

"Kadhimiya."

The driver twists his mouth as if thinking for a minute. "A few
blocks out of my way, but I could take you for eight thousand."

I bite my lips at the outrageous price. I have no time to bar-
gain, so I nod and climb in the front seat without waiting for his
response. It could take me an hour to get a taxi if I don't want to
pay what most drivers ask for.

"*Allah bil Khair.*" May god bless you with a good evening.

The driver smiles. "*Allah bil Khair.*"

The old red and white taxi departs and I brace for the customary chitchat. The driver glances at me so often I fear we'll
crash if he doesn't focus on the road.

"Want to hear a story about the war with Iran?" If he'd just shut up, I could think and plan my next steps.

I want to groan but instead I nod.

"We lived near the border, you know, and I saw the Iranian children blow up. Ayatollah Komeini sent his own people—the children, I tell you, the children—to walk through the mined fields before his troops. I saw them blow up, I was close—well, not too close, of course, but my father's binoculars were good enough...."

I let his jabber drop onto the background and focus on what's ahead. I'll gather a few changes of clothes, my passports, some equipment, eat something, then get to the airport. I'll get in my plane and fly somewhere for a few days. But where? I can't go to Jaddeh, they'll track me there. Besides, what would I tell my friends?

Jonathan invited me to Israel.

If I could get my hands on some good intelligence, I could redeem myself for anything, everything. But I can't just fly to Israel with no clue what to look for, and I can't contact our intelligence department.

The Russians. The caller this morning said he would make contact tonight at a Lebanese restaurant in the Green Zone.

This is crazy, but it also seems like Allah's will. I could trick the Russians into providing intelligence, then go see Jonathan and gather the information Al-Mahdi wants. Then they'll know I'm no traitor, no matter what Hussai says of me. Better yet, I'll prove there's no better candidate for the position of full general. And once the job is mine, it'll be in my power to end the war as soon as possible and help Al-Mahdi restore peace and justice to the Arab world. If Allah wills.

13

General Atartuk's fingers curl like claws as he paces back and forth around Hussai's hospital bed.

"This is a terrible mess, terrible. Al-Mahdi will not be happy. He'll want proof."

Hussai maintains a somber expression, despite his desire to grin.

"He shot me. What more proof do you need?"

The general stops, brows raised, and stares at Hussai. After a few seconds he resumes his pacing.

"A Russian spy... Al-Mahdi will want to crush him. You must provide some evidence."

"He confessed! I just need access to his phone records."

"Unbelievable. Farid is the last man I would deem a traitor."

"More than a traitor."

"But how can he be a Zionist as well as a Russian spy?"

"Farid has no sense of loyalty, General. He spied for both the Jewish pigs and the Russians. He sells information to the highest bidder."

"I don't know, Hussai, something here doesn't fit. How did you come to be in his office while on suspension? I should have you face the Council for this infraction."

Hussai lowers his head and spouts his rehearsed answer.

"I had a trail on Farid. I suspected his ties to the Russians and the Hebrews and thought I could find something in his office. I know I was suspended, General, but I love my country and the caliph. Uncovering a spy seemed a noble reason to disobey. Wouldn't you have done the same in my place?

The general clasps the metal rail of the bed and sighs. "Well, I'm shocked, but pleased. I didn't expect much when I assigned you to counter-espionage. I misjudged you."

Hussai purses his lips. The biggest shock will come when Hussai takes Atartuk's job.

"I'm just serving my country."

"I'm sure Al-Mahdi will recompense you. He's generous with those who serve him well."

Money would be good, for sure. Although Hussai doubts the greedy Al-Mahdi would willingly make him rich.

"And what will you do about Farid?"

"We will hunt him down."

14

The sun will set soon, but tonight I must miss my prayers. The taxi drops me off a few blocks from my apartment, where someone may already be waiting for me.

I cut through a back street and into an alley. A dozen lines hung with clothes hang across it like mismatched veils. I duck down and weave through the entangling fabric. Suddenly I can't see anything. I fight the burka, pull it off my head, and toss it to the dirt. It's royal blue with embroidered flowers around the headpiece.

I push the rest of the clothes to one side and run to the end of the alley toward my apartment. I stop at the corner and glance both ways. There doesn't seem to be any surveillance from this side of the street, but I shouldn't take a chance like that.

I need a disguise.

Back at the alley, I pick up the burka, and pull it over my head. It barely fits and my beard itches against the fabric, but it'll do.

I cross the street and am glad to find I can move easily. I always thought these things would make it hard to walk. I notice the burka barely covers my knees. I must look ridiculous. I run across the street, up the stairs, and into my apartment.

Everything looks clear, but my heart has never pounded so fast. I pack all I need in less than five minutes and head out.

I reach for the knob but it turns before I touch it. The locked bolt comes to a halt. I hear a click, like the safety of a gun.

The silenced bullet splinters the wood as I twist and run toward the kitchen, reaching for my gun.

The door swings open and hits the wall. Two soldiers come in. "Stop, Major!"

I fire in their direction, and they both duck. I slide the kitchen window open and shoot again, hitting one of them in the foot. He cries out, and I recognize soldier boy's face as I step out onto the window ledge.

The scarred colonel opens fire and misses by a centimeter.

The ledge is so narrow there's barely room for my heels, and that's if my back is against the wall—but my backpack is tilting me forward.

Clinging to the window frame, I turn sideways and reach for the neighbor's window at the corner of the building. I brace myself against the glass and move my feet around the corner so I'm standing on a different side of the building.

There's nowhere to go from here—a flat brick wall extends for meters all the way to the end of the wall. I look down. The roof of the shop next door lies three or four meters below.

I jump.

I KNEEL on the edge of the roof but see no vehicles or soldiers in the street below. Did the colonel and soldier boy come alone? Why these two?

Their vehicle must be somewhere, on a neighboring street perhaps.

Feet first, I hang from the concrete border and drop to the street. The colonel must be busy attending to soldier boy.

Or maybe not. I hear fast steps, and the building's door opens. I sprint away.

"Stop right there, Major."

He's close behind me, close enough to shoot me in the back. I cross the street and head toward the alley.

"You're under arrest, Major, don't make me take you down."

The back of my neck tingles, and I push forward. Once into

the alley, I dive for the laundry curtain. I hear two shots, feel their wind above my head as I land on the ground and roll on my side.

I peer beneath the clothes and see his boots approaching. I ready my gun and slide the barrel between a blanket and a pair of underwear. Allah knows I don't want to kill him, but I have to leave here alive.

To my left, a couple of steps lead to a narrow door. I grab a shirt, crawl up the steps, and stand with my back against the wall.

The barrel of the colonel's gun comes into view. As the colonel rips the clothing apart I throw the shirt in his face, following with my fist to his cheek and a kick to his left knee.

He moans and drops to the ground on his good knee. He tries to point his gun in my direction but I push him all the way to the ground and step on his wrist. The gun drops from his hand and I take it.

It looks like I may have fractured his knee, but I don't stay to confirm his prognosis.

15

The artificial plants in the café across from the Lebanese restaurant shield me as I wait for the Russian contact. I won't show up until nine, lest I become more vulnerable to their spying.

It's a good thing I never mentioned my new plane to my superiors—though there's always a chance they'll find out. My one hope is that no one awaits me at the plane as they did at my apartment.

Five minutes before nine, people begin walking out of the restaurant, including the staff. I leave a few bills at my table and cross the street. The restaurant door is locked and a burly man motions from inside that they're closed. I just stand there half a minute–he must let me in, if this is where I'm supposed to make contact.

The man looks more like an ill-humored bodyguard than a restaurant owner. Perhaps he is a bodyguard. He rolls his eyes and comes to the door.

"We're closed, go away."

I shake my head.

"I'll call the police."

I need that information. The man walks to the back and returns with a revolver. Could this be a trap? He taps the glass with the barrel and nods to his right, indicating I should really leave.

I spread my arms, palms up. "I just want some information."

He narrows his eyes, staring at my chest, then opens the door, waves the revolver in the air, and points between my eyes. It seems I came to the wrong place.

He shoves something against my chest. "Get out of my restaurant."

Startled, I grab the object. He retreats into the restaurant.

The thing in my hand is a cell phone. I glance to both sides of the street and decide to go west, where the alleys are darker.

Five blocks later, as my heartbeat is returning to normal, the phone chirps. I answer the call but say nothing.

"I'm glad you showed up." It's the same voice from this morning. "Please pardon the rudeness, but we are taking no chances."

"Haven't you taken a chance already, leading me to your hideout?"

"The restaurant? That's nothing. We just borrowed the place for a while."

Clever.

"Are you ready to hear my proposal, Farid?"

"Speak."

"Good. Now, you are a brilliant man and have probably guessed something about our origin and perhaps our intentions."

I keep walking.

"Your silence is fine. I'll take that as a cautious yes. I want to know your price, if any."

"This is an information business, isn't it?"

"Correct."

I feel a lump in my throat. Am I a traitor, as Hussai claims? Allah knows I would never harm my country. What I'm doing today is for the greater good.

"My price is information, then."

"Interesting. What type of information?"

"I want intelligence about Israel's current defenses and their capacity to respond or initiate an attack."

The Russian laughs. "You've told me a lot just asking that question, Farid. That is good."

"Not enough."

"I like you. And I think I can help you. But first, I need to know I can trust you. Liking does not equate to trusting. If you can provide me some verifiable information about your army's movements and plans, I can give you what you need. Think about it and I'll contact you again."

"No. I want the information now, tonight."

He snorts. "Is that so?"

"Write down these coordinates."

"Coordinates? All right, wait a second, I was not expecting this."

I sneak into a deserted alley and close my eyes, trying to remember the exact location of our rookie platoon in training.

I give him the coordinates. "You can confirm this by satellite images. We have troops moving into that area in preparation for a campaign against Yemen. The caliph wants them as part of the caliphate."

"Is that so? All right. Let me confirm this. If I find it to be correct, then I believe we can begin a profitable relationship. I'll call you back within forty-five minutes."

THE CALL comes twenty-two minutes later, while I'm still on my way to the airport.

"Farid, we retrieved the information from the satellite and can see the movement of troops in that area."

"Now it's your turn to tell me what I need."

I glance at the taxi driver, who doesn't seem to be interested in eavesdropping—still, I decide not to say anything incriminating.

"Fair enough," he says. "West of Jerusalem, there is a military base, Tel Nof. They have moved a few large trucks in and out in the past couple of days. They come in with a concealed load and leave empty."

"What load?" I say, but I know.

"We're not sure, but we suspect they might be nuclear weapons, considering the security around the hangar."

Israel hiding nukes—that information is gold if I can back it up without revealing my source. Disarming those nukes will be necessary to ensure Al-Mahdi's victory and end the war sooner.

"What do you plan to do with that information, Farid?"

I grin. "I'll have to confirm it. Contact me in a couple of days."

I cut the call and throw the cell phone out the window.

16

The hangar lights scare away the shadows and reveal a lonely single-engine plane—cost me all of my savings and most of my earnings. It was worth it for just such a time as this.

Twenty-five minutes later, I'm ready for the two-hour flight to Jerusalem. I stare into the black sky and try to ignore the events that brought me here tonight, focusing instead on things ahead. Like Jonathan and Benjamin, my childhood friends in the West Bank. They lived in one of those Jewish settlements sponsored by the Israeli government to defy the Palestinian authority over their territory, but we met on a barren hill between my village and their settlement. How ironic—we swore to be friends forever, Jonathan even said he would become a pro-Palestinian activist some day, a peaceful Israeli lobbying for the Palestinian cause. For a time I also thought I would become a political leader: the one who would finally sign a permanent peace agreement with Israel, the leader who would teach his people to love Jews and Arabs alike.

Until the day I turned fourteen, and my uncle Abdullah presented me with a copy of the Qur'an.

"I will show you the path of Islam," he said. "I must step up for my brother and do what is right." He shook his head. "Your father is proud of calling himself a secular Muslim, but there's no such thing. You are either a true Muslim or a *munafiq*."

Somehow, he convinced my father to let my brother and me stay at his house in Gaza for a season, and so I went to experience an incredible spiritual enlightenment—and hatred.

Uncle Abdullah's home was a monument for the Palestinian cause, with a life-size poster of Yasser Arafat commanding the living room and Palestinian flags everywhere.

"I want you to meet my son, your cousin, Ali Muhammad." My uncle's eyes shone with pride at the sight of his four-year old. The boy had a green bandana on his head and rectangular pieces of wood strapped around his abdomen.

"Hello, Ali, I'm your cousin Farid." I pointed to the rectangles. "What are those for?"

He grinned and lifted his chest. "My martyr bombs."

My uncle clapped. "How many Jews are you going to kill, Ali Muhammad?"

"A hundred-hundred-five."

"*Allah-o Ahkbar, Allah-o Ahkbar.*"

ISRAEL. HERE I am again.

I shut off the plane's engine, grab my backpack, and step out. An Atarot airport official waits by the retracting steps.

"Hello, sir. Passengers?"

"None."

"Just the pilot, then. Is the aircraft yours?"

I look around the echoing hangar. "Are you working solo?"

He shrugs. "Hey, we just reopened a year ago. And the Sabbath just ended, what do you expect?" He stares at the turboprop while I lock the plane. "Good bird. A Pilatus, right?"

"Yes, a PC-12."

"I love these little planes. Almost bought one once."

He has a longing stare. I tap the side of the plane as if petting a puppy.

"It's a magnificent machine. Maybe I could let you take it for a ride sometime?"

His face brightens. "Really? Do you mean that?"

"Well, but there couldn't be any record of it, you know—"

"Why would I add that to the records?"

"I mean, there can be no record of a Pilatus parked here."

He cocks his head, probably trying to decide whether or not I'm serious. A flashing red light shines through the hangar windows above us.

He looks up. "Security patrol, doing rounds."

My neck muscles tense. Why do they need flashing lights to do rounds? Did they see my plane? If they ask for my passport and start inquiring about the reason for my visit...

I clear my throat. "You must decide, because I don't have much time tonight."

"Decide on what?"

"About the ride... all I ask in return is a small favor, a small omission."

He widens his eyes, then looks at the plane.' "I'm not sure that's a fair price. We don't consider such an omission as small here in Israel."

I hear the static of a radio outside and glance up at the red flashes.

"Would a deposit help?"

He shrugs. I reach for the bills in my pocket and hand them to him—about 300 euros.

He smiles as he does a quick count and stuffs the money in his pants.

"And you'll let me fly it?"

"Can you do it?"

"Don't offend me."

The flashing lights depart.

He narrows his eyes and glances down at his clipboard. He then takes a long look at the aircraft and drops the hand with the clipboard by his side. I turn and trot away.

"Wait, what's your name?"

"Tomorrow. I have to go now."

Come on, Jonathan, answer the phone.

"Shalom."

It's him.

"King David Hotel in two hours."

"Fa—"

"Hush. Later."

Click.

I dial a second number on the pay phone, not sure if it's still valid. Someone answers at the third ring.

"Diefendorf." His thick German accent brings a flood of memories.

"So you're still in Jerusalem, old friend."

Augustus Diefendorf gasps and for a moment I fear he'll hang up. His voice breaks slightly when he speaks again.

"Yes, I am. Are you?"

"Close."

"Maybe we will cross our paths one of these days, do you think?"

"I'd like that, one of these days."

"Maybe we can arrange something." He's cunning—and discreet, knowing his phone may be tapped.

"But I'm lost in one old runway. I think it used to be a refugee camp."

"I'm sorry to hear that," he says. "Maybe someone will find you."

"I hope so."

We hang up.

MY FLASHLIGHT marks the way as I walk down Route 60. Augustus arrives forty minutes later in an old Audi A4. He's one of the few European recruits of the Palestinian cause still left in Israel.

I get in the car and put a hand on his shoulder. "Good to see you, my friend."

His green eyes shine behind glasses. He raises one of his white bushy brows.

"Your visit is unexpected but welcome. I don't want to venture speculations as to why you're in Israel, but you must tell me now if you are in trouble."

"No trouble. I just came to visit some old friends."

Augustus starts driving. We don't speak for a few kilometers.

"What do you need, Farid?"

"Not much, really. Only a means of transportation and a few gadgets."

He sighs. "This is a time of peace, but no one believes it will last. Your visit makes me think this peace is about to end."

The lights of the city appear in the distance and excitement blossoms at the realization that I'm back in Jerusalem. Maybe I'll get a chance to visit the mosque at the Temple Mount and worship with my Muslim brothers.

"All I can lend you is a Kawasaki Ninja 500, but you must take good care of it. I just bought it from a Jewish mechanic who bought it six years ago but only rode it a handful of times."

"Thank you. What about a video camera? A really small one, with tons of memory for several hours of recording."

"Are you a tourist now?"

"I also need a gun and a satellite phone."

"Not a tourist, then."

"And shekels. I'll pay you back."

"With what? Iraqi money?"

"Euros, I have them with me."

Augustus rubs his white stubble, staring far into the road ahead. "At least you didn't ask for explosives. Ran out of those."

"Why?"

"Ibrahim took all I had this past week."

"I just saw him yesterday—in Baghdad."

Augustus shrugs. "He didn't say what he plans to do, and you know I never ask."

My gut chills. Will Ibrahim attempt to attack Al-Mahdi?

17

The loud roar of the Ninja's engine and the aroma of gasoline are exhilarating. Augustus left me waiting at a park for half an hour—he's careful not to let anyone know where he lives—but the wait was worth it.

I speed through Sultan Suleyman, past the Islamic quarter, and keep going west, rediscovering landmarks and intersections in modern Jerusalem. I arrive at the King David ten minutes before my appointment, park the bike opposite the hotel, and wait behind a tree. Four minutes later I recognize Jonathan in the dim light of the street, walking with a woman. They stop and exchange some words. The woman, slender with long silky black hair, places a hand on Jonathan's neck for a few seconds, then walks away. Jonathan goes into the hotel. Who is she?

After another five minutes, I walk around the front garden of the hotel, away from the main entrance. The staff door is easy to find and I make my way to the lobby through narrow hallways and rushing employees.

From behind a column I spot Jonathan, sitting on a purple chair, fingers tapping his knees and eyes fixed on the entrance. His face has hardly changed beneath that new beard, although his hair seems to be thinning. He's wearing a kippa, the Jewish skullcap. He never did before. Perhaps he has become more committed to his faith, just as I have to mine. He always sided with me in the uninformed discussions we had as boys about Palestine's right to become an independent state. But of course time will have changed him into a different person. It changed me.

Of the thirty or so people in the lobby, only two could be surveillance: a man with a brown fedora pretending to read but glancing up every few seconds, and a slim woman wearing jeans and a t-shirt, obviously out of place here.

While there's no reason to believe I'm being watched, perhaps he is. So I wait.

Two minutes later the woman leaves. Soon afterward, a heavy-set woman walks up to fedora man and speaks down to him, flapping her hands. His wife, for sure. His expression turns sour, he stands and follows her toward the elevators. I walk over to Jonathan without letting him see me.

"Your wait is over."

"Farid! Shalom, shalom, *Mah Shlomcha?*"

"Follow me."

Jonathan hurries to keep up. "I was so afraid you wouldn't come, really, I mean, you never answered my message, well you did answer it, but not until tonight—"

"I'm sorry to be late."

"No problem, no problem, I was anxious, really, but now I'm glad to see you…. Where are we going?"

"Over here." I lead him out of the hotel through the staff door to a coffee shop down the street. We sit in a semi-dark corner, away from curious gazes. Good manners would have me socialize for an hour or more before I get to the point, but tonight I must be rude.

"Tell me what troubles you, Jonathan, your message was quite disturbing."

"Where to start, where to start? My mother passed away five months ago and my father is ill and I am unemployed… but the reason I called, really, is that my brother disappeared a week ago—"

"Wait." This is a deep family crisis, but I'm in far worse trouble myself. "It saddens me to hear this, my friend, but how can I possibly help you?"

"Please help me find Benjamin, or my father will die. He's like a Joseph to Israel, my father's beloved son, the—"

"Why don't you go to the local police?"

"I have. They say hundreds of people have disappeared and they don't have the resources to deal with it."

"Hundreds of people?"

"Maybe thousands." He's waving his hands as he talks. "Some say it's like the disappearances more than three years ago, only this time fewer people and only in Israel, as far as I know. You remember the vanishings?"

"Of course, I saw it in the news. But nobody I knew vanished, so we all thought it was some sort of ruse created by the Americans."

"I don't think so, because it happened all over the world."

"Perhaps Allah struck them down on our behalf."

Jonathan's hands suddenly fall to the table and he stares at them. Did I offend him?

"Is that what you think happened to my brother?"

"I don't know what happened to your brother."

"I thought you could help me, really. You were always the best at hide and seek."

I want to laugh. "Is that why you called me? Because I was good at a child's game?"

Jonathan shakes his head, still staring at his hands. "There's more." He wets his lips, raises his chin and looks around. "Someone from Mossad approached me three days ago and said I should stop looking for my brother because I would never find him."

Why would the Israeli intelligence service involve themselves in this? A surge of memories of Benjamin rushes through my brain. He was the most introverted boy in the West Bank, and a talented student.

"I'm afraid, Farid, but you're brave, a soldier, so I thought perhaps you could... you know, at least try?"

Benjamin is likely dead, though I dare not say it. Poor Jonathan—he probably knows but won't admit it. I surprise myself with my next words.

"Have peace, we'll find your brother."

18

When washed in sunrise, Al-Mahdi's palace seems to reflect a glorious aura. Hussai feels a tingling sensation that starts in his bandaged shoulder and runs down his arm and all through his body.

He tries to shake this new emotion off. He doesn't know what to call it, excitement or nervousness, but in any case it would be better not to experience it again.

"Is this your first time in the palace?"

He's even forgotten he's not alone. Hussai turns to the man leading him through the majestic halls. He nods and rubs his right forearm, careful not to touch the shoulder. The wound pulses as if it's alive.

The hallway runs in front of him for hundreds of columns, and it feels as if they've been walking for hours. The walls are pictographic murals with stories, obviously from the Qur'an. Stories he has heard but whose details are foggy.

Even the present is unclear. Why is he here? Why rush him out of the hospital at six in the morning? He tried to call the general, but Atartuk wouldn't answer his phone. He thought to use his wound as an excuse not to go, overcome by panic when he was summoned to the palace. This is his first one-on-one audience with the caliph, but he has been in meetings with Al-Mahdi in which he saw proud men reduced to rubble. What if the caliph sees through him and learns he's not been truthful about the incident with Farid?

The guide stares at Hussai and slows his pace. "You must

purify yourself and dress properly before coming into Al-Mahdi's presence." A frown wrinkles his face. "We must do something quickly."

Hussai observes the little man, pristine but ridiculous in his 17th-century Effendi costume with his pointy soft shoes, shiny green pants, and a green piece of fabric wrapped around his belly and over his shirt like an ancient belt. As long as they don't make Hussai dress like that, he could use a change of clothes. His uniform is stiff with sweat, gravel, and dried blood.

They walk through a narrow opening in a wall, which Hussai would never have noticed by himself, and come out to an adjacent hall, still elegant but not as elaborate as the previous one. The walls are bare of paintings and the ceiling is as high as a regular house ceiling. Servants walk up and down this lesser hallway.

"Follow me, please." The guide takes him to a white room three doors down. "Wait here."

One minute later, the guide returns with a bundle of folded clothes and a towel. "Please don't take long. Al-Mahdi will not wait if you are a second late. You have twenty minutes until your appointment." He bows his head, exits the room and locks Hussai in.

Two meters from him, there is a depression in the floor. Hussai walks to it and peers down. A bathtub. That's the only thing in the room, except for a silver hand mirror resting near the tub. This place is full of madness.

He unfolds the clothes with his free hand and shakes his head—a pink and yellow Effendi costume.

"WASH THIS and bring it back." Hussai hands his uniform to the little guide. "I'm not going out in this."

The guide takes a look at Hussai and laughs. "Pardon me." He covers his mouth. "I'll see what I can do."

Hussai imagines punching the guide in the face. He looks

down at himself again. The small pink shirt ends right above
his bellybutton, and the pants look shrunken, mismatched with
his boots—there's no way in the world the pointy shoes would
fit his fat feet. If he puts the shirt on it will be painful to take off
the arm sling.....

He hears giggles and looks up. Fool people, making fun of
him. He steps back into the room and slams the door.

HUSSAI SITS cross-legged in a large sofa, passing a hand over his
clean uniform. All he needs now is a few pain pills and fried eggs
to improve his morning. For some reason, he's not as afraid to
see the caliph as he was thirty minutes ago.

General Atartuk storms into the amphitheater-like hall.

"I'm late." He stares at Hussai, eyes wide. "What are you doing
sitting there? Come quick."

Hussai smirks and stands.

"Make haste, Hussai, or we'll upset him."

The general strides off and Hussai follows him through a
flight of stairs, down a carpeted path, and into a huge terrace
overlooking Baghdad. Al-Mahdi stands by the stone rail, his
back to the newcomers.

The general halts a few meters from the caliph and waits with
his head bowed. Hussai bows his head like the general but ven-
tures furtive glances to the caliph, who seems to be in a trance.
He can't see the caliph's face but can tell his head is tilted up, as
if breathing in the smells of the city.

"Is this not great Babylon, which I have built for the house
of the kingdom by the might of my power and for the honor of
my majesty?" Al-Mahdi turns to them with a smile that makes
Hussai's heart beat faster.

"*Aasalaamu Aleikum*, Great One." Hussai jolts at the sound
of his own voice saying these words. He did not intend to talk,
much less call him by that title.

"Brigadier Hussai, welcome." The caliph's sharp gaze makes Hussai look away. He wants to flee. He wants to stay. Nausea crawls up his throat. It would be better just to stare at the floor and swallow his bile.

"I must hear your story from your lips and judge its truthfulness. The general's account is quite disturbing."

Hussai gasps, willing the rhythm of his heart to calm, but it only races faster. This is his opportunity to drown Farid and promote himself. He must find the strength to lie convincingly. But his head feels light and the ground is unsteady beneath his feet.

"Perhaps you prefer to sit before you speak, but I wish to stay in the morning air. It enhances my genius."

The general leans to Hussai's ear. "Speak, you idiot."

"What is wrong with him, General? He seems to be wobbling."

"I don't know, my lord, they just brought him from the hospital, the doctors assured me he was well...."

Hussai senses the caliph walking toward him, then grasping his wrist with an icy hand. His head clears but a bitter taste overwhelms his mouth. The ground feels firm again under his feet. He stares at the caliph.

"Take off that sling, Hussai."

"What?"

"Do it," the general says.

The caliph slaps the general's face. "Stop echoing my orders."

"Forgive me, my lord. It won't happen again."

Hussai fumbles to release his wounded arm from the sling.

"Good," Al-Mahdi says as he rips off the bandages and grabs his wrist again.

Hussai wants to cry out but every sound is lost—just as the pain in his arm is lost, totally gone.

"Peace to you, servant of Allah." Al-Mahdi releases Hussai's wrist and ambles back to the veranda. "What is this tale about the major general in my army spying for infidels and attacking Muslims?"

Hussai shakes his head. The caliph has healed him. How? Is he being too gullible, the lack of pain only the power of suggestion? He must focus, must answer the question.

"Farid tried to kill me, my lord." Al-Mahdi raises his chin and narrows his eyes. "I had been tracking Farid. He had contact with elements in Russia and Israel, I'm not sure why—"

"Indeed, my lord." The general waves a few stapled pages in his hand. "I obtained the telephone records and there are incoming calls from Jerusalem and Moscow."

"Only incoming calls? No outgoing?"

The general flips through the pages, mumbling. Hussai can sense the doubt in the caliph's expression. He can't let the general ruin this chance.

"I confronted Farid about the calls and asked him if he was a spy. He didn't deny it but instead fired at me."

"You should be dead. Farid is the best soldier in my army. Why would he miss?"

The caliph and the general stare at Hussai. He twists his lips, searching for the right words that he may live to see his fifty-first birthday.

"Only by Allah's mercy am I alive. God protected me. *Allah-o Ahkbar.*"

Al-Mahdi and the general exchange looks."Wait here," the caliph says.

"I DON'T know how, Hussai, but you have found favor in his eyes," the general says when he returns in less than fifteen minutes. "He believes you. Maybe because he just met you, it's easier for him to see some promise in you. I still doubt the whole story is true. How did you two end up at the base? You told me your version, but why was Farid also there?"

Hussai stands and locks eyes with the general. One day, very soon, he will have his payback, and the general will regret his words and his contempt. "If Al-Mahdi believes me, that's all that matters."

The general's scowl is met with Hussai's smirk.

"Is that all he said, general?"

"The caliph wants you to be his guest for a special dinner tonight."

"I'll be happy to attend."

Hussai turns his back to the general and walks away.

19

I wake suddenly. Where am I?

Sunbeams filter in through a square window near the ceiling. The walls are rough gray stone, emanating the musty scent of centuries-old buildings. Everything clears as my brain settles into the new day. This is Jonathan's home. We got here so late last night I haven't yet seen anyone in his family.

My bladder wants to explode and my stomach is aching for food. As soon as I sit up, my back complains. This is the hardest mattress I've ever slept on.

I stretch, rub my face, and venture outside the tiny room. The narrow blue door across the hallway looks like the bathroom. As I reach for the knob the door yanks open to reveal a young woman wrapped in a towel.

"Aaahh!" The shout pierces my ears, then the door slams in my face.

Noises all around, no doubt in response to the scream. I hurry back to my room, suffering the pain in my bladder and the image of the woman's uncovered shoulders, glistening with tiny drops of water from her wet black hair. Forgive me, god, for these thoughts. I've only seen burkas for years.

Agitated voices seep through the cracks around my door—there's a man, what man, where did he go, are you sure, call the police, is he still here. Then Jonathan's voice above all the others, asking for silence, explaining that it's Farid, remember Farid, the neighbor's son in the West Bank, he came to visit, oh yes, they remember, please call him, they want to welcome me.

Conversation ceases, and there's a knock on my door. I open at once and try my best morning smile.

"Shalom, shalom."

"Shalom, Farid!"

"You look so different now."

I vaguely remember the aged father and unchanged aunts, uncles, and cousins. But the woman in the towel isn't here. I think she's the one I saw walking with Jonathan to the King David Hotel.

"How long since we saw you last?"

"Probably twenty-five years, right?"

"Yes, that must be it."

I lose track of who's talking. "Excuse me." I can smile no more and dart through the cramped hallway and into the bathroom.

JONATHAN'S FAMILY lavishes me with attention. Everybody does something around the house, supposedly preparing breakfast, while Jonathan and I chat at the table. Well, he chats while I think about the woman in the towel.

The beautiful woman. She can't be Jonathan's wife—most likely a cousin. But I must not think of this, I must not mar Zainah's memory.

"Coffee and juice for our guest." Aunt Esther and her daughter Dina set enough cups and jugs on the table for the whole neighborhood.

"And here's your Israeli salad." The large bowl in front of me brims with tomatoes, onions, cucumbers, and what smells like coriander. Salad for breakfast—only in Israel.

What would the Caliphate Council members say now if they saw me? I should be in Baghdad, saying my prayers.

The family gathers around us, the table cluttered with bread, olives, fried eggs, and more—plates and arms entangled. I reach for the bread and sigh when I see it's unleavened. It must be the Passover season. Jonathan leans close to my ear.

"Don't mention our talk about Benjamin."

I nod.

The front door opens, and in comes the woman in the towel, face shining. "Did I miss breakfast?"

She wears tight sports clothes. She must have been out jogging. Why would she bathe before exercising? She ambles to the table, inspects the food, apparently not noticing me, and climbs the stairs to the second floor.

"That's our sister, Taliah." I gape at Jonathan, who spreads his bread with butter, then looks at me and speaks with his mouth full. "Cream cheese? It's goat cream cheese, very fresh, really, you must try it."

"Sister?"

"Aha." He nods as he takes a bite.

"Ah, you know her not." Jonathan's father, David, says from the opposite side of the table. "Taliah was born in my old days, like Isaac to our father Abraham... although she is nothing like the meek Isaac."

I expect him to say more, but the old man shakes his head and begins eating his salad.

Taliah appears a few minutes later, now dressed in jeans and a small t-shirt, radiating so much self-confidence it's insulting. How can they allow her to dress like that? In Iraq she would be stoned to death.

"Shalom." Her casual voice is melodious but arrogant. She kisses her father and sits by his side.

She reaches for some eggs, then looks up and locks eyes with me. All her movements seem premeditated, as if she has planned facing me like this.

"Farid, right? You gave me quite a shock this morning." I smile and look down to my food.

"Hmm, you're a Muslim, right? You don't speak to women."

Aunt Esther taps the table with her fork and I look up. "Taliah, please."

Taliah shrugs. "What? I'm just saying...." She stuffs her mouth with olives.

In no time Taliah is talking about political news and international events in her musical voice. The family forgets me, their guest, and focuses all their attention on her. Unbelievable.

This woman has a power like none I've seen. Not even Zainah was so bold... or so beautiful. The curve of her lips as she speaks is a vision. Her tanned skin is flawless, and there's something in those clear brown eyes that disturbs my soul.

I grind my teeth. By Allah, I must cast away these thoughts. She's a Jew and I must not look at her this way. I have allowed myself to befriend unbelievers, but I must set limits. And I must remain faithful to Zainah.

Why remain faithful to the dead?

I shake my head. I promised to love Zainah forever, and I shall love her in paradise.

Zainah is dead.

Not for me, not for me, not for me.

"Not for me," I say.

All eyes turn to me. The temperature in the room rises ten degrees in a second.

"Please excuse me."

I stumble from the dining table as fast as I can.

FINALLY, I bow down my forehead in prayer toward Mecca. Doing Salah in Jerusalem is a spiritual privilege. *God, you know my faith is sincere, be merciful and forgive my evil thoughts.*

"Farid?" Jonathan knocks on my door, but I keep praying. He knocks a dozen times until I rush my way through the end of the prayer and let him in.

"Farid—you scared me, really, leaving so abruptly, my father is worried and wonders if we offended our guest. Was it something Taliah said? Oh, *abba* chided her already, so she won't be saying foolish things around you anymore. Truth is, she became really upset, said a few unpleasant words about... well, you, and the Muslims, and—"

"It's all right, you don't need to tell me more."

He nods and smiles. There's so much my childhood friend doesn't know. He never met Zainah, he knows nothing about my adult life.

Jonathan slumps on a chair. He's dressed like a Jewish schoolboy, with a white shirt that wrinkles around the small protruding belly and pressed black pants covered in fuzz balls. He looks so harmless and naive.

"How did you get my phone number in Baghdad?"

"The Internet."

"It's listed on the Internet?"

"Not listed, really, not in the white pages, because there's no such online registry in the Middle East, but I hacked an official Iraqi database."

"You're a hacker?"

He shrugs and nods. I try to picture him doing something illegal.

"I had to read your files, just to make sure it was you," he says. "Not trying to pry, really, although what's hacking but prying, right? In any case, it was very instructive to read about your accomplishments and brilliant career—really, my most sincere congratulations to you. Major general, huh?"

I smile, sit on the bed, and lean against the wall. "So how much do you know about me?"

"Well, just what the official records say, really, and maybe a little more. I actually ran a script to feed any new information added to your files, just to keep track, but now that you're here, I can pull it off. I only did it because I wanted to reach you, really, no wrong intentions, just because of Benjamin—"

"Can't you find something about your brother as you did about me?"

He looks down at the floor. "I must admit I haven't been able to hack Mossad's firewall, their encryption codes are in the hundreds of digits."

"Is that why they contacted you? Do they know you tried to hack into their computers?"

"I don't know, but it's possible. Very likely, really."

"We need to do some field work, then. Let's go."

THE NINJA roars as I push it pass 80 km/h, and Jonathan claws my jacket. His face is pressed against my back and his arms wrapped around my waist. I have pity and slow down to 70, but he doesn't detach himself until I go below 40. At this turtle's pace I can actually hear the city drone: honks, chatter, the ancient murmur of its stones. We round the Christian and Armenian quarters and head into east Jerusalem, toward the Mount of Olives, where the scent of a hundred flowers awaits us—the chrysanthemum, the anemone, and... it's been so long I can't remember any more.

Jonathan taps my shoulder. "Turn right on the next corner and go south."

He leads me through some new territory until we reach a three-story building with peeling blue paint and white patches smeared with black, perhaps colored by smoke.

"Is this where Benjamin lives?"

Jonathan nods. "Our father never approved of him living alone, for the longest time, but in the end it was better, really, because he wanted to convert us all."

"Did he turn to Islam?"

"Sorry I didn't tell you before. Benjamin is a Christian."

Benjamin became a blasphemous idolater, believing god is not one but three?

I shake my head and walk to the building. I push a door with cold iron bars and come into an echoing foyer with a narrow winding stair.

"Where exactly does he live?"

Jonathan points up. "Third floor, third floor. I've come twice during the past week, but he never answers the door, or his phone. He used to visit us several times a week."

"Did he travel at all?"

"Many times, but he always phoned when he was away."

We climb the stairs to the third floor. A royal blue door stands at the end of the almost non-existent hallway—there's roughly a square meter of floor between the stairs and the entrance to the apartment.

A crash shatters the silence on the other side of the door. We glance at each other. I fumble with the knob—it's locked, of course. The old door opens easily enough when I smash my shoulder against it. Jonathan runs in after me.

"Benjamin? Little brother, be here, please be here."

The apartment is in shadows, dust dancing in sunbeams that filter beneath the hem of the curtain. I slide the vinyl screen and the light bursts in, making me wince.

The place is small and impeccably tidy but for an open book on the bed by a propped-up pillow and a half-empty glass of water on the nightstand. A broken vase lies on the kitchen floor.

I hear a noise to my left and spin around, drawing my gun. Two green eyes stare at me from the kitchen counter. Jonathan laughs and presses a hand against his chest.

"Just a cat!"

The cat leaps to the floor and brushes its tail against the pantry door.

"It must be hungry," I say. "Why don't you find some cat food while I look around?"

I replace the gun on my waist and move to the bed to pick up the open book. A Bible. I drop it and shudder. The nightstand drawers are empty and the closet has but a few changes of clothes.

"He lives an austere life," I say as Jonathan squats to fill the cat's bowl. "Does he have a job?"

"He always talks about the imminent end of the world, it's annoying really, but he believes it, so I suppose his life is consistent with his beliefs. Why would you accumulate possessions if the world is going to end soon?"

What nonsense. "Are all Christians like this?"

"I don't know, but it's not like I've befriended a lot of Christians in my life."

Come to think of it, I've never spoken to a Christian. All I know about these people is what my imams and schoolteachers have told me—that they're infidels who believe God has a son, who actually think the son of Mary is God. How can Benjamin believe such—

"*Gazlonim! A broch tzu dir!*" Thieves, a curse on you. A coarse voice from the hallway.

20

A wrinkle of a woman stands at the door, spitting Yiddish curses I never heard in my thirty-nine years but whose meaning is more than clear. She pulls a wireless phone from her apron's pocket. Her face, which already resembles a dog's, shakes like a bulldog's jowls.

Jonathan runs to her. "Please, don't call the police, I'm Benjamin's brother. Look, I was feeding the cat, and thieves would not do that."

The lady looks at the feline. "I love that cat. But you don't look much like Ben." She shoots me a quick bottom-to-top glance. "Who's that Arab?"

"He's a friend, we mean no harm, really. Have you seen Benjamin? Do you know where he is?"

She narrows her beady eyes on him. "No. And I don't like you, or that Arab. Take your filth out of here now."

"Please, lady, I need to find my brother, my father is dead worried about him, really, and I'm worried too—I have no news about him, so please tell me what you know."

She looks Jonathan up and down, then says, "It's Sunday. If he's back, he's at the Christian church by the school."

"Thank you, thank you, really, we'll look for him there, we're—"

"Let's go, Jonathan." I grab his arm and pull him out, bumping the bulldog lady in the process. "Take care of the cat, woman."

Her Yiddish curses follow us as we run down the stairs.

I REMOVE my helmet and look at the church's entrance, still sitting on the bike. Jonathan hurries up the stone steps, halts at the top, and turns to me.

"Will you come, Farid?"

"I'll wait for you here. Just go inside and see if Benjamin is there."

Jonathan nods and walks in through the arched doors. This neighborhood smells like moss, and every sound seems to come from a distant place. A mild discomfort sets in and I get off the bike. The discomfort grows worse. It's as if an invisible presence is nagging my soul. I must get away from this place.

I am a sinner, I need repentance.

What? Where are these thoughts coming from? Why am I even considering this? Repentance for what?

I am a sinner.

I rub my temples and pace around the bike. What's taking Jonathan so long? He's been there almost two minutes. He just has to look around and—

"Shalom."

A chubby white man gets out of a red Hyundai Accent. He stares at me with a happy smile.

"Hi, I'm Mike Stein, one of the deacons here. Are you coming to our service?"

His English is perfect, his accent pure, not like the English of my teachers at King Abdulaziz University. An Englishman perhaps? Maybe American? He extends one hand but I keep mine in my pocket. My old imam would say that a Christian American is the devil himself.

He retrieves his hand but keeps the smile. "*Ha'eem ata me'daber eevreet?*" Do you speak Hebrew?

This man is being cordial and respectful to me and I should respond in kind. That is my Muslim duty. I'm not waging jihad against him at the moment.

"*Ken, anee m'daber eevreet.*" Yes, I speak Hebrew. "And English as well." I smile, self-conscious of my accent.

"Excellent. Are you waiting for someone or coming in?"

"Do you know Benjamin Ben David?"

"Ben, of course, he's one of the elect. How do you know him?"

The elect? Is that how Christians call each other?

"He's an old friend I haven't seen in years."

"Oh, wonderful. I just got back from Jordan—been away for two weeks—so I can't say if your friend is here or not. But you know, if you come inside with me, perhaps I can help you find him."

"Thank you, but—"

Jonathan darts out of the church. "Farid, Farid, take me as far as you can from this place."

He stops at the sight of Mike.

"This is Jonathan, Benjamin's brother."

Mike opens his arms. "Wonderful. Big brother or little brother?"

Jonathan shakes his head. "Excuse us." He pulls me to one side, an arm around my back. "Benjamin isn't there, but they claim to know him. These people are crazy, really, they say my brother is one of the one-hundred-and-forty-something-thousand elect from the tribes of Israel and that the end of the world is near and some other crazy stuff, really, they wanted to pray for me or something like that—"

"Calm down, Jonathan—"

"No, Farid, really, I'm even more worried about Benjamin now that I see what he's gotten into, really, a Messianic Jew is what they called him in there.... I know you're a devout Muslim, Farid, but honestly, all this religious stuff doesn't fit me."

I raise my brows and glance at his kippa. He touches his skullcap.

"Oh, this, yes, I only wear it to please my father, really, but I couldn't care less about Judaism."

"You keep surprising me."

He peers over his shoulder and nods at Mike. "Who is he?"

I look in Mike's direction and he seems to take it as an invitation, because he comes our way.

"Do you guys want me to pray with you?"

Jonathan widens his eyes and I can read the terror in them.

WE JUMP on the bike and I drive away as if chased by an army. I can feel Jonathan's chin on my shoulder.

"He's waving goodbye at us, what a crazy man," he says.

How ridiculous to flee from a harmless, deluded person—but that's not what I'm departing from, is it? No, what happened back there is unexplainable and somehow terrifying: that sudden discomfort and thoughts of repentance... the strange Christian talk, their—

"Watch out!" Jonathan screams—just in time.

A bus speeding past the traffic light at the intersection is headed straight toward us. I pull the brakes and slide the back wheel to my right. The screeching bike turns one hundred and eighty degrees and Jonathan loses his grip on me. The draft left by the bus blows against my trembling back and I realize Jonathan is not on the bike.

"Jonathan?"

"Here." He moans and grabs my right leg.

I take off my helmet and look down at him splayed on the pavement. A black circle is painted on the street.

"When did you fall?"

"Just help me up."

I pull him up with one hand. "Did you hit your head?"

"Yes, I'm dead, can't you see? This is the last time I ride with you. I never liked motorcycles, much less now that you almost got me killed."

He frowns and his hands shake. He sits on the bike and grunts. If he wants to be angry, fine. Better angry than scared to death.

I set out again but don't hear his chatter this time. When we reach Jonathan's house he gets off the bike before I shut it down and strides in, closing the door behind him. I can't recall seeing him so upset before. I go into the house and find old David sitting in the living room, reading a book.

"Shalom, Farid." His voice is similar to Jonathan's but has a tired tenor to it.

"Shalom." I bow my head and then look up towards the stairs. "Please excuse me."

He smiles an ancient smile and I climb the steps before he says anything. Upstairs, the narrow hallway lays silent like an empty catacomb. I knock on Jonathan's door, wait, then knock again.

"Are you hurt? Do you need anything?" Music comes alive inside his room. "Jonathan, say something." The volume of the Jewish pop escalates. I sigh. He'll cool down eventually. I hope.

Inside my cell-like room, hours pass and the smell of damp grows worse. There must be a leak somewhere.

How long have I been here? The clock says 4:22, but no, it can't be. That would mean I've only been locked up for twenty minutes or so.

I lie down, sit, lie down again, then finally stand. Discomfort spreads like a rash. I must go ahead with my initial plan and go to the base the Russian mentioned. Tonight after everybody is asleep, I'll do it.

Maybe I should rest, so as to be refreshed for the mission tonight. But my discomfort hasn't left. To make things worse, I barely fit in this bed. My nose tickles and I sneeze. The humidity will kill me if I stay here.

I wipe my face and walk out to the hallway. My throat contracts, begging for saliva. I need water.

I hear an increasing murmur as I descend the stairs to the cramped living room. David's rounded body is slumped on a chair, holding a book in his palms, right in front of his face. He stops whispering and looks up at me.

"This is so very interesting and astonishing. Come, Farid, sit and let me share this with you."

I glance at the book but can't tell what it is. He is my host and I can't refuse. How bad can it be to hear the old man for a few minutes?

"You're kind, thank you."

He smiles as I sit opposite him, rather self-conscious. David's gaze is an embracing pool of goodness and I wonder what memories I bring to him. He regards me for so long that I have to look away, to the cloth covering the table between us: faded blue with golden stars of David embroidered on its hem.

His eyes narrow as he brings the book closer to his face. "Listen to this passage from the prophet Ezekiel: The hand of HaShem was upon me, and HaShem carried me out in a spirit, and set me down in the midst of the valley, and it was full of bones; and He caused me to pass by them round about, and, behold, there were very many in the open valley; and, lo, they were very dry. And He said unto me: 'Son of man, can these bones live?' And I answered: 'O L-rd GOD, Thou knowest.' Then He said unto me: 'Prophesy over these bones, and say unto them: O ye dry bones, hear the word of HaShem: Thus saith the L-rd GOD unto these bones: Behold, I will cause breath to enter into you, and ye shall live. And I will lay sinews upon you, and will bring up flesh upon you, and cover you with skin, and put breath in you, and ye shall live; and ye shall know that I am HaShem.'"

Bones and flesh? Why is he reading from his Jewish Bible?

"Quite interesting. Do you believe in prophecies, Farid?"

I don't know how to respond, but he seems oblivious to my discomfort.

"My father survived the Holocaust," he says. "He had not conceived me yet, no, because I was born after that monster Hitler and his Germans had been defeated... but this passage right here..." He taps the open book with his index finger. "This is the fulfillment of what happened when the Holocaust finished. My father, and all the survivors from the concentration camps, were but dry bones with thin skin, they seemed death, but they lived again."

His eyes shine as he speaks, but suddenly he blinks and stares at my face, as if trying to read my thoughts.

"Why would I say this? Because that's the only interpretation I can fathom. See, it then says…" He returns his attention to the book, searching something in the page. "Here. Then He said unto me: 'Son of man, these bones are the whole house of Israel; behold, they say: Our bones are dried up, and our hope is lost; we are clean cut off. Therefore prophesy, and say unto them: Thus saith the L-rd GOD: Behold, I will open your graves, and cause you to come up out of your graves, O My people; and I will bring you into the land of Israel. And ye shall know that I am HaShem, when I have opened your graves, and caused you to come up out of your graves, O My people. And I will put My spirit in you, and ye shall live, and I will place you in your own land; and ye shall know that I HaShem have spoken, and performed it, saith HaShem.'" David grins. "Indeed he has!"

A chill runs though my bones, and I'm not sure why, since these words are strange and foreign to my mind. They don't have the chanting rhythm of the Qur'an, of Arabic, but a certain magnetism stirs me.

"Can you see it?"

I shake my head. "What?"

"There was no land of Israel for centuries, only Palestine, but in 1948 the State of Israel was born again. My parents came from Poland, and many other Jews came from all over Europe to this land, just as the prophet said, the graves—those Nazi camps— opened, and HaShem's people came to their land."

21

An Al-Mahdi guard lifts one section of the green curtain and the caliph slides into the palace auditorium. All noises cease. Hussai's fingers tickle and again he experiences the odd energy he felt when Al-Mahdi touched him that morning, when he was healed. Well, not healed, because that's impossible. It's just coincidence that he feels better, that his wound no longer hurts.

A bitter taste fills his mouth and he frowns at his tea. The cup is empty and he realizes it has been for some time.

The caliph greets the hundred or so people with the wave of his hand. *"Allah-o Ahkbar."*

"Allah-o Ahkbar," the crowd responds.

Al-Mahdi sits on a golden chair that resembles the thrones of old, surrounded by his personal guards. This dinner with him feels more like a legal audience than the personal meeting he expected.

One of the guards steps forward. "Tonight, publicly, for the first time, you are given the privilege of declaring your allegiance to Muhammad Al-Mahdi, direct descendant of the Prophet, the twelfth caliph of Islam, the Awaited One, the Lord of the Age, the rider of the white horse, who goes forth conquering and to conquer."

Hussai looks at the men around him. Most have chests moving up and down, eyes wide open, pursed lips. Are they feeling the same mix of emotions he is? Are they frightened and fascinated? Do they want to storm out of the palace yet still surrender their will to the caliph, even if it means crawling over ice to bow before him?

Where are these thoughts coming from? It's as if a soundless voice were whispering in his ear.

The guard extends an arm toward the caliph with an open palm. "May Allah curse and slay you if you refuse to come tonight. Now come and drink of Al-Mahdi's love, talk only of him, and experience the happiness and abundance he will give you."

Hussai's feet move him forward along with the crowd until they form a line to the throne. Even to his not-so-devout eyes, this seems like a sacrilege: worshipping a man, when only Allah must be worshipped. But it also feels right, like a duty bestowed from above.

HUSSAI'S HEART is a runaway horse. A tremor runs through his arms as the man in front of him moves away and it is his turn to greet Al-Mahdi. He wills himself to look into the caliph's face, so close for the second time. A perfectly fitted headpiece covers Al-Mahdi's bald forehead. The high hooked nose is oddly shaped, as if a surgeon made an error during reconstruction. This makes no sense, of course—why would the caliph have plastic surgery?

"Lord… Caliph…" Hussai's tongue twists and he can't untangle it.

Al-Mahdi grins, showing a V-shaped gap between his front teeth. "Hussai, do you love me?"

"Ah, yes, my lord."

"Good. Tell me how much."

Hussai wets his lips and glances to the guards on each side of the caliph, whose stares seem sharper than their drawn swords. He touches his shoulder.

"I have risked my life for you, my lord, and will do it again."

Al-Mahdi nods. "Yes, I know. You will risk your life again and again for me. And I will give you everything you desire." He turns to a guard on his left. "Bring a chair or stool and put it here."

The guard walks down from the platform, takes a chair from

one of the tables, and carries it back to the left of Al-Mahdi's throne.

"Come, Hussai, sit by my side and learn true devotion."

Hussai wipes his sweaty hands on his pants, climbs the podium, and staggers toward the chair. Why him? He remembers his father, one of the wealthiest men in Baghdad, always sitting in places of power. Perhaps it is his destiny to sit by Al-Mahdi.

He glances at the caliph, who receives a little man in a red-and-white checkered turban. Al-Mahdi sits with grace and confidence, never leaning forward or dropping his chin. Hussai straightens his back and imitates the caliph as best he can. The little man dips his head.

"Lord Al-Mahdi, the Awaited One, you are after the likeness of Prophet Muhammad, a descendant of Fatimah, and the caliph of Islam. I pledge my allegiance to you."

"May Allah bless you. Go in peace and feel my love."

Hussai lifts his gaze to the line: at least sixty people remain. He listens to the first dozen or so before losing interest. His back aches and his legs need to stretch. He moves his neck in a semicircle and catches a glimpse of General Atartuk in the far corner of the auditorium, speaking on his cell phone. Although the General is harsh with his army, he's always sheepish and pathetic around the Caliph. But it is obvious that this annoys the Caliph. At least that's what Hussai perceived that morning when the Caliph slapped Atartuk. Al-Mahdi's fame for cruelty dates from his days as a militant—surely, he would do more than slap him if the general commits a serious offense.

If Hussai wants to stand out, he has to be different, has to be bold. And now the caliph turns to him.

"Enough for tonight. I will do something different now."

Hussai blinks and looks at the line. "Yes. Perhaps they could make a collective display of devotion?"

"Such as?"

"Such as crawling on their knees and bowing down."

Al-Mahdi smiles. "I like your thinking, but the time has not come for that yet. My people will do that after I rule the world, but we must be patient."

Al-Mahdi starts to leave but Hussai clears his throat. "My lord."

"Yes?"

"General Atartuk did not pledge his allegiance tonight. But he should be first, as an example to the rest."

"Where is that fool?"

Hussai points to the general, who flips his cell phone closed and strides out of the auditorium, never glancing in their direction. Hussai keeps his pointing finger up until the whole assembly sees it and virtually all eyes are on the departing general.

Hussai smirks. "What shameful behavior. When the soldiers hear, they'll look upon you with contempt. This cannot be allowed. Your authority has been challenged."

Now eyes fix on the caliph, who returns the stares with a stern frown. He seems to ponder for a few seconds, then speaks.

"I will punish him, but you must choose the punishment, Hussai, as you are his accuser."

A shiver runs through him. This is his moment, to gamble his destiny with one sentence. The caliph foretold he would risk his life again and again. This will be the first time.

"My lord Al-Mahdi, following the tradition of the Caliphate Council, the general must be beheaded."

22

The GPS screen glows in the dark, and the cold air is a welcome distraction from my conversation with David. The man is deluded.

Not a car on the road to Rehovot—only my bike, the roar of its engine piercing the night. Tel Nof Israeli Air Force base is just a few kilometers away, so I head south on Highway 6.

As I take the exit, I see a sign that says this is an electronic toll highway. I press the brakes and pull over. I reach for the binoculars in my bag and look down the road. Cameras and sensors line the highway. I'll be caught on video as soon as I enter the road. Too risky.

The GPS shows an alternate route: down highway 44, right on highway 3, east on route 411. I let it guide me until it warns me I'm driving away from my destination. But I can't stop now. I was hoping for a hill, any cover to hide the bike, but the terrain is flat in this part of Israel.

Less than a kilometer away, right before entering the town of Mazkeret Batya, I find an isolated gas station. I park the bike in the back and check my position: If I run across the fields, I'll reach the base in about ten minutes. I set out in the name of Allah.

I'm feeling fast tonight. Surely god is with me. The base's thick outer fence is in front of me sooner than I expect. Behind the barbed wire, they've erected a three-meter-high concrete wall. I climb a tree and catch a glimpse of the runway from the top. The air smells of jet fuel. But there are no jets on the runway.

Through my binoculars I see in detail the buildings across

the runway. Two soldiers stand by a hideous metal structure, a cross between a hangar and a warehouse. White lamps seem to emanate a vapor around the place. That must be where they keep the nukes.

I pull out the small video camera Augustus lent me and make sure the date displays on the viewfinder: Sunday, April 21.

"Tel Nof Israeli Air Force base, 2200 hours. Intelligence mission. *Allah-o Ahkbar.*" I zoom in and pan over the base before turning the camera off. This video will prove my loyalty to Al-Mahdi.

Keeping a safe distance, I round the double-wire fence and stop ten meters from a narrow access road. A few hundred meters away lies the first of at least two checkpoints before the entrance. I can't go any further without being spotted.

A pair of lights flashes through the air and I fall to the ground. A truck creeps along the road toward the checkpoint. The sign on one side of the cargo cabin reads: REHOVOT LAUNDRY SERVICE.

The speed limit is low enough to allow me to run after it. When the truck slows to a stop as it nears the checkpoint, I step on the back bumper and pull myself onto the roof. Judging by the voices, the first checkpoint seems to be manned by only two soldiers, who question the driver briefly and let him continue. Up ahead, the second checkpoint looks like a well-lit gate with a tower nearby. I must act now, where the road is dark.

I jump onto the roof of the driver's cabin and smack it twice with my fist. It has the desired effect: the truck stops and the driver steps out to see what's going on. I leap down and knock him unconscious with a jab to his temple. I grab his hat and badge, stuff them in my pocket, then tie his hands with his own belt and gag him with one of his socks.

He looks like an Arab. Guilt knots my stomach, but someone will find him later on the side of the road.

Back in the truck, I don his cap and start the engine. The good thing about driving this slow is that it gives me time to think. On the passenger seat rests a clipboard with some sort of paperwork. I can't read with such poor light, but I think it says—

"Stop!"

An Israeli soldier I hadn't seen waves me to a halt ten meters from the gate, then motions for me to roll down the window. I smile and slip my gun under the seat.

"Shalom."

"You're a few hours late."

"Too much work, too much traffic."

The young soldier—barely twenty—frowns when he stares at my face. "Hey, I haven't seen you before. What happened to the other guy, what's his name?"

I throw a quick glance at the driver's badge. "Mustafa."

"Yeah, Mustafa."

"He's not feeling well, sir."

His gaze becomes more penetrating. "What's wrong with him?"

"Appendicitis, I think. They called me this morning to take his shift."

"And what's your name?"

"Ali, sir."

"Show me your ID, Ali."

"They didn't get me a badge yet, I just started this morning." I grab the clipboard and offer it to him. "I'm sure I'll have it by next time, see, here's all the paperwork."

He looks at the clipboard. "I don't deal with that, just leave it on top of the clerk's desk at the building where you drop off the bags. You know where that is?"

"They explained how to get there, but…"

"It's the first white building on the left, you won't miss it." He starts for the gate. "Carry on, very slow."

As I move forward, I notice my shirt is covered in sweat. The soldier motions to his partners at the gate.

"Laundry guy. Check the truck."

My muscles tense as the vehicle is surrounded by soldiers—
one standing in front of the truck with his weapon ready, another
peering inside the cabin, a third holding a mirror to see beneath
and on top of the truck, a fourth opening the cargo area. I keep
my hands on the wheel and weigh my options. My faint whisper
is almost a thought. "In the name of Allah, the Beneficent and
Merciful..."

"Clear, let him in."

THE CLOSEST building, a white box covered in dust, must be the
one I'm supposed to go to. I park behind it, take off the cap, pull
out my camera and my bag, and jump onto the gravel. The area
is clear. The guarded metal building I saw from the tree would
be on the north end of the runway, which is on the east side of
the base. The stars point my direction.

I round the truck, walking away from the illuminated paths.
The moon lights the path like a sign from Allah, who surely is
with me if I've made it this far. A cool breeze sways the trees and
drops the temperature. I shiver and zip up my light jacket.

Fifty meters or so from the metallic building, I crouch behind
a bush and zoom in with the camera. The two guards haven't
moved. There's no way to pass them unnoticed.

This side of the base is eerily quiet. Even the wind has ceased.

Staying away from the guards, I amble around contiguous
buildings until I'm on the opposite side of the structure. No
wonder I thought it looked like a hangar—that's what it was at
some point in time. The large door has been replaced with black
metal sheets that seem to be sealed together. But why is the exit
not facing the runway? If there's a way in past those guards, I
must find it soon. I go to the side of the building, on the lookout
for cameras and to my surprise find a ladder fixed to the wall. I
glance around and climb up.

At the top I step onto a flat roof, wide open like an industrial terrace. The roof feels solid, but I fear it will creak and squeak if I walk on it. I test it with two short steps but hear nothing.

Ten meters to my left, three or four shafts protrude from the flat surface, and not too far from them sits a humming air conditioning unit. I take out my flashlight and inspect the shafts, peering into the largest one. The flashlight pokes a yellow circle in the black emptiness of the ventilation chamber, revealing dusty walls and a thick gray pipe twisting along the middle of the shaft. Looks as though I've found my way down.

MY ELBOW hits a sharp edge and the pain reverberates through my arm. I lose my grip on the flashlight and it drops into the pool of darkness below. Two seconds later there's a clang, and the dry crack of broken plastic. There's a spare mini flashlight in the side pocket of my pants, but I hate to risk losing that as well.

The air is warmer at the bottom, with a smell of fresh paint and solvent. I turn on the flashlight and see I must crawl through a tunnel. How far?

I clench the light between my teeth to free my hands, wipe the sweat off my forehead, and get on my hands and knees, just as if I were praying. The flow of air is stronger here and the paint smell becomes more intense, more concentrated in this smaller shaft. The skin of my damp palms feels like velcro ripping off fabric every time I lift a hand from the thin metal. The shaft seems to shrink like a funnel. My shoulders kiss the walls and my head bows level with my back. A burning sensation hits my neck and every muscle in my body screams to stretch.

Not now, not after all this crawling. I rest my weight on my elbows and wave the light into the passage ahead. The shaft swallows the narrow beam.

Sweat drips off my chin. I have to get out of here. I point the flashlight to the upper wall of the shaft and move it forward. It certainly seems like the narrowing is incremental. What a waste of time.

I bite my lips, turn the light off, close my eyes, and crawl backwards. My right leg tingles. Please, god, let it not be a cramp.

Eager to reach the larger shaft, I jump to my feet and hit my head against the pipe. An echo swirls in my skull. It doesn't matter, but it hurts.

I hear human voices and hold my breath.

"... at least, that's what I think."

"I know, but the commander said increasing security would only bring more attention to the base, and the missiles will only be here a week...."

The voices outside, now gone, sounded like they came from the opposite direction of the funnel shaft. I make the light dance over the dusty wall and see a grid over a square hole, just a few centimeters above the floor. I pull the grid and it bulges. Two more tries and it comes off.

I point the light in: a textured black surface. How strange. I reach for it, and it stretches against my fingers. I rip the black plastic. I should have seen this before squeezing myself down the other shaft. It's been more than an hour since I came to the base and I still haven't recorded anything. At least, thanks to the conversation I heard, I know the Russians were right.

I creep through the hole and emerge in a room. Masonry tools are piled everywhere, and in the light from a hallway outside I can make out a half-dozen cans of paint, stacked like a pyramid in the corner. No door, only a doorframe. To my right the hallway ends at a wall. To my left it seems to open to a larger area. There are a few offices and rooms, and somewhere out there lies what they're protecting.

The sound of quick steps drives me back into the tool room. I place a hand over my gun. The lights in the hallway go off. A door closes, resounding through the building. That must be the main door with the guards.

I'm alone in the building.

A WHITE light shines over the open area at the end of the hallway. It's a spotlight, hanging from a long cord in the middle of a massive room with a ceiling as high as the building itself.

This is a hangar—one with no airplanes, only trucks. And what seemed like sealed sheets of metal from the outside is actually an electronic gate. I turn on my camera and round the five trucks, recording everything, then focus the lens on my face.

"The Israeli Army keeps this equipment in a disguised hangar inside the Tel Nof base. One of the trucks is loaded with a missile launcher and six missiles, with what seem to be ten nuclear warheads each. The missiles carry the radioactive warning label. A second truck carries what appears to be a large portable radar with the insignia of the army of Israel. I believe this to be an anti-missile system."

I press the stand-by button and check out the equipment. The Israelis are not supposed to have any weapons, as part of the peace covenant. This must be an improved version of the Arrow anti-missile system the UN confiscated from Israel three years ago, much better than anything we have in Iraq. The target acquisition radar is larger and probably more accurate, and the missiles look new. I must get this information to the caliph.

I'll become a hero. No one has done this before. A chill of excitement makes me shudder. Allah the Merciful is gracious toward his servant.

A light shines to my left. I duck behind one of the trucks. A guard walks into the room, pointing his flashlight here and there. He must be making rounds. Dread punches my stomach. My bag lies on the floor between two of the trucks, right in the guard's path.

He walks closer and hovers over the bag, peering into it with his flashlight while I slip around the missiles, positioning myself behind him. He leans forward, his hand reaching for the radio on his belt. I lift my gun by the barrel and reach him in two steps— he hears me and turns toward me. The butt of the gun misses the back of his head and hits his nose. But his body doesn't budge—he's a rock of muscle as big as me. He grabs his gun.

I throw a low round-kick against his legs, and he falls forward, dropping his weapon. I kick it underneath a truck and knock the guard unconscious with the butt of my own gun. I pull out the camera's memory card and place it in my pocket, then put the camera in my bag and search for an exit other than the shaft by which I entered. The front of the hangar is guarded but the back door isn't. Why? It's a huge door, made for huge equipment. I find a panel on one side of this door with a series of buttons and a glowing red light.

Will it open quietly? I doubt it but pass my hand over the light and watch it turn green. The whole panel illuminates. I look up—a camera above the panel stares back. Damn.

Out, I must get out. I press random buttons and the immense gates bulk open in the middle, then stop. A screen on the panel flashes a message: Incorrect Code. CLOSING.

I sprint toward the opening and slide my body through just in time, feeling the metal scratch my chest. My bag is stuck between the gates. I pull with all my might but it won't come through. As I let it go, the sound of the camera being crushed makes me cringe.

The next sound I hear is the faint beeping of an alarm.

23

The calm in the air is suspicious. I crouch behind a building facing the base perimeter and close my eyes. I must get to a vehicle. My bike is unreachable now. If I tried to get over the barbed wire fence? Smashed like a fly, that's how it would end for me. My people would never know—Al-Mahdi would never know I laid my life down for him. And would I be in paradise? Allah will surely take into account my life of prayer, fasting, and alms. But I have not prayed five times a day these past few days, and I had evil thoughts about a woman—

A light comes on inside the building, spilling out through the window above me. I peer around the corner and see the flashing red lights of an ambulance. Why do I think of eternity? I need only survive this night.

The back doors are open but the cabin seems empty. I move as close as I can and take cover behind an olive tree.

A short, slight man wearing a reflective vest emerges from the small building, pushing a gurney toward the ambulance. He places the gurney in the back and closes the doors, then walks to the driver's side. I dart around the vehicle to meet him and put a hand on my face.

"*Tuchal La'azor Li?*" Can you help me?

He nods. "*Ken. Mah Yesh?*" Yes, what's the matter?

I pull my hand off my face and he looks at me intently, his eyes narrowing. I grab his head by one ear and smack it against the ambulance. Pity pricks me when I see the wretched little man moaning on the floor. He's not unconscious, but I don't hit him again. Instead I push him inside the building, my gun pressed against his back.

This is the base's clinic. We go past the reception and into the first room.

"Get in there. Is there anyone else here?"

He shakes his head. Should I believe him? There's no time to find out. I must leave the base as soon as possible.

I point to an empty gurney in the corridor. "Lie down there and don't make a sound."

He complies, and I tie him down with the gurney straps, then gag him with gauze. This is taking precious time. Why didn't I just knock him out?

The corridor is still empty when I return but I lock the door of the room anyway. I cross the reception area, leave the hangar, and in seconds am driving the ambulance toward the gate.

The soldiers at the gate nod and one of them waves as I drive off—as if they knew I was coming. I shiver with cold made worse by my sweat-drenched clothes. I shake off my weariness and focus on the asphalt ahead. A light shines to the north. Of course, that's the checkpoint where I got on the laundry truck.

I turn on the siren and accelerate to 100km/h. Two soldiers stand in the middle of the road, one of them waving at me to slow down. I keep my speed and press the horn. Come on, get out of the way. My muscles stiffen when the other soldier points his weapon at my windshield.

By Allah, I'm not going to stop. I switch the lights to high beams and keep honking, less than thirty meters from running over them.

"Move, you idiots."

At the last breath, the waving soldier steps aside and pushes his armed partner out of the way. I zoom past.

"Thank you, god, for allowing me to escape. *Allah-o Ahkbar.*"

Now, where's my bike?

Radio static startles me. "Central, we have an issue in the

north hangar." They must have found my bag. I reach for the radio on the copilot's seat and bring it closer to listen to the exchange.

After a few kilometers I see a sign pointing to Jerusalem. I'll have to apologize to Augustus for losing his Ninja.

A moan from the back of the ambulance. Of course, the patient in the gurney. He must be very sick if they were driving him out of the base.

I try to ignore the moans. The radio exchanges let me know they've discovered the unconscious man in the hangar. There's quite a commotion, but I've been gone more than twenty minutes and am now on the outskirts of Jerusalem. This is quite a potent radio.

"Central, we just heard from the medic at the clinic. Intruder is believed to have stolen the ambulance. Alert police."

I must abandon this vehicle.

The patient coughs violently, my chest hurts just listening to him. When the spell subsides, he moans. "*Mayim...*" Water. "*Be'vakasha...*" Please.

I bite my lower lip and squeeze the steering wheel until it hurts. No, it's not wise to take care of him. The mission is what's important, getting back to Baghdad with the memory card.

This is not what I should do, it's stupid, it's suicidal, I'll get caught....

THE TRAFFIC in the city is worse than I expected but I dare not turn on the siren. All I have to do is get to the hospital between Jaffa Road and Strauss, then drop the patient off. The man's intermittent cough is now unceasing. And I can hear sirens.

Two police cars approach fast, their glaring lights clear in the dawn traffic. Too fast.

I zigzag a few times, then move to the slower lane, hoping the police will pass by, but they close on me. A familiar sound drowns out my passenger's moans—the rumbling clack of a helicopter.

"Hang on, my friend!"

I jerk the ambulance left and put two wheels on the sidewalk. Carts with tomatoes and cucumbers crash into windows. I overtake a sky blue Mazda and veer sharply to the right, cutting in front of a bus and a motorcycle and turning onto a side street.

If most people in Jerusalem aren't awake by now, they soon will be. The yelps in the back are terrifying as the gurney rocks back and forth. The chopper hovers somewhere ahead, its blades deafening. Then I see it descending, menacing like a beast in a bullfight.

I veer right and spot the hospital down the street. The suspension threatens to break as I bob up and down without slowing until I squeak to a stop in front of the emergency room.

The patient keeps coughing as I pull out the gurney and roll it into the hospital.

"A nurse, I need a nurse."

A large woman in scrubs says, "Who are you?"

I point to the cougher. "He needs help. Take care of him."

"Wait, sir, you must register hi—"

"I'm in a no-parking zone, so I must go."

I spin and head for the exit but notice police cars pulling over to the entrance of the hospital.

I run down the corridor, looking for another exit.

24

Hussai smirks at the general's shaky voice.

"Show mercy, my lord, show mercy. I was coordinating Farid's capture, I meant no disrespect to your excellency, you know I—"

"Shut your snout." The caliph's jaw is set. "The timing of your stupidity is utterly inconvenient, but I gave my word."

"What word, my lord?"

"We must have a public display." Al-Mahdi motions a guard forward. "Take care of the plans for the beheading."

Hussai steps away from the rail and leans forward, chin down. "I would gladly arrange everything, if you wish, my lord."

Al-Mahdi regards him as if just discovering Hussai's presence, his eyes lingering on him for a moment.

"No. You brought this upon us and I'm sure you'd enjoy killing the general, but I have to decide what to do with you first."

The general says, "No, please! Not like this… my honor—"

The guard kicks the kneeling general in the cheek and his body slumps on the marble floor like a sack of wheat. Hussai wipes his sweating palms on his pants and tugs at the collar of his shirt. He's swimming in unpredictable waters, but he can't escape the terror and fascination he experiences around the caliph.

A second guard comes and drags the general out. Hussai gazes away at the morning horizon. That could have been him. The caliph has absolute power over life and death. How would it feel to have that authority? Could it be his? Can he be usurped?

"I know what you want, Hussai." The caliph's voice is harsh. "You want to be general."

Hussai's body stiffens, his smirk vanishes. Al-Mahdi walks toward him, each step like a sharp blade in Hussai's abdomen. Why is it so hard to be near this man yet so hard to be apart from him?

"You are cunning—and I like cunning. But it's no joy to lose a general and the most experienced major in your army on the brink of a war."

Hussai stares at the floor.

"I should punish you as well, Hussai. You're an inconvenience."

A drop of sweat rolls down Hussai's forehead, slides over the nose, and drops like a tiny wet bomb on the white marble. He twists his lips and breathes in deeply.

"But that would mean losing a brigadier general as well. I will lead the troops to victory myself. As for you? Prove yourself loyal and useful, and you may become my general one day."

25

The *soulless* *street* *in* front of Jonathan's house feels queer, like a dormant beast ready to attack. I wonder if the police are waiting for me.

It's that time of morning just before shops begin to open and people leave their dwellings, so I'll wait a few more minutes to step out of this public garden and blend into the coming crowd.

I see no signs of surveillance around Jonathan's, but I've been wrong before. Unless they followed me, which I'm sure they didn't, they have no way to trace me to him.

Once inside the house, I must keep a low profile while things settle down.

If I can. The thrill of danger gives me more ecstasy than prayer, I confess—god forgive me.

Taliah comes out of the house, wearing a short, tight purple sports outfit. I try, but I can't take my eyes off her.

I move deeper into the green area and observe her from behind a palm tree, stepping on some flowers in the process. She crosses the street in my direction and trots down the white stone stairs in the garden, passing so close I can smell her lavender scent. I fill my lungs with the aroma.

She takes a trail lined with ancient half columns stained by humidity and green moss. Standing in the middle of the trail, she pulls out a cell phone and makes a call. Maybe her morning runs are more than exercise. Perhaps she knows something about Benjamin.

The call ends sooner than I expected. She places a pair of headphones on her ears and takes off running. I follow her at a prudent distance, and when she turns at a corner restaurant I sprint to catch up. I make it to the restaurant and glance down the street.

Where is she? My breathing accelerates. Cold emptiness kicks my stomach as I search among the passersby. Am I just going to follow her as she jogs? What for?

There. She's at the newspaper stand, trotting in place as she pays the seller. She takes a rolled newspaper and runs in my direction. I scoot into the restaurant's open foyer, under a blue and white canopy-like roof. She passes by with a quick glance into the foyer and keeps running.

I walk out and follow her with my gaze. A city bus parks in front of me, blocking the view. The bus expels a black cloud of smoke as I round it. My chest tightens up and I cough, stumbling forward. A car screeches, honks. I look up and see a bumper just a few centimeters from my body. This woman is going to kill me.

SHE'S GOOD. My jogging trail in Baghdad is flat, but hers is up and down hills, all terrain. Of course, she's much younger than me, somewhere in her early twenties.

She had stopped to read the paper at a fruit stand, but now she's been going non-stop for forty minutes. She turns left on a busy street, after running through mainly side roads. Where is she going now?

She slows, almost to a walk. Why would she take this route? She's up to something, because it's impossible to run in this crowded sidewalk. I have to push pedestrians and stretch my neck above the countless heads to avoid losing her.

A big man in a black coat bumps my elbow. He offers a wide smile. "I'm sorry."

He wears a large beard and two curls of hair descend along his cheeks. An ultra-orthodox Jew. I stare at him for a second, and he offers me a booklet in Yiddish.

"I have no time for this." I push the booklet against his chest and move into the throng of people and traffic, looking everywhere. I can't believe I lost her. I really wanted to... what? I have no clue why I'm following her.

I lean against a white wall, giving up.

"Why are you stalking me?"

My heart jumps at the sound of her voice. I turn and see her lovely face a meter above my head. She's standing on a flight of stairs that lead to a building, her hands on the rail.

"I... can't tell."

She blushes and curses, then says, "Whatever you thought you were doing, you won't be able to do it now. Unless you want to deal with them." She nods to the building behind her. It's a police station.

Two policemen walk out, one of them carrying a clipboard. He holds the clipboard against his side and I notice a picture that's chillingly familiar. I follow the cops from a safe distance, ignoring Taliah, who keeps insulting me.

They stop by their parked car and I kneel, pretending to tie my shoe so I can get a better look at the picture. It's not too clear because of the poor light, but that's definitively my face.

26

Hussai stands atop a bench in one corner of the plaza, scanning the crowd gathered for general's execution. An Al-Mahdi guard approaches him and points to someone in its midst.

"Al-Mahdi wants no videos leaking out of the country. Make that man turn off his camera."

Hussai elbows his way through the morbid onlookers, the stink of a hundred armpits slapping his nose. He reaches the young man with cropped hair holding an old handycam and grabs him by the shirt.

"No cameras." The crowd forms a circle as he shoves the man to the ground, knocking the camera to the dirt. As the young man bounces to his knees to pick it up, Hussai smashes it with the heel of his boot.

"That will keep you free of temptation."

The man weeps, the mob shouts, and Hussai feels foreign spit against his face. He wipes it with his sleeve and pushes everyone aside.

"Get out of my way."

He emerges from the tumult and looks up to the makeshift platform. The general's uniform has been ripped off his torso, leaving only an undershirt that exposes the gray hairs on his agitated chest. The remaining strips of his pants are covered in mud. His hands are tied behind his back and a there's a rope around his neck like a leash.

Such is the fate of the powerful General Atartuk, who survived the Shiite cleansing under Saddam Hussein but not the improvised trap sprung by Hussai Siddiqui. This is Hussai's moment. He doesn't need to be a hero like Farid, he needs only move in the shadows and eat of the dead. The crowd falls silent as the guard reads the sentence.

"By order of Mohammed Al-Mahdi, the twelfth caliph of Islam, Abdul Atartuk is hereby condemned to be decapitated for failing in his duty while in exercise of his position as full general of the Islamic caliphate army...."

Hussai searches the podium for Al-Mahdi, then strides to the bench he used before and climbs up. Now he sees the caliph getting into his limousine. Hussai feels an urge to call out but contains himself. What would he say? Please take me with you?

The caliph looks in Hussai's direction, makes eye contact. There's a connection between them, Hussai can sense it. Then the caliph is hidden behind the door and the limo drives away.

Hussai hears the swoosh of a sword followed by a gasp and a thud. He smirks.

27

They are searching for me. But how could they have put my picture out so fast? I left the base not six hours ago.

Taliah's voice rises like a furious drum. "What are you doing?" The cops turn to look at her. Fortunately my back is to them. "Hey, answer me, you idiot. Now you're not so brave."

How dare she speak like that to a man? My uncle killed his wife in an honor stoning for an offense milder than this.

She rests one hand on her waist and cocks her head. "Do you even speak Hebrew or do I need an Arabic interpreter?"

My hands shake and it's all I can do not to slap her beautiful face. I inhale, exhale. A few meters away, another two policemen walk toward the station. I could drag her away, but she'd scream and call attention to us. And if I walk off, she might yell at me or—

What can I say to appease her, keep her quiet?

"Your brother is in a lot of trouble with the authorities, Taliah."

"Yeah, right." Her nonchalance is so like my wife's when she argued with me that I feel as if I've traveled back in time. "We think Mossad is holding Benjamin, and now they're after Jonathan because he's been asking questions."

Taliah frowns and shakes her head. "What does this have to do with anything? You were following me and I want to know why."

The policemen come closer to us. If I don't turn her to my side soon, who knows what she might do?

"Jonathan tried to hack Mossad's network for information about Ben."

I expect her to laugh or insult me, but her face turns pale and her pupils dilate. "But he promised to stop. Why is my brother so stupid?" Her gaze softens. "I told him he was asking for trouble."

The policemen walk by us and I scratch my forehead with an open hand to cover my face, watching them through my fingers.

"So why were you following me? How is that going to help my brother?"

The officers pass and I lower my hand.

"I'm...protecting you, Taliah, making sure they're not watching you too."

WE WALK through the garden with the columns, not too far now from Taliah's home.

"Something doesn't make sense. If Mossad is looking for my brother, why don't they come to the house and arrest him? He's not hiding. Or is he? No, I heard him this morning upstairs. How did you find out about this? We have to tell him... I don't like this, Jonathan is harmless, they have no right—"

Honesty attacks me. "I'm the one they want. Jonathan is under their watch, and he's so scared I don't think he'll try to hack them again.""

"What?" Her face turns red. "You're so treacherous! What did you do that Mossad wants you?"

"Let's just say I too have been searching for information, through other methods, and I might have committed some illegal acts in the process."

"Oh, great, now I live in a house full of criminals."

She goes back into what I would call thinking mode: narrowed eyes, head lightly tilted forward, her right thumb rubbing her other fingers in little circles. No doubt she is angry.

It's awkward to look at a woman like this, so uncovered. I have been looking at her all morning. It feels wrong, but what can I do?

I used to see women's faces when I was a young man here in Israel, but the Taliban-like rule of the Caliphate Council in Iraq has all but wiped away any memory of a female presence. And yet I tremble when I see Taliah's figure out of the corner of my eye. Now I understand better why the Qur'an says women should "lay down upon them their over-garments, which is more proper."

She turns to me as we climb the stairs out of the garden.

"Do they know you're here?"

"What?"

"The police, do they know you're staying at our house?"

"I don't think so."

"You must leave, you're putting us in danger. Just grab your things and go."

Taliah trots across the street and into the house, as if not wanting to be seen coming in with me.

She can't tell me what to do or when to leave! Who has given her authority over me? But she's right, isn't she? I'm in a lot of trouble and can ruin them if I stay.

I turn the knob but can't open the door. She locked me out. Outrageous.

Jonathan opens the door after a few knocks.

"Come on in, Farid—where were you?"

The whole family is gathered in the living room, watching the TV. The screen shows a newscaster in front of a majestic building, talking about a Passover celebration and a debate over the sacrifice. The camera pans over two men dressed in ancient tunics.

Jonathan whispers in my ear. "Some nonsense about animal sacrifice in the new temple. The orthodox Jews want to resume the sacrifices they haven't done for centuries, but then these two loonies say there's no need for more sacrifice because Jesus was the ultimate sacrifice or something like that. Very confusing, really."

Jonathan's father jumps off his seat. "Hallelujah! A real Passover at last. Did you hear that, beloved? We must attend the temple dedication tomorrow." He smiles when he sees me in the room. "Would you come with us, Farid? You must come. All of Jerusalem will be there."

He wants a Muslim to attend the dedication of the Jewish temple? This poor old man doesn't know what he's saying. But if I go, I could get a chance to see the Dome of the Rock, perhaps slip away and get lost in the crowd—it's unlikely the police will spot me in such a multitude.

"You can't say no, Farid," David says. "That would grieve me greatly."

All eyes are fixed on me, but Taliah's are the most penetrating. I smile. "Of course, sir, I'll come with you."

28

Hussai leans back and rubs the leather armrests at the far end of Al-Mahdi's private plane. His eyes close. How he hates the headaches that come when sleep doesn't.

The caliph is still alert, even after working all night. A hundred conference calls it seems, to or from every leader in the caliphate. Hundreds of thousands of troops now move according to his wishes.

Someone taps his bad shoulder. Hussai squints, then sees the male flight attendant smiling. He should have gotten a new sling. He can move the arm, but it hurts a little—it seems that Al-Mahdi's healing touch was temporary.

How long did he sleep? He glances at his watch. Only five minutes.

"The caliph requires your presence, sir."

Hussai passes one hand over his face and hair, then breathes deep. He has to do this, headache and fatigue notwithstanding.

"All right." He stands, and the attendant moves to let him pass.

The luxury plane, a gift from the Saudi king, has a passenger lounge in the back and a conference center in the middle. Hussai enters the conference room and yawns as he sits at the long table.

Al-Mahdi commands the room with his presence, drawing the gazes of the other four men. Three of them Hussai knows: the minister of defense, the director of intelligence, and the chief of the air force.

But this is the first time he's seen the fourth man, who has a stern face with long hair and a neatly trimmed beard. He hasn't seen a man with long hair in many years, and never in Iraq. Hussai stares, trying to memorize his features, but the stranger faces him with hollow black eyes and he has to look away.

"Now that the liaison to the army is here,' Al-Mahdi says, looking directly at Hussai, "we'll decide who to strike first." His palm smacks an open map on the table.

Hussai leans forward to glance at the map. It shows the Middle East, Eastern Europe, and northeast Africa. Israel is right in the center. The map shows the new world order under the Islamic caliphate, in which Iraq, Turkey, Iran, Syria, and Lebanon are one empire: Babylon.

The air force chief says, "We need to take fast control over the Suez Canal, cut off Israel's supply from the south up to the Gulf of Aquaba."

"Thus taking over the Aravah and the food they grow in the desert," the director of intelligence says. "I have the imagery from the satellites." He throws half a dozen photographs on the table like a poker player revealing a royal flush. He points.

"That's what we formerly knew as the Dead Sea, now a pool of clear waters with fish and green pastures all around the valley. It's one of the few places in the world where food is growing in abundance. Every other day they find a new spring of water."

"All the more the reason to claim the Suez Canal," The air force chief says.

The defense minister clears his throat. "Let's attack Egypt first, then. We'll make them pay dearly for their treaties with the Jews, show them—"

"Not Egypt." The stranger's voice is deep and melodious, coated with charm and an eerie confidence. "Egypt must surrender voluntarily when Al-Mahdi destroys one of its neighbors. Once Egypt is under Al-Mahdi's scepter, others will follow its example."

Al-Mahdi smiles, cross-armed, spending a few seconds on each man's face. Hussai looks at the map and tries to read the names of the countries upside down. He's never been good at geography. He finds Egypt, moves his eyes further down and reads aloud.

"Sudan."

"That's right, Hussai," the caliph says. "Sudan will be the first nation smitten by my mighty hand. We'll drop you and Khalil at Tehran, and you'll go to the nuclear weapons compound and help coordinate the attack on the East. The Afghans and Pakistanis will join the caliphate by tomorrow, like it or not."

Hussai looks at Khalil, the director of intelligence, and nods. The caliph is sending him on a high mission, just like that.

Al-Mahdi says, "I will take control of every nation surrounding Israel. Turkey and Jordan are part of the caliphate and their past defeats have taught them not to resist my desires. The Saudis think pouring money in my coffers buys their safety, but they will bow or meet the sword."

The stranger laughs. "They will meet your sword, Al-Mahdi."

The caliph continues as if in a trance, his pupils dilated, his voice deep.

"I will smite Sudan so hard that all the nations of the world will tremble in fear."

The stranger laughs again. "Who is like unto Al-Mahdi? Who is able to make war with him?"

"Ethiopia, Egypt, Libya, and even Greece will pledge their allegiance to me."

29

The crowd moving toward the Temple Mount thins as people pass through the Moughrabi gate. Jonathan seems miserable in the warm weather, unlike his father, who beams with happiness. And Taliah, well, she's charming as always with her family but dead cold with me. I meet her hateful glances with a fake grin.

Only now that we're at the mount do I realize we passed through no security gates. They've all been removed. Things have changed in Jerusalem.

My eyes linger on the Al Aqsa Mosque, but the Jewish crowd pushes me east then north along the walls of the mount. I stretch my neck to glance at the Dome of the Rock. Armed guards are posted at the qanatirs, the free-standing arcades that give access to the platform of the Dome. They must be there to ensure no fanatic infidel crosses to our holy site and tries to destroy it. But how I wish I could enter and pray.

Jonathan taps my shoulder. "Farid."

"Yes?"

"It just occurred to me—there's a friend of Benjamin I haven't spoken to. We should really go to see him tonight or tomorrow, don't you think?"

"Sure, why not?"

We come close to the sealed Eastern gate. Further north, more people pour in through the Gate of the Tribes. I gasp when the Jewish Third Temple comes into view, about a hundred meters north of the Dome. Beyond a white wall edged in golden patterns rises a rectangular building that spreads rays of light all around. The crowd halts as if directed by an invisible hand.

"Jonathan, what is it?"

He shrugs, but then his father whispers. "This is holy ground, we have never set foot upon it."

Taliah looks at David with a sweeter gaze than she's ever given me.

"But the temple is here now and we know where the holy of holies lies," she says. "Shouldn't all Jews be able to enter through the courts?"

"If you have been purified, yes, daughter."

Jonathan glances around. "But there are no actual outer courts. The Muslim Dome is too close."

Old David widens his eyes. "That is true, son." He points forward with a shaking hand. "This is where the Women's Court should be."

The two men I saw on the newscast emerge from the temple through an arched door with gold columns and descend the twelve stairs of the temple's platform. One has long disheveled white hair, the other wears his dark hair short.

The dark-haired one spreads his hands toward heaven. "O Lord, God of Israel, there is no God like you in heaven above or on earth below—you who keep your covenant of love with your servants who continue wholeheartedly in your way. You have kept your promise to your servant David, having sent your son Jesus Christ and established his kingdom forever."

The people murmur and shake their heads. The man with the white mane raises one hand and the people fall silent.

"Come forth!"

The audience complies, while a group of men in traditional robes form a human hedge around the temple. Two rails in the middle of the court form a passageway to the temple amid the sea of onlookers. A file of men dressed like ancient priests walk through the passageway, leading cattle, sheep, and goats. Trumpets sound, followed by prayers and recitations. The strange Jewish rituals soon try my patience and I end up glancing at the Dome. Strangely, there are no guards on the north entrance, just a lone man leaning against the columns. I can't see his features from this distance but there's something familiar about him.

I walk sideways to squeeze through the crowd, excusing myself every other second, looking up at the man at the qanatir. He turns to speak to someone inside, someone I can't see, then turns to face the men at the Jewish temple.

His face becomes clearer as I approach. It's Ibrahim.

I MAKE my way toward him, and when he sees me he runs to meet me halfway down the stairs. He grabs my arms, holding me in place, his gaze friendly but questioning. Sweat covers his forehead and a light tremor runs through his hands.

I smile. "*Aasalaamu Aleikum.*"

His voice is but a whisper. "Are you on a mission?"

"What are you up to, Ibrahim? You're the last person I'd expect to see at the dedication of a Jewish temple."

He laughs. "I could say the same, my friend. Tell me your mission, maybe we can help each other." His grasp on my arms is tight. I try to pull away, but he doesn't let go. The tremor in his hands increases.

I take a step back until his arms are stretched too far and he has to release me.

"I talked to Augustus," I say. He glances over my shoulder in the direction of the temple. "Really?"

"Are you planning an attack?"

Ibrahim smirks. "If you don't do anything, someone must."

"You'll endanger the peace covenant."

He narrows his eyes and spits to the ground. "I don't care about any covenants with these pigs."

Ibrahim never minds his words—he's reckless, no filter

between his brain and his mouth. I look around, but nobody is paying attention to us.

A squeaky voice calls out. "Farid, Farid, there you are!, I was wondering where you went." Jonathan walks up to us. "My father is asking about you, really, he was worried, well, he *is* worried, because he doesn't know I found you yet."

Ibrahim raises his brows, his eyes fixed on Jonathan's kippa.

Jonathan extends a hand. "Hello, I'm Jonathan, a friend of Farid."

Ibrahim grimaces and scowls at me. "So you're befriending pigs?"

For some reason I look up to the qanatir. My chest tingles when I see my cousin walking down the stairs.

I call him. "Ali Muhammad."

He doesn't turn but keeps walking, his eyes fixed somewhere ahead of him. He wears a jacket and his right hand clutches something.

No. Could it be? Ali strides toward the temple.

"Where's he going, Ibrahim?"

"Where else? To paradise."

FEAR ASSAULTS me. "Ali, no!"

I try to run after him but Ibrahim embraces me and pulls me back. I gnash my teeth, twist my torso, push my arms out to break his hold. He loosens his grip enough for my elbow to swing against his ribs. Ali is entering the passageway. I step forward—and fall, face flat on the ground, Ibrahim holding my legs.

"Let him, you fool, you'll just blow up with him."

I lift my head and shout. "Ali!"

My cousin sprints toward the temple, shrieking. "*Allah-o Ahkbaaarrr...*"

In a blink, the white-haired man appears at the end of the passageway. He extends one arm and a flame bursts on the ground between his legs. The flame turns into a line of fire that runs toward Ali and consumes him in a matter of seconds, only a heap of ashes remaining when the fire vanishes.

I choke and tear up. Who are these men? What kind of weapon did they use to kill my cousin?

Warm breath fills my ear, Ibrahim's breath. "We'll keep trying until we destroy them."

I roll over and push him off. "These stupid attacks will never give you victory." I stand and look down at him. "Only Al-Mahdi will conquer the world for Islam."

Jonathan grabs my arm and pushes me toward the crowd. "The police are coming, come *on*."

Ibrahim spits at my feet. "You're next, traitor Zionist."

Jonathan pulls me harder until we're lost in the crowd. I look back and see Ibrahim running toward the Dome. The Israeli police close in, but as soon as Ibrahim crosses the qanatir, four Arab guards appear out of nowhere and block the entrance. They'll never get into a Muslim holy site, they have no authority there.

This is the second time someone has called me a Zionist. I'm no protector of the Jewish nation—I'm a servant of Allah. But who will believe me?

30

Hussai rolls his eyes at Khalil's pointless chit-chat and seeks distraction in the scenery outside the car's window. He came to Tehran seven years ago on a business trip, trying—fruitlessly—to recover some earnings from his father's Iranian investments. The city has a different color now, even from this distance. The mountains are devoid of snow, devoid of green. The grass at Azadi Square must be scorched.

The driver glances at them in the rearview mirror and speaks in broken Arabic.

"Compound other side, far from center." He points to a radiation detector inserted in the car's stereo slot. "City radioactive. We go round."

"How long will it take us to get there?"

"There?"

Hussai clenches his fists. "Khalil, do you speak Farsi?"

Khalil shakes his head.

"The compound." Hussai points to his watch. "How long to get there?"

The driver nods. "Ah, yes, yes, three hours."

Three hours in this rattling car? This mission seems more like punishment than promotion. And the shoulder is sore again. He pulls out the bottle with painkillers and swallows four, then closes his eyes and leans his head against the window. Sleep is slow to come, but he eventually drowses off.

"HERE, HERE," the driver says.

The road to the Iranian compound looks like the route to a mining shaft. Then the view changes: a large stone and steel building emerges from the base of a mountain.

The heat rises to unbearable levels, even for an Iraqi, and Hussai feels there is more to the heat than the weather. The facility is disappointing until they enter—it's state-of-the art, impressive despite its dated decor.

The Iranian host who guides them—his name is Saeed, if Hussai is remembering correctly—is a mix of scientist and veteran, with a rugged soldier's face behind thin-rimmed glasses.

A long flight of stairs descends into a natural rock tunnel lit with fluorescent tubes.

"We started building this facility in the early 2000s," Saeed says. "No foreign missile can get us under the mountain here."

After too many steps, the tunnel opens onto to a small leveled space with a guard and a steel door. Saeed punches a code on a pad and scans his thumb.

"Security is a priority, as you can see."

Hussai rolls his eyes. Is he supposed to be impressed?

The door slides open and they walk into another tight space—an elevator without buttons, only a keyhole where Saeed inserts a key to activate it.

"How deep are we going?" Khalil says.

"Not down, up." The elevator zooms for ten seconds, then the door opens to reveal a bright room. "This way, gentlemen. We use the natural caves in the mountain, but you'd never notice this is a cave. We're encased in a huge metal tunnel."

Saeed leads them through a maze of pipes, computers, and people in white coats. They come to a meeting room with a bare table and half a dozen metal chairs. Saeed looks at the Iraqis over his lenses.

"Tell me now, please, the motive of your visit."

Khalil glances at Hussai, who shrugs.

"I'll be direct, Saeed, we don't have much time," Khalil says. "Al-Mahdi wants the rest of the Muslim nations to join the coalition...."

"Yes?"

"And attack Israel."

If Saeed is surprised or struck by any other emotion, his face doesn't show it. He stares at Khalil and waits.

"Al-Mahdi wants to send a message to the Afghans and Pakistanis from here."

"A message?"

Khalil nods. "A nuke."

"Do Afghanistan and Pakistan know it's coming?"

"Technically, no. Though Al-Mahdi asked them in no uncertain terms to join the coalition immediately."

Hussai smirks, remembering the conference call the night before with the Afghan and Pakistani presidents.

"They said they'd discuss it with their cabinets," Khalil says. "But Al-Mahdi doesn't wish to wait."

"Hence we're here," Hussai says.

Saeed nods and stares at the roof for a few seconds, then looks back at them. "Al-Mahdi should be pleased knowing we have some long-range missiles in this compound, we call them Shahab 3, capable of carrying nuclear warheads. They have a maximum range of two thousand kilometers—enough, I think, to hit both Kabul and Karachi."

Karachi? Hussai shifts in his seat. Ayad, his younger brother, lives in Karachi. He hadn't thought about him until this moment. Why would he? Karachi always seemed so far away.

"Excuse me," he says. "I must use the restroom."

"Indeed, to the left of this room," Saeed says.

He steps out and pulls his cell phone from his pocket. No service, of course. He walks past the restroom to an area with several men in lab coats, working on odd machines, and approaches a young man typing on a laptop.

"I must use a phone," he says.

"There are no public phones here," the man says in perfect Arabic. "Try the office on the other side." His gaze focuses on one side of the computer and Hussai follows it. A satellite phone lies on the table, right by the keyboard.

"This is not a public—"

What a fool. Hussai grabs the satellite phone. "It's an emergency."

"You can't—" Hussai pushes his chest and forces him back to the chair.

"I won't take long." He pats his holster, making sure the young man sees it, then walks away, and dials Ayad's number.

It rings a couple of times. He won't answer if he's with a patient. Four rings. Damn it, Ayad, pick up.

"This is Dr. Ayad Sidiqqui, please leave a message." Beep.

"*Aasalaamu Aleikum*, brother... listen, once you hear this, I hope in time, make plans to leave Ka—"

A hand pulls Hussai's shoulder.

"Give it back." The satellite phone owner stands there, hand extended, now brave with an Iranian soldier by his side.

HUSSAI FOLLOWS Khalil and Saeed down a flight of stairs and through several bulky steel doors. His discomfort mounts. What an idiot, calling a soldier to recover his phone. And he had to return it, no point getting shot again. This isn't his territory, he must be careful. But he's worried about Ayad, has been his protector all their life together. Ayad was never interested enough in the family business, never savvy enough for their father's taste. And while the family lived in Pakistan, Ayad distanced himself from the abuse and found respite at the medical school in Karachi. When it was time to return to Iraq, their father didn't even ask Ayad to come with them. Hussai missed him for a while but was happy to remain his father's favorite—until senility robbed him of all peace and he began treating Hussai as badly as he had treated Ayad.

"Hussai, are you listening?"

He looks up at Khalil's silly face. "I need a smoke."

"No smoking in here," Saeed says.

Hussai pulls a pack from his back pocket and puts a cigarette to his lips. Saeed snatches it from his mouth.

"I said no smoking."

Hussai clenches his fists. Fortunately for Saeed, an automatic door slides open and they enter a chamber with a dozen screens and a million pegs and buttons. His fists unclench and his thoughts drift away. What is this place? They have nothing like this in Iraq.

Saeed waves his hand like a bored tour guide. "This is the command center, we'll guide the missiles from here. Any particular preference on the specific targets? Military bases? Government buildings?"

"But it's a nuclear missile," Khalil says. "Won't it destroy more than a building anyway? Wouldn't it affect the whole city?"

Saeed shrugs. "The missile—"

"They must surrender to Al-Mahdi and commit their armies to the coalition," Hussai says, seizing a chance to save his brother. "We must keep the government alive, the military intact."

"What do you propose?" Khalil says.

"Hit a different city, one that hurts their national pride."

Saeed shakes his head. "If we don't cripple their defense they might respond at once... against Iran."

"Khalil, you call the Afghan president right after we launch the missile and begin negotiations." Hussai's voice is calm now, authoritative. "He will yield to us."

"That's not the plan we agreed on," Khalil says. "Al Mahdi wants no further—"

"The caliph gave me authority to make these decisions." Hussai wets his lips. He needs a smoke, soon. And if he's going to be the army general, he has to start acting like it now.

"Are you questioning my authority, Khalil?" His loud voice draws the attention of the technicians in the command center. "We can settle this now with a call to the caliph. Do you want to disturb him?"

Khalil grimaces. "You're exaggerating, Hussai. And you're new—surely you can't expect me to obey whatever you say."

Hussai takes one step toward Khalil and puts a hand on his shoulder while whispering in his ear.

"I got rid of General Atartuk and Major Zadeh. It wouldn't be hard at all to get rid of you."

"You speak harshly to me but are soft with our enemies. Where is your loyalty, Hussai?"

Hussai steps back and faces Khalil, looking him up and down as if deciding what to do with him.

"You're too stupid to be the chief of intelligence. You should be called the chief of fools."

Anger simmers in Khalil's eyes.

"Would you like to know why I find you foolish?" Hussai says. "It's foolish to think we're simply punishing infidels. No, we are demonstrating power so we can gain allies. I want the Afghans and the Pakistanis on my side—and I'm not about to blow up half of my future army because you think it's fun to nuke your Muslim brothers."

Hussai blinks, surprised at his speech. He's always considered himself a clever man, but not always a man good with words. This new ability is proving useful.

Khalil crosses his arms over his chest and says, "Very well, then, let's try your way. But you'll take full responsibility if it fails."

"Of course." Ayad had better repay him some day.

31

Black shadows draw themselves on the walls of my room. It must be four in the morning. My body thinks I'm going for a run today, but I'm not. This isn't Baghdad, it's Jerusalem, a city of insane events. The image of Ali burning at the Temple Mount tormented me all night. I'm drained.

The shadows are blurred by a blue light. I must be going in and out of sleep. How much time has passed?

A buzz comes into the silence—someone's alarm clock. Given the absence of music, it must be a news program. Nobody turns it off, and I hear heavy steps. A door creaks and slams, and then Aunt Esther screams. I jump out of bed, pull a shirt over my head, and run toward her room. Aunt Esther is just two doors down the hall, but I can't get to her because the whole family is already standing like a hedge around her. She's talking and shaking and moving her hands.

"Attacks, attacks in many countries, it's a war!" Aunt Esther's voice, near hysteria. "The radio says we may be next!"

"Calm down, auntie, we'll be fine." Taliah. "Nobody will dare attack Israel again."

"Yes, there's a peace covenant, nothing to fear, really," Jonathan says.

So it has begun. But today is Wednesday, the day I'm supposed to report back to base and plan the attacks. Have their plans changed? Who's attacking who? I have to find out.

"Excuse me, but I must hear this." I wriggle my way through the circle of pajamas and into Aunt Esther's bedroom.

The faintly sweet odor of old age fills the room, which seems like a remnant from a long gone era: black and white photos of the first days of the state of Israel, lavender wallpaper, heavy wooden furniture. The white radio alarm clock with bright red numbers has to be the sole item manufactured in this century.

"You are listening to National Israeli Radio, back with the news of the hour. At two in the morning today, Iraq launched a unilateral attack against the nation of Sudan, using weapons of mass destruction. Early reports coming from the capital city of Khartoum estimate the death toll in the thousands and rising. According to the Associated Press, toxic gases have reached virtually all of the eight million people in the city and its metropolitan area...."

Incredible. That's the sarin gas in the missiles Raskolnikov showed me. But why did Al-Mahdi attack Sudan, a Muslim country? We should be waging jihad against the infidels, not our brothers. The sword is for those who refuse to convert. What are the caliph's plans?

"The attack against Sudan comes only a few hours after the Afghan capital was hit by a land-to-land missile that destroyed many buildings in downtown Kabul. The United Nations and the international community are silent against this new offensive of the so-called Islamic caliphate, and only Israel has criticized the atrocity of this attack...."

I'm taken aback by the tone of this opinionated newscaster, but even worse is hearing reports of my own army on a civilian radio.

"In a broadcast twenty minutes ago, Muhammad Al-Mahdi, the president of Iraq, demanded Sudan's total surrender to his authority and the Islamic caliphate and threatened Egypt and Somalia with biological weapons. During his speech, Al-Mahdi said that unless Egypt and Somalia give him total power over their government and military, these countries will suffer the same fate as Sudan. The governments of Egypt and Somalia have not yet responded. Egypt has long since established a security agreement with the State of Israel, to the dismay of many Islamists. Many expect Al-Mahdi to break the peace covenant with Israel and attack."

David grunts. "Who does he think he is? Hitler?"

"Worse than Hitler." Taliah shakes her head. "This man is killing people of his own beliefs." I hate what she's saying, but anger makes her all the more beautiful. "He has the delirium of all terrorists. They're fanatics, crazy beasts."

I hear my voice ring out. "The world will be better off, even Israel, when Al-Mahdi and Islam take dominion over every nation."

Shock—no, stupefaction—is on the face of every member of the ben David family

"I should have known," Taliah says. "Shame on you." She speaks quietly, but the hatred in her eyes is like a blow. I hear other voices but I see only Taliah.

"What have you become, Farid?"

"Don't kill us!"

"Jonathan, why is your friend talking like a terrorist?"

"I don't know, Aunt Esther, really, I don't know. Farid?"

"I'm going to faint."

Still looking at Taliah, I say, "I'm not a terrorist, but I serve in Al-Mahdi's army. I'm an emissary of Allah, the only true god, and Muhammad, his prophet."

David lifts one trembling finger and points to the door.

"You, sir, have betrayed our trust, insulted our nation, and blasphemed against HaShem. Please leave my house."

IN MY room I pull my gun from under the pillow and tuck it in my waist. Good thing I slept with my clothes on. What else do I need to take?

Jonathan appears at the door. "What are you doing? Are you—"

I brush past him. He grabs my arm as I head down the stairs. "Let me go, Jonathan."

"No, please wait, let's solve this some other way. I still need you to find… you know who."

I yank my arm away and he stumbles forward, bumping into my back in the middle of the stairs. I grab him to make sure his feet are balanced, then head for the door. He follows and tries to get hold of my shirt.

"Where are you going anyway? You must stay, really."

Sunbeams blind me as I open the door and step out of the house. "Thanks for your hospitality. I hope you find Benjamin."

"At least tell me where you're going to be, call me or whatever." He steps in front of me, blocking my way. "Don't let—"

Crack!

Jonathan's body jerks and tumbles forward against me, making me fall backwards through the open door. A second shot nicks the doorframe. I lie on my back, push Jonathan's limp body to one side, and roll to my feet inside the house. I pull out my gun and kneel by the window.

A man darts from behind a car and keeps running.

Blood flows from Jonathan's neck, forming a pool on the beige carpet. By Allah, they'll regret this.

I'm out of the house and see the runner down the street, descending the stairs to the garden. I check for traffic and cross the street two seconds before a dumpster truck rounds the bend, its horn blaring. I reach the stairs and fire at the fleeing man. The bullet hits a column.

At the bottom of the stairs, I dive to the ground. The rock scrapes my left palm and the knuckles of my right hand. I pull the trigger before losing momentum.

As I stop on my stomach, a moan breaches the air. The shooter, less than twenty feet from me, drops his weapon and presses one hand against his forearm. I see his full face now. He scowls at me and reaches down for his gun with his good arm. I leap to my feet.

"Don't do it, Ibrahim."

He spits and glances at the gun on the floor, his hand still not grasping it. Sirens, screeching tires, and the murmur of a crowd hover like a cloud of noises above us. So soon? The police will find poor Jonathan bleeding out at his doorstep. Now there's no going back.

Ibrahim's eyes focus on my hands. Blood drips from the sleeves of his black shirt.

Female voices cry from the street. "Down there, down there, tell the police!"

His gaze shifts, and I move forward. He raises the gun. I fire three times.

I CHECK Ibrahim's pulse. Nothing. Too bad, but my heart aches to think of Jonathan. He didn't have to die like this.

On the street above, two teenagers scream their lungs out. I shoo them with a wave of my gun and they vanish, though I can still hear their cries. I could climb up the stairs and see if I can get to Jonathan, but why risk it? The police are already there. And he's dead. I saw his body stiff and bloody, the bullet hole at the base of his neck, and I can imagine his spine perforated, his family wailing as one, Taliah blaming me, hating me even more if such a thing is possible.

Approaching footfalls, too heavy for shouting girls. I rush into the depths of the garden and seek my way out, running away in the name of Allah. Again.

32

Everywhere I turn people are riveted to the television. I peer into a modest deli where unfinished breakfasts sit on empty terrace tables. Inside, a screen shows glaring images of exploding buildings and dead bodies. I move into the restaurant. I have to see this, and in any case I can see three policemen about eighty meters away.

I thought I'd lost them. One of them points and they all stare at me. They draw their weapons and I dash into the deli, avoiding the dozen figures standing in front of the television. The kitchen is behind the counter. It must have a back door.

On the TV screen is a group of children's corpses scattered on a dusty field, a soccer ball still in their midst. I feel nauseous. What kind of jihad is this?

I kick open the kitchen's door and storm inside. The room startles me. It's a sealed cube with no windows and no exit, crammed with a sink, an old oven connected to a gas cylinder, and a long wooden table in the center brimming with vegetables. I push the table against the door. Lettuce and tomatoes fall to the floor, and a tree of broccoli gets smashed between the edge of the table and the wall. An onion rolls away to my left and hits a half-closed door. I follow the onion and discover a pantry.

Loud voices from the restaurant. The policemen must be harassing everybody, asking for me, but I don't believe they saw me enter—

The kitchen door thumps and the legs of the table squeak against the tiles. I push the table back and press the lock. The door thumps again but the table doesn't move this time. I step into the pantry. A stainless steel freezer stands below a modest window. Could that be my way out? Even if I break the glass I'd have to remove the frame just to fit through the hole. No time for that. Of course, I could blast a way out, blowing up a wall with the propane gas.

I return to the kitchen, disconnect the oven's tube from the gas cylinder, and open the valve. The gas hisses at me. A second cylinder is behind the oven and I pull it out, making it hiss too.

A man screams orders in Hebrew, but I can't understand it, as if the gas has fuzzed my mind. The thumping stops. They may try to shoot the lock open, which would ignite the room.

I run to the pantry and slide behind the freezer as the gas continues hissing. May the will of Allah be done.

THE LOCK clicks and the door shudders, but there's no shot, no blast. It sounded more like a key. The table squeaks and voices fill the kitchen. God knows my intention is not to kill these men, but I can't be caught. Now that the door is open, the gas must be dissipating.

What is that screeching sound? The low hissing stops and I can picture one of them turning the cylinder's valve off. There's an exchange, hard to follow, but I think they said something about evacuating. It's this freezer's hum that muffles every word from outside. The cord is at my feet and I unplug it with a kick.

A faint scent of gas reaches my nose. I only heard one valve, so they haven't closed the other yet. This wait will kill me.

I must finish them or scare them away. What is it suicide bombers do before triggering the explosives? Worship, of course.

The pantry's door knocks against a wall, a light switch clicks, and the room turns brighter. I stick my gun out around the side of the freezer. The sparks from the gun in the gas-filled room will cause an explosion. *"Allah-o Ahkbar, Allah-o Ahkbar."*

I fire three times.

A wave of heat engulfs me. The large freezer mashes my body against the wall and shards of glass rain down. My hand burns and I drop the gun.

For a moment, there's no sound or movement, just the scorching air and the brightness of the flames. Somewhere in the restaurant, the fire alarm goes off. The sprinkler spits water on the pantry, not enough to put out a candle.

The freezer's back panel pushes my ribs, and as I try to shove it away my left hand draws back, burning, stinging, charred by the fire. I finally get the freezer off and free my body. The pantry crackles like stove wood. *Ya rabb tukali 'alek.* O Lord, I put my trust in you.

I peer around the thing, not exposing my whole body, keeping my left hand close to me. The door to the kitchen is burning, my way out is sealed, and soon this room will be filled with smoke. I look up to see the rising thick black cloud charring the ceiling, escaping through the window.

No—through the hole where the window *was!*

33

Taliah holds her wailing father in her arms, his torso slumped against her. She swallows hard, trying not to cry, and closes her eyes as the paramedics lift the body of her brother and bear it away from the house.

How can she console him? How can he endure so much pain?

"Oh, *abba*, I'm so sorry, *abba*."

Her father's sobs shake his whole body and reverberate through hers, shaking the tears out of her eyes. She can cry, it's fine, that's what Jewish women do: mourn their dead. But tears are also a sign of weakness, and her people can't afford to be weak. She won't cry.

But she is. Crying.

She wipes her cheek. Tears of anger, that's what they are. Anger against the lying terrorist who brought this tragedy on them.

She must be strong now, she must hold the family together. *Abba* is too old and both her brothers are gone. She looks up at the relatives on the other side of the room. A cacophony of laments from aunts and cousins fills the place, frustrating the young policeman trying to get a statement from someone, anyone. He looks around, then nods and walks over to her, somewhat awkwardly, flipping pages on a note pad. As he approaches, a man bursts into the house.

"Shalom, shalom!" It's Rabbi Ben-Zur, who reaches them in three long strides. "David, David, what a calamity!"

David lifts up his wet face and shakes his hand. "Rabbi, thanks for coming."

"But of course, my friend, I had to come, I must help with the *mitzvah*, there's so much to do and you should not burden yourself. I'll supervise the cleansing of the body and the *tachrichim* shroud. The burial—as soon as possible, of course."

The policeman clears his throat. "I'm sorry to disturb you, but we'd like your permission to perform an autopsy."

"You shall not disfigure him," the rabbi says. "You shall not desecrate his body."

"Let me remind you, this is a murder investigation,"

"Is it really necessary?" her father says.

"The request is a formality, sir. We'd prefer to have your consent, but a court order is—"

"Divine law is above every human law," the rabbi says. "He won't give his consent—will you, David?"

Her father presses Taliah's hand and she turns to him. She sees his watery eyes, his exhaustion. He can't—won't—argue, it's bad for his health.

"I'm sure there's no need for a full autopsy," she says. "All you need to do is extract the bullets to match with the killer's gun. I can point you to the killer."

She's aware of all the eyes fixed on her.

"What are you saying, my daughter?"

"Farid. That imbecile jihadist shot him."

David gasps and covers his face. Her heart crumbles as she sees her father's pain, but she must settle this. Once they catch Farid, they can mourn in peace.

The policeman writes in his notepad. "You know the perpetrator?"

"He was a guest of my brother, a false friend."

"Where is he now?"

"I don't know."

"You must come to the station and provide a full statement and a description of the subject."

She nods.

The policeman stops writing and looks at her. "Did you witness the murder? Did you see this man shoot the victim?"

The last time Taliah saw Farid was in Aunt Esther's room, when they argued over the radio.

"Miss? Did you hear my question?"

"Yes."

The policeman looks at her intently. "Yes you heard my question, or yes you witnessed the murder?"

"Yes to both."

OUTSIDE HER house it's as if the world has stopped, the bustling street all but deserted. The policeman walks her to the police car, where half a dozen people are leaning over the open doors as if trying to hear something. She pokes one of them in the shoulder.

"What's going on?"

"Shush!"

A raspy voice speaks over the car radio.

"Not only have these nations conceded to Muhammad Al-Mahdi's demands, but it seems the leaders of Egypt and Ethiopia are stepping down to give control to Iraq's appointed generals."

"And what are they planning to do? Is Israel safe?"

The raspy voice is back. "Nothing is definitive as yet, but my military sources say they think they know Al-Mahdi's plan—to take over the Suez Canal and close Israel's access to the ocean."

"What would they gain? The caliphate already has access to the ocean, with Turkey and Syria—"

"This is more than geopolitical strategy, I fear. This is about food, Israel's food. Now he can use the gulf of Eilat and attack from the south, plunder our riches…"

"May the Lord protect us."

"Yes, our army must set…"

Taliah steps back, suddenly light-headed. What's going to happen to them? An invasion? Arguments about an autopsy seem so trivial now. But what else can they do? Jonathan must be buried and mourned. She can't stop the Arabs from attacking Israel.

She covers her ears and looks up as a plane flies above her. A formation of five or six fighter jets zoom across the leaden sky.

34

Eyes and hand burning, coughing from the bilious smoke I inhaled before escaping, I roll on my side and rise to find myself in a narrow street paved with cobblestones. If only I could lie here for a time and let my eyes and my chest recover. Not an option.

After a few paces I feel my breath regain its normal rhythm and my eyes welcome the fresh air. My singed hand stings and throbs hideously, but there's nothing I can do about it for now.

The sound of jets draws my eyes to the sky, where a formation of six F-35s flies—fighters the Americans sold to Israel without hesitation, though they only let our air force buy the F-16s, during the transition after Saddam was thrown out of power.

If the F-35s are in the air it's because Israel fears attack. I must contact Augustus and plan my escape from Jerusalem.

The streets are becoming more empty by the minute, with everybody frightened and many running to find shelter. That's good—it allows me to run without calling attention to myself.

A young couple waits at a bus stop. The man is tapping his left foot and looking at his watch. The woman clutches his arm, her lips white and her eyes fixed on the sky, as if waiting for the flash of a missile strike. The man moves one step forward, and I notice the woman's protruding belly. This girl with her brown skin and Arab features doesn't look like Zainah, but pregnant women always remind me of her. The woman keeps staring at the sky and I look up too. Yes, bombs will fall and end the couple's life, destroy her child—and they're probably not even Jews.

THE JIHAD'S MESSIAH 153

I don't understand the softness coming over me. Perhaps it's the result of being on the wrong side of the battlefield, standing on the target instead of firing the missiles.

I must flee.

I glance back over my shoulder at the couple. The bus speeds down the street toward them but it's not slowing down. The man shouts, to no avail. The woman looks my way with pleading eyes, but there is no help for them, the street now almost deserted. She opens her mouth to say something but I turn and run. A knot forms inside me as I recall my dream with the bomb and Zainah, only now this woman is exploding along with my wife.

No hope for her. I must save myself.

A FEW streets away I find a pay phone and dial Augustus's number. No answer. I try again.

I smash the receiver against the cradle and rub my temples. I have no transport and no place to stay. Augustus was my best hope.

A faint blast sounds in the distance, followed by another—closer—that makes the phone booth rattle.

So it has begun. Outside the booth I see clouds of smoke spiraling into the sky.

The missiles fall as I move through the city searching for refuge and avoiding military patrols. I reach Mea Shearim Street—if I remember correctly, I'm not too far from the city limits. But it will be dark soon. I should stay hidden for a while, then try to get a vehicle.

I turn into a narrow alley ending in a courtyard. A man with black stockings and a long black coat is locking the gates of a shop, his hand trembling as he turns the key. This is the *haredim* district, the exclusive quarter of the ultra-Orthodox Jews.

"Shalom!" I call out to him, but he turns and walks away. If I want to engage him I must speak Yiddish, which I hardly remember, because many of them won't speak Hebrew. The man disappears from sight and I'm left alone with the sound of destruction engulfing the city.

I would rather not enter the home of these strange Jews. I try the gate of what appears to be a bakery, but it's firmly locked. Other doors yield the same result.

The sun has set, and only the flash of anti-missile fire illuminates the city. A distinct building catches my eye and I walk across the courtyard. The synagogue is also locked, but unlike the others I've tried it has an old wooden door that swings open with a single kick.

Inside, a gloomy hallway ends in a room brightened by candlelight, one of those Jewish candleholders with seven arms. I know it has a name but can't recall it. I hesitate as I approach the room where they worship. My heart beats faster, though there's no cause to fear. No one will follow me here. I must wait until morning, then escape once the raids are over.

It's long past the time for prayer. This is not a place my imam would approve for *Salah*, of course. But I must pray, no matter the place, I must seek the favor of god and pray for salvation from destruction.

Back in the hallway I stand and recite the solemn intention. "*Allah-o Ahkbar.*"

A shock wave follows my words and my face touches the ground even before I've bowed down. My ears ring with pain, my nostrils fill with dust. I turn on my back, just in time to see the roof and walls of the synagogue collapse.

35

Taliah glances over her shoulder to the back of the synagogue. The funeral service crowd is thinner than expected. Most people went to a shelter upon hearing news of the impending attack. Only her family and a few close friends are here to honor Jonathan. Even the cantor is missing—the rabbi chants the psalms himself. He seems tense, glancing at the windows every time he hears a noise from outside.

Taliah stares at the pall covering the closed coffin, bites her lips, swallows the tears that try to spill out. She's going to miss Jonathan so much. And where is Benjamin? He should be here by their side. Ever since becoming a Christian, he spends less and less time with the family. She told him she respected his decision though it broke *abba's* heart, but she couldn't accept his moving away. Well, it wasn't entirely his fault—father told him an apostate would not live under his roof, and unless Benjamin renounced "that messianic Christian nonsense," he had to go.

The space her brothers have left is unbearable. They were the only men who treated her with respect. The rest of the imbeciles she meets can't stand that she's smarter than them. Oh, how she longs to get out of Israel—

A deep boom rattles the windows, and everybody gasps. The rabbi puts a hand on his chest and tries to regain his composure, addressing the bereaved.

"Now let us recite the *El Maley Rachamim*, the prayer for the soul of the departed...

"God full of mercy who dwells on high

Grant perfect rest on the wings of Your Divine Presence
In the lofty heights of the holy and pure who shine as the
brightness of the heavens to the soul of Jonathan ben David
who has gone to his eternal rest as all his family and friends
pray for the elevation of his soul.
His resting place shall be in the Garden of Eden.
Therefore, the Master of mercy will care for him
under the protection of His wings for all time
And bind his soul in the bond of everlasting life.
God is his inheritance and he will rest in peace
and let us say Amen."
"Amen."
The rabbi looks up as if waiting for an explosion to echo the
"amen." But the room is silent now.
"I believe David would like to say a eulogy for his son. David?"
She looks at her father, who lifts his chin for a second, the only
gesture he can manage to acknowledge the rabbi. *Abba* seems to
have aged ten years in the past two hours, his tear-washed face
wrinkled with grief and exhaustion. His body trembles as he struggles to rise, and Taliah slips an arm around him to steady him.
   The rabbi extends a hand for David to walk to his side and
face the congregation, but he stays by his chair, his back to the
crowd, his gaze to the ground. The aunts wail in the background
and Taliah claws the sides of her chair, her nails leaving marks
on the old seats.
   "Jonathan, my dear son..." David's voice breaks off and he
pauses for a few seconds, then looks at the coffin. "Jonathan, my
first born, the apple of my eyes, how it pains me to bury you...
I trusted my old eyes would not see more loved ones part from
my side, but now I have outlived you...."
   A sob escapes Taliah's throat and she covers her mouth, shuts
her eyes. She has to be strong for her father, she's not a little frail
woman, she—
   Another sob bursts out like a hiccup. No, she can't break down

now. Her eyes well up and she runs to the back of the synagogue, hands covering her face. She can feel the eyes of everyone on her and a new sob forming in her chest. She tightens her lips and wills the sob to die inside her, but it turns into a choking force. Air, she needs air.

She stumbles through the door. The air reeks of burned tires and tastes like dust. Taliah bends over and retches. Then the sobs come like a train from a long tunnel.

A RAPID succession of explosions, not too far away, slaps Taliah out of her shame and sadness. Something stirs inside her like a boiling hand gripping her guts: fear.

White smoke taints the firmament, and two jets strike above the city. One plane seems to be pursuing the other, the one in front turning and twisting.

Who is who? She can't tell. The chased plane turns, almost 180 degrees, to return from where it came. The other plane makes an even faster turn and positions itself again behind the first plane—there's a streak of red and orange leaves, and Taliah discerns a missile. It cuts between the two planes in a matter of seconds. The jet in front makes an evasive maneuver but is hit on its right wing. A flame lights up the darkening sky.

The plane winds down in a chaotic spiral. She can see more details now: the dark green paint and the pointy tip. Even the noise is clearer, more frightening. The burning jet looms larger.

Taliah screams and races away from the synagogue. A shadow passes over and she looks back at the building just as the charred plane smashes into its roof and sidewall.

THE SYNAGOGUE collapses like bowling pins, releasing a thousand sounds of breaking things. Taliah thinks she can hear the screams of the mourners inside, or is it her imagination?

She stands frozen in the middle of the street watching a cloud of dust and smoke settle over the rubble. Raw shock numbs her senses. She walks forward like a zombie, but this is not her grave. This can't be. Maybe there are survivors?

All she can see as she draws close is a heap of rubble barring the way. Lightheaded, she nonetheless climbs over fallen beams and destroyed furnishings. It takes her a few minutes to get over to the main area of the now roofless synagogue, and once there she must round a large piece of the fallen jet.

The air feels hot and thick. The flames of the burning machine are restricted to the south corner of the building, about twenty meters from her. On the ground lies shattered glass, bricks, wood, tiles—and body parts. An arm here, legs and shoes there, a smashed head to her left.

Taliah's numbness dissolves and pure horror bites her like a viper. If at least she could faint and remain unconscious, maybe die as well—no, she doesn't want to die. But death is all around her.

She looks across the room, where Jonathan's coffin remains unscathed. A sliver of hope pierces her mind. Not for long, though. Near the coffin, where the front row of seats stood, is a large beam. Beneath it, the crushed bodies of her family.

Then a miracle happens. After more than three years, it begins to rain.

36

Red circles move across my eyelids, and I open my eyes to squint at the sun pouring through the ruins. Whispers and noises envelope me, not too far but not too close. I hear men bemoaning the destroyed temple and realize where I am: the synagogue in the Mea Shearim district.

My mouth is dry as an old Ottoman parchment and my head aches. I must have a concussion. My body lies in some sort of pocket among the rubble formed by odd angles of the fallen walls. I'm alive and in one piece, thanks be to god.

Now I remember. My plan was to abandon the city. But is it necessary? It all depends on the outcome of the attacks and whether Al-Mahdi's army strikes again by land. Perhaps I can find my way back to my army. But thanks to Hussai, the scarred colonel, and soldier boy I'm surely a wanted man—and I can't expect a fair trial in the middle of the war. Nor can I show up empty-handed, but I do have the camera's memory card. I check my pocket to make sure it's still there. It is.

Light filters through the rubble less than two meters from the ground. I reach up and remove some rocks—why are they wet?—until there's a big enough hole for me to go through. Worn out bearded faces under traditional black hats stare in confusion as I poke my head out. I mutter "Shalom," but I'm not sure they hear it. I'm not all the way out—my legs seem to be stuck in the hole, something pulling at my pants. A nail?

Almost a minute goes by as I try to wrest my body from the hole and the men discuss me. No one has offered help, they seem more interested in theorizing about my presence here and the religious significance of an infidel—I think I understood that word—emerging from their fallen temple.

I pull harder and feel the fabric of my pants tear, but at last I'm free. I stand among them, brushing at my clothes and faking a smile.

"Shalom."

The expressions on the faces of the six men range from anger to surprise. The courtyard is quite different from the one I saw last night. The large cistern in the middle is but a pile of wet rocks. Shattered glass and human remains clutter the floor. There's no fire still burning, but the facade of one building adjacent to the synagogue looks freshly blackened.

The synagogue itself is unrecognizable. No one who saw it before could tell there was once such a building in this place. I wonder how I survived.

SOUTH OF the ultra-orthodox quarter, I cross Ha-Neviim Street and cut through the Russian compound. The green dome of the Russian cathedral seems unscathed.

The air strike has done a great deal of damage but not as much as I expected. Al-Mahdi must have other plans for Jerusalem. The attack has created enough havoc to occupy the Israelis, perhaps distract them while he conducts a full invasion, but it hasn't rendered the city useless. And apparently he didn't use any biological weapons here. In fact, the city looks washed by rain.

A convoy of Israeli military trucks speeds down Shivtei Yisrael, a dozen at least, oddly familiar. Of course—they're the trucks I saw at the Tel Nof base. I take cover under a porch but doubt they'll notice me. Where are they going? Where am I going?

There's only one place I think I could blend in, and that's the Muslim quarter in the Old City. But what would I do in the poorest area of Jerusalem? I must find my plane and return to

Baghdad. Once there I can show them—but it's too late, is it not? By the time I get to Baghdad, Al-Mahdi's army may have taken over Jerusalem and my discoveries may be useless—in fact they're useless already. What good is it to know that Israel has an anti-missile defense system after the air raid? What good is it to know about their nukes if they'll use them the first chance they get?

No, I can't return to Baghdad now. I must return to my plane and—

Crack! Crack!

Shooting so soon? Adrenaline races through my system, making me feel alive.

I move south, then east, following the song of the bullets. They feel closer.

The deserted streets soon turn into a crowd, and it feels like I've travelled back in time to my militant days in the refugee camps. A mob throws rocks, bottles, and homemade grenades at the Israeli soldiers barricaded at the other end of the street. Some of the men wave Palestinian flags while chanting the name of Al-Mahdi, their savior.

These men have waited for this moment for years. These are Ibrahim's brothers. A trail of white smoke flashes, and a truck splits in a ball of flame. The action freezes as everyone admires the explosion, but soon a combination of gunshots and tear gas envelops the Palestinian mob. I throw myself behind a red sedan with broken windows and a thousand bullet holes.

The pungent smell of the gas reaches me and I cover my face. I could use some water. In what direction is the wind blowing? I don't hear the shooting now, and the men are dispersing. Another rocket flies out of a window. This is my chance.

I run from the car, away from the gas, even as a burning pain gnaws my skin. I cough and spit and keep running until my chest heaves with mucus. My vision blurs with tears and my nose is a torrent. This will pass, this is temporary, I must remain calm.

I take off my contaminated shirt and extend my hands in

search of a wall to regain my balance. I find it and bend forward, spitting as much as I can to avoid swallowing the chemicals in the gas.

My vision starts clearing after five minutes or so, but my ears feel plugged. I see the spit on the floor and my dirty boots.

A cold finger pokes my bare shoulder and I hear an indistinct mumble. I look up and discover a masked soldier pointing a Galil rifle at me.

37

Hussai stops the truck and jumps off onto the boiling sand of the Syrian desert. He scans the area with his binoculars: past the dunes, six or seven kilometers away, rises a short range of orange mountains, rugged rocks like rustic bricks piled haphazardly atop each other. Maybe there he will find a suitable cave.

When Al-Mahdi asked him to plant fake Torah scrolls in a Syrian cave to further the cause, he said this was a "practical matter, a strategy of war against the Zionists." If the Nazis had used similar tactics against the Jews, why couldn't he? These fabricated volumes of the Torah are supposed to refute the Jews and convince them of the truth of Islam. But why does Al-Mahdi suddenly trust him so much as to reveal make Hussai an accomplice to his deception?

A cave, that's all he needs. If he can't find one in that range, he'll have to call the whole thing off, which could enrage the caliph.

He gets back in the truck and drives until he reaches the steep mountains. He remains in the car, waiting for the dust to settle. Along the sand, his tire trail zigzags out of view in his rearview mirror. How to eliminate his tracks? He'll worry about that later. He gets out and wipes his nose—his new allergies are becoming a problem.

After assessing the slope, Hussai grabs the duffel bag from the back of the truck and begins the ascent. Panting, he reaches the end of the slope and the beginning of a vertical wall of natural rock. He leans against the sandstone and puts a cigarette to his lips, then reconsiders. More than nicotine, he needs oxygen.

His head spins. Why did he let himself get so out shape? He was never an athlete, but during his days in Moscow he could keep pace with the Russian soldiers at the track. Now...

He glances at his protruding belly and groans between gasps. With a hand on the rock, he rounds the wall and cranes his neck up, searching for an opening. As he turns on the east face of the mountain, he spots a large cave three or four meters above. At last, some hope. He examines the wall and finds rocks he can use as steps. With a deep breath he pulls himself up.

He unwinds his bag and points his flashlight around. The place is large enough for two adults to sleep inside but not to stand. A few blackened rocks are piled in one corner—someone made a fire here not long ago. Hussai throws the rocks away and makes a note to hide them afterwards. In the space left by the rocks, he notices a hole in the wall, covered by even more rocks. He pulls away a couple dozen more hiding an opening, just the right size for a large man to crawl inside. He peeks in, pointing the flashlight.

A natural rock chamber opens up before his eyes. He gasps in excitement and hits his head against the rock. The flashlight falls and rolls into the new cave, forming moving shadows on the walls.

Hussai crawls to the center of the chamber, grabs the flashlight, and points it up. High enough so he can stand. Perfect! What are the odds of finding this cave on his first expedition? God must truly be guiding him. He wants to shout *Allah-o Ahkbar*. He's never felt so religious in his life as he does now, working so close to Al-Mahdi.

He extracts from his bag three antique clay vases that look like museum pieces. Except that one of them has a tracking device within its base. Hussai places the items in one corner of the chamber and crawls back out. He seals the entrance with rocks and exits the cave.

So that's it. He reads the coordinates in his GPS and transmits them to the caliph. Now he must disappear.

AFTER AN hour's wait at the top of the mountain, Hussai hears the faint roar of the caravan from afar and sees the cloud of dust on the horizon. Al-Mahdi and his entourage. An uncomfortable sensation settles on his shoulders. What if it's too obvious a farce—and poorly planned at that? He rotates his shoulders and pops his neck. No, the caliph is too smart. He'll sneak into the crowd later, when they arrive. Knowing he couldn't leave without creating another trail, he hid the truck on the opposite side of the mountain and sent Al-Mahdi a message to approach the range from the west, avoiding the route Hussai took to get there.

He tries to wet his dry lips but even his tongue feels dusty. And he has so little water left. The sun beats on him and he wipes his forehead. Stupid missions. This one should be done by a soldier, not a general. The only one in the army who seemed to work hard was Farid, now demoted and wanted for treason.

Hussai smiles. If he got rid of Farid, no doubt he can pull this off.

The cloud on the horizon turns into a hazy line of vehicles. At the speed they're going , they'll reach the mountain in less than forty minutes. He could easily wait for them to get closer, then drive around the backside of the range and cut through the valley further west, so as to catch up to the last vehicles in the caravan. When they notice him behind, they'll think he's a latecomer just catching up with them.

That plan is much better than sitting around in the sun. He turns back and begins his descent.

FROM WITHIN the small crowd at the base of the mountain, Hussai sees Al-Mahdi get out of the black Hummer, surrounded by guards and journalists snapping pictures.

What will he do now? Perhaps he will bow down and pray or enter some sort of mystic trance. So far, the caliph has been unpredictable, which for some reason Hussai finds delightful. He moves to the front of the crowd to have a better look and stands between two television cameras.

Al-Mahdi, in a white garment with a white cape and turban, waves his guards behind and ascends a few meters up the slope. All eyes are fixed on the caliph, whose back is to them, his cape undulating in the wind coming off the mountain. When the wind dies, Al-Mahdi turns, spots Hussai in the crowd and looks at him for the briefest of moments, then begins to speak.

"Last night, I had a vision—a vision of this mountain and the secrets that lie within. The archangel Gabriel appeared to me and revealed the place I will show you. Just as it has been foretold, I have led you here to bring forth the truth. You are witnessing the beginning of the triumph of Islam over all religions."

An electrifying thrill prickles Hussai's skin, even though he knows it was not an archangel who led the caliph here. He looks around at the journalists and diplomats and soldiers. Nobody asks a question, no one objects to the bold words of the caliph.

A deep sense of expectation emanates from their faces, as if the wind has infused them with faith. The atmosphere turns thick, and Hussai feels numb, his vision hazy. He closes his eyes and massages his eyeballs with his thumb and index finger. A shadow passes through his mind, and everything seems to shift. He knows his reality is different, but how and why he can't tell.

Hussai opens his eyes. Where is he? Who are these people around him? A large mountain rises up before him and the Al-Mahdi is climbing toward a cave. His guards push two men with cameras up the slope.

What's going on? Hussai blinks, confused, glancing at the men with cameras and notepads, at the trucks and the desert behind them. Then he remembers: Al-Mahdi had a vision from heaven about something hidden in this mountain, and Hussai came with all these journalists to witness the event.

What will Al-Mahdi find in that cave? He can't wait to find out. *"Allah-o Ahkbar!"*

38

The twenty or so men crowded with me in the back of the military truck stare at each other in mute horror. Naked shoulders heave as they pant, their torsos stained with blood and dirt. Three Israeli soldiers watch over us.

My body is pressed against the wall nearest the driver's cabin, my left leg and arm touching the next Palestinian prisoner, but it seems I'm a world apart. I used to be a Palestinian fighter, yet I cannot empathize with these men. Have they even noticed me? No one has crossed eyes with me, their gaze always wary of the soldiers.

I sink in on myself as the truck bumps over uneven ground, and I can picture a cloud of red dust trailing our transport. The trampled rocks make a crushing sound almost like rain under the tires, though I think I've forgotten the sound of rain. I've forgotten many things, it seems. Where is the passion that moved me to fight for the Palestinian cause? I watch these bearded, beaten men who fight for freedom and realize I've lived on borrowed hatred for too long. Hate the Americans, hate the Jews, hate Sunnis, hate all infidels. My uncle, my imams, my country—they gave me a gift of hatred and I drank it all down, sometimes against my true heart, but I did it anyway and became drunk on violence. Addicted to it.

Noises change outside. We're slowing down. Voices, then a clanking sound, something like a gate being opened. I feel the terror around me increase. On another occasion I would be plotting escape, weighing my options, but now I feel as if a mountain of exhaustion has been dropped on me. They took my gun, beat me in the back and in my hungry stomach—there's no strength left in me, just soreness that wants to turn into despair. I won't let it, of course, I must remain hopeful. *InshAllah*, I will find a way out of this.

The truck stops and the soldiers rush us down into the hot day. We're surrounded by thirty-meter-high concrete walls topped with barbed wire. As the gate is closed, I see a rocky hill in the distance and a winding dirt road. Three guards stand near the gate, a few more glance down from nearby watch towers.

The soldiers who brought us here exchange a brief conversation with the guards. I try to read their lips, but a guard shoves me forward to follow the rest of the prisoners. They herd us through an empty courtyard surrounded by a double-wire fence and into a brick building. The door closes behind us and I have the sour notion that I won't see the sunlight again.

THIS IS what it has come to. One day I'm reaching the zenith of my career, in line for the position of army general, a few days later I'm handcuffed in a ragged uniform in a Palestinian prison, my back against a wall, waiting to be tagged and entered into the system.

And it all started with a smirk. Hussai's infuriating smirk. Perhaps it's the will of Allah that I'm here—perhaps it's my punishment for refusing to be a martyr for jihad. But what difference would have it have made to kill myself and a handful of Jews? Would it have changed history? Would it have gained freedom for Palestinians? No, no, no. Everything is the same and only Al-Mahdi can change things. Can he? Yes, of course, because he's the Awaited One, the giver of peace and prosperity. He will bring peace to the world—by waging war.

Why this irrational hatred against the Jews? Why must we slay them, slay ourselves, and slay our children in the process?

The voice of my imam plays in my head: "Because that is the

will of god, as revealed to his holy prophet, peace be upon him."
I don't understand anymore, imam. I did, but not anymore. I
have lost conviction, may Allah forgive me. Convince me again,
imam, convince me again.

The imam's voice: "Remember what the prophet said....
That the last hour would not come unless the Muslims will fight
against the Jews and the Muslims would kill them until the Jews
would hide themselves behind a stone or a tree and a stone or a
tree would say: Muslim, servant of Allah, there is a Jew behind
me, come and kill him."

I press my eyelids hard, seeking a different voice speaking
words that would bring peace: Zainah's voice.

"Next."

I open my eyes and see the back of the man before me moving to the desk, ankle chain clanking on the floor, walking like a
lazy monkey. Monkey? I exhale and the words from the Qur'an
come to me, Allah's curse over the Jews: "Be ye apes, despised
and rejected."

These words bring no peace, and my heart aches as I think
of Jonathan, then Zainah. I think of her a dozen times a day at
least—she is a ghost chained to my soul.

"Hey, you!" A guard pushes me forward and I steady myself
before I fall on my face. "You're next, didn't you hear?"

I move toward the counter, where a woman types on a computer. "Name?" She doesn't even look at me.

I'm a wanted man—worse, a high official in Al-Mahdi's army.
I could lie, but I can see the digital panel that reads fingerprints.

She asks again, in Arabic. "*Ma esmouk?*"

"Ali Muhammad." As soon as I hear her typing, I close my
fists, raise them up, and smack the panel so hard it cracks. The
woman jumps from her seat and moves back, reaching for her
taser.

I hear steps behind me. I duck, spin around, and punch the
guard in the stomach. My chained feet stumble, my rear meets

the floor. The guard recovers quickly and swings the butt of his gun at my head. I block with my arms. Pain shoots through my left forearm, then through my ribs as a boot kicks my torso.

Hands yank me up and turn me on my belly. My face smashes hard against the dirty floor and my body jerks until they tire of kicking it. Finally they drag me to a different place, an enclosed room, and dump me in a corner. I look up and see the guard I punched glaring at me while talking with a couple of huge guards—fresh tormentors. I can't hear what they say but from their nods and the clenching of their fists, it's obvious what will happen next.

I'm glad to see there are no fingerprint panels in this room.

39

When I come to, all I see is a lone yellow bulb in the middle of a gray ceiling. I'm lying on some sort of metal bunk with no mattress, worse than the bed at Jonathan's. I move and every muscle cries foul. I let out a deep moan.

"Hey, Keith, he's awake!" A high tenor voice, speaking in English.

"Finally!" A face comes between the bulb and my eyes, but I can only make out the white hair. "How are you feeling, my friend? Do you understand me?"

"Speak to him in Hebrew, maybe he speaks Hebrew."

"And since when do I speak Hebrew, Micah? You're the Jew—"

"No, my parents were Jewish, I'm an American."

"Well, that's what I meant. Didn't they teach you—"

"I understand," I say in English. My voice is hoarse and my lips parched.

"Here, drink some water." The white-haired man brings a bottle to my mouth. I gulp it and my head starts to clear. "Better?"

I try to sit but only manage to rest on my elbows for a few seconds. My burned hand is wrapped in a bandage.

"Take it easy, buddy, there's no need to strain yourself."

Buddy? What word is that? My jaw hurts. I grimace.

"It must hurt really bad, huh?"

"He'll be all right."

"Hey, what's your name?"

I stare at him for a few seconds. Do I want friendship with these Americans? Well, he's being kind to me.

"Farid."

"Well, Farid, welcome to the best prison cell in Israel. I'm Keith. You're in good company—right, Micah?"

Micah waves a hand as he climbs onto his bunk. "Whatever."

"They must have put you here cuz they know we'll take care of you. Cheap bastards don't have a doctor on site, expect us to do their work. Excuse my language, but these guards get on my nerves."

"That's because you're a Christian," Micah says. "Don't expect the other inmates to care for a new one."

"You talk as if I were the only Christian—what happened to your faith?"

"Oh, whatever. I'm tired now, I'll take a nap."

"Tired of what?" Keith says.

"FYI, I cleaned all his wounds and monitored his heart rate."

Keith bursts out laughing. "His heart rate? What are you now, a cardiologist?"

"Shut up, Keith." Micah turns his face against the wall, lying on his bed.

I shake my head. They put me with the Christians to torture me.

Keith winks at me. "Don't pay attention to Micah, he's always been a rich brat, never mind he's in his forties now, but you must understand, it's not easy being jailed in a country that's not yours...." He runs out of steam, stops for a second. "You don't talk much, do you?"

I rub my jaw and breathe in deep. My ribs hurt. "Thank you for the water."

"You have a funny accent, where are you from?"

"I was born in Israel but haven't lived here for years."

"Sounds like me, born and raised in Ontario, moved to New York in my twenties," Keith says. "Where'd you learn English?"

"May I have more water?"

"Sure." He hands me the bottle.

I sip the water and lay my head on the bed, closing my eyes to avoid his gaze. It feels awkward, talking to this man about my life. But I need to find a way to escape, and this man may have the information I need.

"How long have you been in this prison?"

He smiles. "Close to four years. We came to Israel some time before the war with Iran… Want to hear my story?"

I shrug, hoping the story isn't an epic.

"Man, I'm so glad to be able to talk to someone besides Micah."

He tells me about his life in New York as a chef, how his first restaurant failed, how he met "well-heeled" Micah at a fundraiser, whatever that is, and how he convinced him to invest in a new restaurant that turned out well, so well they opened three more.

Halfway through his tale I sit and take a better look at the hermetic cell with four bunks, a toilet and sink, a locked metal door with a peeking slit for the guards. When I turn my attention back to him, Keith is talking about his wife, about her faith. He didn't understand why she was so committed to her church, began having more fun traveling with Micah than spending time with his family.

"So Micah had started this non-profit to help needy people in Israel—he had this idea of giving back to the land of his ancestors, you know—and he asked me to come to Jerusalem with him to see if this Palestinian organization that was giving food and clothing to the refugees in Gaza was legit. Little did we know, these were Hamas guys, and when the Israelis checked our paperwork they accused us of funding terrorists." He pauses to assess my reaction, but I keep my expression neutral. "So we figure we'll get a good lawyer and he can show we're squeaky clean, we had no idea Hamas was involved, but BOOM! War breaks out and everybody forgets about the trial. Everything in the States was a mess, not just because of the energy crisis but because the Rapture decimated the population, and—"

"Excuse me, but you're using a lot of words I don't understand."

"Oh, you don't understand...what? What did I say? Was it *rapture?*"

"That's one among many."

"Sorry, it's a common word among Christians, and even many Jews have heard of it in the media, so I thought—"

"I'm a Muslim."

Keith's face turns somber. "A Muslim, eh? Yeah, I don't know why I assumed you were Jewish... silly me, you know, because you mentioned, yeah... hum, I'm not making any sense now." He turns to glance at Micah, who's snoring on his bed.

What an interesting reaction. Everything changed in a second. The mere knowledge of my faith turned his rambling into a string of incoherence, of fear. But he should have expected a Muslim in this prison, especially if they bring Palestinians here.

"What are you afraid of?"

Keith puts his face between his hands and murmurs something I can't understand. He looks up after a minute.

"I'm sorry, Farid. I don't know how to explain what came over me, but I'm okay now. You were saying?"

Should I push him further? I want him on my side, so I can get information from him, but I'm also curious.

"Are you afraid of Muslims, Keith?"

"Not at all, why would I be? You know, unless..."

This could be amusing, but I'm not enjoying myself. In fact, a headache is threatening, and I wish I had some pain pills.

"I won't hurt you, please calm down."

Keith says, "I'm sorry," then goes and shakes Micah awake.

"What now?"

"He's a Muslim."

Micah looks at me. "Doesn't surprise me. So what do you want me to do?"

"Should we tell him?"

"He won't like it."

THE WATER I just sipped burns in my stomach. Do they have terrible news of things that happened while I was unconscious? All
I can think of is another defeat for my people, an Israeli victory
over Al-Mahdi. But the Chosen One cannot be defeated.

"What I want to tell you won't be easy to hear," Keith says.
"It may offend you."

"It will," Micah says.

"Is it about Al-Mahdi and the Islamic army?"

Keith looks astonished. "So you already know?"

"Know what? Is the war over? The invasion failed?"

"Ah, no, not that I've heard."

"Right," Micah says. "The guard's mood would be better."

The headache has eased. The caliph's army is still in the battle.
"*Allah-o-Ahkbar.*"

They exchange quick looks, then Keith says, "As a Muslim,
do you believe in Jesus?"

I nod. "Isa, the son of Mary, yes, he was a prophet."

"Not just a prophet, Jesus is the Son of God."

"No." I shake my head. "Allah has no son, it's a blasphemy
to say god has a son."

Keith shakes his head. "Jesus himself said he was the Son of
God, and the Bible says whoever denies He is the son of God is
the Antichrist."

I lean forward. "Nonsense."

"I'm sorry to let it out like this, Farid, but I must tell you the
truth and explain my reasons if you'll let me."

A fire burns inside me, a power stirring in my chest like the
anger that drove me to shoot Hussai. Even my skin feels hot.

"What truth?"

"The truth about the Antichrist, the enemy of God who wants
to take over the world. That Antichrist is the same person now
attacking Israel—Al-Mahdi."

"You're deceived by a lie and I shall silence you." I clench my
fists and charge toward him—.

Keith jumps to his feet and points at me, palm out.

"In the name of Jesus Christ, be still!"

Every tender muscle on my body contracts in a spasm, my beaten-up legs buckle, and I fall forward onto the floor.

40

The top of Hussai's head feels as hot as the desert around the base. In moments like these, he wishes he'd yielded to the council's wishes and worn a stupid turban. He wipes the sweat from his upper lip and stares at the ranks of soldiers gathered under the scorching Jordanian sun. The military base buzzes with activity, finally under Al-Mahdi's jurisdiction even though the king of Jordan resisted at first. Hussai had to make escalating threats until the monarch walked out of the room, then turned at the door.

"Tell the caliph he may use the base and the soldiers. One last time."

Hussai hasn't communicated that last phrase to Al-Mahdi, expecting it will be useful when he becomes general and needs the favor of Jordan—he'll remind the king of those careless words and how he kept them from the caliph, hence sparing his life and his nation. Then again, it may not be necessary, if Al-Mahdi decides to trample Jordan after he's done with Israel.

The soldiers chant as they wait for the caliph to appear and inspire them with his customary war speech. The chant began as a murmur, growing like a wave, resounding through the base, over and over again: "No to Israel! No to the devil! Al-Mahdi is the bridge to heaven!" It has gone like this for more than a half-hour. They're probably as bored as he is.

The wait before the slaughter, a new holocaust, a new intifada. But it's so hot and there's no breeze at all. Back in Baghdad Hussai would be napping in the open courtyard of his home, gorging on *masgoof*, the barbequed fish, or some *pacha*. He searches his mouth for the taste of his last cigarette, three or four hours ago now, but his mouth tastes like sand.

His cell phone rings and vibrates twice. He pulls it out and sees the voicemail icon. But the call didn't come through. The list of missed calls shows nothing. He dials and listens.

"Hussai, we must speak again. I have good news for you, you'll like it. I'll call later."

Raskolnikov. Ha, they must be so afraid they're ready to offer him some cash in exchange for information—or more, perhaps they want more. He deletes the message.

The overwhelming drone of a Hercules plane drowns out the soldiers' chant. Hussai looks up as the whale-like aircraft lands. Six more follow in succession and taxi down the strip as near to the hangars as they can. All movement ceases, and the Jordanian and Iraqis at the base fix their attention on the aircraft. The sun shines in the cloudless sky, highlighting the Iranian flag that covers a good portion of one side of the planes. This is the Persian regiment of the Islamic caliphate's army.

The rear doors of the Hercules open in unison and hundreds of marching soldiers step out. Black flags hover over them as they swarm the base.

"*Allah-o Ahkbar! Allah-o Ahkbar!*" The soldiers erupt in a chant again as they cheer the coming of their allies.

"Feeling lucky?"

Hussai spins around and sees Khalil, wearing a pair of Rayban sunglasses that make him look like a giant fly.

"Do you think you have what it takes to lead the black flags of Jihad?" Khalil's lips twist in a sly smile.

He wants to play with words, it seems, provoke him into saying something that might be used against him later. Hussai looks over at the Iranian soldiers before answering.

"Al-Mahdi is the rightful leader of Jihad. I am merely a servant of Allah."

"A servant? What happened to being a general?

Hussai's cellphone chirps. He glances at the caller ID: Raskolnikov. He must really want to make contact.

He feels breath too close to his shoulder.

"Not answering?" Khalil says. "Who's calling?"

Hussai scowls at him, then walks toward the platform where Al-Mahdi will soon speak. Khalil reaches for his shoulder. Hussai recoils.

"Listen, Hussai. The day you threatened me you earned an enemy. And the rest of the security and war council is on my side. You're by yourself, so you better watch your back, you hear me?"

Hussai bites his upper lip. If he only had a knife to stab this insolent fool. Patience. He must plot Khalil's fall, but in the meantime, this warning can't go unchallenged.

Hussai can't see Khalil's eyes behind the sunglasses, so he focuses on a point in the middle of the lenses.

"Look around you, Khalil. Observe the soldiers—they're on my side, *they* watch my back."

Khalil shakes his head—a sorrowful expression on his face, as if he pities Hussai. Infuriating.

"I doubt you'll come back alive from this war," he says.

41

Taliah perceives the dawn creeping through the window, feels the vertigo of shadows receding in the darkened room. What day is it? Has she been awake all night? She can't remember falling asleep in the old padded chair, but time, how much time has passed? This is at least the second dawn after the tragedy. Or is it the first? No, the first was in the makeshift hospital where they were treating all the wounded. A gallery of images flashes: the bloody shirts, the missing limbs, the silent screams under the deafness caused by explosions, the smell of burned flesh and fuel.

It didn't happen last night but the day before. Just one day and two nights, then? But it seems so long ago....

The emptiness of this house is unbearable. She can still see the falling jet! Better to focus on something else if she is to survive.

For what?

Sudden cramps make her shift in the chair and she stretches her stiff curled legs. Her hands are numb from clutching her mother's photograph against her chest. She looks down at the black and white picture of the woman with the sly smile and passes a finger over its face, from forehead to chin. Her lips quiver and she rests the photo on her lap.

"There, *ima*, rest in peace, don't you worry about us."

She thinks about the bodies of her loved ones and how the army forbade her to make burial arrangements—too many dead and too much chaos for funeral services. Outrageous.

Where is her family now? Where are their spirits? In Sheol, in Abraham's bosom? Are those stories even true? Abba was such

a good man, a true keeper of the law—he surely earned passage
to paradise. If there is such thing as paradise...

SHE MUST have drifted off. Sunbeams shoot into the living room.
Taliah squints. Her eyes sting as if a thousand needles are prick-
ing them. She opens them in stages, taking in her surroundings,
and for the first time notices how decrepit the house is—from
the faded wallpaper to the curtains that must pre-date the birth
of Israel. And the ancient door with...

She walks to the door and examines the odd hole in its frame.
It looks like a bullet notch. Not far beneath it, the carpet retains
the smudge of Jonathan's blood despite the cleaning efforts of
the synagogue ladies.

If her brother hadn't been shot, her family would be alive.
If her brother hadn't brought Farid to the house. He no doubt
murdered Jonathan in cold blood and may have started this war
against Israel. Didn't she hear from his mouth that the country
would be better off if it fell under the Islamic regime? Taliah
should have turned him in when she had the chance. They hosted
a spy, an enemy of her nation, and he brought disaster upon them
all. But it's not her fault, it's Farid's. She looks again at the bullet
mark on the frame. If only she had a gun and knew how to use
it, she'd search for the terrorist and take revenge, as the Torah
teaches—tooth for tooth, eye for eye. What's to stop her? Fire-
arms can be bought anywhere. Could she do it?

She extends one hand to trace the hole with her fingers—
Someone knocks at the door. Once, then twice.
Taliah stares at the door in perfect stillness.
More knocks.
"Who is it?"
"Police." She inches the door open. "Shalom." It's the same
officer that took her statement when Jonathan was shot.
"Please excuse me for the time of my visit, but the police force

is being deployed to help the army, and this was my only chance to come and see you."

Taliah frowns. Why would he want to see her?

"I, um, must report to my superiors at zero seven hundred hours."

She considers closing the door on his face, but then she'd be back alone in the house, alone with her pain.

"May I come in? I have important information I must share with your family."

I don't have a family.

"What information?"

"About your brother's shooter."

"You caught him?"

He nods.

THE POLICEMAN—AARON, he calls himself—sits in Taliah's grieving chair in the living room and leans forward, both hands on his knees.

"The extracted bullet matches the gun we found by his body, with his fingerprints on the trigger. "

"You found his body as in 'dead body'?

"Correct. And he has been identified as a Palestinian terrorist, long wanted by the police."

Of course, she knew the police wanted Farid. Well done, justice is served. A sudden hollowness bites her soul. But she should be happy he's dead.

"Who killed him? The police?"

"No, miss. We have the description of the suspect from a couple of witnesses, and we are trying to apprehend him as well."

"I don't understand, I—"

"You said you knew the accused, that he stayed at this house. Is this the man?"

He pulls out a photograph and hands it to her: a lifeless face with abundant beard around a twisted mouth, a face she has never seen before.

"His name is Ibrahim Azzem. Do you recognize him?"

"This is not him, I told you already, the man who killed my brother is named Farid."

Aaron looks perplexed. "Are you positive?"

"Well, he could have made up that name, my family knew him as Farid, but that's not him, I'm sure about that."

He frowns and says, "I've interviewed dozens of your neighbors myself, and three separate witnesses have said they saw the man in the photograph shooting at your house from across the street that morning. The store owner by the corner, the lady two houses down from here, and her son. But you say this is not the man."

He stares at her with an openness she finds insulting, as if he's trying to read her mind. What can she say? This is all new information to her, things she had not considered. Who is this man in the photo and where did he come from? What did the neighbors see? What happened that morning?

"Tell me, miss, where exactly were you that morning?"

Her mind swirls. "I— I was upstairs with my father when we heard the shots, and—"

"You were upstairs?"

"Yes, we were all scared, then we came down...."

She stops when she sees his face turn stern. He digs into a pocket again and pulls out a notepad, flips some pages and reads for a few seconds.

"On your statement of April twenty-fourth you said you saw the suspect shoot the victim. Now you state you were not present at the scene but heard the gunshots from upstairs. Which statement is the truth?"

Weakness runs through her body like lightning, her vision blurs.

"But I know Farid killed Jonathan, I know it, I know it, he's guilty, he's the cause of my pain, he killed my whole family, he—"

A sob cuts off her words. Her body shakes uncontrollably and then the sobbing turns into wailing.

42

The sweat on my skin is sticky but cool. My fever has broken. I hope morning is near, because the string of nightmares has driven all rest away and I can't find any comfort in prayer—as if a presence in this cell clouds my mind every time I attempt to recite the Qur'an.

Weakness and nausea.

I know what this is, dehydration, but I must have an infection as well. Was I delirious or just talking in my sleep? At some point in the night I remember Micah—or was it Keith?—pressing a cool cloth against my forehead, offering water. Why do these two strangers keep caring for me? How can they be blasphemous and kind at the same time?

Such a mystery. I've never been so close to a Christian. I always kept out of their way when I was young, immersing myself with my own people, following my uncle, learning from my imam. Now I share a cell with two Christians who say God is three and not one, who actually believe the prophet Jesus is God. Worst of all, they believe Al-Mahdi is... no, it's blasphemous even to recall that evil thought.

The light comes on and the door bangs. Outside, a voice barks an order in Hebrew, something like "back up." I hear locks clank and then the door swings in to admit a pale figure in the ragged prisoner's uniform who places a tray on the floor. The voice that barked before, a guard, orders the server to retreat. He obeys and our cell is locked again.

"Are you awake, Farid?" Keith says with a jovial tone. "Didn't

I tell you this was the best prison cell in Israel? We have room service and all, you see."

Micah moans. "Yeah, room service, but have you told him why?"

"Well, that's just a minor detail, you know, what matters is, they bring us the food here and we don't have to go to the dining area."

"Yeah, cuz the Palestinians would tear us to pieces once you start preaching to them. They almost killed us once."

"Isn't it a good morning, Micah?"

"Whatever."

Keith gets off his bed and I close my eyes. Perhaps he'll think me asleep and shut up.

"Oops!"

"What?" Micah says.

"They just brought two rations."

"Well, they must expect Farid to go out with the rest."

"But he's sick... ah, it's okay. I'll give him mine." Amazing. What's with this guy?

"Suit yourself."

"You hungry, Farid?"

I try not to move but the mention of food makes my stomach growl. I haven't eaten in at least two days. How long have I been here?

"Wake up, man, you need some food."

I look at him and his wide grin. He has crouched by my bed and holds a bowl and a spoon in his hands.

"If you can't do it I'll be happy to feed you, but you're a big guy and maybe won't like that, so at least try, okay?"

I tell my body I must eat, I must reach for the food, but it doesn't listen. Never have I felt so powerless.

"You need at least a little of this to regain your strength, right?" He puts a spoonful in my mouth, a starchy mass that tastes like nothing I've eaten before. "Weird, eh? I don't know what it is, but

I think there's some fiber in there, maybe some carbohydrates. The protein comes at lunch time, so don't worry, you'll get some kosher food courtesy of the Israeli government."

Micah laughs. "Kosher? Yeah. Why would they bother feeding us that?"

I turn sideways and try to grab the plate from Keith as he and Micah start arguing about the origin of the prison food. The bandaged hand is a nuisance, so I unwrap it and stretch the fingers. It feels hot but better—still, I won't risk touching things gratuitously. The white mass in the bowl lacks any appeal, but I must recover from this sickness. I've eaten worse. At the side of the bed lies a bottle of water. I drink it all.

As I finish eating, Micah waves a hand at his friend and places a pair of headphones on his ears.

"Whatever, Keith."

Keith takes the bowl from me. "You're done, eh? Good."

I let my body slump on the bunk again and close my eyes.

"You know what, Farid? I'll pray for your healing."

Next thing I know, Keith puts his hands on my head and my chest and begins to say a prayer that sounds more like a command, not so much speaking to God but to me... to my sickness? His hands are warm, very warm in fact, and for some reason I don't move away. Awkwardness, embarrassment, and a bit of fear stir in my chest until he finishes and moves away.

What was that? The nausea is gone, although I'm still weak. My head is clear but my body weighs a ton.

Keith sits on his bed and looks at me for a while, as if studying me.

"Farid, do you believe in prophecy?" he says.

I think of old David reading an alleged prophecy from his Jewish Bible about the Jews coming out of the Holocaust. That could be interpreted any way, I'm sure. But the truth is Islam has prophecies as well. How else would we have known about the coming of Al-Mahdi? The Hadiths talked about him. Those

NICK DANIELS

who recorded the words of the Prophet, peace be upon him, say he foretold that the world would not come to pass until a man from among Muhammad's family, whose name would be his name, ruled over the Arabs.

Do I believe in prophecy? Of course, I could tell him, because I know the Islamic traditions regarding the Mahdi, the traditions spoken by the Prophet… the Mahdi will fill the earth with equity and justice as it was filled with oppression and tyranny, and he will rule for seven years. The Mahdi will offer the religion of Islam to the Jews and Christians—if they accept it they will be spared, otherwise they will be killed.

Jews and Christians must convert or die. Muslims will live. Sharia will rule the world.

Horrible images flash through my mind: the piles of dead children in Sudan, the devastation Al-Mahdi has caused in Muslim countries with his biological weapons. I do not comprehend it. From a ruthless tyrant like Saddam Hussein, perhaps, but from the Chosen One?

"You must know well Islamic prophecies, right?" Keith says. "I mean, that's what they taught the kids in Palestine for decades, the coming of their Messiah, who would conquer Jerusalem and set them free. I bet they say the stories are fulfilled in the new caliph."

I stare at him for what seems like an hour. His gaze is clear, and I see no hatred in those eyes. He reaches for a book under his pillow and opens it. "Let me read some of the Christian prophecies to you. Some have happened, some will happen in the next few days."

A groan, a word of protest—something—must surely emerge, but no sound comes from my mouth. I'm mute. And listening.

"You see this, Farid?" He holds a book in his hand. "This is the Bible. And in the Bible, there's a book by a prophet named Daniel to whom God revealed what would happen in the end times." He turns some pages. "Six hundred years before Christ, Daniel wrote about the peace treaty between the Arabs and Israel, and it says this about the ruler who makes the treaty: He will confirm a covenant with many for one 'seven.' In the middle of the 'seven' he will put an end to sacrifice and offering. And on a wing of the temple he will set up an abomination that causes desolation, until the end that is decreed is poured out on him."

He arches one brow. "Does it sound familiar? We are in the middle of the seven-year treaty, and it won't be long until the Al-Mahdi army comes through and ends the sacrifice at the new temple. You'll see, if we're alive, the abomination he performs there—whatever it is."

What am I supposed to do? Convert to Christianity just because his bible talks about a seven? I have no strength to knock him down, but I could at least debate him, show him the superiority of Islam.

"Our..." I can speak now! "Our traditions are more specific than that."

"How so?"

"The Prophet said there would be four agreements between the Muslims and the infidels. The fourth would be mediated through a person from the progeny of Aaron and be upheld for seven years. The prophet Muhammad said: He will be from my progeny and will be exactly forty years of age." Now I smile. "I know this well because we recited it when we celebrated Al-Mahdi's return from signing the treaty. Al-Mahdi was forty years old when he came to power."

"Very good, buddy. You know your part, right? I can also quote prophecies, like the verse from Zechariah that says : 'I will gather all the nations to Jerusalem to fight against it. The city will be captured, the houses ransacked, and the women raped. Half of the city will go into exile, but the rest of the people will not be taken from the city.' Bet this is what will happen when Al-Mahdi's army gets here. They'll only gain control of half the city."

"Why are you telling me this? What do you want to prove?"

"I'm telling you this so when it happens, you'll believe."

I sneer. "Are you guessing the future now?"

"Haven't you been listening? I've told you what Al-Mahdi's going to do, according to the Bible. He's gonna take over half of Jerusalem, end the sacrifice at the new temple and do some sort of abomination—oh, and the Bible also says: 'He will oppose and will exalt himself over everything that is called God or is worshiped, so that he sets himself up in God's temple, proclaiming himself to be God.'"

I can't help but laugh. I'm feeling sorry for this deluded man.

"You know nothing about Islam. There is no god but Allah, and Muhammad is his prophet. Al-Mahdi knows that, he believes that. No true Muslim would ever proclaim himself as god or even follow someone who claims such thing."

He shrugs and smiles. "Really?"

Micah springs up from his bed. "It's happening, it's happening!"

"What's happening?" Keith says.

"The invasion. The news says the Islamic Army is about to cross the dried-up Jordan River, hundreds of thousands of soldiers, tanks, trucks, the whole enchilada."

Keith whistles. "They're on their way toward Jerusalem?"

Crushed by my own army? How can I let them know I'm here? But wait, this is a Palestinian prison—they should liberate us. Yet the resolve of this army is like a jaw of iron crushing everything in its path.

Micah's face reveals an excitement I haven't seen so far, as if he's just come alive.

"It's all true, then. I mean, I believed it before, but now ..." He pauses and presses his lips together, listening to his radio. "Sounds like the Two Witnesses have gone wild preaching about the impending destruction.—"

"What are they saying?"

"They...' He presses one finger against the ear bud. "They're quoting Jesus, something about when you see the abomination of desolation in the holy place...."

Now Keith starts quoting. "' 'Woe to those who are pregnant and those who are nursing babies in those days! And pray that your flight may not be in winter. For then there will be great tribulation, such as has not been since the beginning of the world until this time, no, nor ever shall be. And unless those days were shortened, no flesh would be saved; but for the elect's sake those days will be shortened.'"

"Yeah, I think that's it."

I'm mesmerized by the ominous words, the mention of pregnant women and nursing babies bringing bitter memories. The mix of contempt and pity I felt during my exchange with Keith begins to recede, replaced by an irrational dread. What will happen when I die? My people have deemed me a traitor, I've been imprisoned without glory, fled from martyrdom, have befriended Jews and now, it seems, even Christians.

O ye that believe. Take not the Jews and the Christians for friends. He among you who taketh friends is one of them. How I wish my inner imam would shut up. I'm no Zionist, and I'm certainly no friend of these two lunatics.

"Farid?"

Keith throws something at me and I catch it.

"Keep that, one day you may want to read it. It'll save your life."

I scan the cover of the Bible and put it aside. The last and only time I ever held a Christian Bible was at Benjamin's apartment a few days ago.

"The ministry of the Two Witnesses is about to end—right, Keith? I wonder what has happened to the one-hundred forty-four thousand elect."

The elect? Where did I hear that before?

Keith turns to answer Micah. "The Bible calls them the first fruits redeemed for God. I think the Lord will take them to heaven at about the same time as the witnesses. Maybe He did already. Like a second rapture?"

Rapture, there's that word again, but I'm sure I heard something about the "elect"' before—in English, because the sound
of the word is what triggered the memory.... Of course! The man
at the Christian church that wanted to pray for Jonathan and me
called Benjamin "one of the elect."

Could Keith know what happened to Benjamin?

"Please tell me," I say, "what do you mean by the word 'rapture,' and who are the elect?"

Both their faces look like they don't know whether to they're
more surprised or happy. Then Keith smiles, and it's the kind
of ingenuous smile you hardly ever see and just have to return.

"Sure," he says, and I smile back at him. He leans forward—
eagerly, intently. His excitement is almost contagious, no matter
what nonsense he's going to spout. I'm actually enjoying this.

"After Christ rose from the dead and before he ascended to
heaven, he told his disciples he'd come back some day."

"We Muslims know Isa the son of Mary will come again to
help Al-Mahdi establish Sharia on earth."

Keith looks like he's trying to swallow a smile. " I know, and
I have my say about that, too, but you asked about the rapture.
So anyway, the Bible says that in the end times, Christ is going to
come for his church—the dead rise to go to heaven first, then those
who're alive disappear from the earth and meet him in the sky."

"Disappear?"

"Yup, happened almost four years ago, all over the news—I
mean the disappearances, not the rapture, nobody caught *that*
on tape. The newscasts got it all wrong, speculating all sort of
nonsense."

I search his eyes for any sign that he's joking—the guy does
have a sense of humor—but he's dead serious. I've never given
much thought to those disappearances, why would I? The rumor
among my people was that it was a ruse by the Americans. This
explanation, this rapture, is the craziest, most absurd thing
I've heard so far, even more far-fetched than the scripted news.

Yet Keith says it with such conviction that I find it hard not to believe him.

"So that's what you call the rapture?"

"In a nutshell, yeah. It's like a Jewish wedding, when the groom comes to his bride without much notice and takes her to the place he prepared for them, like—"

"Why didn't you go up, if you're a Christian?"

He looks at me, then stares at his hands. "I didn't believe in the rapture... back then, you know. So I missed it."

I raise one brow, hoping he'll go on, because I truly don't understand. Then Micah jumps off his bunk.

"Keith believes the rapture wasn't a gift for every Christian, like salvation, but a reward for being faithful. You see, we weren't real followers of Jesus, just Christians by name, going to church every now and—"

"We didn't have faith." Keith looks up at Micah. "'Two will be together in the field, one will be taken and the other left behind.' My wife was taken, but I wasn't."

How cruel, this God who would make distinction between his followers. Is Allah like that?

"The truth is," Keith says, "that I only believed in the rapture—and became a real Christian—after it happened. That's when something clicked and I began to study prophecies about the end times."

Micah nods. "And that's how you figured out the role of Islam in the coming of the anti-Christ, right?"

"Who else?" Keith says. "Who else would readily accept a leader filled with so much hate? Nobody in the West would follow such a man." Keith nails his eyes on me. "But Muslims, well, that's a different story. They've been waiting for centuries for the appearance of a leader, a Messiah, that would subdue the world under Islam. And all those Islamic traditions about the Mahdi have an amazing and diabolical parallel to the Antichrist of the Bible."

43

Sometime in the middle of the night, a swooping noise disrupts my sleep. A siren.

I sit up and listen up. Boots rush outside and above, while my cellmates rustle in their bunks.

"Another air raid?" Micah says. Keith mumbles something. "Keith? Do you think it's an air strike, man?"

"No." I turn to them, even though I can't see their faces. "The troops are coming, you heard it on the radio."

"So?"

The light comes on and we all stare at the bulb for a second. Micah looks apprehensive, not terrified, but he passes his hands though his hair again and again. Keith looks like a man giving precedence to his hearing above all senses.

"They're here," he says.

I nod, thinking of my troops, the advancing tanks, the thousands of armored trucks: Al-Mahdi's army, like locusts decimating a field.

"Close, for sure."

Micah clears his throat. "Maybe it's something else, maybe a prisoner escaped, maybe…"

Keith sets his eyes on me and offers a smile. "What do you think will happen next, Farid?"

I linger on his warm, caring voice. He's spoken blasphemies against my god and my faith, yet he treats me with such guileless kindness I find it difficult to hate him, even to resist him.

"They won't attack a Palestinian prison," Micah says. "Right?"

"How will they know it's Palestinian?" Keith says. "It has the flag of Israel."

"Duh. This is the West Bank."

Keith shrugs. "Does it really matter anymore? It ceased to be Palestinian territory years ago."

I shake my head. "That's all beside the point. My army occupies by destroying everything in its path, unless it has an order to preserve something."

Keith raises his brows. "*Your* army?"

I sigh. "I'm a commander in Al-Mahdi's army."

"Well, that explains a lot," Keith says, looking at me intently. There's nothing negative in his look. I can't figure it out.

The noises outside intensify. No direction for the prisoners, no warnings or assurances, only running. Then I hear the unmistakable sound of a helicopter landing. I wonder if the guards are fleeing, leaving us locked behind.

"So, Farid, what's your title there in the army?"

"Major general."

Keith whistles. "Major General Farid, eh? Bet the Israelis who put you in this puny cell don't know that, do they?"

"Probably not."

"Interesting… so you know how they fight and stuff, right? Are we likely to survive this night?"

Micah leans forward, eyes wide open.

"If Allah wills it."

We're silent for at least twenty minutes, listening to what we can't see. Then we hear the last clacks of a helicopter and the commotion stops. No more footsteps or shouts. Nothing.

"What's up?" Micah says. "Where'd the guards go?"

"Away, I guess."

A wave of shouting erupts from all directions, along with clangs and bangs.

Keith nods. "Seems like the other prisoners reached the same conclusion."

The shouts are muffled by a boom, and the walls shake. Micah jumps from his bunk. "What was that?"

"Praise be to God, He is our rock and strong tower." Keith closes his eyes and begins to sing. His voice is deep and strong as he sings a simple but mesmerizing tune, something about a God our help in ages past—

A second, louder boom rattles our bunks, but Keith keeps on singing. Micah joins him, sweat covering his forehead. "Our hope for years to come...."

I must prepare for whatever comes. I put on the soft shoes of my prison uniform and walk to the metal door. It has no handle, nothing to grasp—it's sealed to the walls like a reef to the sea bed.

BOOM!

The tanks are firing at will. Perhaps there's resistance from the Israelis near this compound. Not good. The prison buildings could catch fire. If Al-Mahdi's army had a clear path to Jerusalem, we'd have a better chance of remaining intact. On the other hand, with no guards and no liberating army, we could be stuck here for days, without food. There's no way to guess what will become of this insignificant prison. How long until the caliphate takes control of Israel and appoints a leader to review the state of the prisons?

As sure as Allah is god and Mohammed his prophet, I will find a way out of this cell.

Micah and Keith are seated side by side on Keith's bunk, each with an arm over the other's shoulder, murmuring prayers. Their eyes are closed and tears run down their cheeks. What's strange is that they don't look sad or fearful—their faces glow, almost white, even though the cell's only lamp emits a dingy yellow light. Even as he sheds tears, I can discern Keith's wonderful smile, now also lighting nervous Micah's face.

My hands tingle and I rub them against my pants. I feel suddenly weak, drawn to them and their strange spirituality. These men do things I've never seen, as if they actually connect with their deity. I rarely find deep pleasure in my *rakas*, although I've taught myself to be at peace when I recite my prayers. It's the soothing repetition of the Arabic words that liberates my mind from daily worries, at least for the moment. But tears of happiness and ecstatic adoration of God? This is totally foreign to me, but seeing them I know it's real.

I take a step closer and listen to their words. The room keeps shaking and the booming continues, but that all seems distant now, even unimportant. A closer explosion shakes the ground and I'm pulled out of...whatever. Micah's favorite word.

Escape, that's what I should be seeking. I glance at the dirty toilet. It must drain somewhere, and the pipes could lead me outside.

"We have to get out of here," I say. "You can help me and live—it would be faster—or stay here and get blown up. Come, let's see if we can break a hole into the ground under the toilet."

Keith grins. "Planning to flush yourself down a tiny pipe?"

I shrug and walk to the toilet, searching for the knob to cut off the water. As I lean forward, a wave of sound and concrete pushes me head first onto the floor. My ears ring and everything goes dark.

44

$\mathcal{D}$ust and shards of stone stick to my tongue. I spit them out.

My body feels intact, though my ears ring from the blast. I push against the floor and drag myself up. The roof and one whole wall of the cell are gone, as far as I can tell in this scarce light—probably a street lamp or a floodlight from a prison tower.

I am a fugitive of death. Sooner or later I will meet my fate.

To my right lies a shadowed pile of rubble where Micah's and Keith's bunks were a minute ago.

"Keith? Micah?"

A moan from within the debris.

"Who is that?"

"Fa-Farid? Are you okay?"

"I am, thanks to Allah, what about you?"

"I… I don't know."

I step on the scattered rocks and narrow my eyes, seeking a human form in the mountain of bricks and concrete. A twisted piece of metal sticks out from the debris, and beneath it, an arm reaches. I grab the hand.

"Is this your hand, Keith?"

"What hand?"

So it must be Micah's. I shake it.

"Micah, can you hear me?" I wait, then feel his wrist for a pulse, There is none. Gently I let go of the hand "I'm sorry, Keith. Your friend is dead."

A few seconds pass. "Not dead, he sleeps."

"What?"

"His spirit has entered the presence of God."

How can he sleep and go to God? "Are you injured?"

Again, he takes some time to respond. "Yes, very badly." His breathing sounds harsh. "I think all my bones are crushed from the waist down... and my head, my head is bleeding."

I hear the familiar roar of tanks in the distance and look up at the dissipating dust. I can escape now, get out of this cell. But I want to show kindness to this man who has been so kind to me.

BOOM!

The building shakes again. The tanks keep targeting the prison. Screams from other inmates rise and fall, mixed with wails and cries for help.

Keith gasps. "This is it. Forgive me, Farid, if I have offended you. I just had to speak the truth. And I'm going to do it one more time. God is love, Farid. God *is* love."

I bite my lips, not knowing how to respond. Although this man is sorely misguided, he took care of me. I can't just leave him behind. He'll suffocate in there, and he needs medical treatment.

I bend over and begin to remove rocks, throwing them to one side.

"I'm going to save you, Keith." I remove two large bricks and grab hold of a heavy piece of concrete.

"No, Farid. Jesus has already saved me. Tonight I'll be with Him in heaven. You're the one who needs to be saved."

Me? I let go of the concrete. What kind of man cares more for another man than himself as he lies dying?

"You don't know what you're saying. There's still a chance—"

"No, listen to me, Farid. Jesus loves you, now and for eternity. 'For God so loved the world that He gave his only begotten son so that whoever believes in Him will not die but have eternal life.'"

A cool breeze surrounds us, but it's Keith's words that chill my bones. God loves me? My imam never said that Allah loves me. The Qur'an says Allah does not love sinners, or transgressors.

It's obvious from the Prophet's words who is hated by Allah, but there's no declaration of love for his followers, none whatsoever. This cannot be.

"Allah loves not those who reject the faith. He will punish me if I reject the teachings of the Prophet and the Qur'an. I must fulfill my duty as a Muslim to earn the favor of Allah."

"Christians believe no one has to earn God's love, Farid. He loves us all—including every Muslim, every Jew—no matter what we do. He can't help it because that's who he is. God *is* love." He pauses for a moment. "If you're killed in this war, Farid, would you go to paradise?"

"*Insh'Allah*. In the day of judgment I will know."

"You can know now, if you surrender to the grace of Jesus." His voice turns raspy and he pauses to gasp for his breath. "He died on the cross... for your sins, so you won't have to be judged. Would you accept his forgiveness?"

A heavy burden settles inside me and I remember the voice I heard at Benjamin's church—I am a sinner and must repent. Yet it's distant, this thought that God loves me and forgives my wrongs because another died in my place. My imam taught me that Jesus was never crucified, that Judas the traitor was crucified, while Jesus was taken to heaven.

"God loves you so much, Farid."

His voice seems to stretch into agony. I stare at the debris, unwilling and yet wanting to believe these shocking words from the mouth of a dying man.

"How do you know God loves me? How am I supposed to receive that love?"

A draft of air stirs the dust and I can hear the tanks getting closer.

"Keith?"

This is the loneliest moment of my life.

45

What a terrible night to die.

Sprinting down the hills of Palestine, numb with the sounds of war and the smell of burning flesh, I fear a bullet will end my life. Why am I ashamed of my fear? I've valiantly faced worse than this, killing and almost killed. It's the uncertainty of what lies beyond the grave.

Not until tonight have I seen a man so at peace with the time of his death. Not even my brother had that lucidity before blowing himself up—caught on camera, I saw the sweat on his forehead, the quivering lips, the trembling of his body. The Qur'an promises paradise for jihadists. I must die and kill my enemies so I can walk into paradise. Otherwise I must earn Allah's favor with my fervor to his teachings. But in the past few days I've missed my prayers again and again. I have failed in my duty, and not for the first time.

Just as the voice of my imam visits my head from time to time, I now hear Keith's voice: "God loves you so much."

How can God love me? What have I done to earn his love? But Keith said you don't have to earn it.

The cries of women in the village down the hill bring me back into the physical world. I should walk to the village and search for new footwear and clothing to replace this uniform. The boots I stole from the dead guard are too tight for my feet, making me dread every step.

The edge of the town is marked with concrete barriers decorated with graffiti clamoring for the liberation of Palestine. A path from the hill leads to a hole in the barrier, probably made by a rocket. I slip in and come to a rundown house surrounded by clothes lines. Perfect. But as I search for a suitable shirt, all I find are women's or children's clothes.

A continuous rata-ta-ta fills the air, and blood stains the ground. In this old house I seem to be alone. I make my way through a back door and come into a single room divided by hanging bed sheets—a main living area, a bedroom, a kitchen. Candles light the living room.

The knob of the front door creaks and I slide behind one of the sheets into the bedroom, where a cot lies on the floor. I crouch against one wall and peer through an opening. A panting woman hurries in and fumbles with the lock. She has long black hair, slender arms, a terrified expression, and a big belly. A memory of Zainah giving birth to our son numbs my body and soul for a moment. By Allah, I must retain control of my senses.

The woman leans forward beside a window and brings her face near the candle on the sill. She looks so young, not older than twenty, and I discern a lovely face behind her mask of fear. Her beauty is not the maddening allure of Jonathan's sister but more like the sweetness in the face of a pretty child. This woman, this girl, is a stranger to me. Jewish or Palestinian, I can't tell, but seeing her like this, so vulnerable, so innocent, so pregnant, makes her feel like a sister. She blows the candle out.

The door rattles and she flinches, letting out a cry. A thump makes the hinges turn, the old wood swings open, and a soldier walks into the house, ogling the girl. She steps backward, shaking, not withdrawing her eyes from him. The soldier leans his M-16 against the wall and wipes his mouth with his forearm.

He advances, closer to the candles, and I get a good look at his uniform. An Iraqi soldier, one of my fighters. The girl trips and falls backwards. She grabs her belly and screams as the soldier falls on her. My soul cringes, for I cannot fathom vicious rape during war, despite the implicit consent of the Prophet when his warriors raped Arab captives. Clerics have debated rape for centuries, both condemning and encouraging it, but the reality of jihad is this—what's happening here , right now, right before my eyes.

How can I protect this girl without being disloyal to Al-Mahdi's army? If I were a full general I would never allow this. I glance at the crying woman being subdued like an animal. I hear the voice of my imam: "A woman may be likened to a sheep—even a cow or a camel—for all are ridden."

I'm really getting annoyed with my imam right now. What if this was Zainah? This girl is a human, not a beast, not a thing to be used by a lustful soldier. I see his face twist and rage strikes me like a flooding river.

I rip the sheet away, grab the M-16, and smack the soldier's head with the butt of the rifle. A crack, a groan, and he collapses over the girl. I lift the body and throw him aside.

The girl stares at me with eyes wide, tears streaming, her chest rising up and down violently. As I grasp what I just did, I realize I'm almost hyperventilating myself.

I'M BACK in Al-Mahdi's army.

At least in uniform, if not in rank and authority. I can blend in with my fellow Arabs. I now have hanging over me not just Hussai's false charges but a verdict from Allah: I have killed a Muslim, when I unintentionally fractured the rapist's cranium.

The girl is safe for now, but what about the rest of the women in Jerusalem? I leave the village of ransacked houses and make my way to Jericho Road, which leads to the city. Here I see the bulk of the Islamic caliphate army with its black flags, troops moving forward like a storm, covering not only the road but the land around it. Many nations have answered Al-Mahdi's call to war. Certainly Israel is on the brink of destruction.

I hold my distance so I can go wherever I want without drifting into the line of command. I can't imagine obeying the orders of a captain. Perhaps there's hope and I may regain my honor, plead for Al-Mahdi's mercy, and uncover Hussai's deceitfulness.

Dawn must be at hand, and I should take advantage of the dark. Once Jerusalem falls, Al-Mahdi will appear and proclaim it the property of Islam. I must be there to present my case before him.

The army moves at a steady pace, truck after truck, tank after tank. I drift northwest into the maze of tombs and pebbles in the Jewish cemetery. In the distance I can see the walls of the old city and beyond them the Dome of the Rock. I should try the route nearer to the Mount of Olives, where it will be easier to stay hidden. Hopefully no one will attack a lone Islamic soldier

—unless I encounter a group of Israeli soldiers.

The path around the catacombs of the prophets is deserted, as are the grounds surrounding the church of St. Mary Magdalene, but there's a presence in these Jewish and Christian places, like a finger always pointing at me. My imagination, what else?

As I pass the Garden of Gethsemane, I sense the pounding of the army close by. I run with all my might through the fields, ignoring the passing vehicles, cutting through the trees, until I reach the Lions gate and enter the old city.

The sight greets me like a slap. Islamic soldiers crowd the narrow streets, rampaging, unloading equipment, pitching tents. The whole area within the walls is a military base.

"Soldier!" I turn at the harsh voice and glance at the insignia on his arm. A captain, of course. Life is full of ironies. "Report to the Temple Mount immediately." His finger points south.

Seeing no better place to go, I comply.

46

The scene at the Temple Mount is even stranger than the rest of the old city: a half-dozen television crews broadcast the chants of an agitated Palestinian mass demanding the destruction of the Jewish temple, which is now guarded by soldiers of Al-Mahdi's army—I among them.

The sun has come out and I face the crowd, pretending to do my duty but dreading the two crazy men behind us. What is the purpose of guarding the temple if nobody dares attack it anyway, not as long as the two witnesses stand there?

Their voices echo through the mount, raising the hairs on the back of my neck. "Listen, O people of the earth, the day has come, the day of rebellion, and the man of lawlessness has been revealed, the son of destruction is on his way to the holy temple. He opposes and exalts himself against every so-called god or object of worship, and today he will takes his seat in the temple of God, proclaiming himself to be God. The mystery of lawlessness is already at work, the lawless one is among you, but the Lord Jesus will bring him to nothing by his coming. The coming of the lawless one called the Mahdi is the work of Satan, for you have refused to love the truth and so be saved. For that reason, God has sent you a strong delusion, so that you may believe what is false, in order that all may be condemned who did not believe the truth but had pleasure in unrighteousness."

The words excite the multitude like fire. They bother me, but I've heard worse from Keith—it's as if my mind has become impervious to the blasphemies of the Christians.

One of the soldiers keeping guard beside me grunts. I glance at him and he shakes his head.

"They must be put to death. May Allah curse them."

"What are the orders?"

He doesn't turn to look at me but talks between his teeth, knowing we're not allowed to chat.

"Maintain the peace and protect the temple until the caliph arrives."

So Al-Mahdi is coming here? Good news. Maybe this soldier can tell me more about what's happening.

"What's the situation in the city? Are the Israelis holding up?"

His eyes dart around, checking to see whether anyone is watching us. "I heard we have control of the old city and most of east Jerusalem. The Zionists have bunkered themselves on the west end."

"So we have half the city." Half. Keith said something about Al-Mahdi taking half the city.

The sound of a chopper causes everyone to look at the morning sky. It has the swords of Islam on one side. The caliph has arrived. The first lieutenant coordinating the temple guard begins to shout.

"Go, go, move everybody and make room!"

We form a tight line and push the crowd toward the stairs leading to the Dome of the Rock, then return to our places. As the chopper comes down, the witnesses start clamoring again. My bones grow cold as I realize their voices are raised above the deafening sound of the helicopter.

"Behold, the son of lawlessness, who comes to profane the temple. He will take away the regular burnt offering and set up an abomination that causes desolation. Let those who are in Judea flee to the mountains. 'Let the one who is on the housetop not go down to take what is in his house, and let the one who is in the field not turn back to take his cloak. Alas for women who are pregnant and for those who are nursing infants! Behold, there will be great tribulation, such as has not been from the beginning of the world until now, no, and never will be.'"

My heart pounds against my flesh like a boxer hitting a punching bag. How can I want to flee the Mahdi, the one in whom I've placed all my hope? He is the Awaited One, the caliph of Islam, the jihad's Messiah.

The chopper's blades lose momentum and come to a stop. From the platform of the Dome of the Rock, eight men descend at a trot, bearing black banners. They go past the helicopter and halt a few meters from us, then set the banners so the poles are touching the ground.

This is one of the greatest moments of Islam's recent history. We have the Temple Mount—what we lost in 1967 we have taken back today. How can I doubt that Al-Mahdi is Allah's messenger? He has fulfilled the prophecies, united the Arab nations, and expanded the rule of Islam around the world.

I should be joyful, not fearful. My dread begins to falter. Yes, what a privilege to be here and witness the victory of Islam over Judaism. This is not how I expected it to happen, but at least I'm here. *Allah-o Ahkbar.*

I can't help but smile when the door of the chopper swings open. The caliph will come first, followed most likely by General Atartuk. The first to emerge is an Al-Mahdi guard, then another. They stand to one side and the caliph steps out. The TV cameras point at him, the crowd cheers, the soldiers stand firm and lift a hand in salutation—myself among them.

Al-Mahdi waves to the people and walks toward the journalists who seem to have appeared out of nowhere. A small podium with a microphone waits at the top of the flight of steps to the Dome, right by the qanatir. It wasn't there a minute ago.

The caliph ascends the steps. As he begins to address the audience, my eyes turn to the helicopter, where I see the shape of someone getting out. I recognize the uniform and the insignia immediately—it's a general. The face under the cap, however, is not Atartuk's.

My guts burn. It's Hussai.

47

As Hussai descends from the helicopter, he blinks and feels, again, a shift in his internal landscape. It has happened over and over the last few days, particularly when coming in and out of the caliph's presence. The shift is like awakening from a dream—the idyllic state, of course, when Al-Mahdi is close, and a hypnotic calmness takes hold of him. He can't explain it, but it seems his love and veneration for Al-Mahdi have suddenly grown. Although it feels as if this reverence has been here all his life—his memories are lapsing lately—he can only point to a few instances of feeling overpowered with love for Al-Mahdi, and all those instances in the past couple of days.

"This way, General Sidiqqui."

The captain in charge of the Temple Mount regiment extends one hand toward the steps to the Dome of the Rock.

General Sidiqqui. He likes the sound of that. Al-Mahdi surprised him when he came down the mountain with the Jewish scrolls and announced that Hussai was going to be the new general. This is the only vivid memory he has of that day.

Hussai reaches back into the helicopter for his briefcase and is about to follow the caliph up the stairs when something catches his attention. To his left a line of soldiers keeps guard beneath black banners, and beyond them lies the Jewish Temple. The whole structure seems to glow, and from behind the columns of the wall seems to shine a light like the halo of dusk over a clear horizon.

A dormant desire stirs in Hussai's chest, the lust for gold that drove him to seek the position of general. The riches of this temple…no, he now wants to serve the caliph, to give his life for the cause of Islam. Still, he can see himself stripping the gold off the walls, taking away the utensils, even plucking off the precious stones the Jewish priests carry on their chests.

Someone taps his shoulder. "General?"

Hussai grunts and turns toward the captain. "I'll stay here."

The captain nods.

He'd rather not be in front of the cameras. Let the caliph have the glory, he'll be happy with the gold. The growing crowd chants and Hussai thinks he'll see a replay of the scene from the Jordanian base, but Al-Mahdi raises one hand and silences the expectant faces. His smile is affable but his eyes are serious, almost cold. Hussai prepares to let his soul sink deep into Al-Mahdi's words—even before he speaks, everybody knows that only truth and knowledge will emanate from his mouth.

"Hear, O my people, those gathered here in this holy place, and those around the world." The caliph stares into a camera zooming in on him. "Today, we reclaim the Temple Mount for Islam!"

A deafening shout erupts from the multitude. "*Allah-o Ahkbar, Allah-o Ahkbar!*"

A thrill takes hold of Hussai, a kind of exaltation he hasn't experienced since he was a child. The caliph quiets the people again.

"East Jerusalem is ours, and we will fight until the opposition ends and all submit to me. I will have no rivals.

"Hear me, you Jews and Christians, convert to Islam today or die by the sword. I am a merciful leader. All you must do is renounce your blasphemies and declare that there is no God but Allah, that Muhammad is his messenger, that Al-Mahdi is the Messiah."

The caliph takes a green headscarf from one of his guards and ties it around his forehead. In gold and white, the headpiece bears the two crossed swords of Islam and the words, *Bismillah Alrahman Alraheem.* In the name of Allah.

"The infidels must wear this badge of allegiance on their foreheads or right arms as a symbol of their conversion, as must all the believers called to fight for god's cause, my cause.

"Hear O Muslims, the Qur'an's call to jihad: Fight and kill the unbelievers wherever you find them, take them captive, lie in wait and ambush them using every stratagem of war. This is my call today: Muslims, fight in Allah's cause, Al-Mahdi's cause. Stand firm and you will prosper. Help Al-Mahdi, obey me, give me your allegiance, and you will be victorious. *Allah-o Ahkbar.*"

The crowd is louder this time, and even Hussai screams at the top of his lungs. "*Allah-o Ahkbar, Allah-o Ahkbar!* Al-Mahdi is the bridge to god!"

A voice like the roar of a lion cuts through the chants.

"Jesus Christ is the King of Kings and lord of lords, the son of the most high God!"

The voice comes from one of the two witnesses at the entrance of the Jewish temple.

Al-Mahdi lets out reverberating laughter, but when he speaks his voice rings with anger. "Verily they are disbelievers and infidels who say, 'Jesus is God.'"

One of the witnesses, the elder of the two, steps forward and proclaims in a voice stronger than Al-Mahdi's, even without a microphone: "'Christ Jesus, who, though he was in the form of God, made himself nothing, being born in the likeness of men. He humbled himself by becoming obedient to the point of death, even death on a cross. Therefore God has highly exalted him and bestowed on him the name that is above every name, so that at the name of Jesus every knee should bow, in heaven and on earth and under the earth, and every tongue confess that Jesus Christ is Lord, to the glory of God the Father.'"

Al-Mahdi rolls his eyes. "Christ was merely a messenger. Many were the messengers that passed away before him. See how Allah does make His signs clear to them, yet see in what ways they are deluded!"

The caliph is quoting directly from the Qur'an, for Hussai has heard those words before.

"O Christians, do not be fanatical in your faith, and say nothing but the truth about Allah. Isa, son of Mary, messenger of Allah, bestowed his Word on Mary and His Spirit. So believe in Allah, and say not Trinity, for Allah is one God. Far be it from His Glory to beget a son. That is a blasphemous lie."

"Who is the liar but he who denies that Jesus is the Christ?" the witness says. "This is the Antichrist, he who denies the Father and the Son. 'No one who denies the Son has the Father. Whoever confesses the Son has the Father also.'"

The people move their heads from side to side as each man speaks. Hussai's legs tremble. How dare these men challenge the caliph? Perhaps he should do something, perhaps he should order the guards to fire at them. But he feels glued to the ground and can only stare, helpless, at Al-Mahdi, who shakes his head like an adult who's losing patience with a child.

"Have you no understanding? You know well I am the truth. In his confrontations with the Jews and Christians of his time, the Prophet Muhammad, peace be upon him, chided the infidels for subverting the revelation from Allah and changing the books, for certainly the texts of the Jews spoke about Muhammad, and they knew it, but through evil schemes vanished every mention of him from the Torah." He points at the witnesses. "And you Christians did the same, changing the words spoken by Isa, the son of Mary, who proclaimed the words of Allah and the coming of one greater than him, Muhammad himself."

"Jesus said, 'I am the way, and the truth, and the life. No one comes to the Father except through me. If you had known me, you would have known my Father also.'"

The caliph opens his mouth to speak, but the younger witness lifts a hand and keeps talking. To Hussai's amazement, Al-Mahdi lets him.

"'Christ is the image of the invisible God, the firstborn of all creation. For by him all things were created, in heaven and on earth, visible and invisible. 'For in him all the fullness of God was pleased to dwell, and through him to reconcile to himself all things, whether on earth or in heaven, making peace by the blood of his cross.'"

With a red face, Al-Mahdi yells, "Allah has cursed you for your unbelief! A scripture came to you from Allah confirming the truth of Islam, and you denied it! Allah's curse is on you!"

The two witnesses step back, as if they've said everything. Their countenance is calm, —unlike Al-Mahdi, they seem impassive. Shouldn't Hussai be issuing orders? But what? The stories he has heard about these two are enough to keep him at bay. But he's the general now, and others can take risks for him. Yet he feels unable to do anything but watch events unfold.

After a few seconds, the caliph regains his composure and speaks to the crowd.

"Not three days ago, I led my people into the desert, where you witnessed the discovery of some ancient Jewish scrolls so ancient and so delicate they certainly predate any such existing texts. The experts who have examined them report a ninety percent probability that these were the actual copies written by the hand of Moses. How is that possible, you may ask? Only god could have known the exact location of these scrolls, and that is why I have found them and today we will reveal the truth. For after examining the ancient texts, untouched by evil hands, Islamic scholars have concluded that they in fact prophesied the coming of Muhammad. And not only his coming, but my coming, the appearance of the twelfth caliph of Islam, and of this day, when the true revelation of Allah will be given, when you will know Allah with your own eyes, because you have seen me."

48

Cold sweat streams down my temples and I fear I'll be sick. I'm not weak or in pain—this is more a divine terror, a strike of lightning every time the two men behind me speak. I tense, trying to ease the irrational tremor. It gets worse.

The people cheer Al-Mahdi's words and drink of his speech without thinking. Am I the only one noticing this? Two or three times he has referred to himself in the same manner as Allah and the Prophet. We all know he is the Awaited One, and I could certainly see him being as honorable as the Prophet, but it seems as if...

Then I remember Keith's words. No, no, no. This is nonsense. How could he know this? But Al-Mahdi *is* exalting himself as God. This is blasphemy—Allah is the only god. Or is he implying that... No, impossible. The Christians say that God became man, but Allah is beyond incarnation, beyond anything in this earth.

Al-Mahdi trots down the steps with a fixed stare of hate toward the Jewish temple, toward the witnesses. His guards follow him, the crowd parts before him. The men with the black banners step aside, and I find myself in his path. I'm just a few meters away as he marches towards a confrontation I dread to witness.

For this is the final test. Al-Mahdi's jaw is set and I see murder in his eyes. But these men have burned their enemies alive. My cousin was engulfed in flame.

The air feels thicker, and a chill raises the hair of my body. It's as if I've become soft and fragile as a child. No, I am a warrior, I am strong, I am....

Al-Mahdi stops less than two meters from my position and looks past me to the witnesses. One of his personal guards pushes me aside and I take two steps back. Now I'm not facing the Dome of the Rock but have turned to my left, waiting for the world to end before my eyes. My hands feel like flour, and my grip on my weapon loosens.

I catch a close look at Al-Mahdi's profile over the guard's shoulder. The face I always longed to see, the face of the man I served wholeheartedly, the face that inspired my every step. Al-Mahdi has held my dreams for so long, all I've wanted is to serve in his army and bring peace to the Arab world. I expect those feelings to flood me again.

But they don't, there's nothing. He passes by and leaves me empty. No rekindled dreams, no emotions welling up, nothing but an empty feeling. What's wrong with me?

My mouth feels dry and I realize my jaw hangs open. The void is so strong that time seems to slow and the world a mirage in the desert.

Then the guard moves forward and Hussai steps in front of me.

MY STARE is so intense that surely he will turn and see me. What then? What will happen the instant he recognizes me? He could make a scene and ask for my arrest, but would he? That would mean interrupting the clash between the caliph and the Christian prophets, turning the attention of the world away from Al-Mahdi. Hussai's not stupid.

The question is, what am I going to do? Hope he doesn't notice who I am or finish what I started the day I shot him? He got rid of me, and somehow he got rid of Atartuk. I underestimated him dangerously.

His uniform looks new and a size too large, the cuffs covering part of his hands. His protruding belly is well disguised under the coat. The cap hangs over his forehead a bit too low. But he is general and I'm not. He may smirk for an hour straight if he wants—for he has defeated me.

But that could change. The fact that he's in and Atartuk is out means that in times of war nothing is set but fate is determined by God. Strength returns to my fingers and I grasp my rifle with a new vigor. I could shoot him now... and be shot back. Still, it would be vengeance. He robbed me of what was rightfully mine, and he must pay for it.

He nods, as if answering someone—the Mahdi, perhaps?—and looks down at the briefcase in his hand. He opens it and extracts a tube. He places the briefcase on the ground, unscrews the lid of the tube, and slides out a rolled paper, a scroll. He finally extends his arm and offers the scroll to the caliph.

Al-Mahdi unrolls the scroll and holds it up as if to read it. If this is one of the ancient Torah scrolls he mentioned in his speech, why is he holding it like a magazine instead of an archeological finding? And does he know how to read ancient Hebrew?

Apparently he does, for he addresses the witnesses, who listen with raised brows and crossed arms, looking amused.

"Listen to this, you evil-doers, you who are cursed by Allah. Moses had commanded the Israelites to prostrate themselves, and his Lord spoke to him, and they heard His voice giving commands and prohibitions so that they understood what they heard. But when Moses went back to the Jews, a party of them changed the commandments, changing the name of Allah for that of Yaweh. This is that which Moses wrote in the book of Deuteronomy: 'Hear, O Muslims, Allah our God, Allah is one, and there is no God except Allah. And thou hast loved Allah thy God with all thy heart, and with all thy soul, and with all thy might. And it hath been, when Allah thy God doth bring thee in unto the land of the Arabs which He hath sworn to thy fathers, to Abraham, to Ishmael, and to Isaac. Cities great and good, take heed to thyself lest thou forget that Allah will send thee a Messenger, who will bring thee the holy Qur'an.'"

The white-haired witness unfolds his arms and a staff appears in his hand. He points to the scroll in Al-Mahdi's hands.

"You have devised lying words and utter falsehoods against the Lord. Your words shall perish and so will you."

As he speaks, the scroll dissolves into dust, which the wind blows back in the caliph's face. A collective gasp sucks the oxygen from the Temple Mount.

Al-Mahdi shrugs and turns to Hussai, who hands him a second scroll. He points at the witnesses with the rolled scroll.

"Why do you persist in denying and rejecting the revelations of Allah?" He unrolls the scroll. "Ah! The book of Genesis, the unaltered book of Genesis." He begins to read. "And Gabriel the messenger of Allah said to Hagar, 'Behold thou art conceiving, and bearing a son, and hast called his name Ishmael, for Allah hath hearkened unto thine affliction; and he is a wild-ass man, his hand against every one, and every one's hand against him— and in the last days, from his descendants I shall bring forth the Messiah, the Mahdi, who will fill the earth with equity and justice as it was filled with oppression and tyranny.'"

The other witness points a finger at the caliph. "'And the beast has been given a mouth uttering haughty and blasphemous words, and it has been allowed to exercise authority for forty-two months, starting today. God has allowed him to make war on the saints and to conquer them. And authority has been given to him over every tribe and people and language and nation, and all who dwell on earth will worship it, everyone whose name has not been written before the foundation of the world in the book of life of the Lamb who was slain.'"

This time, the other witness's staff hits Al-Mahdi's hands, and the scroll falls to the ground. The caliph scowls at them.

Why are they provoking him? Maybe they want him to attack them so they'll be justified in defending themselves and killing Al-Mahdi. But he cannot die, not yet. He has so much to conquer still, so much to do for Islam.

I've never seen Al-Mahdi lose his temper, but his reddened face and fiery eyes tell me I will. He turns his back to the witnesses, strides toward his guards, and grabs two swords from them. He brandishes the blades above his head and approaches them, an elegant but terrifying figure. The blades fly down and stop a few millimeters from their necks, but they don't even flinch.

"I can kill you right now and I know you won't touch me," Al-Mahdi says, "for you yourselves have said that authority has been given to me over all the world. And that includes you. So bow now and worship me if you don't want to die."

They reply in unison. "Fulfill the apostle's prophecy: 'And when they have finished their testimony, the beast that rises from the bottomless pit will make war on them and conquer them and kill them, and their dead bodies will lie in the street of the great city that is called Sodom and Egypt, where their Lord was crucified. For three and a half da—"

Al-Mahdi lets out a terrible shriek, pulls the swords back, then thrusts them into the witnesses's stomachs.

49

For an eternal second I believe this is all a dream, until the crowd breaks loose in shouts of celebration. Two bodies lay on the bloody ground, Al-Mahdi standing over them. He spits in their faces and walks to the temple, not even bothering to retrieve the swords jutting from their limp bodies.

It all happened as Keith said. But Al-Mahdi is victorious, the Christian prophets dead. What does it mean? Did the Christians know they were going to be defeated? If so, what's the point?

The crowd presses in, their shouts louder, their eyes thirsty for blood.

"Keep them away from the bodies!" Hussai shouts. "Form a perimeter around the corpses, now."

The soldiers hesitate but obey. I move to the farther side of the circle—if the mob gets a chance, they'll dismember the bodies and drag them through the streets. Who among the Muslims does not hate these witnesses? Al-Mahdi has rid us of two men who closed the sky for years and sent plagues outside of Israel. Yet the power in their words and deeds today was unmistakable.

The human circle sways like a palm tree in a sandstorm, then breaks, as one of the soldiers is pulled away by the mob—he falls to the ground, and the people in front trample him. The crowd in the back keeps pushing. We'll all be trampled soon.

I point my rifle to the sky and let loose a round of bullets. The crowd scatters like cockroaches. Encouraged, the circle advances, soldiers showing their barrels to anyone who still wants to come for the bodies. I glance back toward the Jewish temple and see Hussai entering the ornate doors. Not sure why, I follow him.

As I sneak into the outer courts, a man in some sort of ancient priestly attire runs toward me, trips, and falls to my feet. He lifts his teary eyes and wails, then speaks in Hebrew.

"It's gone, it's gone! The glory of Elohim has departed the temple. Sacrilege! The gentiles have entered the holy of holies." He pushes past me.

The holy of holies? I scan the area, the columns and strange items around me, then cross the roofless court and climb a flight of steps to an immense golden gate. It's locked, so I enter through a door on one side and come to a smaller courtyard. The building in its center is the tall structure we could all see from outside. The fragrance of incense lingers in the air and there's a large water basin on one side—I guess the basin serves as a purification area, like we have in our mosques.

The place seems desolate. I continue up the steps to the main building. A sudden mix of sadness and fear chokes my throat as I reach the entrance. Does this place have some sort of power? I step inside past thick curtains, then stop. Ten meters from me, maybe less, stand two of Al-Mahdi's guards, their backs to me. I get behind a curtain and peer in. Further into the place, Al-Mahdi paces frantically, knocking over every item in his way, spitting on the floor.

"No, stop!" In one corner on the far side there's a bearded man hanging by his arms as two guards keep him on his knees. His face is smeared with blood and his garment—the same priest-like attire of the man I encountered outside—is torn in half. "You are desecrating the temple!" he cries.

"That's the whole idea, worthless pig." Al-Mahdi strides toward him and slaps his face, then looks at his hand with disgust, picks up a cloth from the floor and wipes it. "Chop his head off," he tells the guards. He then looks at the wide-eyed priest. "At least you gave me an idea. I will find the Ark of the Covenant and make you Jews sacrifice swine on it, every day. Then I'll make you drink its blood and eat its meat until you vomit."

My heart sinks at such cruelty and humiliation, and my head swirls. Is this the man I want to serve? But who else would I follow? This is all I know.

A finger taps my shoulder. "Move out of the way, soldier."

I turn and meet Hussai's eyes. His lips part, his brows all but meet in an expression of incredulity. For a split second I think he's afraid, until his mouth makes a smirk, as if he finally grasps the irony of it all. It has not escaped me.

My breathing accelerates. I know he's going to say something clever and haughty, but his voice will call attention to us, and I don't want to face Al-Mahdi in his mad ferocity.

"Farid, Farid... you just come to me like—"

I thrust the butt of the rifle into his stomach, pushing him away from the entrance. Surprise makes him lose his balance for a moment, but I was too close to swing hard, so he regains his footing before reaching the edge of the steps behind him.

He tries to snatch my rifle from me, unsuccessfully, so he swings a kick at me. His boot hits my left ankle. A bullet of pain shoots up my leg, and I let go of one hand on the rifle. He twists it to point at me, moves his hand to the trigger. I strike his fingers with a punch, smashing them between the metal and my hand, then slam my elbow against his cheek. In a last move, I risk freeing my other hand from the gun and punch him in the jaw.

Hussai's body jerks and he flies down the stairs on his back. The sound of his screams reverberates throughout the temple. I glance around, weighing my options. He's trying to rise. I can get to him in a few steps—but the rifle got caught in his oversized coat and is now in his hands.

I hear hurried steps inside the building and know Al-Mahdi's murderous guards will soon surround me.

HUSSAI STUMBLES to his feet and holds the M-16 in front of him, ready to fire. His face is flushed with anger, his hair disheveled without the cap, his clothes in disarray. The guards storm out of the building. I lift my hands and move back swiftly, hoping he won't pull the trigger if I'm surrounded by the guards—I know firsthand Hussai's aim is poorer than average. Almost intentionally, I trip and fall backwards against one of the guards. He catches me and throws me to one side. I flip in the air to face the ground and land on my hands under my chest. I couldn't be more vulnerable than I am now, so I wait for a blow.

No gunshots, no threats. Not even a kick in the stomach. What's going on here?

"What's going on here?"

I'm startled at hearing my thoughts out loud, and from Al-Mahdi's lips. He's here. That's why nobody touched me.

"Lord Al-Mahdi—"

The caliph cuts Hussai off. "Wait a minute, Hussai, I want to hear this man's version first. Soldier?"

I get to my knees and lift my head slowly. "It is a long story."

I see a hint of a sly smile as Al-Mahdi recognizes me. He examines me from feet to head and puts a hand on my shoulder.

"I knew I would see you again, Farid, but didn't expect it to be here." He opens his arms. "In my new temple."

His new temple? He's appropriating a Jewish temple for Islam?

"Put down that weapon, Hussai. You might shoot somebody." The paternalistic tone in Al-Mahdi's voice makes me feel better, but only for a moment. It's just like he treated Atartuk, like a stupid child.

Hussai frowns, then complies. I return my eyes to the caliph, whose face turns serious.

"Are you a traitor, Farid? Have you given your allegiance to the Jews?"

"No, sir, never."

His penetrating eyes examine me and I feel ashamed, not

sure why. It's as if I'm naked and exposed, as if he can read all my doubts, all the terrible things I've heard about him and almost believed.

"Good. I believe you." Relief floods my chest. "Still, you will have to prove it."

"Yes, my lord Al-Mahdi, I was spying on the Israelis, obtaining intelligence for you. They have nukes and anti-missile—"

The caliph waves a hand. "I don't need intelligence any more, do I? I'm the conqueror. No, I have a better idea than that, Farid." He rubs his chin and grins. "We've captured about a dozen Jewish priests and let one escape so he can spread fear among the other Jews."

All relief is gone.

"Show me that you love me, Farid, and that you hate the Jews. Show me your allegiance by beheading the Jewish priests."

50

Hussai bites his lower lip, refusing to believe this is happening. How has Farid again found favor with the caliph?

Three guards run inside the building to bring out the beaten priests, tied up in one of the storage rooms. Hussai takes the steps to the platform, observing the silent exchange between Farid and the Al-Mahdi. He can't let Farid redeem himself. With Al-Mahdi's capriciousness, Farid could well end up with Hussai's new job.

"What if he refuses to kill the priests, O exalted one?" Hussai says.

Al-Mahdi studies Farid. "He must do it. It's my desire, hence his duty."

Farid's face is stern. He's thinking this through, his gaze lost in the distance. Hope rises in Hussai's mind. Perhaps he was right all along.

"He's a Zionist and a lover of Jews, your excellency. That's what I've always said. If he refuses, he must be put to death. And I would gladly hold the sword."

"I decide who dies and who lives." The guards return and Al-Mahdi addresses them. "Line the priests at the foot of the stairs, tied to one another. And bring one of the TV reporters inside. We'll make this a public execution, a display for the world to see, and there will be no Jew in Jerusalem that does not fear for his life."

Farid turns to look at the caliph, his eyes wide, sweat beading his forehead. Al-Mahdi just smiles. Surely he has noticed Farid's hesitation, his silence speaking for him. A true jihadist would have jumped in celebration by now. He won't do it, that much is obvious. Or will he? His reputation is that of a professional killer, merciful with women and children but cold-blooded with enemy soldiers. He has raided and ambushed hundreds of men.

Bile crawls up Hussai's throat. Despite Al-Mahdi's healing touch, his arm still hurts from time to time, all thanks to Farid.

"He won't do it, he loves the Jews more than his country." Hussai's voice has a slight tremor.

Farid shoots a quick, hateful glance at Hussai, then nods at the caliph. "If I may speak my mind, sir, I must confess my reservations."

Yes, he reveals his true colors.

"You may speak your mind, Farid, but I hope you won't disappoint me."

"Far from me to disappoint you, sir. It's just that I'm dressed as a simple soldier, and your people will wonder why am I conducting judgment when you, O excellent Caliph, are the righteous judge. It should be the general who performs the execution."

Al-Mahdi shakes his head. "You know the Qur'an, Farid, you know the Prophet called unto others to execute Allah's enemies and even lauded those who cut the head off his adversaries." He regards Farid for a moment. "You say the general should conduct the execution." Al-Mahdi looks from Farid to Hussai, then back at Farid. "Well, if that's what you want, I will make you general."

Hussai feels punched in the stomach. The caliph is mad.

"My Lord, pardon me, but—"

Al-Mahdi waves one hand. "Don't fret, Hussai, you can be a general too. Didn't Alexander the Great have four generals? I can have two, or twenty if I wish. My empire will be greater than his, and like the Prince of Greece I will rule the whole world."

Hussai's fingers clench the M-16 in his grasp. The rage that boils in him makes his body shake like a kettle. He turns his eyes to the priests, kneeling with their heads lifted up. Al-Mahdi's guards push them so their faces touch the floor, but they slowly rise again until their bodies—from the knees up—are straight. What a prideful people, what a revolting view.

Hussai is suddenly overpowered by numbness. He sees Al-Mahdi and Farid walking down the steps, The caliph puts a hand on Farid's shoulder.

"You have always been my most capable asset in the army. I thought I had lost you, but here you are. Whatever happened between you and Hussai, it's in the past. I'm willing to forget about it, I won't even ask you anything. All you have to do to become general is kill a handful of my enemies. No need to fight, just cut off their heads. So, what say you?"

51

General Farid Zadeh. Unbelievable. No more a traitor, not a fugitive of two countries, but full general of Al-Mahdi's army.

I would have to share my authority with Hussai, but that can be remedied. He escaped once–I won't miss a second time. He deserves to die. He's a hypocrite, a false Muslim, and a traitor. He tried to kill me and frame me for treason. My vengeance is justified.

As for the Jewish priests… if I don't kill them, one of the guards will. According to my imam, Allah will reward me if I kill these Jews.

Yet even the thought of beheading anyone is repulsive, much less innocent unarmed men, priests in their own temple. I know this is an infidel's temple and there is no god but Allah, yet the power of the witnesses, the prophecies, the survival of the Jews throughout history—all this is testimony to the existence of their God, something I can't deny.

I feel as if a cloud covers my mind and blurs my vision. Then I realize my eyes have watered. I turn away from Al-Mahdi and wipe my face. A movement across the courts catches my eye. Two men hurry toward us. One carries a video camera, the other a handful of bags with cables and equipment.

They begin to set up the camera and Al-Mahdi signals one of his guards to give me his sword. I weigh the weapon in my right hand, look up at the camera on its tripod, then down at the twelve priests condemned to die—simply for serving their God.

How could I have been drawn into this butchery? If I refuse, who knows what will happen to me? Most likely Al-Mahdi will react with rage and have me killed.

"Are you ready, General Zadeh?" Al-Mahdi's deep voice reverberates in my soul. "Show me your loyalty."

I swing the sword as if I'm practicing, hoping to buy time because I don't know—I'm not sure—what to do. It's a horrific act, yes, but perhaps it's worth it. I think about myself two weeks ago, several days before this anti-adventure began, when I would have done anything to become a general, maybe even worse than killing a dozen innocents. What has changed? I have changed.

My eyes fill again and my surroundings turn hazy. I can just make out Al-Mahdi talking to the camera, gesturing and pointing to the priests, but not his words. There's only a distant ringing in my middle ear and the sound of my own breathing. Then the voice of Keith: "God loves you so much."

How can his God love me, a Muslim? If he loves me, he must also love these priests. Why then would he allow me to kill them? Shouldn't he protect them? If he doesn't, then he's not much more God than Allah.

I feel as if someone in heaven is laughing at my thoughts. I shake the sensation off and walk around the priests, hardly noticing the tears in their eyes. I must not feel mercy, just finish the job, saving them from torture and slow death in a dungeon.

This is the will of Allah.

Al-Mahdi glances at me, penetrating my mind in a second. I can hear his voice although he doesn't open his mouth. *Do it, Farid, kill the Jews.*

Self-conscious, I stand with my back to the temple's sanctuary and point to one of the priests in the middle. The cameraman pans over the group and appears to zoom in on the man I picked. If the God of the Jews is real, he won't let me kill his priests. If he doesn't stop me, then I shouldn't fear, for Allah is the only god and killing Jews is a good deed in his eyes.

I mutter under my breath to the invisible God that supposedly loves me so much. "I dare you to stop me."

The blade swings back and my heart roars like a jet as I focus
on the victim's neck. Still, I hesitate.

A blast pierces the air and the priest jerks before I swing the
sword. The priest slumps to the ground, face first. Blood stains
his back.

HUSSAI'S RAPID panting is the only sound in the first seconds after
the echoes of the rifle die in the air. His face is twisted in rage.

"Only the real general should execute the Jewish apes."

A pool of blood extends around the dead priest's body, and
the others begin wailing as only Jews can wail. What did just
happen? Did God really stop me? I look back at Hussai, trying
to comprehend his behavior. One thing is clear here. We can't
both be generals.

"That's why Al-Mahdi asked me," I say. "Because however you
got yourself named general, it was certainly not for your merits."

He points the M-16 at me and gives me that infuriating smirk.
"Look at the mighty Farid, who everybody called the 'rock,' all
afraid, knowing he's going to die."

Al-Mahdi steps between us, facing the rifle.

"You're so amusing, Hussai." Al-Mahdi laughs. "That line
about the 'real general executing the apes' was first rate. And
shooting the priest, well, I didn't expect that. I'm tempted to keep
you. But don't you ever—" He snatches the rifle from Hussai with
one swift move. "—walk over my authority again." He presses the
barrel of the M-16 against Hussai's forehead. "This is my show,
and everyone does what I command. *Only.*"

"Yes, my lord...." Hussai's voice trails off.

"I feel like blowing your brains out right now."

"You are merciful, my lord, just like Allah."

"Yes, just like Allah." Al-Mahdi nods. "You always know how

to appease me, Hussai. Now go and fix your uniform, you look like a schoolboy."

Hussai hurries away without looking back and I shake my head. That sounded like a father chiding his son. More and more, the man I thought I knew begins to feel like a mad dictator, not unlike Saddam Hussein.

Al-Mahdi turns and regards me with an undecipherable expression. I feel as if a chasm separates us. .

"Now we can go on with the plan," he says. "Pick up your sword."

The sword lies right beside my feet, but I don't remember when I dropped it. He walks to a safe distance and I bend to retrieve it. I stop halfway, my hand extended but not quite enough to reach the hilt. What makes me think I'll have any say in this war, even as a general? Atartuk was but a sheep before the caliph, and Hussai is no different. Even I am about to comply with his thirst for blood.

In my heart, I know the truth: This is not what I want. This is not who I am.

I straighten, leaving the sword on the floor. The caliph—I don't even feel like calling him Al-Mahdi any more—is instructing the cameraman to switch the mini-disc in the camera for a new one to get rid of the previous footage. Two of the guards disappear inside the building, carrying the body of the dead priest, while the other guards are focused on the caliph. Hussai is nowhere to be seen. Less than fifteen meters away lies the exit to the temple's outer courts. Beyond that, Jerusalem. I head for the door, unnoticed.

52

Hussai steps out of the wash room—the only modern thing in this ancient design—dragging his feet. What got into him? Al-Mahdi is so furious he dreads meeting his gaze.

He can always deal with Farid later. He did it once and he can do it again. So why did he fire that gun? He should have known better. It was as if an invisible hand pulled the trigger for him.

He observes the scene: priests, guards, reporters, the caliph. Where is Farid? A man is crossing the outer courts—his back is to him, but it's Farid. The door closes, and Hussai strides toward it.

As he enters the outer courts, he sees Farid sprinting through the temple exit. Why is he running? There's only one explanation: he's deserting. Now, that's a good reason to kill him.

He runs after his prey.

OUTSIDE THE temple, hundreds of soldiers have moved onto the Temple Mount to control the excited crowd. It sounds like a market but looks like a war zone. Hussai sees a soldier walking fast, about five meters away. He grabs him by the shoulder. The soldier spins around. It's not Farid.

"Sir?"

"Never mind, soldier. Carry on."

All soldiers look alike in uniform.

"General?"

Hussai turns to his right and sees a young soldier covered in sweat. "Yes?"

"What should we do with the bodies, sir?"

The two lunatics lie dead where the caliph left them. Damn. He doesn't have time for this.

"Just leave them there for now." Hussai scans the crowd again.

"What about the people, sir? They want a peek at them, same with the journalists."

"Set up a fence or something and let the world watch." Yes, that would be please Al-Mahdi, who loves making a show out of everything."Spread the word that this is an event to celebrate, tell the journalists. No, wait. I should tell them that." He nods at his own cleverness. "Now, go and do as I said."

"Yes, sir."

Whatever made Farid change his mind about killing the Jews is irrelevant. What matters is he's gone and Hussai remains the sole general of Al-Mahdi's army. He wonders if he should tell the caliph of Farid's desertion. Perhaps not. Al-Mahdi will notice the absence anyway, probably already has, and will be angry as a demon.

After a few minutes, a group of soldiers installs a barricade around the dead bodies and the journalists gather around it. Hussai starts toward the group but a sudden fear seizes him. What if Farid comes back? He'd thought he was free of him before, but he showed up at the temple. Farid may return to kill him, he may even join the Jews and find his way back.

He must do something.

From the temple gate, the two reporters who witnessed everything inside come out running. Their faces are pale and their hands trembling.

Hussai walks over. "What's going on in there?

"I'd rather not say."

That bad.

"Did you record anything after the first incident?"

The cameraman shakes his head. "No...the caliph became, well, quite upset."

"That's an understatement," the other reporter says.

"Quite mad, I should say."

Hussai tries a stern expression. "Mind your words, or you can be in serious danger."

They nod. An idea grips Hussai—an idea that will make it impossible for Farid to gain the allegiance of the Jews.

"Now, I can pardon your irreverence and spare your lives if you cooperate." He pauses to make sure he has their attention. "Tell me, can you edit the footage you have to make it appear that the man with the sword actually killed the priest, instead of me?"

The cameraman thinks for a moment. "It wouldn't be very smooth, but I can show him lifting the sword, then cut to the image of the dead body. Sometimes this is done when you don't want to be too graphic with the images of killings. I'll just have to avoid showing the wounds closely."

"Good. We'll do that, then broadcast it on Israeli TV."

53

The terror that made me flee the Temple Mount is beginning to fade. I'm surprised nobody stopped me and questioned me. I slow down in a deserted street where the only noise is the rhythm of my boots on the pavement. I halt to catch my breath among empty stores and lifeless facades. I'm very close to the wall surrounding the old city.

The bright sun hits me hard and the light's reflection on the windows makes me squint. A figure moves atop a roof—

I dive to the ground and roll to one side as a bullet ricochets in the narrow street. The figure. Is he by himself? If it's an Israeli soldier, he might be in the company of others. I might be ambushed. And I have no weapon.

Keeping my back against the wall of a nearby house, I seek a way out of this street. I start running once I reach an alley and feel an overwhelming thirst. I can't keep going like this. I kick open the door of the first dwelling on my left and move from room to room. A lavender scent fills the empty house. In the bathroom, I let the water run and drink. I wash my face and listen for any signs of danger.

Nothing. It's strange they didn't follow me. Well, this is still the old city, which is now under the control of the Islamic caliphate. The Israelis may come over the wall to survey the positions of our troops from a safe distance, but I don't think they'll venture deep inside the city.

I dry my face with a damp green towel and regard myself in the mirror. Water drips from my unkempt beard and my eyes are bloodshot. The stolen uniform looks a bit too small on me and feels tight under my arms. Staring at my reflection, I realize my life no longer has any direction. I've no dream to pursue, no career to occupy my days. I know nothing about my future and it feels so... well, it's odd to think this way, but I feel liberated. There's still some sort of emptiness in my soul but somehow there's also a prodding to move forward, to find a new path, even though I have no idea what it is.

"This is my chance for a new start," I tell the man in the mirror. I find a razor and begin by shaving my beard, then take the uniform off.

When I finish, I walk around the house. In the couple's bedroom, a chest with clothes provides what I need: a pair of jeans and a shirt. The shoes in the closet are too small for my feet, so I keep the boots. After changing my clothes I walk to the kitchen and eat olives, grapes, and bread. May Allah bless this family.

A new clarity fills my head and I even consider sleeping for a while, but it's not safe. The owners may return, or the apparent ceasefire may end. One thing I know: if I want to rethink my life I must do it away from the army, away from Al-Mahdi and Hussai, away from Baghdad. Maybe I can go to Jaddeh. But that would mean revisiting places I frequented with Zainah, and I'm not ready for that. I'll find a destination later.

I eat the last grapes in the bowl and wipe my mouth. The food is heavy on my stomach. I wander around the house, intending to retrace my way to the exit, but find myself sitting on a bed, then lying down. Just a few minutes, no more. I close my eyes.

THE REVERBERATING echo of an explosion wakes me. Was it in my dream or in the real world?

I feel lighter now, rested, must have slept for two hours at least. Too much time wasted. I must sneak into west Jerusalem and find a vehicle, return to my plane. It's dangerous, almost suicidal, to fly out of a war zone the day after an air raid, but it's the fastest way to get out of the city.

I jump out of the bed and leave the house. I can hear the *ratatata* of machine guns and the hovering choppers. I run, wary of roofs and open doors. In civilian clothes I'm a target for any side. I don't know if the Israelis will shoot civilians, but if they catch me crossing to their side of the wall I bet they won't take chances.

The sounds of shooting increase as I move south along the wall, although I can't see anyone. I wish I had a weapon.

Further down the wall I notice the faint smoke of a bullet exchange, about fifty meters away. That's the Jaffa gate. I crouch behind a fountain and inspect my surroundings. There seems to be shooting at the small square that separates the Christian and the Armenian quarters.

On one edge of the square, very close to the wall, a line of tall trees rises. I dash for them and climb the tallest. The thin branches sway as I cling to them—one of them snaps and I lose my footing. I reach out with both hands toward the wall and stop the fall. That was close.

The top of the wall is less than a meter above me. I swing my weight back on the tree and climb one more branch, praying it won't break, then jump. I reach the edge of the wall with my hands, pull myself over, and look toward the modern city. The street lies ten meters below. Not a safe jump. But not too far from where I stand, another palm tree stands like a ladder, a fair distance from the wall. That's a jump I can make.

INSTEAD OF a large army base like the Old City, west Jerusalem looks like a circus of panic. Long lines of stalled cars trying to go past checkpoints and barricades, shouting and horns blaring, distressed soldiers directing an evacuation for which they were obviously not prepared.

The police and the army pay no attention to the people running by, but still I switch sidewalks whenever I see anyone in uniform approaching. In this evasion game, I must move away from main roads and into the neighborhood streets. Soon I'm so focused on where not to go that I lose track of my path and end up walking without direction. I pause at an intersection and try to orient myself. The old houses and colorful stores look familiar. Of course—I'm not far from Jonathan's house.

Sadness tears at my heart. I brought this on Jonathan, didn't I? And I was so rude at the end with his family, just to defend the caliph, that madman. It's only fair that I offer my apologies and see if they need help evacuating the city. Yes, that's what I'll do. I just hope Taliah doesn't kill me when she sees me.

54

Taliah looks out the window to the frantic crowds fleeing the city. She should be doing the same. She lets the curtain
fall over the window and steps back into the dim light of her
room. It's time to survive. An involuntary snort, a self-pitying
laugh, comes from her mouth. That's what she said two days ago,
when she thought she had grieved long enough and it was time
to move on, even to take revenge—if she could—on Farid. But
then the policeman came.

She thought about this hard and long, concluding that Farid
was in fact protecting Jonathan, that he went after the shooter and
killed him. The thought didn't make her feel better. Things got
worse with the news about the invasion, the explosions and firing without end, each rattle of the windows bringing to mind the
image of the jet falling from the sky and destroying the synagogue.

So she collapsed into oblivion once again, crying for *abba*
and Aunt Esther, for Benjamin and Jonathan, for mother—and
for herself, for she died too, the woman she used to be passed
away with the rest of them.

She pulls a crucifix Benjamin gave her a few months ago from
under her sweatshirt and looks at it. She can't be seen wearing a
Christian symbol, of course, but it's the only token she has from
her brother and she's only now started wearing it. Her eyes flood
with tears.

"Enough!" Her shout echoes in the hallway outside her door.

She wipes her cheeks and walks to the bathroom to wash her
face, then sits on the closed toilet, a towel in her hands. Yes, this

is enough, for if she stays here she will die at the hands of those Islamists—what terrible things she has heard about the invading army, barbarians like no others. The small hope that the Israeli army would repel the invaders was crushed when the soldiers came with the announcement of voluntary evacuations.

How will she escape? Without a car, without money, without a clue how to defend herself. Without her customary toughness, something that seems to have died with her family. But she must, because she is strong and clever. She's a woman of the world, no matter that she's only twenty-three. She can do anything. She'll find a way. A sob chokes her and she covers her mouth with one hand.

"I can do this, I can do this." Taliah repeats the phrase over and over as she lies on her bed, hugging her legs. "Can I do this?"

A loud noise makes her jump out of bed. Someone's knocking at the door.

Taliah bites her knuckles as she approaches the door. She shouldn't be scared. If it were an invader, he wouldn't be knocking. Perhaps the police are going around to check on residents who haven't evacuated yet. She reaches for the knob but doesn't turn it.

"Who's knocking? What do you want?"

She hears someone, a man from the sound of it, clearing his throat.

"It's Farid."

She stiffens. Why has he come back? Can she trust this Muslim? He's one of the enemies, by his own admission. He may not have killed her brother, but that doesn't mean he's well-intentioned. What if—

"Taliah?"

She stares at the dark stained door, picturing the mass of the man on the other side. Some of the hatred and anger she felt toward him a few days ago returns.

"Taliah, I... I just wanted to see how your family is doing and, um, to say how sad I am for what happened to Jonathan, how much I regret my shameful behavior with your father and with you."

These words don't fit the image she has of Farid. Is that really him? She swings the door open. Sure enough, the man at her door resembles Farid, although there's something different about him—the clean-shaven face and the tight white shirt that reveals the contour of his muscles. He's even wearing jeans, looks a lot like men she's gazed upon with interest at her favorite cafe on Ben Yehuda Street. He offers her a shy smile.

"Shalom."

"What do you want?"

"To apologize and see if—"

"You said that, but what is it you really want?"

His face twists in what seems sincere confusion.

"The truth is what I said. I don't blame you for not believing me, since I lied to you before. Please, Taliah, accept my apology."

She purses her lips and narrows her eyes. He sounds convincing. She'll hold judgment until her intuition tells her she can trust him.

"Well, I acknowledge your apologies. Is there something else you want?"

"Yes, I'd like to speak to your father."

Taliah feels a massive weight descend. She shakes her head.

"Is he not home or you won't let me speak to him?"

She shakes her head more vigorously.

"No? Which of the two?"

Her eyes fill with tears.

"Taliah, what's wrong?"

She turns away and runs up the stairs, hating herself for not being able to contain the tears.

WHEN TALIAH comes back down fifteen minutes later, she finds Farid in the living room, leafing through her father's Torah.

"Don't touch that. You don't believe it, so don't profane my father's Bible."

Farid closes the book and sets it down on the coffee table, then looks at her.

"You're alone."

"Do you like to state the obvious?"

He puts a hand up. "No need to be offensive, it's just my indirect way of asking about your family."

"I don't like indirect speech."

Farid blinks and nods, then stares at her, waiting. Although she can't let herself trust him, she dreads to be alone again. His company is an odd comfort.

"They passed away. Every one of them." She looks down at the floor and her voice quivers. "I'm the only survivor of a most improbable accident."

Farid stands and bows his head. "What a tragedy. I'm so sorry, Taliah."

She takes a deep breath and pushes the pain to a corner of her heart, then becomes aware of the awkward silence between them. Seeing this strongly built man in such a sheepish attitude makes her want to snap at him, but there's no strength left in her. If they remain quiet, that would be all right, but she doubts he would stay for the sake of giving her company—and protection, for he could defend her if something happened. How can she ask him to stay without showing her vulnerability? She'll have to sound very neutral.

She attempts a kind, but not too kind, expression and voice. "Do you want some water?"

Farid gives her the faintest of smiles. "Sure, yes. Thank you."

She walks to the refrigerator and pours two glasses of water. As she turns to take them back to the living room, Farid stands at the door of the kitchen. She lets out a soft gasp.

"Is there something I can do for you?" Farid says.

His tone and gaze are honest, aren't they? But why would he want to help her? She knows nothing about this man, except that he used to be a childhood friend of her brother's and that the Israeli police want him for whatever crime he committed. She hands him the glass of water and steps back.

He takes a sip. "Thank you." Now he gulps the rest in less than five seconds. Then comes another silence and she feels that she can't bear this, that he must leave, the sooner, the—

The sound of a siren comes and goes outside the house, and she hears distant shooting. She clutches the glass in her hands like a shield, but a shivering fear invades her. She closes her eyes for a second, then opens them and looks into Farid's.

"Are we safe?"

I could lie to Taliah, comfort her with vague assurances, but to what point or purpose?

"For now," I say, "this part of Jerusalem is safe, but it won't be for long. The Islamic Army is large and—"

"Are you a spy?" Her tone isn't harsh, it's matter-of-fact. "Isn't that your army? Why are you here?"

"That's a very good question. I've deserted my army."

Taliah raises one brow.

"You don't believe me?"

She shrugs. "It doesn't matter."

What's going on in her mind? By Allah, women are confusing! In any case, I did what I came to do. Things are worse than I imagined, but that's the nature of war. I must stick to my plan and get out of Jerusalem.

"Thank you for the water. Again, I'm deeply sorry for your loss." She's clutching her glass so hard she might break it. "I must go now, Taliah."

Her lips quiver and her head tilts up as if she wants to say something. But she freezes, so I walk out of the kitchen—just as the windows rattle with the waves of a distant explosion, almost like a mild earthquake.

"Farid? Wait."

I hear the sound of the glass hitting the counter. She hurries out after me.

"Wai…" The word trails off and she takes a deep breath. The sight of her shakes me to the core. When I met this woman a few days ago, she was as bold and outspoken as anyone I've ever seen. Now, even her voice trembles.

"Where are you going?"

"Away from the city, out of the country. You should evacuate as well, while there's time."

"I don't know where to go."

"Your government must have shelters or refugee camps somewhere. I've seen some buses leaving toward Tel Aviv. Maybe you should try to get on one of those."

I glance at the clock on the wall. A quarter past three. Not many hours of sunlight left. I must hurry, try to make it to the airport.

"Is that where you're going now, to Tel Aviv?"

"No, I'm leaving the country, I have a plane."

Her eyes light up. "An airplane?"

"Yes, and I must go now."

I turn again but she reaches for my arm. An odd thrill shoots through me then passes, leaving only annoyance. I stiffen my arm and she releases it.

"Take me with you, in your plane. I'll pay you."

"I don't need any money, I just need to survive this war."

"Please, Farid, please."

She's actually begging me, incredible. "Take one of the buses, it's safer."

"I've never been on a bus," she says. "Don't you know buses are easy targets?"

"For what?"

"Suicide bombers."

I chuckle. "I doubt a Palestinian group will try that now—"

"I'll take my chances with you." Her voice rises and I see a hint of the old Taliah. "You owe me that much. Do you want me to accept your apologies? Then take me with you."

As WE stride against the crowds, trying to find transport north, I could kick myself for letting Taliah come with me. Sneaking into a truck or borrowing—well, stealing—a vehicle can be complicated enough for one person much less one person and an unpredictable female.

I can see the wall of the old city in the distance, which brings back the madness at the Temple Mount.

I lead Taliah in a direction that won't intersect with Al-Mahdi's half of the city. She trots along without complaining—or talking at all, for that matter. Her eyes flutter and her muscles tense every time we hear shots, but other than that she holds herself together. Is it pride or is she really that brave? A few days ago I'd have known the answer, but after seeing her at the house, I have my doubts.

We're both sweating after more than half an hour of moving about the streets. There aren't as many soldiers in this part of the city, but some looters are roaming around, breaking into shops and even churches. They seem to be Palestinians. They must be plundering while they have the chance, before the caliphate imposes Sharia.

I stop at a corner as three men across the street break the window of a shop with a rock the size of two fists. The glass shatters and an alarm goes off. Taliah stands behind me and looks around my right arm. She doesn't touch me, but I can feel her breath on my skin, smell the clean aroma of hers, some sort of natural soap.

"Are we going to walk all the way?" she says.

"Those men won't mind us, don't worry." The men are hauling stuff out of the store now.

"If they get away with that, can't we get away with using an abandoned car?"

I'm surprised by her suggestion but try not to show it. "I doubt someone will leave a car behind when they need it to evacuate."

"What about that one?" She points down to the end of the street to her right, at a yellow Volkswagen camping van.

We run toward the van. She arrives first and tries to open the driver's door. Locked. She's reckless, not checking to see if the owner is around. I scan the sidewalk and the dwellings near the vehicle. Everything seems deserted.

When I turn back to her, Taliah is already getting in the van through the sliding door on one side.

"Let's go." She gets behind the wheel, grinning like an excited little kid, then her grin turns into a frown.

"Do you know how to start a car without a key?"

"What kind of person do you think I am?"

"Do I have to answer that?"

I should be sorry the old Taliah is back, but I'm not. I gesture for her to move over. I'm an engineer by profession, so I should be able to figure this out, right? I take the driver's seat and stick my head beneath the steering wheel, holding my breath as I search for cables in the dark. I saw one of my university classmates do this once, but that was a long time ago.

Unable to see, I'm feeling around—I don't want to make a fool of myself in front of Taliah—when I hear the engine come to life. How in Allah's name?

Simple. The keys are in the ignition. And Taliah is smiling at me—the first time ever.

"I found them in the glove compartment."

I don't know what to say, so I just mutter, "Good," and shift into first gear.

56

Taliah screams when the van skids, avoiding a truck coming their way.

"We almost crashed!"

Farid ignores her—how dare he?—and struggles to control the vehicle. What a lousy driver. He grinds his teeth, and she can see his white shirt is drenched in sweat. Repulsive. And she thought she'd be safe with him.

Farid stops the van and hits the steering wheel with his fists.

"No wonder they abandoned this piece of rubbish."

He doesn't look at her, which infuriates her even more. The ease of their escape has given her new confidence. She's the one who saw the vehicle and found the keys. What has he done so far to protect her? He's been running around the city, clueless. She wonders if he even has a plane. If he can't drive a car, how could he fly an aircraft?

Farid gets out of the van and slams the door. He crouches out of her sight, probably looking at the front tire. The engine is still running and she feels her skin prickle. She could drive away and leave him behind. After all, she can't be sure he's trustworthy. She begged him to take her along in a moment of weakness. She knows better, she has never needed men to make her way in life—well, she's needed her brothers and her father, but they're family. She unfastens her seatbelt, then hesitates when Farid stands up. She holds her breath. He walks to the rear of the van.

Taliah slides over to the driver's seat and checks the side mirror. Farid crouches to inspect the tire and frowns. This is her chance. She steps on the clutch and shifts gears. There's a harsh scraping sound. She sees Farid standing. Her foot presses the gas pedal—too hard. The van screeches and jerks forward, throwing her body along with it. She lets out a cry. The road takes a sudden, sharp turn, and she veers hard to the right. The van doesn't respond—the wheel seems to resist her turning and pulls back to the left. There's something very wrong with the steering.

This is why Farid stopped in the middle of the road. She presses the brake as the van jumps onto the sidewalk, headed straight toward a street lamp.

Taliah heaves and shakes, tears filling her eyes. What has she done?

The door swings open and Farid puts a hand on her shoulder. "Taliah, are you hurt?"

She shakes her head. The engine stopped once she released the clutch, but she fears the van will move forward and hit the lamp post, just a few centimeters away. A sob sticks in her throat like a needle. She lets her hair cover her face and looks down as she staggers out of the van. Farid moves to one side, and she sits on the sidewalk, head between her knees. How childish she has been, how irrational. She feels her cheeks burn. The tears that flow are tears of anger.

She looks down and sees Farid's boots. He stands there for a while.

"Are you sure you're not hurt?" he says finally.

"I'm fine."

"Good. We can't stay here, so let's go."

She wipes her face, throws her hair back with one hand, then looks up at him, squinting a little. The fact that he doesn't scold her only makes her feel worse. If he were angry she could hide her embarrassment in retaliation. But his face, though stern, shows no vexation.

"If we continue north on Route 60 for five or six kilometers, we'll reach the airport."

She nods at the van. "Do you intend to drive that?"

"No. The tires not only have low pressure, they're unaligned and really worn. It wouldn't surprise me if the rods and the steering rack are rusted, too. It's too hard to maneuver. We'll be better off walking or finding a new vehicle."

Walking six kilometers with war at their heels? He's out of his mind, but she bites her tongue. After that scare a few minutes ago, she wouldn't want to get in the van again.

Farid starts walking west, presumably toward Route 60.

"You better move, Taliah."

She sighs and follows him.

57

After busying himself in pointless tasks and avoiding the caliph for two hours,, Hussai returns to the temple. Judging by the somber eyes of Al-Mahdi's guards, the worst has passed.

All that remains of the condemned priests in the courtyard is a pool of their blood. The air smells of death. Someone must have executed them, and someone must yet be punished for Farid's escape. Hussai shudders just thinking about the caliph's anger.

In the center of the temple, that which the Jews call the Holy of Holies, Hussai finds Al-Mahdi seated on a throne-like chair. From a safe distance his mood appears to be calm, and he nods with eyes closed at a man in a white robe beside him.

Hussai can only see the man's back, but there's something familiar about him. He waits for a moment, afraid to interrupt, his mind rehearsing again the story he's concocted to explain Farid's escape. The caliph opens his eyes.

"There's my general." He beckons to Hussai, who keeps his eyes on the man in the robe, on his long hair. As he draws closer Hussai recognizes him. It's the eccentric stranger from the caliph's plane. Just like last time, he's materialized as if from thin air, piercing everything with his hollow black eyes.

Hussai stops a few paces from the throne and bows.

"Yes, my lord?"

"It seems Farid is against me after all."

"Yes, my lord, I—"

"Is this man loyal to us?" The stranger points at Hussai, his deep voice sending a shiver down Hussai's spine.

Al-Mahdi leans his head backwards and smiles. "So far, he has been."

The stranger pulls his finger back. "I must see it."

"Hussai," Al-Mahdi says. "Show me your allegiance."

"My lord?"

"Kneel and tell me you love me."

Hussai nods and looks down. He feels awkward, uncomfortable. He fights to find the right words, but his skull itches just imagining the stranger's eyes drilling through him.

"I pledge my allegiance to you, my lord Al-Mahdi, I offer my love to you."

The stranger gives a shrill laugh. "That is pathetic."

Hussai looks up, eyes wide.

"Repeat after me." The stranger's condescending tone unnerves Hussai. "I worship you…"

Does he have to endure this? The caliph nods. Hussai clears his throat.

"I worship you…"

The stranger says, "I worship you, Lord of the Age, the Awaited One."

"I worship you, Lord of the Age, the Awaited One."

"Praise belongs to Al-Mahdi, Lord of the World, the Merciful, the Compassionate, Master of the Day of Judgment." Hussai gasps. This man is reciting the Qur'an, inserting the name of the caliph in place of the name of god. Is this right? He looks at Al-Mahdi, sitting on a black and golden throne, and a sense of awe overwhelms him, a thrill of ecstasy that blurs his thoughts and fogs his surroundings. Yes, it is right. The caliph is worthy of this praise. He can't look at Al-Mahdi and fail to see his divinity.

Hussai repeats the stranger's verses, each word like a nail sealing his fate to the will of Al-Mahdi. The stranger laughs.

"I see it now, he can be trusted."

"Excellent, excellent." Al-Mahdi leans forward. "I wish you to do something for me, Hussai."

"Anything, my lord."

"Bring my statue to Jerusalem, the one in Baghdad, and place it here in the temple."

"I will, my lord."

The stranger offers Hussai a rolled newspaper. "The Jews are fleeing to Jordan. Bring them back."

Al-Mahdi nods. "Better yet, slay them."

58

Night falls as we approach the airport. "What's going on here?" Taliah says.

There is indeed an eerie atmosphere at the terminal. A crowd of about forty people tries to enter, but three policemen block the doors and motion them away.

"They've closed the airport for some reason."

"I'll find out," she says.

"Wait—"

But she already hurrying to the terminal's entrance, where she taps the shoulder of a dark man with curly hair. I hear their conversation as I catch up with her.

"They won't let us in." The man has an Indian accent. "I want to use my plane and leave, but they're not giving reasons for the closure."

"Where will you go?" Taliah asks.

"I heard the king of Jordan has opened the borders for Jews who want asylum. I'm going to Amman. A friend lives there."

"Why would the Jordanian king do that?" Taliah says. "He's an ally of the Islamic caliphate."

The Indian shrugs. "He changed his mind, I guess."

"Could it be a trap?"

I say, "That's a possibility—"

"I'll take my chances," the Indian says, "but I don't want to remain in Israel."

"But if you have a plane," Taliah says, "you could go any-where. Why not a safer place?"

He shakes his head. "The Islamists control all the countries around Israel, and my little plane won't take me too far in one leg."

Taliah purses her lips and looks over the heads of the crowd at the sealed doors. I turn to the man.

"How long have you been waiting?"

"Three, maybe four hours."

This is useless. Of course the army will want control of the air space and every plane they can get their hands on. I must get to my plane before they do—if they haven't already. The risk afterwards, will be to get shot down while on the air. I place a hand on Taliah's elbow.

"Let's find another way in."

She looks at my hand on her arm and then at my face, but in the shadows of the night I can't read her expression. I pull my hand away and realize this is the first time I've touched her.

"We can go around the building and climb the fence toward the runway. I think I can find my way to the hangar where my plane is parked."

We follow the outer gray wall of the terminal until we reach the fence, parallel to the runway and about three meters high. I look at Taliah.

"Can you climb it?"

She neither looks at me nor speaks but charges toward the fence and makes her way up in three quick movements. She swings her legs over the top and drops to the other side, stumbling in the dirt.

"Are you all right?"

She grunts and gets up, wiping off the dust. Her eyes dare me to move, as if she's been waiting for ages and her patience is exhausted. I climb over calmly and descend on the other side with my feet on the ground. The hangar where I left my plane isn't far, just a few hundred meters from the terminal. I lead the way again, keeping close to the buildings and the shadows.

Half a dozen trucks move around the runway toward the exit.

"Why don't they drive on the pavement?" Taliah says.

"What?"

"The trucks are on the grass."

It's true, and odd. I step out to take a closer look. Large craters and cracks spread over the runway. No truck, and no airplane for that matter, can use the runway in such a state. This is bad news.

Taliah draws closer to me and gapes at the craters. "What in the world?"

I sigh. "They bombed the runway."

"Who did? The invaders?"

"I don't think so. They'd have used a neutron bomb, something to keep the structure intact. No, I think the Israelis did this themselves."

"Why? It makes no sense." I walk back to the cover of darkness. "Farid, what now? How are we going to get out of here?"

"I must find my plane."

FROM THE outside, I can see lights in the hangar.

"There's people in there, probably soldiers," I say. "So wait for me here."

"Are you mad? I'm not staying here by myself."

"Listen, Taliah. If you want to come with me, you'll have to do what I say." This gets me a hateful look. "Besides, if you're caught here by yourself, you can just pretend you're lost and they'll let you go. If they catch you with me you'll have a harder time getting off the hook. So you have to wait for me here until I see if the coast is clear, all right?"

She nods, glaring at me, and I leave her by the pay phone booth between two hangars.

Muffled voices grow louder as I approach the hangar. The door has a dirty glass panel through which I can see two soldiers standing by the extended ladder of my Pilatus. The lights inside the cabin seem to be turned on, but it's hard to tell from here.

Why didn't they move it out before destroying the runway? It looks as if they just discovered it. A third man shoves his head out from the plane and says something to the two soldiers, who nod and follow him inside. Oh, no. Nobody's going to mess with my Pilatus. I push the door open, scan the hangar, then run toward the back of the plane.

The rear hatch clanks when I release the lock, and I cringe. I wait a few seconds, then open it and crawl inside the kitchenette. As I close the hatch, I hear the door of the hangar open. Past the curtain in front of me is the passenger cabin, where I keep my survival equipment. I move the curtain slightly and peer through. One of the soldiers is standing at the door to the cockpit, his back to me. The other two men must be inside. I grab the sharpest knife among the kitchen utensils and charge with a stealth move.

The Israeli doesn't notice me until it's too late. I press the knife against his throat.

"Release your weapon."

He complies but makes so much noise his comrades look back from the seats and jump to their feet. I snatch the soldier's rifle and point it at them.

"Hands up."

"Farid?"

I crank my neck back to the main cabin at the sound of Taliah's voice. What's she doing here?

"What's hap—"

A rough embrace pushes me against the floor and I land on my back. Taliah screams, the Israelis shout orders, and the soldier over me tries to punch me in the face. I block his fist with my left arm, then stab him in the shoulder. He jerks and I push him aside. The other two stare at Taliah. I jump to my feet and notice the other soldier doesn't have his rifle. He must have put it down when he sat in the copilot's seat. I motion with the rifle toward the door.

"Out, get out of the plane." What I'm going to do once they

get off, I don't know. I must secure them somehow. "Taliah, calm down."

The two guys in the cockpit hurry out the door and Taliah after them. Where's she going?

I stumble forward as pain pierces my leg. Blood stains my jeans where the soldier pricked me with the same knife I used against him. He's soon on top of me and we roll down the ladder to the hangar's floor.

59

Taliah rushes down the stairs of the plane, sure her heart will burst from her chest. She should have stayed outside, but Farid said he would just check and come back. When he went inside the hangar, she thought everything was clear.

One of the two men in front of her nods at his friend while patting something in his waist. Beneath the man's shirt, Taliah can see the butt of a gun. Her fingertips tingle. They're going to kill her.

She can't fight them, not without a weapon, and they'll shoot Farid as soon as they get a chance. The men split up, one walking off to the right, the other to the left. Her eyes follow the man with the gun, who went to the right. She should stay away from him—

She spins around, startled. A series of grunts and thumps erupt from the plane and Farid and the third Israeli soldier roll down the short flight of steps, struggling. Farid kicks the soldier on the shoulder and he falls on his back, moaning. When Farid scrambles to his feet, wincing, Taliah notices blood on his leg. The other two move toward him, and she knows he's doomed.

If they get you with me, you'll have a harder time getting off the hook. She pictures herself in a prison, being tortured for information she can't even fathom. The newspapers would show her photo with a caption saying she's a spy or worse. Her chest feels heavy with fear and she finds it hard to breathe. She puts her face between her hands, seeking the strength that has always resided within her. She must do something, anything.

A fist hits Farid's abdomen. He bends forward and takes a

blow to the back of his head. He falls to the floor, then looks her way. The movement of his lips is clear enough. He's telling her to run while a boot smashes into his side.

He cares about her. Another kick, and this time she hears his desperate voice.

"Run!"

Maybe against her will, maybe just by instinct, she begins to walk backward. His eyes leave her and a deep sorrow washes over her. Why does she care so much about him all of a sudden? She turns to the exit and runs. Something rips inside of her.

TALIAH RACES from the hangar without considering her direction. After a hundred meters she sees the terminal building and a group of about twenty soldiers barricading the entrance. What now? She can't go that way.

To her left a low brick building rises, in sharp contrast to the high hangars. The building is dark, which probably means no one's there. She hurries to the site and finds the entrance, like an oversized garage door, open. She steps into the darkness. Once her eyes begin to adjust, in the gloom she can discern the form of a big truck. The wheels are almost as tall as she is. A passing headlight shines over the truck for a moment. She looks out toward the runway and sees a truck heading for the terminal. But the two seconds of light gave her a glimpse of the bright green fire truck. So this is the airport's fire department.

She feels her way to the front and searches for the door handle. When she opens the door, the interior light comes on. The steering wheel is huge, and on one side two joysticks emerge from a black panel with buttons and lights at the bottom. There's something familiar about the panel. Then she remembers—she once saw a television documentary of a fire in Germany where the firefighters used this type of truck, which shoots water from hoses on the roof.

The light makes her feel exposed, so she slams the door closed and leans back in the driver's seat. She can try and find an exit on the opposite side of the building, one that would take her outside the airport. And then what? Walk all the way to Jordan? If she just could go home—but she has no home, only a house submerged in melancholy.

No, she must get out of the country, and the only safe place seems to be Jordan. All she needs is a vehicle. A vehicle like this truck? That's crazy, she can't drive this thing—or can she? Even if she tries, it would be so obvious the truck is stolen that the army would stop her in no time. Nothing could be more conspicuous than a fire truck speeding through the desert.

She sighs and closes her eyes, then sees the image of the beaten Farid crying out for her to run. Is he dead? Maybe they won't kill him, but he'll end up a prisoner of war. It hasn't been more than ten minutes since she left him, maybe only five. Everything is happening so fast.

An irrational desire to rescue Farid pushes its way into her brain. She laughs at herself but the laughter dies in her chest.

If she were in her right senses she'd run for her life and let the Muslim fend for himself. This is suicidal. So why is she turning on the ignition button?

THE FIRE truck roars as Taliah steps on the gas pedal, hisses when she hits the brake. "Whoa!"

This is a powerful machine. She accelerates again with more caution, and the truck slides forward. If she weren't heading into harm's way, she would actually enjoy this.

The hangar where Farid's plane is parked looms, twenty meters away. There's no movement around it. She has no weapon, her only advantage is this truck. What if she crashed into the hangar? That would take them by surprise, and in the confusion, Farid could escape.

She stops the truck and fastens her seat belt. The truck has no nose, its front just a windshield, headlights, and bumper. If the windshield breaks, she's dead. Who is she fooling? She can't do this.

The door of the hangar opens and Farid steps out. How is this possible? Did he overpower them?

Someone else comes out, a soldier with a gun, and pushes Farid forward. Farid turns his face toward the truck and puts a hand up, deflecting the light from the headlamps. He'll never know it's her. Perhaps she should turn them off.

The soldier also shields his eyes, as do two others that come out after him. They're all focused on her—no, not on her, on the truck—standing there like easy targets. But even if she had a gun, she wouldn't kill them.

She just needs to knock them down.

She turns to the panel on her right and clicks the power switch for the hose system, then grabs the joystick and presses her thumb against the red button. A torrent of water sprays from the top of the truck and jets over the stunned men. Taliah pulls the joystick forward and shoots again, aiming for the armed soldier. The water hits him in the chest and he falls backward.

She giggles and drenches the other two. Farid looks startled for an instant, then bends over and takes the soldier's rifle. Still, he stays there, eyeing the truck .

Taliah laughs, rolls down her window and calls out.

"Farid, come on!"

He sprints toward her, climbing into the passenger seat. Blood covers most of his face and one of his eyes is swollen.

"Well done."

"You're welcome." She points toward the soldiers scrambling up and nods to the joystick. "You wash them, I'll drive."

60

My instincts tell me it would be better to shoot them, but the look on Taliah's face draws me into her game. She has never looked at me like that before—without hostility or fear. She might be afraid, but not of me, not anymore.

I release the rifle and for the moment pretend I'm a firefighter. It does the trick, for the Israelis succumb to the liquid power. The fire truck darts forward and around them. I must grab the roof and the seat to avoid hitting the window with my head.

"Do you know where you're going?"

Taliah shakes her head. "Not a clue."

"There must be an exit somewhere. Keep going straight."

She makes a sharp right turn and I bump my head.

"What are you doing, Ta—"

She winces with her whole body, keeping one eye open. The fence snaps with a clank and thumps against the windshield before flying away. The truck shakes and rattles but soon we roll onto pavement and she gains control with another sharp turn.

I finally breathe after a long moment and blink twice. The oversized mirror outside my window shows the airport fading away, no cars chasing us. Then I stare at her slender little body commanding the ridiculously large steering wheel. Unbelievable.

"I'm impressed." Taliah smiles but keeps her eyes on the road. "Are you all right driving? I can take over."

She glances at me. "You're hurt. I'm not."

"Hurt? Bah, this is nothing."

Even as I speak, my brain shuts off my adrenaline, and a

dozen body parts scream in pain—my cut leg, my tender ribs, my swollen eye, my split lip.

Weakness and malaise settle over me. I lean back on the seat, close my eyes. The pain grows worse as I concentrate on it.

"Surely there's a first-aid kit in here somewhere," Taliah says.

I find it in a compartment right below the joystick panel. I pull the jean up on my left leg and clean the knife wound, then press the skin together, tape it and cover it with gauze. I'll need stitches soon—and some antibiotics. I spend the next ten minutes tending to my other injuries and cursing the men who beat me and made me abandon my plane.

Now we have to leave the country by land. Trying to cross into Jordan means heading east, toward Jericho, which will take us too close to the Islamic army. In fact, they must be all over this area by now. I can't believe Jordan has opened its borders to the Jews. And even if they did, why would Al-Mahdi's army let anyone through?

In an outer pocket of the medical kit, there's an old map of Israel. I take it out and unfold it. The two main crossing borders with Jordan wouldn't be open at night, and no Jew dares travel the King Hussein Bridge. No, we take a different route. I pass my finger over the blue line in the map that represents the Jordan River, long since dried up. In theory we could leave the main road a while, to avoid any kind of border security, then—

"Oh, no. Farid, what do we do?"

A line of about a hundred cars waits in turn at a checkpoint. Taliah, her face pale, pulls over fifty meters or so from them.

"We can't stay in this truck, they'll never let us through." She sighs. "This country is obsessed with checkpoints. Even during an evacuation!""

"I doubt the Israeli army would set up a checkpoint here. Judging from our position and the direction we're heading in, it can only be a Palestinian checkpoint."

"Palestinian? How do you know all this?"

I shrug. "Isn't it obvious? They had all but lost the West Bank after the nuclear war—now they're reclaiming it. And that's how they show their authority, restricting the entrance."

"So there's no way they'll let us through."

More vehicles come to the stalled line. They're definitely not moving. I must come up with a plan.

"Don't go anywhere yet." I open the door and get out of the truck.

The night is cold, but the air seems to wake me from my pain-induced lethargy. The westbound road is almost deserted, with only sporadic traffic. Maybe we could go that way without being hit by an incoming car. Or a bullet?

The big green truck makes me smile. A comic plan forms in my head. What if we fool them into thinking we're firefighters responding to an emergency? Would they attack a fire truck? It's worth trying.

Right by the passenger door, there's a compartment with a black sliding door. My hunch—and hope—is right and I find a few helmets inside. I grab two and walk over to Taliah's side.

"Put this one on and let me drive."

"What are we going to do?"

"You'll see."

She scoots over to the passenger seat and I take a few seconds to inspect the controls.

"Do you know how to turn the siren on?"

"I think it's that switch over there." She points to a red switch. "Why?"

"Perfect. Fasten your seat belt."

"Do you really expect them to move aside?"

I step on the gas and make a sharp turn. She lets out a cry, but the truck climbs with ease over the flowerbed separating the roads. A car speeds by in the far lane. In the name of Allah I pray this works.

With the siren blaring, I drive forth against the traffic, against sanity.

THE CHECKPOINT on the opposite road passes by my window and I sigh with relief.

"We did it."

Taliah points forward. "No, we didn't."

A westbound checkpoint for cars coming into Jerusalem from the East lies ahead. The siren must have attracted their attention, for a spotlight focuses on us. A series of warning shots blasts from the checkpoint.

"This was a bad idea, Farid, a really bad idea."

I head left, over the flowers, back onto the eastbound lane. I hear more shots.

"Get down." I duck and pull Taliah against the seat. The bullets rip through metal somewhere in the truck but not near us.

"Turn that siren off, turn it off, we're going to die!"

I push the truck to go faster and feel it fishtail. No cars before me. The sound of bullets ceases but Taliah is still screaming.

"Calm down, please. There, I turned it off."

She covers her face with her hands and sobs. I want to comfort her, but two pairs of headlights shine on my rearview mirror. The lights catch up fast, the bullets even faster.

61

Taliah covers her ears and shuts her eyes, but the fear doesn't recede. Why are they shooting? Why don't they leave them alone?

"Taliah, hey, Taliah." Farid shakes her shoulder and she buries her face deeper into the seat. Why would she look up if it doesn't sound safe yet? The truck rattles as if hit by something. Taliah's body jerks from side to side and hits the door. She's going to die, she's going to die!

Farid keeps calling, his voice now harsher.

"Taliah, get up. Now." He darts a look outside his window. "Get the rifle and shoot them."

"What?"

The truck rocks violently as Farid cuts in front of the car that's chasing them. He must be trying to prevent them from pulling alongside and shooting. She shudders.

"They're coming your way. Use the rifle now."

"I don't know how."

"Weren't you in the military? All Israelis—"

"*Abba* had connections. He got me a religious exception."

"Too bad, the army would have done you good."

"What is that supposed to mea—"

This time the collision sends her back against the seat, then forward. She bumps her head against the windshield.

"Stop doing that!"

Farid steps on the brake and the truck skids as one of the Palestinian cars cuts in front of them. Taliah stretches her arms

266   NICK DANIELS

to avoid hitting the windshield and her elbow presses against the water canon joystick. She may not know how to use a rifle, but she can shoot water.

A man in front of them sticks his torso out the window and points his gun at Farid. Taliah releases the water and the man is knocked out of the window. She squeaks with fear as he rolls on the pavement. Farid barely avoids running over him.

"Good job, keep doing that."

The fire truck revs up and bumps into the rear of the Palestinian car. She showers the car, which maneuvers out of the way, but Farid moves closer.

"Into the car, now."

Water floods the driver's open window and he loses control, crashing against the trees by the side of the road.

"I did it!"

A series of bullets break her window and zoom past her ear. She screams and ducks down.

"Water them, Taliah, quick."

She can do this. She lifts her head, her body still crouched, and locates the car. She presses the button on the joystick but only sees Palestinian gun barrels staring at them.

"We're out of water."

Farid accelerates and cuts the path of the chasers. "Grab the wheel."

He grabs her left arm and clamps her hand on the steering wheel, then reaches for the rifle between the seats. Taliah feels the truck trembling under the control of her fingers, the weight of the situation sucking the air out of her. She clenches her teeth and tightens her grip. If she had a hard time keeping the truck on the road while using both hands, this is going to be impossible.

Farid's torso pushes against her arm, the muscle stretches, then tingles like a cramp.

"Keep the truck straight. I see them now. Keep your head down."

She dips her head and the deafening clank of the rifle pierces her ear as Farid shoots not ten centimeters from her face. Her ears ring and she loses balance, releasing the wheel. The truck is hit.

"Don't let go!"

Taliah pulls her body back and falls beneath the dashboard. Farid tries to regain control of the truck, but she knows he won't make it, there's no way, they were going too fast. She should have held the wheel. All that physical training, and she's not strong enough. Her chest aches as she realizes this is the second time today that her driving has placed them in danger.

She buries her head between her legs and braces for the impact.

A loud screech. Momentum throws her body forward.

She opens her eyes just in time to see a light invade the interior of the truck, then it's gone. The world spins and she rolls with it. Farid shouts words she can't understand. Something hits her face. Glass shatters. Everything fades to black.

THE SOUNDS reach Taliah as if they're coming through a tunnel—faint and unintelligible, then louder, somewhat coherent. She opens her eyes to a blurry scene, one where she's being dragged out of an overturned fire truck.

"Come on, Taliah, I must get you to a safe place."

Her vision clears and she's aware of everything: of Farid lifting her with one arm around her waist, of the chilly night and the smell of something burning, of the danger that looms ahead. He places her on the ground, her back against one of the trees planted by the side of the road. He kneels and puts a hand on her shoulder.

"There's some blood on your face. Are you all right?"

"I think so."

She takes a hand to her cheek and retrieves a damp finger. She can't really see the color of the smear, but it does feel like blood.

"It's only a minor cut." He points to the tree. "Hide here for a moment."

She watches him run down the slope and cross over to the fire truck, which is resting on its side a few meters away. Prickling coldness creeps over her skin. Her shoulder is sore.

How did they survive? And how did he get her out of the truck? She thinks about the honest concern in his eyes—even his swollen eye—and his ridiculous strength. She shakes her head. She won't allow herself any feelings for this man. But she can't keep her eyes off him.

Using the truck as a shield, Farid crouches at one end, weapon ready, and scans the area. He pulls back. Headlights from a car on the road turn the truck into a silhouette. The car stops and a few shadowy figures step out.

Taliah can tell they're armed. She scrambles behind the tree.

The men get closer to the truck, two of them walking toward the front, where Farid lies waiting. The other disappears around the back. Farid moves swiftly, firing his rifle. The two oncoming men drop. Then he charges forward, flooding the car with bullets.

Her whole body shakes. For heaven's sake, who is this man? He just killed them in cold blood. No regrets, no hesitation. He might be protecting her, defending himself, but such ability to kill is outrageous. He's a savage.

Farid walks toward the vehicle and disappears behind the bright headlamps. He must be there somewhere, checking for survivors, but all she can see is two yellow circles and the outline of the truck. Then a man steps up from behind the truck. Taliah gasps.

The other shooter.

62

The car is empty.
The driver lies dead on the pavement beneath the open door he used as cover. There are three, maybe more, bloody bullet holes in his disfigured face. I'm killing my Palestinian brothers to protect a Jew. I don't want to think this, but it's how I've been trained.

The vehicle is an old Toyota pickup, its paint fading and the body rusting. I shut down the engine and remove the key. The brightness of the headlights dies. I hear Taliah's voice calling my name.

A shadow moves in front of the car, and I duck. A bullet shatters the windshield, but it holds. I wait with my weapon ready, my back flat against the seats. Which side will he choose? "Farid!"

That's Taliah, and she sounds close. Foolish girl, she'll be killed.

I kick the door open and scoot out onto the pavement, rolling, seeking my target.

"Farid, watch out!"

She's running down the slope, calling to the darkness. The shooter stands between her and me. He turns to her, lifts his gun, and takes aim.

I pull the trigger. Both the shooter and Taliah drop to the ground.

I RUN past the body of the Palestinian, not bothering to check if he's dead or alive.

I should have checked the perimeter for more shooters before inspecting the car.

Taliah lies face down on the grass at the bottom of the slope. Bile rises to my mouth and I groan as I crouch beside her. Her back rises and falls—she's breathing.

"Taliah?"

She lifts up her head and gasps. "Ah, it's you, I was so afraid it was the other man."

"Are you hurt?"

She shakes her head and sits on her knees. "I heard gunshots and dove to the ground. Isn't that what you're supposed to do?"

I feel like laughing but just smile. "I'm so glad you're not hurt."

"Did you kill him?"

"I did."

Her face turns somber and she looks away. Awkwardness fills the space between us.

"This place isn't safe." I stand and offer her a hand. "Let's go."

She looks at my extended hand but stands without taking it. "You're right, Farid, let's go."

I WISH I could ignore her and concentrate on driving this old pickup. It runs smoothly, but the wind and sand slap my face without mercy through the shattered windshield. Taliah sleeps on the back seat and all I can think of is her. When she's nice, the vivacity in her eyes reminds me of Zainah. I care for her, yet she torments me. By Allah, I abhor this feeling with all my being.

Jericho shouldn't be more than forty kilometers away. There we can get some supplies for the rest of the trip. Lights flash in the distance—probably another checkpoint. I make a U-turn and search for a side road I passed two or three kilometers ago. I find it and head north, hoping it will eventually turn east toward Jericho. The road is dark and monotonous. I blink and try to will the exhaustion away. My mouth is dry, my eyelids heavy.

I must focus on something or I'll fall asleep. My mind drifts to the back seat. What does Taliah think of me? Does she see me as an interesting man?

Maybe if I analyze our differences, I can talk my mind out of this foolish obsession. For one, she's not a believer, for another she's too young—just look at her smooth skin. I remember our first encounter, with her wrapped only in a towel....

I glance at the dashboard to check the gas. The needle points to the center, half a tank, just like an hour ago. I slap the dashboard with my palm. The thing is broken. We may be running out of gas at any moment—who knows how far the next town is. I must fill up the tank before entering the Jordanian desert.

Perhaps I'm mistaken. I keep glancing at the needle but fifteen minutes later it still hasn't budged. I groan, and as if in response to my frustration, the engine coughs.

"Not now."

Taliah stirs in the back of the cab as the pickup rolls to a stop.

"What is it?" she says.

I get out of the car and look in the bed of the truck, hoping the late owners carried extra gasoline. No such luck. Taliah comes out after me.

"Why did we stop?"

"We have no gas."

She opens her arms, palms up. "What? We're stuck here—in the middle of nowhere?"

"For the moment, we are."

"You didn't check the gas before we left?"

I examine the tank's cap and find the culprit—I probably made that bullet hole when I shot at the pickup.

"This is an inconvenience."

"An inconvenience? You're unbelievable, Farid—"

I wave my hand at her. "Shush."

She puts both hands on her waist. "How dare—"

"Listen."

I point to my ear and close my eyes, breathing in the familiar sound in the air. I kneel and place a hand on the ground, then nod.

"A tank."

"Where?" she says.

"Coming our way, with more vehicles. We must hide." I grab Taliah's arm and pull her into the open. "Let's get away from the car."

We run to a spot fifty meters from the road and crouch behind some rocks and plants. We can't be far from Jericho—the green in this plain is like an oasis in the desert. From here I have a fair view of the approaching battalion. Taliah's rapid breathing distracts me from the road and I glance at her shadow in the dark. I can sense her trembling.

"Are you cold?"

She waits a few seconds before answering. "I'll be fine, what's your plan?"

"We'll wait for them to pass, then go back to the car and spend the night there. In the morning we'll walk to the nearest town."

"Couldn't they help us?"

"I doubt they're Israelis. If they're part of the caliphate's army, things would go very badly for you."

"Stop being a jerk."

There she goes again.

The heavy rhythm of the army raises the hair on my arms. That's the kind of life I'm used to, all I've known for the past twenty years. The lights from the vehicles form a white circle around the battalion, like a spotlight over a performer, and I see the insignias on the tank and the trucks. An Iraqi regiment. Something stirs inside of me, an urge to join my former comrades.

"Where are you going?" Taliah says.

I blink and realize my body moved forward with my thoughts. I can't go back to Al-Mahdi's army. I had my chance and I turned it down.

I wave a hand at Taliah. "I just want to see."

The regiment passes by our car, then stops. One of the vehicles reverses and parks in front of the pickup, shining lights on it.

I retreat behind the rocks just as two soldiers jump off the truck and inspect our car. They talk to each other, then one of them speaks into his radio. He must be talking to his lieutenant or a captain. What are they planning to do? If I were in their position, I wouldn't give a second thought to an abandoned car far from the city. But they seem to be making a big deal about this one.

The soldier puts the radio down and says something to his partner. He nods, takes a hand to his belt, then both walk backward. A wind colder than the desert air fills my chest as I realize what's about to happen. From his belt the soldier unclips a grenade, one of the new kind with a timer, and throws it into the front of the pickup before running to the truck.

"What are they doing, Farid?"

"Ruining our night."

63

The explosion of the car is muffled by a larger blast, many kilometers away. A column of fire rises in the south as a series of missiles light the sky.

Taliah grabs my arm. "What was that?"

The soldiers look mesmerized. They didn't expect this.

"Get down, hide behind the rocks." The engines of the convoy roar and they drive away.

"Farid, what's going on?"

"That's Jericho, an air raid."

I can feel her body tremble. "Oh, no, no. God, how can this be? Not again…" She sobs and I put an arm around her shoulder.

"Stay calm, it's all right, we're far from the city. We're safe." A light breeze rustles my face. The wind is blowing south, southwest maybe. "We have to move north, away from the missiles."

What a frustrating night. I had put my hope on walking to Jericho, but that's out of the question now.

"Come on, we have to get as far as we can from this place."

I pick up a few dry sticks and branches from the ground and start off into the gloom of the Jordan Valley, Taliah at my side.

I GLANCE at the stars to make sure we're still walking north. It's been forty-five minutes, maybe more, since we left the road. I'm sure we'll find a village soon, for there are plenty on this side of the border. I can sense Taliah is growing weary.

The starry night gives me just a faint glimpse of my companion—she walks with her arms around her chest, hugging herself, face down. She must be cold. When we come to the bottom of a low cliff I look up and around, but there's not much to see in the darkness.

"I'll make a fire now."

Her head lifts and I imagine a smile, though I can't be sure. She all but collapses against the rock wall and sits there, her forehead touching her knees. Her silence is a mixed blessing. I'm grateful she's no longer lashing out, but if something is wrong and she doesn't tell me, how will I help her? What if she's hurt or feeling sick? I need to know if she has any symptoms of hypothermia.

"The sweat of my hands damped the sticks a little," I say, just to break the silence. "But they'll work fine."

Once the flames start burning, she lifts up her head. She comes closer and reaches toward the fire.

"I wish I had some food to offer you. I think I can find a cactus, maybe some sabra fruit."

She rolls her eyes. "Good luck with that."

A sour taste fills my mouth. "Why do you keep treating me with contempt?"

She shakes her head.

"You asked to come with me, and I've kept you by my side although you've put my life at risk. You could at least show some gratitude."

"Sure, yes, thank you for everything."

Her snide tone makes my blood boil. By Allah, if she were a man, I'd...

"You're so arrogant you don't even realize how ridiculous your attitude is." She sends one of her lethal looks my way. "You're looking at me right now like you hate me. Why, Taliah?"

"Because this...this is all your fault—you killed my family, and your stupidity brought us here instead of taking us out of the country like you promised. You expect me to thank you?"

"I didn't kill your family!"

"What did Jonathan do to you?"

"What makes you think I shot Jonathan?"

"You may not have pulled the trigger, but you got him killed. Why?"

I have to sit down, have to get through to her.

"It was an accident, Taliah. That bullet was intended for me." I'm not entirely sure this is true, for Ibrahim could as well have been planning to kill us both, but it's what I want to believe. "Without knowing it, he sacrificed himself for me."

Tears stream down her cheeks and she wipes them with a quick, angry swipe of her fist.

"I don't believe you."

I swallow hard and feel the last of my anger drain away. I think I understand.

"Jonathan was my friend, Taliah, my best friend when we were children, and so was Benjamin. I came to Israel because Jonathan wanted me to find your brother. I had no intention to harm him, or any of you."

Taliah stares at the fire with narrowed eyes, and her chest heaves.

"Taliah, I know you're grieving, and I know what it's like, how we try to find a target to blame. I did the same when I lost my wife."

Her eyes flick towards me, then back to the fire. This is something I hate to talk about, never talk about.

"Zainah died giving birth to our first son, eleven years ago. The baby died a few months later from a congenital disease." I pass a hand through my hair. "I blamed my family for my pain. Zainah was my cousin and our marriage was arranged by our families—but we loved each other, we adored each other." I close my eyes and see Zainah's face. I open them and see Taliah, staring into the flames, listening intently. "When the baby died I was convinced it was because we were cousins, so I blamed my father and my uncle. They had brought this tragedy upon us. I hated them for so long. And I learned to hate myself, in a way."

I let the crackling of the firewood fill the air between us. She may not even be listening, but just saying these words relieves me of a choking pain. As if in prayer, I mutter my thoughts to the night.

"It's been a long time since I opened my soul like this. So many years of denial, of suffering. It's so easy to fall into depression and self-pity instead of moving on. I thought I did, thought I had when I gave myself to my military career, but the pain is still here. It burns within me, smoldering, unquenchable, keeping me from happiness. What a sad man I am."

I look up and find Taliah staring at me with tears in her eyes.

64

So this murderous man has feelings, and a story. Is that what she's doing, blaming him to avoid the pain of her situation? In the firelight, this brutish man with a half-swollen eye now seems more sensible, more human. For a moment, he's lost in his own thoughts, and she wonders what it would feel like losing a spouse and a son. She has neither, but she's lost her parents, her brothers. Her life has changed, but it could be much worse. She could have died in the synagogue, she could be alone at the mercy of invaders. She's here instead, not the best place in the world, but not dead. And not abandoned.

"I'm sorry about your wife and son, Farid."

He looks at her, his expression just a bit wary, then nods.

She says, "Perhaps we could start over, you know, give ourselves a chance to be fair to each other. I'm sure we've misjudged one another and stepped on each other's feelings. What do you say?"

He tilts his head back and cocks an eyebrow.

"If you're serious, yes, of course."

"I mean it."

"All right."

"Good."

"Good."

She smiles. Farid nods. Taliah puts her hands on her knees, plays with her hair. They stare at the fire and glance at each other.

"What—"

"We should—"

Great, now they're interrupting each other.

He smiles. "You were going to say..."

"No, you first, tell me."

"All right. I was going to say we should, well, I can do it myself, but if you want to help, it would be better. We should find more wood for the fire. It won't last all night like this."

"Sure, I'll help."

They look for plants growing out of crevices on the cliff, find only a few. After twenty minutes the temperature drops and Taliah's limbs begin to hurt.

"They're just small sticks," she says, "nothing big enough to keep the fire going all night."

"I'll worry about that. You need to get warm." They return to the campsite and rekindle the fire. She sits closer to him this time.

"Sorry I wasn't much help with the wood," she says. "You must think I'm just a useless, spoiled girl."

"I don't think that."

"Yes, you do."

"How do you know what I think?"

Taliah shrugs. "All right, I don't. So what do you think of me?"

"I think you're smart and brave. I saw you in action at the airport with the fire truck, remember."

"Oh, that. I'd never done anything like it. But it felt good. And thanks for the compliment. Anything else?"

Farid pauses for a moment and looks at her, then at the fire. "I think ... I think you're beautiful."

Taliah feels her stomach tingle with a mix of surprise and anxiety. Is this man falling for her? She hopes not.

"Let me say more, if I may. I mean no disrespect here, but this is something I just realized. I'm sure men treat you like an object to admire, or perhaps...worse. They don't know you're smart, which you are, but think only that your beauty gives them liberty to take advantage of you." He shrugs. "You may think I have no right to talk like this, since Sharia doesn't do justice to women in my country. But I learned to think differently, Zainah taught me that. She told me how she felt devalued by our culture and how I should look at women with respect. I haven't always done it, but I know better. I know how women feel, and I think that's why you put up that harsh exterior, so people won't hurt you or use you."

Something breaks in her soul—something she knows should be broken. Here she was judging him by his appearance, which she hates when others do to her, and he sees right through her.

"Have I offended you?"

She shakes her head. "No, but you *have* made me think."

Farid yawns. "We should sleep close to each other. It would be warmer."

"You mean body warmth?"

"I'm not that cold, I just say it for your sake."

65

I wake with a stabbing pain in my stomach. Hunger. My right shoulder hurts too. Taliah is sleeping against my back, so there's no chance of rolling over, unless I wake her. The fire has died but the cliff provides good cover from the wind. This is the coolest we can expect it to feel for the rest of the day. The heat to come makes me dread the rise of the sun. All I can think of now is water.

Water.

I close my eyes again and drift away.

A DREAM, it was just a dream. But I'm panting.

Pink and yellow streaks tinted the sky. I was flying over Asia and Europe, seeing the scorched land and piled bodies. Then I landed in Baghdad and the city burned. In the mist of the flames Al-Mahdi laughed, so powerful the fire couldn't touch him. People engulfed in flames came to him, begging for help, but he just laughed and let them burn.

Never could I have imagined this, not until I saw the true character of the caliph—a bloodthirsty lunatic with delusions of divinity. He will carry the Muslim world astray. Have we all been led astray, as when Muhammad received a false revelation from Satan? How then can we know the truth?

Unless it is as Keith said, and we Muslims never had the truth. Those things he read, those words he challenged me with, I've witnessed their fulfillment. That means…My body shudders just thinking of this. The conclusion is too difficult to accept. I could even accept the truth of Judaism, but Christianity? My imam always said the Christians came from the devil. Yet the devil can be no worse than the man who calls himself the Messiah of Islam. The people don't know what he is, and those who do know—like Hussai—are puppets in his mad hands.

I rub my face and sit up straight. Blood rushes to my head and my scalp hurts.

Taliah stirs and moans, then rolls over so she faces me, still asleep. I stand and stretch my sore legs.

The sun is rising, and we must head east. Our only hope is to find some water at the banks of the Jordan, or perhaps a village near the border. As I bend down to wake Taliah, an ominous thought crosses my mind: this jihad must be stopped before the whole world is destroyed.

THE SUN burns my face like a thousand stinging needles.

I suck in a breath of warm, grainy air, then cough dust through my raspy throat and parched lips. Chills seize my body, and I know what this means: dehydration.

I try to focus my mind on what has kept me distracted these past few hours—plans to defeat Al-Mahdi, either aligning with the Russians or providing more information to the Israelis—but headache and fatigue make it impossible to concentrate.

"Farid, I see a village!" Taliah points to a few rectangular shapes in the distance. "It could be a mirage. Let's go." The shapes begin coalescing into windows and doors and smoke. Taliah gasps. "That house is on fire."

We quicken our pace. My chills intensify and I bend over a few meters from the outskirts of the village, falling to my knees. The air feels so much hotter here. Taliah, who seems to have more strength, walks ahead, past the houses and into the town. A few seconds later she returns, her voice shaky.

"It's not just one house, Farid, it's almost every one of them—
the whole place is burning."

"Did you see any people?"

"No, but I'll go find some water."

She disappears into the town again and I crawl under the
shadow of a brick wall. I can hear the fire consuming the struc-
tures. I shouldn't have let Taliah walk into that place, it's too
dangerous.

I wait, but she doesn't return. Following the wall, I walk into
the village. The fire is thicker toward the center of the town and I
can't go more than three blocks without daring the flames.

"Taliah!"

Where's that woman?

Nausea roils my stomach. I need fluids, now. I find a small
house not yet touched by fire but half destroyed by artillery. I
enter and find fragments of brick, wood, and fabrics scattered
over and around a thin mattress on the floor. Among the mess
lies a dead dog, its body smashed by debris. The sight doesn't
help my nausea.

Past the dead animal, a short hallway leads to two doors—a
bathroom and a tiny kitchen. There's no refrigerator in the kitchen
and the sink doesn't work. I stumble to the bathroom, which
smells awful. Of course nothing comes from the sink's faucet.
My last option makes me want to vomit, but I must do it. I kneel
by the stained toilet and dip my face inside like a thirsty beast.

I WIPE my face and walk out of the house.

My head clears slightly, but the chills and the tingle are still
with me. I guess there weren't many electrolytes in that toilet.
The fire has spread, and I must hurry. I call Taliah's name, again
and again. Maybe she returned to the place where she left me. I
retrace my steps, crawl in the gloom, under the smoke, choking,
coughing, guessing my way back out. I turn a corner, more by

instinct than knowledge, and stumble on something soft. A body.

It's Taliah. I check for a pulse. She's alive.

"Taliah." I touch her blackened face. "Taliah."

I take my shirt off and wrap it around my face like a mask, then lift the unconscious body and carry it on my shoulder. I try to walk fast, but I'm blind to where I'm going. My eyes burn, my feet stumble.

"God, please help me get out."

My chest hurts like hell and I feel my legs giving away. Three more steps, that's all I give myself before I'll surrender. One, two—the air clears. I see some blue between the layers of gray smoke—three. Four and five. And I can breathe.

Voices surround me, there are people here, but my vision is blurred. I fall to my knees, lay Taliah on the ground, and collapse beside her.

66

Hussai massages the back of his neck and looks across the table of his new Jerusalem office to his just-promoted major general.

"Our troops are raiding every Jordanian city, town, and village, as you commanded, General."

"Good, Ergun. That will teach the Jordanian king. Now we round up more Jews for a public execution. I want to know how many are found and killed."

Ergun nods and Hussai smiles at his own cunning. If he can show good numbers to Al-Mahdi, he might earn a star.

He says, "Now, what's the status of the relocation of the Caliph's statue?"

"It has been collected from Baghdad and is ready to be flown to Jordan. The airport here is useless, so we must drive—"

Someone knocks on the door. A lieutenant sticks his head into the room.

"General, you must see this."

Hussai and Ergun follow the lieutenant to a conference room where most of the staff is gathered around a television. The screen shows a crowd in the Temple Mount clamoring for Al-Mahdi, and beside him, the stranger with long hair from the plane and the Jewish temple. The camera zooms in as the caliph raises one fist toward the sky, then opens his hand toward the stranger.

"He is finally here."

The crowd at the Temple Mount becomes silent.

"Who is that?" Ergun says in Hussai's ear.

"That's what I want to know."

The stranger smiles, then walks to a lame man near the front of the crowd and points at him.

"In the name of Al-Mahdi, get up and walk!"

The screen shows a close-up of the cripple's face, fearful and then astonished as he struggles to stand and actually walks a few steps. The crowd goes wild and so does Hussai's staff.

"Did he really heal him?" Ergun says.

Hussai feels his fingers tingle. The temperature in the room seems to drop. The camera follows the stranger as he strolls back to Al-Mahdi's side. The caliph grins and takes the stranger's hand before leaning forward to speak into the microphone.

"My people, I present unto you the prophet we were waiting for: Jesus, the son of Mary."

67

Taliah wakes from delirium, remembering only fragments of the past day. Days? Hard to tell. She has the vague recollection of being carried on a camel, of being forced to drink, eat, take some horrendous herbal tea. What she remembers most, though, is the malaise that accompanied her every waking and half-sleeping moment.

None of her senses delivers anything familiar. The smell of camel sweat in the air, the rough fabrics rubbing against her skin, the shifting darkness in the tent that houses her—all foreign, yet comforting. Her back muscles feel stiff, so she turns in the cot to face the exit. She starts at the sight of a man sitting in a corner of the tent. She can only see his feet and part of his legs.

"Who's the—?" Her own voice scares her. It sounds like an old rusted pipe being opened after many years.

"Drink some water. There's some in that vase over there."

"Farid?"

"How are you feeling?"

She sits and feels a faint dizziness. "Like coming back from the dead, with some death still glued to me." She sips the water.

"Good."

"How long have you been sitting there?"

"A couple of hours, maybe more. I can't take the sun outside, makes me sick."

"Where are we?" she says.

"In a Bedouin camp somewhere in Jordan. Some of their men saw the burning village and crossed over to see if anyone needed help. That's what they told me, though I suspect they also hoped to find something valuable among the rubble. In any case, they saw us and were kind enough to save us and care for our health."

"There's something in your voice, the way you talk about them...."

"I never liked Bedouins."

"Why?"

He leans forward and his face comes into the light. He glances outside. "My family didn't like them. Whatever the reason, I just went with it."

"Now that they saved your life, won't you change your opinion about them?"

"Maybe. I've changed my thoughts about more significant things recently."

They listen to the sounds around the tent for a while. As Taliah feels more awake, she becomes more aware of the sweat on her body and the stuffiness of the air.

"It's so hot in here."

"Yes, the front of the tent is usually open during the day, but I wanted to avoid as much sun as possible. Do you want me open it?"

"Please."

Farid rolls up one side of the tent and light floods in like a gust of wind. She winces, then takes in the view around her. A set of wooden poles sustain the fabric of the tent, which seems to be some woven from sort of hair. Goat hair, perhaps. Three large rugs serve as the floor, and her low mattress is close to a fire pit on the ground. Outside, a dozen men in turbans mingle while kids play and camels stare.

A woman with a black cloth wrapped around her forehead approaches Farid and says something in Arabic, pointing at Taliah. Farid turns to her.

"She says she has prepared food for you, that you must eat."

"Oh, lovely. Thank her, please."

The woman walks away and returns with a girl, both carrying pots and plates. They serve the food on the opposite side of the tent and Taliah joins them. Two men come and sit by their side, and Farid introduces them as father and son. Apparently their family owns the tent.

The woman starts speaking again.

"She says this is called *mansaf*." Farid points to a large plate of rice with meat and nuts. "The lamb is cooked with goat yogurt."

"Sounds wonderful." She looks around for utensils, then at the members of the family, who seem prepared to eat.

Farid smiles. "You eat with your hands."

"Oh, I see."

TALIAH SIPS cardamom-spiced coffee at the entrance of the tent. Farid stares into the horizon, his eyes narrowed on something unseen.

"What are you thinking about so much?"

"Just making plans," he says.

"About what?"

"Do you like that coffee?"

She shrugs. "It's not bad."

"I can't stand it."

He's hiding something. The activity around the camp never ceases.

"Farid, I feel bad that everyone is working and we're just sitting here."

"They honor their guests, that's us, so don't feel bad. Besides, we need to recover our strength."

"I guess so."

A couple of rough-looking young men walk by the tent and stare at Taliah. She's seen them pass by a few times before. Are they stalking her? She scoots closer to Farid.

"Please don't leave me if you can."

The hours leading up to sunset become hard for Taliah as

Farid sits immersed in his thoughts, barely speaking to her. It must be the weight of the war. She's heard that soldiers are often so disturbed after war they can hardly hold a conversation. The wretched caliph has started so many wars in the last few years, no doubt his mind is all in shards—like her life. Taliah's thoughts are like fuel, kindling her grief, turning it to anger against the caliph. She's never wished anyone death, but she desires nothing else for the so-called Al-Mahdi.

Their hostess comes, gesturing and smiling as she talks to Farid. Taliah sighs. She should have learned Arabic when she had the chance.

"What is it, Farid?"

"She says that after prayers the clan will hold some festivities in our honor. There'll be some music and poetry. Aabida wants to know if you would dance."

"Dance?"

Farid shrugs.

THE ROUGH young men loom from time to time, making Taliah uneasy. She tries to ignore them. Despite the feast and the music around her, despite the friendly smiles and the invitations to dance, she can't relax and enjoy. Worst of all, she's clinging to Farid's arm like a girl in love. Not that she's in love with him, but he comforts her, even more so after she heard the story of how he carried her from the burning village. He didn't want to talk, but she insisted, until she got every detail. No doubt he cares about her.

She looks at him, drinking coffee and staring at the musicians—men playing one-stringed violins and metal pipes that stand as flutes. At the center of attention are two rows of women facing each other, singing back and forth in verses. Farid's features have an inherent roughness, accentuated by his still swollen eye, but there's beauty too in that face.

Perhaps she shouldn't be looking at him like that, but the

firm biceps under her fingers turn her mind in that direction—
she's attracted to him. She feels her cheeks burn and looks away.
He didn't notice her blushing. He may not even be aware of her
embrace. Whatever is occupying his mind has a hypnotic force.

"Farid?"

He blinks and turns to her.

She takes a deep breath and releases his arm, his gaze making her self-conscious.

"I hadn't said it before, but thank you for saving my life yesterday."

Farid smiles. "You're welcome." Then he stands and lifts his
cup. "Too much coffee, I must go and relieve myself."

"I thought you couldn't stand the coffee."

She watches him go and finishes the last of her own coffee.
A presence towers over her and she looks up. Two men sit down
by her, one on each side.

The stalkers.

68

Nothing feels better than an empty bladder.
Well, yes, there's something better, and that's Taliah's hands around my arm. I don't know when her feelings toward me changed, but I take pleasure in it. Does she realize I'm at least fifteen years older than her? Maybe she does. Maybe she's just fond of this old man and I'm imagining things.

And besides, I can't think about a relationship now. I have a mission: I must return to Jerusalem, locate Augustus, and find a way to communicate with the Russians. He should be able to track the first call they made to my cell phone.

I walk around the perimeter of the camp, letting the cool of the night refresh my sunburned skin. A short distance from the tents, I spot the shape of the mountains in the night sky. I don't want to leave Taliah alone, but walking feels good after being seated all afternoon. All those hours thinking, sitting by her side, I pretended to plan our escape out of Jordan—but I could think of nothing but her.

Would loving Taliah be a betrayal of Zainah's memory? Oh, what a battle, but in the end, I felt Zainah would want me to be happy. It's unbelievable how I feel right now. From where am I drawing such strength? Last time I felt so giddy was ... when I married Zainah.

Love.

I must burn out all this energy, clear my mind, and concentrate on my mission. Perhaps it would be better not to return to the camp yet. Low clouds hang over the mountains. How odd—a dim glow brightens some of the clouds, but dawn is hours away. It must be something else. I should find out.

The hike up the mountain is easy for the first ten minutes, then a vertical wall threatens to end my climb. The camp below is now a blurry clump of shadows around many small fires, with one big bonfire at the center. I face the rock again and feel for any crevices, then pull myself up. It's dark but I can do this. I lift one foot, feeling for another support, and slip. My body hits the rock and I roll down the path about ten or fifteen meters, coming to a stop on a plateau.

My arms burn from the scrapes and my ego hurts worse. What was I thinking?

I close my eyes and lie here a moment. No bone is broken, no organ is pinned. How many times have I defied death in the past two weeks? Why am I still alive? Certainly not by my own cunning.

I'm alive because of the love of God.

Startled, I open my eyes and see the clouds open to thousands of stars. These thoughts are not my thoughts. And a God who loves sounds more like Keith's Christian God than the God my imam preaches.

Joy and sadness settle in my chest. Joy, for this absurd assurance that God loves me. Sadness because I suspect, almost know, that it is not the god of my fathers.

"I want to know you, God who loves."

Clouds move again between me and the sky, and there's the dim glow. A path to my right rounds the wall I wanted to climb, and I take it, still intrigued by the source of the glow. On top of a large boulder, I get a glimpse of the land on the other side of the mountain.

The flames of a distant fire burn to the south. It looks as if a whole city is burning—just like the village across the border where Taliah and I almost died, just like the fire in my dream.

This is the caliph's doing. He's burning the villages, not only in Israel but in Jordan. I can't wait for the Russians to mount an offensive—the whole Middle East would be burning by then. Al-Mahdi must be stopped now, he must die, and no one can kill him but me. I can get close to him.

A new resolve invigorates me, a strength that seems to come from above. Maybe it is Keith's God. Maybe this is a divine recruitment to act against my nation.

It's ludicrous to think this way, yet I believe it. I spin around and begin the descent. After a few minutes, I realize I feel no pain from the fall. The scratches in my forearms are real, but nothing hurts, even though I smashed my back and legs against the rocks. How marvelous.

Thankful, I glance at the vastness of the sky and feel awe before this newly found God. As I look down the path, I notice a large hole on the side of the hill and walk to it. The rocks form an arc that marks the entrance to a large cave. It would be interesting to explore it when I can bring some light.

At the bottom of the hill I hear hooves pounding the ground, fast but at a fair distance. I walk toward the camp, staying close to the hillside, then cross to where an incoming rider can see me and not run over me. The galloping sounds closer now, and I wait by the entrance to the camp. A camel emerges from the night into the orange glow of the Bedouin camp, a short skinny man on top of it. I lift a hand to make the camel stop.

"*Aasalaamu Aleikum.* What news do you bring, brother?"

The man stumbles off the camel. His face is smeared with dried blood, and he wears no headpiece.

"My brother, I bring terrible news. It's the caliphate's army, they're executing vengeance against the king for offering refuge to the Jews."

"How? What did they do to you?"

"They came to our village looking for any Jews that might be hiding there, demanded we hand over any Jew among us. I didn't know of any, but a whole Jewish family seemed to be

among our residents. The soldiers killed them, then burned
our houses."

"Is your family well?"

"Allah's will, yes."

"My pain is with you."

"You must know we aren't the first, they've been doing this
great injustice everywhere. And now they're moving north, right
in this direction. Warn your people. And woe to you if there are
any Jews among you."

69

"*Hal takallamu lloghat alarabi?*" the bearded stalker says.

Taliah's hands turn cold and her heart pumps with terror. What in the world is he saying? Is he threatening her?

"English?" the second stalker says.

She looks at the young man on her right. He has a wide smile with one broken tooth. She nods, forcing her mind back to the language she learned at school but hasn't used for years.

"Yes, English."

"Arabic no?"

She shakes her head.

"Me English, a little. My name is Omar. He is my brother Abbud."

She didn't expect any of the Bedouins here to speak English. The bearded Abbud speaks to his brother in Arabic, probably asking what they've been saying. Omar answers him and nods. Closer, they seem gentle. Her muscles relax and her heartbeat returns to normal.

"You no Muslim," Omar says. "We see you no pray."

Taliah tenses again. Where is Farid when she needs him the most? Next time she'll go with him wherever he goes, even if it's to evacuate his bowels.

Omar grins. "You Christian?"

"No, no, I'm Jewish, but liberal, not Orthodox at all. Not really religious. And I have nothing against Muslims, you're a great people."

"So why you carry cross?"

Omar points to her chest and she realizes Benjamin's crucifix is hanging loose above her shirt. She tucks it away.

"It's a gift from my brother. A Jewish Christian—no, a Christian Jew."

A look of disappointment crosses Omar's face as he translates to Abbud. Does that mean they won't kill her?

"We think maybe…"

"Yes? What?"

Omar leans closer and whispers. "We think maybe you Christian, like us."

"You're Christians?"

"Yes." Both of them are beaming.

"Does anybody else in your clan know?"

"No. Danger for us."

So that's why they were so interested in her. These poor souls are secluded in their beliefs.

"I'm sorry I'm not what you expected, but don't worry, I won't tell anybody."

"Do you want to be Christian?"

Taliah laughs, then covers her mouth, seeing Omar's blank expression. He's serious.

"I don't mean to offend you, Omar, but people don't just change their religion like that."

He frowns and shakes his head. "No understand."

Taliah sighs. "All right, how do I explain this? I must have a reason to become a Christian, a reason to believe. Do you understand? Why would I become a Christian?"

His snaggletooth smile returns. "Jesus loves you."

"What kind of reason is that?"

"Love."

DESPITE THE disapproving looks of some of their fellow Bedouins, Omar and Abbub stay by Taliah's side, talking in Arabic and broken English.

Omar shrugs. "They no understand me, no worries."

"Where did you learn English, Omar?"

"American missionary teach me. He teach me also about Christ."

"When was this?" she says.

"Years ago, he show me Jesus movie and explain gospel, explain end of times. I wanted to believe, but too much afraid of my family."

"What happened to the missionary?"

"He go up to heaven with Jesus."

"Oh, he passed away. I'm sorry."

Omar laughs. "No, no sorry. Is good."

"Well, I guess for some people who believe in heaven, it's good to die."

"He no die. He go up to heaven." Omar motions with his hands as if he were snatching something up from the ground, up into the sky.

"He went up to heaven while he was alive?"

He nods with the smile of a little child. "Yes. All Jesus believers go up to heaven in rapture."

Rapture? That's a fancy word for a guy whose English is so limited. What kind of brainwashing is this?

Omar points to his chest. "After he raptured, I no afraid anymore, I believe in my heart Jesus is God, my savior."

Abbub interrupts, obviously wanting to know what's going on, and Omar talks with him. Taliah looks over her shoulder, hoping Farid will come back and rescue her from this conversation she might enjoy but can't understand a word of. Omar and Abbub are kind of cute, but they're cute fanatics and a bit crazy. She'll just thank them for their interest and extricate herself. She stands and turns to face them.

"Excuse me, but—"

Farid appears from behind a tent, running toward her, a short man following him.

"TALIAH, I must take you away from here."

"Why? Who's that man? Why does he have blood on his face?"

On the opposite side of the bonfire, the short man talks with the leaders of the tribe, motioning with his hands and almost weeping.

"It's not safe to stay here, not for you," Farid says.

"I don't understand."

She switches her gaze between Farid and the newcomer. Farid's anxiety is contagious and her chest feels heavy.

"Hello, my name is Omar."

Farid frowns at Omar's greeting. "Why is he speaking English?"

Taliah shrugs. "Because he doesn't speak Hebrew. He's been speaking to me in broken English for a while."

"What does he want?"

"To turn me into a Christian."

Farid's eyes widen. "Really?"

"Tell me what's going on."

The music stops as the leaders of the tribe motion the people to be silent and introduce the newcomer.

"*Fil arabi?*" Farid says to Omar and then they begin to talk in Arabic.

The visitor steps forward and also speaks in Arabic. Why won't Farid give her an explanation? Why isn't it safe for her to stay here? She looks around and sees the faces of the listeners cringe and pale in fear. Then the man shouts louder, something ominous enough to prickle her skin. A few heads turn toward her.

Maybe Farid is right. Maybe she's not safe.

70

The excitement of finding a Christian, who can explain more about the God who loves, dies away when a fierce discussion erupts around the fire. The leaders send the messenger away with some women to provide him water and food while they discuss the news with the tribe.

Aabida, our kind hostess, stares into Taliah's eyes, then speaks to the leaders and points at her. Taliah's face is tight with fear. I stand by her side.

"Go into the tent, now, Taliah. Wait for me there."

"Why is everybody staring at me?"

"I'll explain later, go now."

"No! Explain now, I want to know."

"Would you listen to me for once? It will be easier for me to contain them if you're not here where they can see you."

"I'm not leaving your side. If they can harm me here, they can harm me in the tent. I feel safer with you."

That's a good point. And the knowledge that she feels safe around me causes a feeling quite inappropriate for the situation at hand.

"All right! Stay, then."

Aabida is saying her guest is a Jewess—Taliah was heard speaking Hebrew with me—and she will bring ruin to the tribe. More than half the people agree with her and want to hand Taliah over to the army when they get here.

One of the leaders, an old man with only a whiff of white hair on his head, says that to dishonor a guest in such a way would be a transgression against their traditions, their Bedouin culture.

My first impulse, of course, is to tell them we'll leave at once. But I'm not keen on going back to the wilderness so soon, fleeing a powerful army on foot. It could mean death for both of us.

I step forward. "Listen to me, brothers, please. You have been kind and hospitable. You saved our lives once, so please don't take them away now."

"Are you a Jew as well?" a man asks.

"No, but her fate is my fate." I lock eyes with several of them, then look at the old man who defends us. "You honor your traditions by honoring us, but you should not endanger your people. Just give us a camel and some provisions and send us away."

"A camel?" a woman shouts. "You're crazy."

The old man looks down to the floor, then back up at me. "You may depart when you wish. But your request for a camel must be made to the family hosting you."

Aabida says, "We have but one camel and cannot do without it."

Her husband stands by her side. "True, we can't give you our animal."

"Can anyone help us?"

All heads shake vigorously. Omar and Abbub stand behind me.

"We want to come with you," Abbub says.

"Yes, to Petra, that's the only safe place for Jews and Christians in all Asia."

I turn around and face them. "Petra? How do you know this?"

Omar smiles. "That's the place of refuge, God will protect us there."

I don't see the logic in that, for Al-Mahdi's army can enter any place, including Petra, but I'll play along if it serves my purpose.

"All right, Petra. Do you have any camels?"

They both shake their heads. Perfect.

The crowd gets excited again and people begin to shout.

"Hand them over!"

"Apprehend them."

"Their lives for ours."

What are my options? Something is wrong here.

The messenger returns to the gathering and I walk toward him. Taliah grabs my hand and comes with me. I take him by the arm and pull him to one side.

"The Mahdi's army will come here and trample everything whether they find Jews or not, right?"

"How do you know that?"

"It used to be my army. It's like a monster that destroys everything. I saw what they did across the border in a village in Israel. I saw the city burning down south."

He says, "I must return to my people. I fulfilled my duty by warning this tribe."

"First you must tell them this, so they'll know to protect their possessions and their lives. Tell them handing over the Jews is no safeguard."

"I will do no such thing."

"Taliah, step back." I grab the man by his shirt and bring his face close to mine. The blood on his face is oddly smeared, and the skin beneath it seems intact. "Where did the blood on your face come from? Whose blood is it?"

"What do you mean? It's my blood, they beat my face."

"Wrong. Your face has not a single bruise or cut. Who do you work for?"

"I...I'm just a farmer, nothing more."

I take one of his hands and examine his palm. Smooth. "You're a terrible liar." With a quick spin, I flip his slight body and he lands near the bonfire, facing up. The tribe gasps.

"This man is an impostor. He works for the caliph's army and his only purpose is to inspire terror." I kick his testicles and he squeals like a rat. Then I pick a branch from the pile of wood by the bonfire and light its top in the flames. I bring the burning branch between his legs, close but not touching them. "Tell them what's going to happen, tell them what the soldiers will do."

"I don't know what you're saying. You're a crazy Jew lover."

"They'll come and burn every tent, right?" I let the flames lick his pants and they catch on fire. "Just like this."

He squeals again and rolls on the ground, gasping and crying, until the fire is quenched. He buries his face in the sand but I lift him up so he's facing the bonfire.

"There's much more heat in here to make you talk."

He drops his head. "It's true, it's true."

"Say it louder, what's true?"

"The Mahdi's army will destroy and kill everything in its path. You'll die if you don't flee."

Panic rises like steam among the Bedouins and each runs to his own tent or drops to the ground to wail. I call Omar and Abbub and point to the impostor on the ground.

"Keep an eye on him and don't let him escape."

They grab him by the arms and drag him away.

Taliah says, "What will we do?"

"I must help these people."

"Wait, why was it not safe for me? They all seemed to blame me for something."

"No one is safe. I'll explain later. Come on, I have an idea."

I lead the way to the corner where the heads of each family are gathered in a somber discussion.

"Excuse me, brothers." They look at me with fear. I don't blame them. "Do you know about the cave in that mountain?" They turn to see the mountain I'm pointing at. "That's your chance of survival."

71

A few hours after the scene at the bonfire, Taliah and I are at the base of the mountain.

"Omar and his brother seem to know the mountain and caves well, and they're in charge. Everything and everyone are in the cave. Except for that." I point to the half-torn tent and the scattered items lying on the ground that should give the appearance of a hasty escape.

"Yes, except for that. And the camels."

A dozen camels lie sleeping on the ground on the opposite side of the camp.

"Grab a branch or a cloth and erase the few visible tracks leading to the mountain. I'll use the camels to create a track heading west. Hopefully that will mislead them."

Taliah puts her hands on her waist. "That's a lot of tracks to erase, why don't you do that job instead?"

"Fine, if you can make twelve camels obey you, go ahead and take my job."

She looks over at the animals sleeping on the dirt and grimaces. "It's not as if it were desert sand, right? There aren't that many tracks anyway."

"Right."

Taliah picks up a branch with dead leaves from under a dry bush by the hill and begins to work. The she turns to me.

"How long do you think we have?"

"I expect them to show up soon after dawn."

"What if they come before that?"

I nod at the mountain. "I sent someone to the top to be on watch. He'll let us know."

She seems content with that. When she's not looking I trot over to the camels and wake the three boys who take care of them. They'll lead the camels toward one of the wadis to the west and find a place to hide them. The wadi has a hard bottom and the camels won't leave tracks there. The boys ride a camel each and drag the rest with reins. I accompany them for a kilometer, then return to the camp. Taliah is still working on the tracks when Omar and Abbub come running down the mountain.

"What happened?"

Omar bends over and places his hands on his legs, panting. "They're coming. We could see their vehicles moving fast. They'll be here in minutes."

"Let's go." I run toward the hill, motioning them to follow me and calling for Taliah. She looks at me with a blank stare and I realize I spoke in Arabic.

"Sorry. Leave that now, they're almost here."

"So soon?"

Halfway up the mountain I stop Omar and tell Abbub to keep going with Taliah.

"Omar, do you know a good spot from where we can see them but they can't see us?"

He thinks for a moment and nods. "Follow me."

We trudge around a steep cliff with loose dirt and hide behind a boulder sticking out from the mountain. We have a wide view of the camp, and down below on my right, I can see a section of the trail that leads to the cave.

Dawn is upon the valley.

The platoon arrives three minutes later, creating a cloud of dust and noise. The soldiers examine the camp, kicking the remains and pointing to the tracks. I hope the camel boys have made it to their hiding place.

A faint whisper distracts me and I turn to Omar.

"What are you doing?"

"Praying."

It's certainly a fitting moment to pray, but who can pray while danger looms below us? A group of Al-Mahdi's soldiers is moving around the foot of the mountain, too close for my liking.

"They're up to something down there. Maybe Taliah didn't erase all the tracks."

"Someone's coming, Farid."

"Where?"

He points to the trail, where two Islamic soldiers march with weapons ready.

"They're going to find the cave," I say.

"Don't worry, God will protect us. He is our deliverer."

I keep my eyes on the soldiers. "Is there another way to catch up with them? I must surprise them, but I can't go over the cliff unnoticed."

"Have faith, just pray with me."

No, I can't stay still and let them trap Taliah and the Bedouins. Maybe I can distract them, make them chase me away from the cave. I'd be arrested or killed, but the Bedouins would be fine, and Taliah would be saved. I move out from behind the boulder and round the cliff—and discover a crevasse in the rocks, large enough to let me reach the trail and attack them. With my gun ready, I head into the crevasse.

72

The two soldiers come into view, well within range. Two quick shots would take care of them, but I don't want to draw attention. They stop a few meters away and look up the trail. One of them points ahead.

"What do you think that is?"

"Looks like an oil lamp hanging from a tree."

"Odd, isn't it? Let's check it out."

So much for Omar's prayers. I have to do something.

As they start uphill again, a strong voice calls. "Hey, privates!"

The two soldiers turn around and a third catches up to them. "Did you turn off your radio? The captain's been calling you."

"Sorry, sir. I lent my radio to Ra—"

"Never mind your excuses. We're clearing the area immediately. The general has ordered all troops to move north to Arbel. We're to set up a defensive perimeter for the caliph's visit to Lake Tiberias. Move out, you two. Now."

The soldiers trot down the mountain.

"Are you all right, Farid?" Omar's voice startles me.

"They left, everyone will be fine."

"I told you to have faith. God is in control." I nod, wishing I had faith like that. "God loves us, Farid, that's why he helped us."

It seems this God who loves me, who called me to kill the caliph, has just told me where the caliph's going to be.

"Omar, do you know how to get to Lake Tiberias?"

"Yes, our tribe settled there for a season."

"What about the mountains of Arbel, do you know the area?"

"Arbel is one of my favorite places in the world. Abbub and I used to explore the caverns there when we were younger. Why do you—"

"I want you to take me there."

"But we should go to Petra, that's—"

"Petra can wait. I must go to Arbel immediately."

I spin and start for the cave, Omar following me.

73

Taliah tries not to gag as the soup of odors in the cave threatens to choke her. If she could only stick her head out and breathe real air—but with her luck, she'd probably alert an Islamic soldier of their presence. Not that it would be hard to find them. The crying babies and the singing goats should alert the whole platoon.

Abbub smiles and says a few words in Arabic, but she can't even smile back because of the nausea. A new odor hits her nostrils and it's just too much. She pushes people and animals out of the way and heads for the exit.

Farid and Omar appear along the gentle slope to the mouth of rock. Her heart jumps.

"I was worried about you!"

Farid smiles. "All is well. They're gone."

Omar runs past her and says something in Arabic.

"What did he say?"

"He's going to tell the others."

"Oh, all right. I need to breathe, so I'll wait outside."

"I'll come with you."

The air of the mountain clears her head. Farid looks at her intently.

"What is it?"

His mouth twists into a silly smile. "I must leave for Galilee."

"I thought we were going to Petra. What's in Galilee?"

"Lake Tiberias."

"Why do you call it that? It's the Sea of Galilee, and there's nothing there. We should be going south."

"I don't have time to explain it now, Taliah. You wouldn't understand."

Taliah puts her hands on her hips. "Of course I don't understand, because you hardly speak."

"Look, the Islamic army is moving north and I must leave as soon as I can."

"Are you mad? Why do you want to follow them?"

"We'll go south after I'm done. You stay here with the tribe and I'll be with the two brothers."

"Hey, that's not fair. I can't stay here with these people. I'm not one of them, I don't speak their language. If you want to get rid of me, at least be honest and—"

"No, no. It's not like that. I'd like you to come but it's dangerous."

"That's an understatement, Farid. Please. Tell me what it is that you want to accomplish."

He looks at her for a long moment, then says, "I must kill the Caliph."

"Are you serious?" Fear grips Taliah's heart. "This… this is suicide. I mean, I know someone has to kill that madman—for my family's sake, I'd do it if I had a chance—but that's not something you just do—"

"I know the implications. That's why I must go by myself and you must stay here. Omar and Abbub will lead me there."

"Do they know what you plan to do?"

"They'll know when they need to know. I won't tell them unless I have to."

Taliah's fear mushrooms and she wants to scream at him to forget it, to flee with her. She's lost everything—she can't lose Farid.

"How can I persuade you not to go?"

"You can't, Taliah. It's my destiny."

"Then take me with you."

"Too risky. Not a chance."

Of course he's right. What was she thinking, asking him to

take her along in an assassination attempt? She looks back at the cave and feels the nausea nagging her again. If she's to avenge her family, she must help Farid. She grips his hand.

"I'd rather die a brave woman than live in hiding like a coward."

74

From a lookout on Arbel Mountain, Hussai observes the dried-out Lake Tiberias and the land of Galilee extending toward the Golan Heights.

A slight headache creeps in as he thinks about the tasks ahead. Setting the stage in preparation for Al-Mahdi's revelation of the site of the Jewish Ark of the Covenant should be easy enough. What worries him is the military defense of the caliph himself. What if the Israelis ambush them?

His leap to general didn't exactly come with battlefield experience, and he has been relying too much on Ergun, which sends the wrong message about his own competence. But the major general does seem to know his way around here, even explaining the history of the place to Hussai. Apparently, Jewish rebels used the numerous caves in this mountain as forts against the Romans in the first century.

Now the caliph says the Ark is in one of those caves. They'll have to wait for Al-Mahdi to reveal the exact spot, which only he knows. Although Hussai suspects the creepy stranger knows more than he says—the stranger who's said to be Jesus, the son of Mary. People call him by his Arab name, Isa.

All Hussai knows is that the sight of this Isa chills his marrow. A few hours ago, he took a couple of soldiers with him into the caves—where he arrived before anyone else—and came out alone. Hussai hasn't seen the soldiers since.

The radio buzzes. "General Sidiqqui, are you available?"

"Yes, Ergun, what is it?"

"The last regiment has arrived from the south. The troops are taking position in Migdal. What are your orders?"

"Establish a perimeter around the mountain and have some men search the villages in the area for any hostile activity."

"What are you expecting to find, General?"

"Do as you're told, Major. Over." Hussai clips the radio back on his belt and stares down the cliff. On the plain below, a crew of workers is installing two large screens to display live video feed of the caliph entering the cave.

He glances at his watch. They'd better be ready. Al-Mahdi will arrive in less than three hours.

75

Taliah bends forward with her hands on her knees It's been more than two hours since they left the mountain and at least an hour since they lost track of the army up ahead.

"I'm so thirsty," she says to Farid in Hebrew. Farid looks at Omar, then speaks in English.

"We need water, Omar. Did you bring any?"

"No water, I drink all. Abbub can find some."

Farid frowns. "He can?"

Omar speaks to Abbub in Arabic. He grabs a stick and walks around poking the ground. The rest of the crew stops to watch.

Taliah whispers in Farid's ear. "What's he doing?"

He shrugs. "I guess he's looking for water."

"But it's dry. How is he going to find any?"

Abbub is concentrating on a depression in the riverbed with a darker color. He reaches for a sharp rock and starts to dig a hole. Omar runs to Abbub and bends on his knees to help him dig.

"Come on, Taliah, let's see what he found."

When they get to the hole Taliah says, "This is useless. The river has been dry for years."

Omar looks up and hands her a knife. "You make hole with this."

"I don't want to ruin your knife." She's not about to scoop dirt for nothing. But after ten minutes of frenzied digging, a brownish liquid seeps into the hole. Her eyes widen.

"Is that water?"

Farid nods. "Now we sit back and wait. The rest of us, that is, because that's all you've been doing."

She's too embarrassed to answer back. The hole fills slowly but steadily.

"Is it safe to drink it?"

Farid shrugs. "The ground doesn't look contaminated."

"But the Jordan received raw sewage from the pipes near the Sea of Galilee."

"That was more than a decade ago."

Taliah tastes the dust in her dry mouth. Even the brownish water seems inviting. Omar and Abbub scoop it with their hands and drink. Farid motions her to drink but she hesitates. He waits, then drinks himself.

He must be thinking she's a spoiled girl who can't survive in the desert.

"Excuse me." She pushes Farid aside and kneels by the hole, telling herself not to look at the water as she brings it to her lips.

76

Omar points beyond the parched bed of Lake Tiberias. "Mount Arbel is in that direction."

I can glimpse the army in the distance, as well as a crowd
gathered at the base of the mount.

"Yes, I see it."

We're both crouching behind a large rock on the west shore
of the lake.

Taliah is a few meters away, while Abbub keeps her company,
sharpening a stick into a spear. He doesn't know my purpose for
coming here, but his manner of passing time is ominous. I'm
about to penetrate the ranks of the most powerful army on earth,
and all we have is a stick.

"Omar?"

"Yes?"

"I need to borrow your knife."

He hands it to me and I weigh it in my hand. The handle is
rustic but the blade is sharp. "Where did you get this?

"I made it."

"Good workmanship. I'll take care of it."

"What will you do with the knife?"

"I'm not sure yet, but I just may need it. All I know is that I
must get to Arbel, unseen."

Omar surveys the scene intently for a moment. "We can
take you."

"Unnoticed?"

"Do you see that rift on the lake? An earthquake three years ago opened an underground passage to the caves in the mountains. Abbub knows them well."

THE UNDERGROUND entrance to the cave provides the coolness my skin was longing for. Still, the air is harsh and dry. We walk for what seems like hours through a monotonous dark passage. Sunlight makes its way in every now and then through holes above us.

"Can't they make a torch or something?" Taliah says. "I keep bumping against the walls."

"We can manage with the light we have for now." As soon as I say this, the low roof brushes my head. "Just be careful."

The cave becomes darker after a few hundred feet and Abbub stops us.

"Wait."

"What's that sound?" Taliah says.

A whirling noise invades the darkness. My muscles tense and I fear we've been discovered. A light shines on the cave's wall to my right.

I call out. "Who's there?"

Abbub laughs. "It's just my wind-up flashlight."

Flashlight? These Bedouins are more prepared than I thought.

"We can continue now," Abbub says.

"Farid, what's going on? What did he say?"

"Everything's fine. Let's go."

The path sinks into a depression for a stretch, then turns into a steady ascent.

Taliah grabs my arm. "We've passed four forks with different tunnels. Do they know where they're going?"

"I believe so."

She clings to me, and although it makes the walk harder, her closeness distracts me from my fatigue.

"How are you feeling?" I say.

"Not really sure. Afraid, perhaps, but I try not to think about it."

"Good. You're a brave woman."

I can't see her face but I hope there's a smile on it.

"Thank you, Farid."

"This is it," Omar says.

I look around as we come out of the tunnel and into an open rock chamber. Faint gray light filters down from some point above us. At least a dozen tunnels open into the chamber from different directions.

"Is this a natural formation?"

"Most of it," Abbub says. "They may have blasted or drilled through in some places."

"Now," Omar says, motioning to the tunnels. "Where do you want to go?"

"A high point where I can get a glimpse of the army. Without being seen, of course."

Omar and Abbub discuss the options while I explain to Taliah what we were talking about in Arabic.

"This way," Omar says after a while, and we follow Abbub up to a cave on our left. Fifteen minutes later, a light shines in front of us.

Taliah sighs. "The sun at last." She hurries past me. "I want some air."

I grab her hand. "Not yet. We must make sure nobody can see us."

I walk toward the mouth of the cave. The sunlight blinds me and I visor my eyes with one hand. The cave opens to a small lookout on the southwest side of the mountain, halfway to the top. I'm stunned by the beautiful view. So much peace in this—

A motorized flapping deafens me and I jump back into the cave as a helicopter hovers just five meters above the lookout. The chopper rounds the mountain, then it's out of view.

Taliah and the brothers join me as I go back outside. I lie flat on my stomach and stick my head off the cliff to peer down at the base of the mountain. The helicopter lands on a flat spot in the midst of a crowd of at least two hundred people, not counting the soldiers all around the perimeter of Mount Arbel.

I'm too far up to recognize faces without binoculars, but fortunately, two immense screens have been set up to broadcast whatever it is the caliph is doing. One screen stands against the base of the mountain, and I can only see its back corner. The other screen stands opposite to the first, further from the mount, giving me a full view of the show.

A low, indistinct voice reverberates from a speaker system and the echo makes its way up the slope. The screen shows a close-up of the chopper and I recognize it as the same one that landed at the Temple Mount. Sure enough, the door opens and Al-Mahdi steps down, dressed in white like an ancient king.

Out of a black Hummer near the chopper comes Hussai and a man I've never seen before. Tall with long black hair, this man walks with an air of confidence unsurpassed even by the caliph.

"Who's that?" Taliah lies flat on the ground beside me.

"I couldn't tell. Maybe a foreign leader who's made an alliance with the caliph."

Just like he did at the Temple Mount, Al-Mahdi steps behind a microphone and addresses the crowd, his speech clear despite the echo.

"My people, listen to my voice, that you may hear magnificent things I have for you. Today I will reveal the most sought-after archeological artifact in history, the lost symbol of Allah which the Jews distorted and claimed as their own. Today, I will uncover the Ark of the Covenant."

The crowd claps and cheers.

"The Ark!" Taliah cries. "How can he—"

Al-Mahdi's voice booms out. "I could say it was Gabriel— the angel who spoke so many times with the Prophet Muhammad, peace be upon him—who revealed the location of the Ark to me. But let it be known that such angelic visitation is no longer necessary, as the divine nature of the Mahdi is revealed...."

He's at it again, making himself equal to God. Am I not right to kill him? He's fallen under the spell of power, just like the Egyptian pharaohs or the Roman emperors. What's worse is that everyone follows him blindly, as if they too are under a spell. He'll lead the world astray, consuming everything with his madness.

A hand shakes my shoulder. "Farid? Look, they're moving out."

I blink and look at the small humans, then at the screen. The caliph and his guards get back into the helicopter. Hussai tries to follow but Al-Mahdi waves him off, motioning instead to a cameraman to hop inside. The blades begin to rotate and the screens jump between views outside and inside the helicopter, which ascends and flies out of my direct view. But on the screen I see it hovering over the mountain, then trying to land on a flat surface on its far side. After a few minutes, the pilot brings it close to the ground, the door opens, and Al-Mahdi and his entourage jump to the side of the mountain while the chopper's still in the air. One of the guards throws a large case to the ground, no doubt containing the equipment to dig out the Ark. The crowd cheers and claps when the caliph walks with confidence toward a cave. The helicopter returns to the foot of Mount Arbel, and the screen shows Al-Mahdi at the mouth of the cave, giving orders to his four guards.

Is that all Hussai could provide for the caliph's protection? I wait to see if the helicopter bring more guards or people to dig the alleged Ark out, but the pilot shuts down the engine and Hussai doesn't lift a finger.

Four against one, then. Dangerous but not impossible. I begin in the name of... I begin in the name of the Christian God.

77

I stand and say in Arabic, "The moment has come."

"Moment for what?" Omar says.

"What did you say, Farid?" Taliah says in Hebrew.

I speak English. "He's in a cave. I can surprise him."

"Are you out of your mind? Shouldn't you plan better if you want to kill the Mahdi? You don't even have a gun."

Omar widens his eyes. "Kill?"

"There won't be another chance," I tell Taliah. "He only has a handful of guards, and we have the brothers to guide us."

Omar steps toward me and speaks in Arabic. "My English is limited and maybe I didn't understand. What is it you plan to do?"

I sigh. "I plan to assassinate the caliph. I need your help to get to that cave on the other side."

Omar shakes his head and turns to his brother. "Do you hear that, Abbub? He wants to kill the Antichrist!"

Abbub grimaces. "It is for God to kill him, not a man."

"God may take too long. I can finish this now."

"We won't help you," Omar says.

"But it's your God, the Christian God, who's called me to kill Al-Mahdi. Don't you see he's going to destroy all Christians?"

They both sit on a rock with stern faces. Omar speaks after a few seconds.

"The Bible says Jesus himself will destroy the Antichrist."

How can I argue against that? Going against their Bible won't help my cause.

"Well, maybe Jesus wants to use me to destroy him."

Abbub crosses his arms and looks out toward the lake. "If Jesus wants you to do it, then he'll lead you there, not us."

Omar nods and gives me a cold look. "Yes, let Him lead you there."

I STRIDE down the tunnel toward the chamber that connects to many caves. All things were working in my favor until these two decided to quit on me. Cowards. That's what they are. All that talk about Jesus killing the caliph is an excuse to hide their fear. But I don't need them. I can do this by myself.

"Wait, Farid, wait for me."

Now what? I don't have time to explain everything. I turn around, ready to send Taliah back to the brothers, but she throws her arms around my neck.

"Please, be careful. I've lost everything—except you."

My anger against the brothers evaporates, even my determination to kill retreats to the back of my mind as I return her embrace. Her warm cheek rests on my chest and her hair brushes my chin.

"I don't know what happened up there with Omar and Abbub, but I guess they don't want to get involved. I just want you to know you can count on me to help you, however I can."

"Thanks, Taliah."

She draws back to look into my eyes. All I want to do is kiss her, but I contain myself. I must focus on what's ahead. There'll be time for love later—if I succeed.

"It's too dangerous, but perhaps you can help me find the cave where Al-Mahdi is. Once we find it, I want you to come back here to safety, all right?"

She nods and gives me her best smile ever. Then she reaches into her pocket and offers me something almost as good—the dynamo flashlight.

"How did you get it?"

"I snatched it from Abbub's hands before running after you."

"Great thought."

We reach the tunnel chamber and head to the opposite side of the one we just exited.

Taliah points to a group of four or five cave openings.

"It must be one of these."

"Assuming the tunnels go straight up, like the one we already used. They could as well lead down deep into the ground."

"So what do you suggest we do?"

"Let's listen for any sounds coming from the caves. You check those two on your left and I'll check these ones."

I venture a few meters into the closest cave. No sound from within, not even a draft; only the slight rustle of my own body. I retrace my steps and go into the next cave—this time walking even deeper until darkness covers me completely. Nothing here.

God, is it really you calling me to do this? If so, I need some guidance.

I feel my way back into the chamber. .

Taliah's face brightens. "I thought you'd found it and had carried on without me."

"How would I leave you? You have the flashlight."

"Ha, ha, very fun—"

A distant blast echoes in the chamber.

"Where did that come from?"

"From there."

Taliah points to a couple of caves in a section we haven't explored We run to them and I hesitate. Both seem dark and still. But Taliah's right. The sound came from this side of the chamber. They must be blasting rock to look for the Ark.

"Are you waiting for another sound?" she says.

I must decide, gamble on one of them. "Let's go right."

We step into the gloomy cave, walking as fast as caution allows. The little flashlight isn't much help. We continue for four minutes or so and my hope begins to fade.

"Farid? Should we try the other cave?"

"No, let's keep going."

After a few minutes we come to a three-way fork.

"Now what?" Taliah says.

"Do you feel a breeze or air coming from any of them?"

She waves a hand in front of her face as she pokes her head inside the caves, while I walk a few paces into each of them.

"I think I felt a draft in both of the caves to the right."

I sigh. "Actually, all three caves carry a draft."

"So they all lead to the outside?"

Standing at the entrance of the middle cave, I feel a sudden itch on my eyes. I wipe my face and point the flashlight to my fingers. Dust.

"I found it."

78

Like the rest of the crowd, Hussai's engrossed by the images on the screen. The first blast with the portable excavation equipment didn't remove as much wall as they intended, and Al-Mahdi is ordering two of his guards to blast the rock again while he waits outside. The cloud of dust settles and the screen shows the guards again, setting up the small charges of TNT necessary to tear down the wall without blowing up the whole cave. Hussai has his doubts—he's never heard of archeologists using dynamite to dig a site—but it's not his job to think or offer an opinion on such matters.

One of the guards turns away from the wall, then back to his partner who's still crouched by the explosives—he seems to be stuck. Finally the guards stumble to their feet and head for the exit.

The camera zooms out as the charges go off, and dust fills the screen.

The guards lie on the ground, their clothes smeared with blood. One stirs, then lifts his head. The other two guards come to his aid and bring him to the caliph, who seems impassive. Will Al-Mahdi heal him?

Hussai's radio buzzes and he brings it to his face. "General, I think we should send the helicopter up to bring the injured down."

Why didn't Hussai think of this? "Yes, Major, exactly what I thought. Go ahead and instruct the pilot."

A guard kneeling by the one on the ground speaks loud enough for the camera to pick up his voice. "He's alive. Unconscious, but alive."

The image turns to Al-Mahdi, who talks directly into the camera. "Do not worry, my people. All will be fine, they will be healed. Just wait and see what my—"

The deafening noise of the helicopter drowns out his voice, and all eyes follow its ascent. Hussai notices the lone figure of Isa, standing where the chopper was parked seconds ago. Did he intend to get on the helicopter? Isa glances at Hussai and he looks away, feeling uncomfortable. Well, he'll have to wait for a later trip.

In the meantime, it seems Al-Mahdi has entered the cave with one of his guards, the camera one step behind.

79

A second explosion creates a cloud of dust and such tingling in my ears that I have no doubt I'm in the right cave. If the Ark of the Covenant is really here, they may well destroy it. Obviously, the caliph is not an archeologist.

The cave clears and I advance. At one point I must crouch and walk in a squat position, but then the ceiling rises up again, and the rock around me brightens. In the distance I can hear a helicopter flying away, but closer to me, there's the unmistakable voice of the caliph.

I stop behind a large column of rock at the back of the cave. Less than ten meters away stands my first obstacle—one of Al-Mahdi's guards. His back is to me but his hands are at his sides, ready to pull either the gun on his right or the sword on his left side. Beyond the first guard stands a second, pulling a large artifact from behind a pile of debris. A man with a camera follows his every move. The guard manages to move the artifact half a meter outside of the wall, then stands for a respite. How much would the Ark of the Covenant weigh if it really is covered with pure gold?

The cameraman steps to one side and Al-Mahdi comes into view. He walks to the guard and pushes him aside. He regards the artifact for a moment, then pulls off what seems to be a thick mantle. The wing of a golden angel emerges first, then the rest of its body. Next, a second angel and a box beneath it, engraved all around. It's not as beautiful as I imagined. In fact, it's somewhat disappointing. But the caliph claps once and beams for the camera.

Everyone in the cave seems engrossed by either the Ark or

the caliph. This is my chance to take them down. No mercy. If I succeed today, I will stop this mad jihad and bring the peace Zainah longed for.

I pull Omar's knife and surprise the first guard, covering his mouth with one hand and slitting his throat with the blade. He jerks once but I twist his neck to finish the job. I lay him on the floor, clip the knife on my belt, and take the gun from his holster.

As I switch the safety of the gun, the second guard sees me coming and reaches for his weapon. I fire three times and he drops to the dirt.

Al-Mahdi turns, startled, his black eyes on me. There's no fear in his countenance, no hesitation as I approach with the gun raised in front of me.

"My dear Farid, you come to me again."

He doesn't glance at the gun, not even for a second. He just stares into my eyes.

A cold draft blows out of nowhere, chilling my soul. I tell myself to pull the trigger and finish it, but my finger is numb. His gaze bores deeper and I look away for an instant.

"You think you must do this, Farid, but that's not true. You're just confused and upset by this turn of events." He takes a step forward, I take a step back.

Why did I do that? I'm armed and he's not. I should kill him now.

The caliph motions to the cameraman to come closer. "My people, do not fear. Men cannot harm me. This happened for a reason, so you will witness the unveiling of my divinity." He turns to me and reaches for my weapon.

"No!"

He stops as I press the barrel against his forehead.

80

Hussai glances around at the paralyzed mass of people. Jaws drop and every eye is nailed to the screen. The only voice he can hear is the major's, blaring through the radio, asking for his orders.

But the caliph wouldn't want anyone to steal his show. He himself said they shouldn't fear. If Al-Mahdi is really divine, then Farid won't be able to kill him. Hussai turns the radio off and listens to the caliph's words.

"I am your lord, Farid, and you know it in your heart. You are drawn to me, not because you want to destroy me, but because you want to serve me."

Farid couldn't bring himself to kill the Jewish priests, much less Al-Mahdi. But what if Farid is a Zionist after all? What if the lies he made up about Farid are actually true? It all fits. His presence here at Arbel makes more sense if the Israelis sent him to assassinate the caliph.

He can't let this happen. Everything would collapse before Hussai could use the war to his advantage. Besides, he knows better now—he's seen the power that resides in the caliph, he's seen the fulfillment of the prophecies in his lord Al-Mahdi.

Ergun comes running to him. "General, I tried to reach you on your radio…"

Hussai looks past Ergun's shoulder and sees Isa talking to the helicopter pilot, who landed with the wounded guard not two minutes ago.

"General, I just received communication from our base in

Jordan. They've detected a fleet of aircraft coming our way. I think they're hostile, probably Israelis."

Ergun's words slip from Hussai's mind. All he can think about is stopping Farid. He looks over to the improvised helipad. Isa is getting on the chopper and the blades begin to turn.

"Do whatever you have to do, Major. I'll do what I must." He runs to the helicopter.

81

"*Release your anger, Farid.* Release your weapon and surrender to my will. Serve me as you know you should. Be one of my generals and regain the respect and honor of your men. You know this is what your heart desires."

My chest is tight and I choke on my own resolve. The wintry air revolves around me. Serve him or kill him? I stare at the ground and feel my strength falter.

"Serve me, Farid. Serve me and live forever surrounded with glory and wealth. This is what I promise to those who pledge their allegiance to me."

The caliph pushes the gun from his forehead with confidence, and I let my arms be moved until the gun falls to the ground. An eternal moment passes between us and the whole world swirls around me. My body swings forward and he catches me, placing both hands on my shoulders.

"Stand up straight." His voice is now harsh and authoritative, not conciliatory as before.

I lift my eyes to him and try to straighten my back. I must look pathetic. What will he say now?

His hands are still gripping my shoulders. He smirks.

Of all the expressions he can muster at this moment, he decides to smirk. I glance around at the dead guards, at the camera broadcasting death, and I know the last thing I want is to serve this madman.

"Now, Far—"

His eyes widen in surprise—the only time I have seen such

a look on his face— and his trembling hands reach for his chest. Blood spurts out onto my arm as I twist the knife inside him. When I release the grip on Omar's knife, Al-Mahdi's body slumps to the floor.

82

Hussai jumps off the helicopter. He darts for the cave without waiting for Isa, fumbling with his holster, almost tripping as he pulls his gun out.

No one will stop him this time. Farid will die today.

A jet thunders above him and the sound of explosions ripple around the mountain. He looks up at the sky. The Israelis are attacking, that's what's happening. He'd better take cover inside the mountain. Just then, a man emerges from the cave. Hussai lifts his gun, ready to shoot, but realizes it's the cameraman. He keeps the gun pointed at the journalist.

"Halt. What's going on inside?"

"This was not supposed to happen, this was not supposed to happen." He talks like a robot.

"What was not supposed to happen?"

"Those were his last words." He points to the camera but his eyes are tormented. "I have it right here."

Dread seizes Hussai. "Is the caliph dead? Is the killer still inside?"

He nods. "He told me to get out."

Hussai feels the eerie presence of Isa behind him and looks back. The man seems unshaken, walking with confidence toward the cave. But he could be killed as well. They all have underestimated Farid, but no more.

He runs to the mouth of the cave, presses his back against the exterior rock and peers inside. No bullets come his way. He erupts into the cave, firing into the air four times. The bullets ricochet and he freezes. The caliph lies in a pool of blood with a knife handle sticking out from his upper left side, close to his heart. By his side, the gun he saw Farid point at him. Hussai bends over to find a pulse. Nothing.

A few meters away, deeper in the cave, lies a dead guard. Hussai walks to him and sees the blood around his neck as well. Farid is a butcher. Tracks on the dirt lead to a tunnel further in and he feels a cold wind pushing him toward it. That's the escape route. He turns his radio on as an explosion shakes the ground.

"… under attack, we are under attack. General, please respond."

Hussai speaks into the radio. "Repel the attack, Major. I'm in pursuit of Farid—"

A grunt from the entrance of the cave distracts him. Isa comes in, pushing the cameraman back into the cave. What is this man up to?

The explosions outside become stronger, and so does the wind that pushes him deeper into the cave. He clips his radio back into place and rushes after Farid.

83

Even the darkness of the cave can't hide this death. It's still here, under my nose, the stench of his blood. And in front of my eyes, the shadow of unbelief that crossed his face at the last moment. He discovered he was just a man after all, and I've shown the world his human nature.

No gladness fills my heart, nor remorse—only a anguished void between my chest and my stomach. I thought it would feel different to fulfill one's destiny, to answer the call of God. But I feel somehow that this isn't over, that my calling has just begun.

I reach the convergence of the four tunnels. The light has dimmed and I can't tell which one leads to the rock chamber below. The mountain rattles and a shower of small rocks hits my head and shoulders. The roof of the cave is crumbling under the explosions outside. What in the world is going on out there?

I hear steps approaching from one of the tunnels, but which one? Is someone coming after me? I check my waist—I dropped the gun and left the knife. What am I going to tell Omar? Worse, how am I going to defend myself?

The steps sound closer, somewhere to my left. A shadow emerges and I leap at it.

"Aahh!"

"Taliah?"

"You almost killed me!"

I get off her and help her to her feet. "I'm sorry, I thought I was being followed. What are you doing?"

"I heard the explosions and you were taking too long, so I

came back to look for you. Omar and Abbub are in the chamber
below, waiting for us."

A new explosion shakes the cave and more dirt and rocks
fall to the ground. Then I hear another sound.

"What's that?"

"I think they're trying to bring the mountain down."

"No, something else." I point to the tunnel that leads to the
caliph. "From that cave."

84

Hussai holds his breath, listening to the echoing of voices ahead. Was that Farid? He wipes the dust from his shoulders and points the gun forward.

Two meters ahead, the tunnel opens. The voices fall to whispers, then cease. Hussai strides forward, firing twice. The bullets nick the walls at the same time as the mountain shakes.

A silhouette vanishes into a cave to his left and Hussai darts after it. His right foot slips at the entrance and he must grab the wall to balance himself. The footsteps echo ahead and he fires into blackness. No moan or thud, only the dry crack of bullet against rock. No point wasting ammunition.

He replaces the gun in his holster and feels his way through the cave, hands extended before and above him. The last thing he wants is a bruise on the head. What if he falls unconscious? Nobody knows where he is. He unsnaps the radio from his belt.

"Come in, Major."

Faint static. Of course, there's no signal inside this cave. It's too late to go outside and call. Apparently, Farid and whoever's with him know these caves well. He can't give them more time to escape. A boom from above loosens more debris and Hussai ducks as golf-ball-size rocks fall upon him. The attacks must be really intense out there. He quickens his pace and scrapes his legs against the rocks, but after a few minutes he catches a glimpse of faint light. He reaches for his gun and slows. As before, he plans to burst in opening fire, not giving anyone a chance to shoot him first.

He halts and holds his breath. He hates the silence, broken only by the pounding of his heart. They could be lying in ambush, but as far as he knows Farid may be unarmed. Still, his accomplice may have a weapon.

Hussai inches forward, then stops. A swooshing sound pierces the air and he takes it as a signal, He storms into a large natural chamber and opens fire. In one second, he realizes two things— he's alone in the chamber, and the swoosh is that of a missile. Where did it come from?

The mountain shakes horribly and the ceiling of the chamber cracks. Hussai runs back to the tunnel just before tons of rock fall from above.

85

We must head north, Omar tells me over his shoulder as we run through a cave we haven't used before. "It's easier to find shelter in that direction than south in the valley."

"Just lead the way and we'll follow."

Drenched in sweat and covered in dust and dirt, we look like survivors from a mud slide. I haven't told them what I did, but Taliah must know, because she thanked me for avenging her family. I just nodded.

The rift in the lake opens up over our heads, and suddenly we're under the open sky.

"There's the north shore," Abbub says, pointing ahead a few hundred meters. "Once there, we must seek the riverbed."

We reach the shore. A large mass of rock bars our way to the east. To the west, the Islamic army forms a line of defense around Mount Arbel.

"We must climb or walk around this rock," Omar says.

What would I do if I were still fighting as major of the army? The Israelis are coming hard with their air force, but it seems Hussai was prepared with anti-aircraft weapons.

Taliah lets out a shriek. "No, not again!"

I spin around and see her staring at the sky. Above us, a ball of fire drops with furious speed.

"Incoming jet!" I wave my hands at the two brothers and grab Taliah, pulling her into the rift with me. Omar and Abbub run toward me. As I duck, the jet smashes into the rock mass. Shrapnel follows a cloud of fire and smoke that envelops the air above.

I fall flat on my face against the rock. Heat penetrates every pore in my body. Am I burning? I open my eyes but everything is hazy.

"Taliah, are you hurt?"

A loud sob is all I get. I crawl until I find her and put my arms around her.

"It's all right. You're going to be fine."

The dust dissipates within a few minutes and Abbub and Omar come to our side.

"We aren't injured," Omar says. "You?"

I shake my head. "Nothing physical. Right, Taliah?"

She wipes her tears and rests her head against my chest. "I'm okay."

"We must go now," Abbub says.

We emerge from the rift once more and round the crashed jet from a safe distance, almost running. Taliah has grabbed hold of my hand and won't let go. I like that.

"The riverbed, there," Omar says and sprints ahead.

While war rages behind us, we step onto the rocky terrain that was once the mighty Jordan River. Omar seems excited.

"There's a village nine or ten kilometers away. We'll find food and transportation there. Then we must flee to Petra."

That sounds too good to be true. "Are you sure the village is still there?"

"We'll be fine. The Lord will provide. Has God ever failed you?"

I think for a moment about my near encounters with death, the miraculous ways in which we have survived and found hope, water, even love.

"No, he hasn't."

He smiles. "That's because He loves you."

86

Hussai is staggering. *Blood* oozes from the back of his head and his right shoulder feels dislocated. He almost died under those rocks. But he outlived the caliph, and as general, he has to clean this mess and get in front of the army and win this war. He'll defeat the Israelis and hunt Farid, even as far as America if he has to.

The explosions wane to sporadic booms by the time he reaches the cave of the dead. He expects to find it deserted, but instead, the cameraman is back in place, filming the most gruesome scene Hussai has ever witnessed. The temperature in the cave is at least five degrees lower than in the caves beneath, which doesn't make any sense.

Isa has drawn a circle of blood around the body of Al-Mahdi, whose white clothes have turned red. The knife he saw in the caliph's chest is now stuck in the ground above his head. The crazy prophet mumbles an unintelligible prayer or enchantment, sometimes speaking in a language Hussai doesn't understand.

Hussai walks closer and every hair on his body stands. His mouth dries up and his knees tremble. Isa looks at him and speaks with a deep guttural voice.

"Behold the beast that exercises the authority from the prince of this world, and who heals the mortal wound of the leopard."

Isa strides around the circle and Hussai's heart seems to stop. He halts by the caliph's feet and drops himself over the corpse, aligning hands with hands, mouth with mouth, eyes with eyes.

Hussai glances at the cameraman, who shakes like a palm tree.

NICK DANIELS

Isa cries out: "Possess him, oh spirit of the ancient serpent, and bring him back to life." He blows his breath in the caliph's purple mouth.

The cameraman faints and drops to the ground. Hussai knows he wants to flee and hide under a rock, but all strength has abandoned him. Kissing a dead body and speaking nonsense, Isa is even madder than the caliph was—

Al-Mahdi's left hand twitches.

Epilogue

Taliah sleeps on my shoulder, oblivious to the jerks of the rattling bus taking us to Petra.

"We're less than five minutes away," Omar says from under his head scarf. We're all wearing them as a disguise.

I nod, confident we'll make it to the rock city without a problem. If we haven't found resistance so far, I doubt we will in the next few minutes. My worries are of a different nature and they come from my reading of Omar's Bible. I've read through the book of Revelation four times already—understanding little— but I keep coming back to the thirteenth chapter, where it talks about a beast that has authority over all the earth.

"Are you sure 'the beast' refers to Al-Mahdi?" I ask Omar.

"The first beast is the Antichrist, yes."

The bus enters the village of Wadi Musa, on the outskirts of Petra, and the passengers begin to collect their stuff. I glance at the Bible to read the troublesome verse again: "The beast seemed to have had a fatal wound, but the fatal wound had been healed. The whole world was astonished and followed the beast."

The wound of my knife? It feels impossible to think that I fulfilled an ancient prophecy, but even more difficult to fathom that the caliph is alive.

The text in my hands is still shaky although the bus has stopped. Why are my hands trembling?

"Taliah, wake up," Omar says.

She stirs on my side. "What?" She squints at the light coming through the windows. "Where are we, Farid?"

"Petra." I return my senses to the Bible and shut everything else out. If all this is true, I must know the end. I lay the book on my lap and pore over the pages, studying each instance of the word beast—I've highlighted the term more than twenty times in the last nine chapters. My head spins with images of wars, plagues, and angels.

I rub my tired eyes and keep on reading. "... the fifth angel poured out his bowl on the throne of the beast... they will give their power and authority to the beast.... the beast, the kings of the earth, and their armies, gathered together to make war..."

My chest feels tight. In chapter nineteen, I find a glimmer of hope. "Then the beast was captured, and with him the false prophet who worked signs in his presence.... These two were cast alive into the lake of fire burning with brimstone."

Someone shakes my shoulder. "Farid? Farid!" I look up at a grinning Omar—he's taken his head scarf off. "You're the last one," he says. "Let's go."

He knows about the terrible doom foretold in this book, and still he looks happy. "This isn't over, is it?"

Omar shakes his head.

I close the Bible and stare at the village, overwhelmed by the tribulations ahead—the gory battles, the tyranny of a supernatural Al-Mahdi, the end of the world. This is all so hard to grasp. I've left jihad for a faith I do not comprehend, yet it soothes my soul—as does Omar's serene face.

"You look so at peace, Omar."

He smiles. "We're on the winning side."

THE ADVENTURE continues with *The Jihad's Prophet*

WWW.JIHADSERIES.COM

About Nick Daniels

NICK WAS born in the late 1970s, in a bustling city in South America. He wrote his first short story in third grade about a explorer lost in the Amazon jungle, then discovered Jules Verne during sixth grade and was hooked into fiction for life.

He spent the next few years reading literature classics (mostly Dostoievsky) and contemporary Latin American writers such as Gabriel Garcia Marquez, Jorge Luis Borges, Julio Cortazar, and Mario Vargas Llosa, plus every book in the library that piqued his interest.

At age fifteen, he decided to write a novel about a woman who loses the ability to love. It remains (thankfully) unpublished.

After graduating from journalism school, Nick moved to the United States to continue his education and write about science and faith issues. He worked as a science writer for several years until he gradually found his way back into fiction.

His first novel, *The Gentlemen's Conspiracy*, was published by Risen Books in 2009.

WWW.NICKDANIELSBOOKS.COM

FACEBOOK.COM/NICKDANIELSBOOKS

CPSIA information can be obtained at www.ICGtesting.com
Printed in the USA
237257LV00001B/8/P